# HIVE KNIGHT

Trinity of the Hive (Book One)

by

Grayson Sinclair

# License Notes

**Hive Knight (Trinity of the Hive: Book One)**
Copyright © 2020 Grayson Sinclair. All rights reserved.
Copyright © 2020 Luciano Fleitas Cover Artist

A Starlit Publishing Book
Published by Starlit Publishing
69 Teslin Rd
Whitehorse, YT
Y1A 3M5
Canada

www.starlitpublishing.com

Ebook ISBN: 9781989458969
Paperback ISBN: 9781989458976
Hardcover ISBN: 9781989458983

# Contents

*Dedicated to Robert Leyendecker*

*For supporting a complete stranger with everything you had. I couldn't have done it without you, bud.*

*"The only difference between the virtual and the real world is the amount of data. We can feel a lot more if we see, hear, or touch something in the real world than in a virtual world.*

*—Asuna Yuuki*

# CHAPTER 1 - DRACONIAN MEASURES

A blast of lightning slammed into the ground an inch away, and I slipped on the wet, mossy rocks, sending me tumbling to the ground. Iron filled my mouth as my ears rang. *By the nine kings of Hell, that was close!*

My racing heart filled with fear as the dragon roared, shaking the earth and conjuring a mass of storm clouds overhead. Thunder cracked, and hailstones the size of my fists hounded us mercilessly.

*Damn, of course, this wouldn't be easy.* I gripped my sword tight in my hands and charged the beast.

"Duran, wait!" Alistair screamed over the thunder.

*Like hell!* Each passing second inched us closer to death, and if we didn't act, we were doomed.

Gil and Levi ran forward, circling the mighty dragon and holding its attention.

The elder storm dragon was deadly; every facet of it screamed at me to flee for my very life. The beast towered over all of us, moving with lithe precision, snapping its jaws at Levi's greatshield.

As dangerous as the creature was, its beauty could not be denied. Its scales glistened like sapphires in the rain as it moved its hulking body to face us. Its massive limbs capped with ivory talons were the length of my longsword; one swipe would rend us in two.

While they bought time, I circled around it, searching for an opening.

Alistair cursed and held his hands towards me, reciting a short chant in Script. He finished and a bright red circle appeared in his palm, a swirling geometric pattern that danced over a pentagram. As it spun, a warmth spread over me.

A tiny notification in the corner of my vision flicked to life as Alistair's spell took hold.

**Damage Boost: 30 seconds**

Such a quick and dirty incantation, but it was enough to give me a chance. I ran in between Gil and Levi while they kept it busy and slashed my longsword across the dragon's chest. The metal bit deep, hewing a chunk of flesh out before I backed away. Blood sprouted from the gash to splash across my face, mixing with the sweat that dripped down to sting my eyes.

*Damn, not as deep as I needed!* It was barely more than a scratch on the massive beast, but it was deep enough to cause the Bleeding status effect, which would only help us as the fight wore on.

The dragon unfurled its wings and rose on its hind legs to claw at Gil. The vicious talons missed him by a fraction of an inch.

The ebony giant bellowed with laughter, taunting it. Gil was a human mountain, easily seven feet tall and stacked with muscle. His chainmail shone from beneath his leather armor in the rain. Gil hefted his enormous battleaxe and brought it down across the right leg of the dragon before backpedaling with far more speed than I'd have credited him for.

The dragon lowered to the ground and stared at us with a hatred that hinted at far more intelligence than any mere beast. It swiped out with its tail, which was half the length of its body and riddled with jade spikes each the size of a dagger. Death whistled past us as we rolled out of the way.

I landed in a puddle formed from a depression atop the mountain. A flash of my features appeared before the rippling water distorted the image. Long, copper hair soaked to a muddy brown, which framed a rugged, menacing face. My hair nearly covered my eyes, which were alight with adrenaline. Even though my heart raced a mile a minute, I had the biggest smile plastered across my face.

Moss and bits of rock clung to my hands as I pushed myself off the ground and retrieved my bastard sword. The rocky, uneven terrain of the mountain made maintaining my footwork nearly an impossible challenge. I stepped over the slick rocks to rejoin my party.

Sparks of lightning curled from the dragon's jade horns, arcing off to strike at random. An errant bolt struck next to Alistair while he was distracted. He shouted over to us, but his words were lost in the storm.

I ran over to him; his fine hair resembled a dirty mop as it stuck to his face and obscured his green eyes. Alistair ignored me as he built another spell. Arms splayed wide open, his palms glowed as he worked his magic. I couldn't understand the words of Script he used, but as the sandstone Script circle flared to life in between his hands, I recognized the spell he was about to cast: *Ground.*

Which meant we were about to be in trouble.

Amid the torrential downpour of rain, a ball of electricity amassed between the dragon's horns and shot out in all directions before arcing back to converge on us. The bolts of lightning hit us and obliterated my senses as a blinding white light seared my vision and ozone burned in my nose.

It took a moment for the world to right itself again, but when it did, I was elated to see that we'd weathered the attack unscathed.

"Alistair, how far is the radius for *Ground?*"

"Fifteen feet, long as you stay close, I can keep the lightning attacks at bay."

*Oh, hell. That's not going to cut it; we're sitting ducks here.* We may have had a counter for the dragon's magic, but it still had half a dozen other nasty ways to end our lives. Realizing its electrical attacks had no effect on us, the storm dragon raged and lowered its head like it was about to charge us. "Shit! Not good! Gil, Levi, cover Alistair!"

Not waiting for their replies, I surged forward to meet its charge. Putting every ounce of speed into my legs, I activated *Holy Blade.* My sword took on an ethereal sunlit glow, and the scents of summertime overrode the stench of ozone. The light from my blade grew as the dragon opened its maw. The jagged, yellowed teeth snapped shut next to my ear as I brought my longsword up in an arc, slicing a deep furrow from the beast's lower jaw to the base of its neck. A few teeth rattled to the ground and drew my gaze for a split second.

Which was a foolish mistake that should have killed me.

It cried out in agony and lashed out with its tail. The tip slammed into my side; one of its spikes speared through my shoulder. Pain radiated through me, and the tail whipped me into the air by the force of its attack. My health bar flashed in my interface, dropping deep into the yellow and then into the red when I crashed into the ground a moment later. My head slammed hard against a rock, and everything went dark.

I found myself dreaming of the past, which was never a good thing.

The tiny hovel I'd called home for the last few months was empty when I pushed aside the thin canvas flap. FEMA only used the highest quality particleboard and plywood in its construction; I'd accented it with duct tape and egg cartons to try and keep in as much warmth as I could, but it wasn't enough.

A small pile of worn, filthy clothing sat on my bed, which was essentially a burlap sack filled with cheap stuffing. It, my clothes, and a thin, itchy blanket were all I had left in the world. After kicking the soiled clothing to the floor, I sat down, disgusted and ashamed with myself. *So close. I was so fucking close this time.*

I looked once more at the fence in the distance and watched as two workers under armed guard patched the two-and-a-half-foot hole I'd spent two weeks working on. I'd been so close, timed the guards' patrol routes, and snuck enough canned food to last a week in a camouflaged spot right next to the fence. All that prep work only to be caught by two refugees who'd gone looking for a place to hook up.

*Maybe tomorrow…tomorrow will be the night,* I thought, scratching at my wiry beard as I curled up against the wall and wrapped my blanket around me. *I'll make a new plan tomorrow.* A comforting lie. I was so consumed by my despondency that I didn't hear it when she approached. A light knock on the doorframe interrupted my thoughts.

"Sampson Acre?"

Her voice was rich and strong, yet she spoke softly as if she were afraid of being overheard. Her words mixed with the constant hum of sounds that came with living in close quarters with thousands of other people, but my name cut through the background noise. She leaned in, only showing me half her face, staring down at me with a waiting gaze.

"I'm sorry, what?"

"Are you Mr. Sampson Acre?"

I nodded, and she entered my cramped home, giving me a proper look at her.

She was pretty, bordering on beautiful. Long black hair flowed past her sharp cheekbones and pointed chin to rest just under her bust. She had full, strawberry lips upturned in a fake smile and light green eyes with flecks of gray dotted around the iris. They held a stark intelligence behind the allure of them.

Her clothes marked her as an outsider as much as her looks. An avocado green sweater and gray denim pants hugged her slim frame beneath a spotless white lab coat. Expensive black trail boots with only a hint of dirt completed her look.

I hadn't seen anyone so well dressed in years; she didn't belong here amid this destitution. A stiff breeze rolled through camp and rattled my canvas door flap, bringing a faint whiff of lavender and vanilla to my nose. It came from her onyx hair, which fluttered gently in the wind. The woman clamped down on the clipboard in her hands, stopping the ruffling papers with her well-manicured fingers.

"What do you want?"

Her smile deepened in its falseness, showing off her perfect teeth. She had a good smile, but it was all for show, and it didn't touch her eyes; they were calm and unreadable. "My name is Dr. Bell, but you can call me Jessica."

She paused, taking stock of me, her eyes flicking up and down. Suddenly I was very self-conscious about my appearance. Usually, it wouldn't bother me what anyone else thought, but she was different—gorgeous, intelligent, and, more importantly, clean. Something I wasn't.

I couldn't remember the last time I'd had a chance to take an actual shower, and sitting here in my stained and threadbare clothing put me off balance. My appearance obviously didn't bother her; she was satisfied with her assessment as a flicker of a grin crossed her lips and her eyes thawed by a degree.

"Would you like to help save the world?"

*What?* I blinked, stunned. *Surely, I misheard what she said?* "Come again?"

She chuckled. It shattered the persona she wore for just a second, giving me a glimpse at the real Jessica. She was laughing at me, but there wasn't any meanness in it.

"I'm sorry. I shouldn't've laughed; that was rude of me. I can't say much, but the organization I work for needs test-volunteers. I can't give away any more details about the project as it's highly classified, need to know, and well…"

"I don't need to know."

"Bingo."

She was too clean and well dressed for this to be a joke. There had to be some truth to what she was offering, even if what she was saying was impossible. *Earth can't be saved; it's been beyond saving for five years now. One look outside this camp will tell you that…besides, even if it could, there's no world for me to go back to.*

I shied away from that thought before it dragged me deeper into despair and shifted to meet her gaze. "Last I checked, this world's fucked, and unless you've figured out a way to get rid of the ghouls, this is a pointless conversation."

The corners of her mouth lifted by a notch, but her cold demeanor returned in spades. "So cynical for such a young man," she said, smirking before flipping through a few pages on her clipboard. She stopped and whistled under her breath. "But you do have a good excuse, don't you, Sammy?"

Cold ice gripped my heart as she said that name. *Stop it, what would Micah say? He'd be devastated at seeing me like this.* "Don't call me that," I snapped.

"Right…Sam?" she hedged.

I stifled my sigh. "That's fine."

She nodded and went back to her notes. "According to FEMA's records, they picked you up six months ago?"

I craned my neck over at the scratch marks on the far corner of the wall. "Five months, twenty-one days," I clarified.

"And in that time, you've attempted escape seven times, is that correct?"

I scowled. "Eight, actually. Tonight makes eight."

Jessica spoke, not looking up from the clipboard. "Why don't you want to stay? You know what lies outside those walls."

My throat burned, and I spat onto the floor. "This is supposed to be a refugee camp, not a goddamn prison. I want to go home."

Her smile fell from her face, pinching her lips together. "You have no home to return to," she said, flipping through her notes once more. "Family: mother, father, and younger brother. All deceased."

*Deceased.* A single word, the lives of my family reduced to a single word on a clipboard.

"There is nothing waiting for you out there but death. Do you want to die?" Jessica asked.

I let the question hang in the air; I didn't have an answer for it, anyway. Jessica just stared at me while I looked anywhere else. I coughed to break the tension in the room. "So, what's your offer?"

"A jailbreak, so to speak. I can get you out of here."

I looked sideways at her. "And in return?" I asked with trepidation.

"Your cooperation in our experiment."

I was getting anxious just sitting on the bed, but with her blocking the doorway, I couldn't leave, so I settled for drumming my fingers in my lap. The dulled sound helped to focus my thoughts. *Well, this is shady as hell, but she's offering the thing I want most. Son of a bitch, I've been had.*

"I'm guessing you won't be explaining anything about any of this, either?"

"Can't," she said with laughter in her eyes. "Classified."

Jessica had me beat; she knew it, too. Before she ever stepped foot in here, she knew exactly what to dangle in front of my face to get me to dance to her tune. I couldn't refuse her. *Anything beats rotting in here. Guess I'll be her little guinea pig.* I climbed to my feet and looked her in the eye. "Okay, I'm in."

"Excellent," she said, extending her hand. "We leave in the morning."

I shook her hand. A thick scar on the center of her palm rubbed rough against my own as we shook. *I don't want to stay, but guess we can't leave tonight, not unless we feel like getting torn to shreds.* I didn't want to stick around this camp for a minute longer, but I wanted to be eaten alive by a ghoul even less.

Familiar clumsy footsteps stomped up to my home and made me go quiet. The canvas sheet was thrust aside as Soph walked in carrying two steaming bowls.

"Hey, Sam, I brought you dinner…" Sophia's eyes lit up when she saw me.

Wearing a thin, holey yellow t-shirt depicting a band I'd never heard of and torn jeans, she barged in without a care in the world. Her face was thin from the years of rationing, but she had a hyper energy about her, that even the apocalypse couldn't get rid of. Her deep sun-kissed skin only accented her sparkling hazel eyes.

Her grin faded slightly as she noticed I wasn't alone. She gave the doctor a once over. "Who's your friend, Sam?" she asked, brushing her walnut locks out of her face to smirk at me.

"Heya, Soph, this is—"

"Dr. Jessica Bell," she said, holding out her hand. "And you are?"

"Sophia," she said brusquely, kneeling to set the two bowls on the floor.

Jessica paused, flicked through a page or so from her clipboard, and looked back up to Soph. "Sophia Hale?"

Soph nodded.

"Ah, well, that makes my job a little easier. I needed to speak with you."

"You offering her the same thing?" I interrupted.

"I am," she said to me before turning back to Soph. "Now, Ms. Hale, I—"

"Don't care, I'm in."

I looked up, shocked. "Just like that?"

She shrugged. "Yep."

"Well, that makes my job a lot easier," Jessica said, tucking her clipboard under her arm. "Be at the front gate first thing in the morning."

With that, she departed, and as soon as the flap closed back, Soph hopped down next to me. She handed me a bowl and scooted close to me on the bed before stealing half my blanket from me.

"Hey," I protested.

Soph pressed herself against me. Her chest squished against my arm as she arranged herself comfortably next to me. "Shut up and eat," she told me with a laugh.

My screaming belly delighted in the salty broth that did little for my hunger but warmed me up nicely. The bowl was empty too soon, leaving me sleepy. I sat the bowl inside Soph's empty one and leaned back.

Soph took the opportunity to cuddle next to me. "Now that we've got food, what the hell did I just agree to?"

I shrugged. "No idea. She wouldn't tell me anything. All I know is that we're leaving this damned camp. Speaking of, why did you agree so fast?"

18

"Because. You're not getting away from me that easy," Soph said, leaning over to kiss me.

Her lips were full and soft on mine, and I responded to the kiss before I could tell myself not to. Her kisses tasted of chicken broth and desire, and Soph pulled me into her, wrapping her hand around my neck. She slid her tongue into my mouth as her kisses grew hungrier, and it was at that point that I pulled away. *I can't.*

"Soph…"

She sighed and eased up but didn't let go of me. Instead, she pressed her forehead to mine and nuzzled against my nose. "I know, Sam. I know," she said, curling up into my shoulder.

Her rhythmic breathing brushed hot across my neck, and her body heat took the chill from the air. I wrapped my arm around her and held her close. "I'm sorry, Soph."

"I know. I don't fault you for it. I'm just hoping you'll let me in one of these days."

"Yeah. Me too."

Sophia's breathing deepened as she drifted off to sleep in my arms, curling toward me automatically.

A rough shove snapped me out of my dream and brought me back to reality. Alistair stood over me, shaking me with one hand while working a spell with the other. "C'mon sleeping beauty, get the fuck up already," he said with one final jerk.

The problem with nightmares is that they linger; when you jolt out of slumber, they leave you stunned and confused until reality sets in, and you can calm your racing heart. I stood and ran my fingers over my scalp, the inflamed, broken skin oozed, and a knot the size of an egg was already forming.

The pain from my forehead, along with trying to shake off my old memories, put me in a dire position in the middle of a fight. I stumbled to my feet, my health bar flashing red, warning me that I was close to death. *Yeah, like I don't know that. Need a health potion.* I was a second away from pulling one out of my inventory when I realized how bad an idea that would be. *I'll be too sluggish after. Can't risk it in the middle of battle.* Though I also didn't want to waste *Divine Heal.*

Gil and Levi were holding the dragon at bay. It had stopped throwing lightning and was trying to slice them in half with its claws. Levi's greatshield was thick enough to withstand even the dragon's onslaught, but they could only hold out for so much longer.

I hobbled over to Alistair, who'd cast his spell and was working on another. His hands held in front of him, fingers splayed as he recited a guttural chant. Two intricate halves of a pentagram formed in his hands. As Alistair wove the spell, the diagram grew more detailed and glowed with intense light before settling on burnt orange and melding into one whole Script Circle.

With a thump of pressure, hundreds of small burning dots appeared through the storm clouds. Tiny, razor-sharp shards of molten metal descended on the dragon and scored numerous lacerations across its tough hide. The effects of *Meteor Rain* were severe, and it bled from dozens of cuts and puncture wounds, Alistair's spell distracted the dragon enough to let me run over without fear of attack.

"Alistair, I need healing."

"Obviously," he replied with a cheeky grin, his dull green eyes lighting up with humor. "I don't have time to do this properly, so it'll have to be fast and hard."

"Bet you say that to all the girls," I said with a laugh.

20

He chuckled but didn't respond as he built a quick version of *Full Heal*. *Oh, this is going to hurt.* In three seconds, he'd primed the basics of the spell, but due to the haste, he couldn't build it properly. Pain made my eyes water and sent my head spinning as my skin stitched itself closed, and my wounds healed. I ground my teeth to keep from screaming, and by the time I let out a breath, it was over, and my health bar was back in the green.

"Thanks," I said, pulling out a mana potion and tossing it to him. "Drink up before you deplete your mana."

He nodded and lifted a shaky hand to uncap the potion and chug the contents. I put Alistair out of mind and focused on the dragon. We'd been fighting for a good while now, and it was still standing firm. *Need to pull out all the stops here.*

"Gil, step back and let me take over!" I yelled, rushing in.

Gil rolled out of the way of a quick swipe, and I stepped in.

The storm dragon bellowed and swung wide at me. Praying my timing was right, I dipped my shoulder as its claws passed a millimeter from my face. Activating *Rush Strike*, a gust of wind swept at my back and propelled me forward at breakneck speed. The radiant blues of its belly were in my face before I knew it, and I hastily drew my hunting knife. I plunged it deep in between its thick scales and used it as a steppingstone to get me on its back.

It roared as my knife punctured its flesh, and in pain, it didn't notice that I'd climbed atop it. I chained the tail end of *Rush Strike* with *Twice Critical*, and my sword blurred, vibrating at such high speed that it appeared translucent. My balance was precarious on the dragon's spine, and I ran in between its spikes to hop onto its snout. My blade sang as I plunged it sideways through one of the beast's eyes and out of the other. Yanking with all my might, I tore through bone and obliterated what remained of its sight.

The dragon roared in utter agony and threw me from its head. I landed in a crouch just as a wave of thunder crashed into me; it knocked me off my feet and to the ground. Half deafened from the roar, it pressed its advantage and summoned a bolt of lightning from the heavens.

I saw it coming, but I couldn't counter it. Alistair was building a complex spell, which limited my options. *If I use* Aura of the Antimage, *I'll blow out his spell. Damn it, no choice.* My only choice was to dodge it. I threw myself out of the way, but I was too slow. Lightning hit my leg as I leapt from the ground.

Pain lanced through me as I landed, and I stared in horror at the blackened stump of where my leg had been moments before. The pain was excruciating, and for a second, I thought I would black out for a second time. Alistair was busy managing his spellwork, so I was forced to use my one healing ability.

I activated *Divine Heal,* and my leg reappeared in a flash of golden light. The subtle scent of sunshine mixed with the stench of burnt flesh. My health bar returned to green as I healed, and a countdown appeared in the corner of my interface, standing at twenty-four hours.

Recovering my senses as quick as I could after having my appendage blasted off, I moved out of range of its claws. The dragon had returned its attention to the other members of my party. Even wounded and blind, it was still an extremely dangerous threat and was trying to tear Gil apart.

The rain lessened with each passing second, and I feared it would take to the skies. I raced forward and swung my sword in an arc above me; my arms trembled with resistance as the blade split a large tear in the dragon's leathery wing. Bright purple blood oozed out of the gash, and the beast roared in agony, turning to face me, which was a mistake on its part.

Not being able to see meant the dragon didn't notice when Gil rushed in with his gigantic battleaxe and used *Sever.* Gil leapt into the air and swung his shimmering axe. He bellowed as he struck the dragon's front leg from its body. The dragon hissed, lighting bursting from its nostrils as it toppled over and crashed onto the earth.

*It's time to end this.* "Gil, Levi. Double guillotine!"

Both of them nodded, while Gil and I exchanged a brief look, we both knew our next move and charged in. The dragon, bloody and weak, picked itself off the ground and roared in rage, swiping out withs its claws in anger. I ducked the dragon's clumsy swipe, which was a terrible move, as having one leg severed and attacking with its remaining front leg sent it toppling over. It crashed to the ground after its attack.

With me having used both *Rush Strike* and *Twice Critical*, I was half as effective as I should be. *I've already used one aura, but now's the time to use the second.* It was reckless of me to have blown so many abilities so quickly, and because of it, Gil would have to deliver the final blow.

Activating *Aura of Speed*, I surged ahead as a soft red outline formed over my skin. The *aura* granted me exceptional speed, so I jumped first, managing to bury my sword halfway through the creature's neck, and was just able to pull it free before Gil jumped. I rolled to the side to avoid his incoming attack. Gil activated his *War Cry*, and my battle fatigue faded as his shout reached me, sending it back down to manageable levels.

Spurred on by the rush of *War Cry*, Gil ran up its torn wing, nearly slipping on the river of purple blood from the gash I'd made. He climbed on the back of the beast and positioned himself in between two of the spikes along the dragon's spine. With another howl, it tried to throw Gil off but couldn't shake the grinning berserker.

The dragon bucked, flapping his gigantic wings and flinging warm droplets of blood to mix with the raging thunderstorm. For a moment, the beast took to the sky, and my heart skipped a beat. Time froze, and I was afraid that we'd just let our quarry slip through our grasp.

Gil never lost his smile as he balanced on top of the massive creature and quickly clambered up to the dragon's neck. His axe glowed silver as he activated his most powerful ability, *Steel-Breaker,* and with a shout that was lost to the roar of the wind, he swung the axe with all his might.

Steel met flesh, and the dragon's head arced from its body.

It fell to the ground, sending droplets of purple blood in every direction as bone crushed in on itself. The body hadn't yet registered its death and remained suspended in midair as the dead dragon flapped its wings one last time. Gil hefted his axe high as the carcass fell back to earth. Gripping one of the spikes tight, he rode it to the ground, jumping off at the last second before it collided with a boulder the size of a house.

He dropped into a crouch and rolled as he hit the ground, sliding on the slick surface and nearly face planting. He leapt to his feet and shouted. "Stuck the landing!"

I laughed, and a triumphant cheer rose from my lips, to which the others swiftly joined in. *We did it!*

# CHAPTER 2 - ALL THAT GLITTERS

As the adrenaline flooded out of my system, I slumped to the ground, the rest of my battle fatigue slowly drained back to zero. The others followed suit, and we basked in our hard-fought victory.

I went and retrieved my knife from the dragon and looted its heart from its carcass. Gil clapped me on the back as I stood up.

"That was one hell of a fight," he said in his trademark baritone. "I know my fatigue was high at the end, how about yours?"

"Man, I was two swings away from collapsing on the ground. That was close."

"Hell of a fight, though," he repeated. "I feel bad about dealing the final blow."

"Don't. That was far too epic for me to complain about. Besides, glory is for suckers. I got what I needed."

"It was pretty cool, but fuck, man, that was terrifying." He held out his fist, which I bumped.

"Won't get any arguments from me. Now go grab your loot and let's get the hell out of here."

"Oh, right, I almost forgot," Gil said with a grin and went off with Levi and Alistair to pick over what remained of the dragon.

I smiled at his back as I watched the three fight over loot drops before focusing on my own prize.

*Combat Results!*
*One Downed (Elder Dragon): 45000 Exp!*
*Total Exp Gained: 45000!*
*Exp: 10000/10000*

*Level Up!*

*Level: 100*

*Stat Points Available: 10*

*Ability Point Available!*

I held off on using my new ability point and pulled up my quest tab; a new screen flared to life in my vision.

*Quest: Legendary Class: Blade Master*

*Type: Legendary*

*Difficulty: S*

*Reward: Class Change*

*Quest Log*

*~~Acquire access to Rogue Class~~*

*~~Acquire access to Paladin Class~~*

*~~Acquire Ability: Aura of the Antimage (Unknown location)~~*

*Acquire Ability: Dance of the Immortal (Seek out Heart of an Elder Dragon)*

Finally, after nearly four years of searching, I'd done it. *My own legendary class, one no one else has yet.*

But I couldn't gloat about it; having a legendary class was something only select few could ever hope to achieve. People would literally kill to find out how I'd obtained it. *Though, even if I shouted it from the rooftops, I don't think anyone else can acquire it.*

Three years of hunting any leads to find the elder dragon only to find it at the very edge of the world. *Doubt there are many more left, not since the elves and the dwarves hunted them to the last centuries ago, or so the legend goes.*

And, even if someone managed to find another one, acquiring *Aura of the Antimage* would be an even more challenging task than taking down a dragon. *Why Evelyn just gave it to me is a mystery. Maybe she's not so heartless after all.* I shook my head and focused on the squishy, dripping heart in my hand.

**Item: The Heart of an Elder Dragon**
**Use item: Yes/No?**
*Yes.*

**Abilities (Choose One)**
**Dragonscale Defense**
**Dance of the Immortal**
**Elemental Resistance (Passive)**

*Dance of the Immortal.* As soon as I thought it, a rush, like a shot of caffeine, ran through me as the screen faded, and my new ability was added to my roster. Which then soon went into my abilities list when I used my newly acquired point. One final screen flared to life in my interface.

**Class change from Swift Paladin to Blade Master**
**Yes/No?**
*Yes.*

I still needed to sort out my stat points, but before I could, Gil called out to me. "D. Over here!"

He sounded excited, so I rushed over. Hidden behind a large mound of rocks and boulders was a treasure trove. An enormous pile of gold and items stood before me, easily up to my chest. It was more gold than I'd ever seen before, millions, a literal fortune, and that wasn't even counting the number of hero-tier items scattered around.

It was by far more gold than I'd earned in all the years since coming to this world. This amount of money was nothing short of a game-changer; it would set our guild up as a powerhouse. *With this much wealth, we could challenge even the Alliance. For once, we could even the playing field.*

"By the nine kings of Hell," I whispered.

"Right! The hell we going to do with it all?" Levi asked.

"The better question is 'how are we going to get it home?'" Gil asked.

He had a point. *No way could we carry even a tenth in our inventories.* We would need some expensive storage chests to store it all in, and even then, it would take several trips to collect it all. I was interrupted from my thoughts by Alistair.

"Guys, do you see that?" he asked, pointing at a dark wooden staff in the middle of the pile.

I tuned him out; it was a magic staff, something I had no use for. I ignored his continued ramblings and went back to logistics when Alistair suddenly bolted and went and grabbed it.

The moment he put his hands on the staff, the pile of gold started to glow. *It's a trap!* "Alistair, run!"

But it was too late. A bolt of lightning fell from the heavens and struck right through him. *Ground* had long since worn off, and he had no defense against the lightning magic; the spell was so powerful, it nearly disintegrated him, blasting him apart and sending a massive wave of force to throw us out of the immediate area. My health bar dropped to half just from how close I was, and it took a moment to recover from having my bells rung.

By the time we'd risen to our feet, the area around where the treasure had been was nothing more than a blasted wasteland, the gold and items reduced to nothing but bits of charred metal and ash. The ground was blackened glass, and Alistair's body was gone. I checked my friends' list only to confirm my fears. A small pile of items and gold remained behind—everything Alistair had on him when he died.

I stared at the spot where Alistair had been moments before, while a small wave of grief rolled through me. *We survived a fucking elder dragon, only for him to die to a stupid trap.* "Damn it."

"Fool," Gil said with a shake of his head. "That was a rookie mistake."

"Yeah, and an incredibly expensive one at that. It'll be god knows how long it'll take him to level back up. That puts the Gloom Knights a man down, and he was our war mage. Markos sure as hell isn't going to step up to the front lines."

"Well, looks like we need to recruit some new blood. We now have two empty seats to fill."

"Let's worry about that later. Let's get off this accursed island first," I said.

"I like that plan," Levi said and bounded forward.

Levi was a brutish man, in every sense of the word. Short brown hair and dull brown eyes. He was only a few inches shorter than me, but he outweighed me by an order of magnitude. Decked out from head to toe in the heaviest plate mail he could get his hands on, he was a real beast of a man. Absolutely nothing could get past that shield of his.

Following his lead, we set off back down the mountain.

Over the next day, we climbed down the rocky mountain and sheer cliff faces, back to the perpetually wet and sad gray stretch of beach where we'd landed our rowboat. Though it was less miserable-looking than when we'd arrived. The storms that gave Stormstruck Reef its name peeled back to reveal bright blue skies.

I nudged Gil and pointed up. "Think the dragon was the cause of the storms?"

"That'd be my guess, but I think we have more important matters to deal with right now."

I followed his gaze out towards the *Delilah*, the ship we'd chartered to ferry us out here, and I knew what he was getting at. "Captain Avery isn't going to let us walk, not when he thinks we have the dragon's hoard."

Levi spat on the ground. "Fucking pirates."

"My sentiments exactly. Well, let's get this over with," I said and climbed into the rowboat and set back to the ship. The *Delilah* was a rough-looking ship, its name painted on the side of the vessel in neat letters, which stood apart next to the worn and somewhat rotted planks that comprised the hull. A brace of cannons lined the deck, with several more protruding below from the gun deck.

As we climbed aboard the brigantine, we were met with a ghost ship. Not a soul was on deck, which only confirmed what we'd suspected. *They'll ambush us when we leave the captain's cabin.*

From a look, I knew the others were thinking the same thing, but I was confident we could handle anything they tried to throw at us, so I sauntered forwards to the cabin without a care in the world, acting like a bumbling fool. "Avery, we're back," I called too loudly as I thrust open the door.

Avery's cabin was what tipped me off in the first place; it was too well decorated for a simple merchant ship. Expensive wooden furniture and a black drake leather chair dominated the cramped space; it was a marvel he could move around at all.

The cabin was empty, and knowing what awaited us, we filed out of the cabin and found ourselves surrounded.

Nearly a dozen men, all dressed in mismatched clothing but all bearing the same hungry scowl as they stared us down. Captain Avery was in the middle of the crowd, leaning against a large wooden crate.

Avery was a snake in human clothing with thin, sour features and weak, villainous green eyes. He couldn't have looked more sinister if he'd started twirling his thick mustache. He cleared his throat as we approached. "All right, you lot. Hand over everything in your possessions, and I may just let you live."

Normally, I'd have just tried to barter, work out a deal that would benefit the both of us, but fresh from the death of one of my friends, I had no mercy to spare. "Gloom Knights, to war," I whispered to the others.

Without waiting for their response, I bolted ahead to the nearest pirate, a thick man with chestnut tanned skin who wielded a length of pipe. He swung carelessly with the rusted metal, slow in his meaty hands. I sidestepped, parried his arm, and pivoted, bringing a right hook to his cheek, sending him to the deck and the pipe spinning out of reach.

Two others rushed in, one unarmed, the other held a wicked fillet knife. I flicked my foot out, catching the unarmed man in the side of the knee and shattering it. He fell to the deck, screaming, clutching his ruined leg.

The knife entered the edge of my vision, and I took a single step back. The blade passed an inch from my face. I shot my left arm under his to grip his wrist, and my right on his tricep, just past his elbow. Pushing with one and pulling with the other, I snapped his arm at the crook.

Taking the knife from his limp grip, I slid it across his throat, turning his screams to a gurgling death rattle.

I ducked the arterial spray and kicked the unarmed man with the broken leg in the face. With him stunned with a broken nose, I jammed the stolen knife home in his eye.

Blood sluiced across the deck and down the side of the *Delilah* in rivers.

In the minute it'd taken me to dispatch those three, Gil and Levi had torn apart the others, leaving only Avery to contend with.

He shook with fear and dropped his sword, staring wide-eyed at us like we were devils. "Please, spare me. I'm sorry."

I shook my head. This trip had brought up too many old memories, and I was out of forgiveness—for him or myself.

"Ask the gods for mercy. You'll get none from me."

***

I cleaned the blood off my knife using Avery's coat and stood up from beside his corpse, careful not to step in the pooling blood.

With the crew dead, we set about looting their bodies and the ship. It seemed Avery was a highly successful pirate, as the cargo hold was filled to the brim with chests of gold and items, though it paled in comparison to the dragon's hoard.

Gil whistled long and slow as he took in the sight. "Well, looks like we still came out ahead during this trip after all."

"Seems so, but we now have the same problem as before. How the hell are we going to move all of this back home?" I asked, searching for an answer. "Lake Gloom is halfway across Nexus, and none of us have leveled up *Sailing*."

Levi just nodded along, not helping the conversation in the slightest. Gil perked up, before groaning.

"What?" I asked.

"All we need to do is hire a crew to sail her back to Lake Gloom…" he trailed off, leaving me to put two and two together.

"Not a bad pl—oh, son of a bitch."

"Yep."

"All right," I said with a sigh and climbed the steps back to the upper decks. "Let's go talk to Miguel."

*He's on the other side of the isle, though. Looks like we're burning our teleportation scrolls.* They were incredibly expensive, but we'd made more than enough gold to cover the cost. We teleported to the gate on the outskirts of Arroyo, which lay just outside the borders of the West Kingdom.

The unmistakable odor rising from Causwick Bay was especially pungent when we stepped out of the gate.

"Must've had a good haul today, judging by the stench," Gill said, breathing through his mouth.

On the many docks that lined the port, seven of them held large fishing vessels, and most of them had a steady stream of workers unloading the day's catch. We walked past the docks towards the center of town, past a slew of worn and rotting wooden buildings. The salt and moisture in the air played hell with the buildings year-round.

"Shit," Gil said, pointing up ahead. "We picked the wrong day to show up."

A fleet of armored stagecoaches and wagons rode past, filled with dozens of armed Alliance soldiers.

"Long as we stay out of their way, they have no reason to notice us."

The coaches headed to the edge of the docks, and the soldiers began loading up crates by the hundreds to the wagons with practiced efficiency.

"Looks like they're loading cargo to take back to Central, so let's get to the Cask before they get done," I said.

The Gray Cask was the only stone building on the street, and it stood out next to its shoddy wooden neighbors. The loud drone of its patrons bombarded us as we walked down the steps to enter the tavern.

If the stench was bad outside in the open air, it was repugnant inside. We were assaulted with a pungent mixture of smells. Ale, wood smoke, and roasting meat mixed with the sour stench of sweat and the rawness of the sea and its bounties.

I tried to ignore the smell and sat down at the nearest empty table. Knowing that we'd be here for a while, I ordered a round. We sat, nursing our drinks for over an hour. I tried to keep my number down, but after the second, I didn't give a shit anymore. Just as I downed my fourth ale, the guest we needed to see swaggered in.

Miguel was a cocky ladies' man, or he styled himself like one in his skintight black tunic and leather pants. I couldn't deny he certainly cut a handsome figure, built with the lean frame of a swimmer, with his jet-black hair and dark skin giving him an exotic air. He looked to be around the same age as myself, give or take a few years, though, in fairness, none of us were as young as we looked.

He didn't even glance in our direction as he entered. He knew we were there; he also knew that we needed his help. No one came or went without him knowing about it and making a profit on the info. He sauntered over to the bar, grabbed a bottle of top-shelf brandy, and took a large swig before setting the bottle down. The bartender didn't so much as a glance in his direction as he walked off; Miguel motioned us to follow him, and we had no choice but to comply.

Down in the basement, Miguel walked over to the far wall and pressed a hidden button on the wall. A false door swung open to reveal a rather spacious and well-lit office. Which was just for show since Miguel didn't need to hide his criminal dealings; he paid his dues to the Merchants Guild like everyone else.

He sat down in a chair behind a large, expertly carved wooden desk, which was more of a work of art than a piece of furniture. "What can I do for you boys this time?" he asked the three of us with a sarcastic tone, though his eyes never left mine.

I suppressed a sigh at the superiority in his voice, and I couldn't even be angry at him. Much as I hated dealing with him, he got the job done every time. "I require your delivery services."

Miguel wore a slightly smug smile on his face as he spoke, "And what, pray tell, is it that you need to be delivered? It must be quite important for you to have come to me." His gaze shifted to one of abject greed. "Did you finally figure out a way to quickly produce more Gloom shrooms?"

I shook my head. "Unfortunately not, I even asked Alistair to try expanding the cave with earth magic, but from what he told me, if we excavate any further, we risk the structural integrity of the rock. Given the location of the cave, a few more gold in my pocket isn't worth having the ground beneath our home crumble out from under us."

Miguel's face fell at my words, and he stopped himself from cursing. "Oh, well. Might actually be for the best right now. Since the demand is so much higher than your supply, we can charge an arm and a leg for each dose, raking in gold hand over fist."

I leaned back in my chair and crossed my arms, staring down Miguel. "That's the first I'm hearing of price gouging. I didn't think our product was selling that fast from the coin we've been getting. You wouldn't undercut your supplier, would you, Miguel?"

Miguel froze for a split second but covered it with a fake smile. "Of course not, my friend. It's just grown increasingly popular this past month or so. Your share will reflect the increased profits, have no fear of that. Now, what was it you kiddos needed from me?" he asked quickly.

I let him change the subject and sat back up in the chair, propping my arm under my chin. "I've recently come into possession of a ship. It seems the former crew left it abandoned. I was hoping you'd be able to lend us the services of one of your crews to sail her back to Gloom-Harbor."

"Oh, if that's all you need, that shouldn't be too difficult to arrange," he said, fumbling at a drawer under his desk for a moment before pulling out a rather large map of Nexus. Miguel unfurled it across the smooth mahogany surface.

"Where is this ship of yours located?"

I leaned forward in my seat to get a better look at the map. "I'm not sure the exact island we landed on, but somewhere around there," I said, pointing at Stormstruck Reef, located near the edge of the map.

He whistled at that. "Morrigan's Feathers! How'd you end up way the hell out there?"

I told him about our hunt for the dragon and of Alistair's death.

"My condolences," he deadpanned.

"Can you do it or not?"

He didn't answer right away. Instead, he reached across his desk and took hold of a small wooden pipe, taking ample time to light it. "Oh, I can do it, but I would need to send two crews out on one ship. Keeping that plus the distance in mind, this won't be cheap."

"How much?"

Miguel took a long draw from his pipe, blowing the smoke straight at us. "Let's call it eight hundred gold for services rendered."

"Done."

I pulled out the heavy bag of gold and thrust it onto his desk. The thump of gold caused Miguel's eyes to light once more. The three of us stood up from our chairs, and Miguel and I shook hands. As I turned to leave, Miguel asked one last question.

"Just out of curiosity, what's the name of the ship you acquired?" he asked, putting heavy emphasis on "acquired."

"The ship's name is the *Delilah*."

He laughed deeply at that. However, underneath his laughter lurked some unpleasant nastiness. "You managed to wrangle Old Avery's ship out from under him, eh?" he said with another chuckle.

"Something like that…is that all?"

Miguel stood up, sudden enough that he knocked over his pipe, sending still-lit ashes tumbling across the wood.

"Hold up a moment," he said. His voice echoed with what sounded like desperation. "I don't think you kiddos know what you've gotten your hands on here."

I was intrigued, though I wouldn't let it show on my face. As far as I was aware, the *Delilah* was just a rundown ship in need of some serious TLC, but it wasn't that at all if Miguel wanted it so badly. Odds were good that he was cooking up some scheme, and I just knew that if it involved Miguel and either plotting or scheming, he would try and cheat us on the deal. I turned to him and tried my best to look as unreadable as I could manage. Getting the better of Miguel was something I rarely achieved, but I would be damned if I let him screw me on this.

"Well, then, why don't you illuminate us on that fact?"

He smile deepened, and I knew what was going on inside his head. I'd just told him that I didn't understand the value of the ship, which couldn't be helped. He was currently thinking of the best way to take advantage of that.

"Well, you see, Captain Avery was…I guess you could call him a former employee of mine."

"He ran smuggling routes for you is what you mean," I interrupted.

Avery had been a sailor and a crook, so the only business Miguel would need someone like that for would be to run goods up and down the coasts of Nexus. Miguel blanched at my words. So used to lording over us, he could forget I could be clever when the occasion stuck me.

"Which makes the *Delilah* a smugglers' ship and not the simple brig I took her for," I continued. *No wonder he wants it. Smugglers' ships are rare and incredibly expensive. Though why the rush, Miguel? Trying to avoid the heavy taxes from the Merchants Guild?*

"Yes, that's it exactly." Miguel finally noticed the mess he had made on his beautiful desk. The embers of ash singed the edges of the map, causing smoke to fill the room. He swept the whole mess off in a rush before the small fire could spread, and ran his ash-stained fingers through his ink-black hair. "So, you can see why I want her back."

"She was your ship?"

"She was indeed. I paid a king's ransom to have her built by an artisan who specializes in such things. I was also paying Avery a great sum of money to sail her for me. The risk in hiring such characters is that one day, his greed got the better of him, and he absconded with my ship and its cargo." He spat on the ground at the thought. "Cost me a fucking fortune, he did."

My heart went out for Miguel there. Really, I promise.

"You want the ship? Well, let's hear your offer?"

"Five thousand gold, plus let's say two hundred silver for the bounty that I had on Avery."

"Hmm," I said. *That's not chump change, but it's also a pittance compared to the money Miguel stands to make running goods up the coast. It's a bad deal, so how about a counteroffer?* "I'll give you the ship. It's yours, but I want ten percent of all the money you make running cargo with her. Plus, the two hundred silver for the bounty. I did earn that, after all," I said, smiling at him.

Miguel paled at the thought of losing so much money. "That...that simply isn't possible," he stammered. "Duran, be reasonable."

"Take it or leave it, Miguel, and hurry up. I haven't been home in months. I want to leave."

He thought about it for a minute, sitting back down in his chair, his hand propping up his chin. "Five percent," he countered.

"Nine."

"Seven."

"Eight," I said.

"Done," Miguel agreed.

We all stood up from our seats again, the wood creaking as we rose. Miguel proffered me his hand once more, and we shook on our new deal.

"You can send the first payment with the rest of our profits when you come to pick up the next shipment," I told him. I picked up the bag of gold I had placed on the desk. While I wasn't thrilled, it was the best possible outcome. We all turned and headed for the door when a thought struck me. "Also," I said, turning back to face Miguel, "You can keep the items hidden in the compartments of the ship, but the gold and the items that are in plain view belong to us."

"Of course," he said, flashing his trademark grin. "I would never cheat my best clients."

*Right, of course, you wouldn't.* We left Miguel's office through the crowd of patrons in the Cask, exiting into the bright sunlight. Once we were outside, we headed back to the teleportation gate. It was about twice as tall and wide as a standard door frame, comprised of polished white marble that gleamed in the sunlight. I'd always found them pretty, even if they didn't match any of the surrounding buildings.

We climbed up the steps to the gate, our footsteps echoing sharply on the marble steps. We stood in line behind several small groups of adventurers waiting for their turn at the gate. "You know, I've always wondered why NPCs can't use teleportation?" Levi mused, scratching at his scruffy hair.

"Don't know, but I know what happens when they try."

Both Gil and Levi perked up at my words. "Well, you gonna share, bud?"

"Sure. During my first life here, back when we'd just arrived on nexus, a group of players wanted to test out and see what would happen if you shoved an NPC through a teleportation gate," I began as we moved forward in line. "They kidnapped a helpless farmhand who'd been in the wrong place when those assholes had gotten bored. Three of the players picked up the NPC and tossed him headfirst into the gate…and from what I heard, they kept finding blood and bits of flesh inside the gate for weeks after."

"That's disturbing," Gil said with a shake of his head.

"Was worse to watch, poor guy looked like a watermelon in a blender when it was over."

Levi turned green. "Well, I can't eat watermelon ever again."

I laughed as we waited our turn, joking and cutting up with Gil and Levi for the next few minutes. After what felt like a lifetime, it was our turn, and we stepped through the swirling mass of blue light to head home.

# CHAPTER 3 - MEMENTO MORI

We arrived at the front gate of the Castle Gloom-Harbor. The dark gray stone looked sallow in the bright summer afternoon, but the soft breeze coming in from Lake Gloom was heavenly. The giant wooden bridge lowered at our approach. I looked up to see one of the guards operating the switch. As we walked through the outer bailey, we passed several of our NPC men at arms, who stood at attention as we passed. I nodded back out of politeness and headed inside.

A trio of our maid staff were in the entranceway, cleaning and polishing to their hearts' content. They too, stopped and bowed respectfully as we approached. "Jade, Ruby, you know you don't have to act so formal with us," I said, turning to Amber. "Didn't I tell you that it's unnecessary to bow?"

"My apologies, lord. But Mistress Evelyn demands it."

I grumbled to myself, but I couldn't do anything about it. *Evelyn and her godsdamned jokes.* "All right, fine. Whatever," I said with a sigh. "Not like I can force her to stop. Amber, would you mind bringing drinks to the guildhall?"

"Right away, lord," she said with another bow and headed toward the kitchens.

"All right, let's get this over with," I said.

I took a left down the hallway to our meeting room. Once inside, I sat back in my chair and called a meeting through the chat in my interface. The three of us settled in to wait for everyone. As usual, it took about half an hour for everyone to rouse themselves from whatever they did to occupy their time and arrive.

Markos was the first to arrive, followed closely by Yumiko and Makenna. Behemoth lumbered in next and went and sat by Levi. I didn't see Wilson enter, but cloth rustled against wood, and I turned to him as he sat down next to me. Evelyn and Adam walked together and sat down in their seats, only to start whispering to one another. Harper was the last to sit down, but that was par for the course. Once everyone had sat down, I got right down to business, starting with the bad news.

"Alistair is dead."

A round of solemn looks passed around the group, though none were shocked by the news. He wasn't here, and I'm sure a few noticed his absence from the guild roster. Soon after, Amber walked in, carrying a large tray laden down with drinks and began serving us.

We held a small vigil, more of a wake really, telling stories about Alistair, an odd ritual considering Alistair wasn't really dead, but it would still be many years before he could level up enough to return. A fact that some people didn't really understand.

"I don't get it," Harper said after draining his mug of ale. "Why don't we just go pick Alistair up when he respawns in two months?"

I turned my gaze to Harper, who had the misfortune to enter the Ouroboros Project when he was only eighteen. As such, his horrible acne clashed with his bright orange hair, which he'd shaved to the scalp on each side of his head leaving a garish fauxhawk which he kept insisting was "dope."

Harper was perpetually a teenager, which, in my opinion, was a hell unto itself. To top it off, he was a brash, impulsive hothead who was generally a giant pain in my ass. His only saving grace was he was the best shot I'd ever seen.

I was about to reply when Wilson spoke up from next to me. "That's not how things work, Harper."

Harper slammed his mug down on the table, spilling some onto his blue shirt, his face red already from one glass. "I don't get it. Other guilds have no issue helping to level up their fallen members, why can't we?"

The vein in Wilson's head throbbed as he let out a deep sigh, running a hand through his swept-back, steel-gray hair. He opened his mouth to respond—probably too harshly—but I stepped in.

"Wilson, Harper's still new. This is the first time we've had a member die on us since he's been with us. And he's right—we operate by a different set of rules than most guilds," I said to my apoplectic second-in-command, turning to Harper. "Because of how we do business, we can't afford weakness. Even if we were to help him level, it would still take a good couple years to get Alistair back up to strength to be of any use to us. That's years where we'd be weakened, and we can't afford it."

"He does make a good point though, dear guild leader," Evelyn said, looking up from the conversation with her brother. "We already have one empty seat, and Alistair makes two. That puts us in a precarious situation."

She made a valid argument, but then again, she was rarely ever wrong. Evelyn shared many of the same traits as her twin brother, Adam. Both were pale as ghosts and had the same silver hair and radiant golden eyes. Adam was taller than Evelyn, though I knew she had more lean muscle than he did. He also didn't share Evelyn's sharp cheekbones and had a more rugged set to his clean-shaven face.

Wilson tugged at his neatly trimmed gray beard, clearly wanting to say something, but we'd gotten off track.

"Look, this conversation can wait till the next guild meeting," I said. "Let's not get into this at Alistair's vigil. I say we adjourn for the day. All in favor?"

A round of ayes echoed through the room.

44

With the vigil wrapped up and our business out of the way, we brought the meeting to a close and dispersed. I headed up to the third floor to my bedroom to take a bath and relax. My room was the first door next to the stairs, and I pushed the heavy wooden door aside and locked it behind me. My room was minimalistic but elegant.

Red oak furniture dominated the bedroom. A large, four-poster canopy bed took up the most space, leaving little room for the wardrobe in the far corner and the nightstand. I had no decorations barring the heavy crimson drapes over my windows that kept the room in a perpetual state of twilight.

A bath enticed me, but I was still a little melancholy about Alistair, and a drink sounded better. I grabbed the crystal decanter on my nightstand, poured a generous measure of whiskey into the glass, and stepped out onto the balcony. Leaning over the dark stone railing, I could see well past the Rolling Hills, which comprised the territory of Gloom-Harbor. The green hills looked almost like a watercolor painting under the bright gaze of the sun.

Movement from above drew my attention to a raven that flew overhead under the sunlight, circling, looking for food. It seemed to take note of my presence at the same time I noticed it, as it swooped down to land on the edge of the railing, looking at me with its large, blood-red eyes. The raven's feathers were sleek and looked like oil under the bright light.

"Well, aren't you beautiful?"

The raven flinched at my words, startled by the sudden break in silence. It started cawing at me and flew away. I chuckled and turned back to the view. The amber liquid burned down my throat, and something wet slid down my cheek, I wiped it away to discover I was crying.

Alistair's death upset me, but it wasn't what was twisting my gut into knots. He was dead, yes, but that wasn't the be-all-end-all. It wasn't a true death for him; he would come back eventually.

She never would.

I drained the glass and threw it as hard as I could over the railing. It shattered on the stone wall far below me. *Godsdamn it! It's been fifteen years, why can't I just forget already?*

Deaths always hit me like this, always brought back the memories I wanted to forget.

"I'm sorry, Soph," I said for the thousandth time, but my words meant nothing. Such things don't burden the dead.

I knew that all too well.

***

"C'mon, sleepyhead. We're going to be late!" Soph shouted as she dragged me out of bed and into the glaring morning sun.

I fought a halfhearted battle to get her to release my hand, but I couldn't fight against her energy, so I settled for gripping her hand tighter and let her drag me along toward the front of the camp.

The gate was open when we reached the entrance, which only happened when scavenger teams were sent out to gather supplies. Parked in front, almost wedged into the gap, was an old retrofitted deuce and a half, outfitted with massive tires for urban crawling and armor plating that looked durable enough to keep out even the ghouls' sharp claws. UV floodlights were fastened around the monstrosity. It looked intimidating and powerful, but it didn't make me feel any safer. *It'll take more than military might to stop them. They're fast, deadly, and just plain smarter than us.*

The truck was full to capacity as we climbed aboard. In the back were two soldiers, though they weren't in standard military gear. No insignia or identification of any kind. They held the demeanor of no-nonsense, motioning us to take our seats with sharp movements, but refusing to speak. Once inside, the truck's loud engines started, and we left the place I'd come to see as my prison for the last six months. *Good Riddance.*

I stared out the window for a while as we rolled through the streets filled with broken cars and broken glass. For a long while, the old world passed me, and I was fine. Then the area started looking familiar. Cold dread filled my gut, and I tried to fight the emotions welling inside, as we drove past my house.

The windows were broken, and the door was shattered off its hinges in thick pieces. A single chunk hung listlessly on the brass hinge, the light wood coated in a heavy brown stain. It looked like someone had splashed a coat of paint, but it wasn't paint. I turned away. My skin beaded with sweat, and I wanted to vomit.

We rode for an hour until we reached an old airport, and the driver pulled the truck into a large hanger. Most of the space was dominated by a huge 747. I'd never flown, let alone seen a plane up close before. It had been painted black and gray, and quite a few spotlights had been fastened to the frame.

As we boarded, we filed in line among several hundred other passengers, just like us. Refugees. Survivors. Sophia and I sat next to each other, holding hands and trying to hide our nerves. *Whoever we've crawled into bed with, it speaks a lot about them that they have access to a working plane, let alone clearance to fly.*

We took off out of the hanger and down the runway. As I'd never flown before, I panicked for a second as we took off, but the view from my window shattered my fear and left me conflicted. It was an incredible, yet very surreal experience.

The sights of the city so far below us were bitter. The once-majestic skyscrapers, towering giants that held so much light and life, were now gray and lifeless, reminiscent of tombstones—a mass grave for an untold number of dead. Yet, despite the horror of what I was seeing, freedom burned within my heart. *Maybe now I can put my ghosts to rest.*

Once the plane had safely landed and shut its engines off, we were led out in a single file line. We'd landed at another airport, though this one was clearly for military use. Several rusting and burned-out wrecks of fighter jets and a few guard stations clustered around with numerous heavily armed soldiers standing watch.

There was a huge building that looked to be an old army command center, lit up like a Christmas tree. Every window burned with bright light. I thought this was where all of us were heading, but we marched past the building to a warehouse situated around back. The rusted, corrugated door screamed in protest as it was shoved open. I expected more rusted metal on the inside, but it was clear that this wasn't a simple warehouse. The walls were reinforced concrete latticed with rebar supports and massive I-beam columns to support the weight of the roof, which looked sturdy enough to survive a bomb strike.

*Maybe it can. This must be a survival bunker leftover from the Beggars' Revolution.* My thought was only confirmed as we were led to a huge freight elevator, and a hundred of us at a time were taken down. Sophia and I were in the first group, and with a heavy groan of metal, we started down.

We descended for almost five minutes. It had to be at least a full mile below ground. With a jarring stop, we reached the bottom.

The elevator opened into a massive man-made cavern. Concrete and steel, from floor to ceiling, stretched at least a hundred feet in the air and as far back as my eye could see. The space was amazing, but the sheer volume of people moving around sent my jaw plummeting.

A hundred thousand souls stared at us as the elevator opened, craning their necks to get a look at the new blood.

I didn't know there was anywhere near this many survivors left. Sophia was ecstatic and kept jerking on my clothes, pointing this way and that, showing off something new she'd seen, while I wasn't as enthusiastic about the sights. It was damned impressive, but when you took away the sheer size of it, it was just another refugee camp.

Without any ceremony, we were led in groups to the showers. The showers were small, one-person affairs, but the water was almost boiling, and I stayed under it for a long time, scrubbing myself with soap till the stream that ran off me and swirled down the drain was no longer tinged with brown. Once I was clean, I dried myself with a towel and found rows of shelves with clean clothes and toiletries, plain white t-shirts and gray sweatpants in every size.

I got dressed and stopped by the sinks to brush my teeth. The mirror was large and spotless, giving me the first good look at myself in a very long time. The years of malnutrition and living in squalor hadn't been kind. My skin was pale and thin, stretched too tight over the bones.

One look at my wiry beard and tangled hair, and I snorted in disgust. I took a nearby electric trimmer to both. When my copper hair filled the sink, I squirted a liberal amount of shaving cream and shaved my face clean. I almost wished I hadn't when I saw the result. With my clean-shaven face and hair cropped so close to my scalp, I looked emaciated and hollow.

I wiped my face and cleaned up my mess before heading outside to wait for Soph.

She arrived about ten minutes later, looking much more refreshed than I felt, and if I thought she was pretty before, with her dirty clothes and grimy skin. It was nothing compared to her now. She practically glowed. She was wearing identical clothing as me, but my eyes were drawn to her chest, as it was apparent she wasn't wearing a bra, and I quickly averted my eyes.

"You look nice," I said with a cough.

She beamed at me, her face flushed by the heat of the water, and ran a hand over my buzzed hair.

"So do you," she said, helping me to my feet.

We waited for the rest of our group to finish bathing, then we were taken to a communal mess room, where teams of chefs worked with the speed of demons to serve several hundred people at once.

After a light stew, we headed deeper into the facility, past bunkhouses, medical tents, sports fields, and even an arcade until we arrived at a heavy steel reinforced door guarded by two guards, both armed with serious firepower.

With a nod from the doctor, they let us pass. The heavy steel door swung open without a sound. Once inside, I found us walking down a large hallway. It reminded me of a hospital. White tile and soothing, non-threatening, beige-painted walls, all undercut with the sharp white fluorescent bulbs, which hummed constantly.

Once the last person filed in, the heavy door swung shut and locked with an ominous click. Soph took my hand and clung to my back as we walked down the corridor, though the identical walls made keeping track difficult. We reached a particularly long hallway with wooden doors spaced about a hundred feet apart. A team of scientists walked out and ordered us into smaller groups of fifteen to twenty each.

Our groups lined up by each of the doors, and we all filed inside. The room was large. Sharp and clinical, surgical even. Floor to ceiling sparkling white tile and stainless-steel carts next to strange machines. The entire back wall was dominated by computer screens and monitors, blinking lights from a hundred different sources displaying a ton of information that I couldn't understand.

There were over a dozen glass tubes in the center of the room, large enough for a full-grown man. Wires and the like sprouted out the top and back, snaking down under the floor. Every one of them was open, waiting. Expectant.

Three technicians brought us all to the side and began going through some preparations. My heart leapt into my throat as my arms were swabbed with alcohol. The sound of rubber gloves snapping sent childish fear spiking through me.

"What's going on?" one of the other refugees asked, his voice panicked.

The others voiced similar concerns all the while I tried to keep my cool. I put on a brave face for Sophia, but I was shaking with nerves. The scientist in charge looked up from his preparations. He saw the looks of fear on our faces and wisely decided to calm us down.

He was a tall man in a crisp, tailored three-piece suit under a lab coat. Middle-aged with deep-set eyes and salt and pepper hair that gave him a roguish appearance. He cleared his throat and spoke, finally letting us in on what the hell was going on. He had a loud, clear voice that echoed in the quiet room, but he forgot his audience and began with a string of words that sounded either incredibly technical or completely made up.

He stopped speaking, mumbling a curse under his breath, and started over.

"Forgive me, I forgot who I was talking to. Welcome to the Ouroboros Project. I'm sure you're all curious as to why you're here," he said, coming over to us. "I won't bog you down with the details since you'd need to be a neuroscientist to grasp the full implications of the technology at hand. But to simplify things, we've broken new ground in virtual reality development, and we believe we've finally cracked the code to digital immortality."

A round of gasps echoed through the room, mine included. *So that's what this is about. Saving the world, my ass.* I didn't agree with virtual reality, or so-called digital immortality. It was nothing but cowardice. *Running away while the ghouls ravage the world topside.*

*Whatever, not my fucking problem anymore. I've got clean clothes and food. That's probably the best I can hope for at this point.*

The man droned on for a bit more, trying to wow us with his words about how they made the discovery, but I tuned him out. I didn't care about any of it.

Sophia was next to me, wide-eyed at his speech, excitement building in her eyes. I smiled down at her, and she caught me looking at her because she tilted her head, smiled, and gave my hand a reassuring squeeze.

When the man was done with his speech, he got straight to the point. "The reason why you're here is quite simple. We need volunteers who are willing to have their minds scanned. We need copious amounts of data to help build realistic virtual worlds, and we can't do it without your help."

I could tell from the tone in the man's voice that it was nothing but fluff and bullshit. He was asking us, but it was clear that we didn't have a choice in the matter. I shifted to look at the door we'd entered. A keyless lock kept us from leaving, and the man carried a pistol under his lab coat. *The others are too wrapped up in the daydream he painted for them. They've been given a modicum of hope, and they're clinging to it.*

I didn't trust any of them, but I had no choice but to go along with it. I wasn't going to abandon Sophia and leave her alone. As the man finished speaking, he asked everyone who was willing to volunteer to step forward, and everyone but me stepped without a second's hesitation. The man gave me a once over, his eyes staring at me unblinking till I relented and followed suit.

"Excellent. Then I will leave you all in the capable hands of the technicians," he said as he departed, swiping a keycard to exit the room.

The technicians led us over to each of the tanks and started hooking us into them. The metal was cold against my skin, and it took them almost an hour to strap all of us in. They slid several needles into my arms and injected me with something that made me sleep and dream.

I dreamed deeply, but it wasn't like any other dream I'd ever experienced before. It was too bright and colorful. I tasted things that lingered on the tip of my tongue, half-remembered sights, and smells of my childhood. It got increasingly vivid until I thought I was reliving my old life.

For a too-brief time, I got to see my family again, got to watch Micah grow up again, see his crooked teeth and caramel eyes wide as he begged me to play with him, repeatedly. It made whatever shady deal I'd struck worthwhile; I'd have done anything to stay like that forever.

I was jolted out of my dreams by intense pain. As if a rod of molten metal had been shoved into my skull. My eyes flew open, and I screamed till my voice tore. The pain dulled by a fraction as more painkillers entered my system.

When I could focus my eyes, outside the glass, a technician stared at me with wide and panicked eyes. He was mashing a button on the console next

Grayson Sinclair

to him as hard as he could, tapping it like it would win him a prize, all while flooding my system with more drugs, which made my eyes heavy.

"What did you do?"

"Uh…uh, you weren't supposed to wake up for that."

"What—what did you do?" I repeated.

"We attached a neural transmitter to your brain stem. It's to help ease the burden of information collected from the machine," he stammered, still pressing the button to pump sedatives into me.

My eyes grew too heavy to hold open any longer, and I fell into a deep sleep from which I did not dream.

I awoke slowly, incredibly groggy, and my throat was dry as the desert. The glass enclosure opened with a hiss, and I tasted fresh air. It was sweet but did little to soothe my parched mouth. The technician watching me lifted a bottle of water to my lips, and I sipped fresh water until it was empty, and I could speak again.

The man threw the bottle in the trash and helped me out of the tube. Itchy dulled pain followed as the IV and other needles were unplugged, and then it intensified as they removed the catheter. I cursed them and tried to stand on my own, humiliated by their carrying me, but I took one step and sprawled to the ground, my muscles unresponsive.

Two attendants helped me into a nearby wheelchair, and I glared daggers at them. They wheeled me out of the room. Before we left, I turned and looked at the rows of tubes. Several of them were empty, but Sophia was still in there, sleeping peacefully.

"Where are you taking me?"

The female technician leaned down and smiled at me. "To get some food and water, as well as speak to the director. He's anxious to make your acquaintance."

54

I wanted to argue, but I was tired, and the prospect of more water shut me up. I was escorted to a room much further down. It was similar to the one that housed the Ouroboros Project. The same white tile. There was a stainless-steel table bolted to the floor and a single chair of the same material, the only other thing in there except for a showerhead on the far wall and a drain in the center.

The male technician stood by the door while the female wheeled me to the table. A pitcher of water and two glasses lay on the table along with a bowl of tomato soup, the reddish liquid steaming delectably. My stomach rumbled, but I was too tired to eat. I leaned over to pick up the pitcher of water but was too weak to lift it.

"Here, let me."

The voice startled me, and I almost knocked over the water. I looked up to see the man who had told us about the project, the director, but on second glance, it wasn't the same man. They looked incredibly similar, but this man had more gray in his hair and beard, more lines under his eyes. *Maybe his older brother?*

He poured me a glass and helped me to drink. When I'd drained it, he sat down opposite me and cleared his throat, motioning for me to eat, but I just stared at him, waiting.

He frowned when I refused. "Not hungry?"

I shook my head.

"Well, then, I'll get to the point. I wanted to thank you for agreeing to join the program. With your help and the help of the others, I believe the project will be a success."

I scoffed at him, to which he smirked. "A cynic. Well, you spent five years in that hellscape above, so I can sympathize, but you still have our thanks."

His praise rang hollow in my ears. The look in his eyes also disturbed me, like I was something to be crushed underfoot—a worm, lowly and beneath contempt. He turned his head and spoke to one of the technicians who wheeled me in here.

"Did you deactivate his neural transmitter?" he asked.

The tech shook his head. "No, sir. You asked us to bring him to you, and we didn't want to waste time."

The director's eyes fell slightly. "I see. That's unfortunate." A hint of regret filled them, which quickly washed away.

He rose sharply in his seat, offering me his hand. I didn't care for his words, or him. I wanted to leave, go back and check on Sophia. *The sooner we get this charade over with, the better.* I managed to stumble up from the wheelchair, my legs trembling with the strain to grip his hand. It was rough with callouses, and he wrapped his fingers tightly around my wrist and squeezed hard. Too hard.

It hurt, and I pulled to no avail; his hand was like iron. Panic-stricken, I looked in his eyes; they held remorse, but it died as he steeled himself. He reached into his lab coat and withdrew his pistol, small in his hands.

At the sight of the gun, I tugged even harder on his hand, but I was too weak. I couldn't escape. So slow, he raised the pistol, and I stared down the barrel. "What are you doing?"

"The transmitter we placed in your skull is far too valuable to waste on a lab rat. I wish you'd just eaten the soup. This would have gone much smoother," he said and pulled me towards him. "You'll remember this, I'm afraid."

I fell off balance to land on the table, soup spilling over to dribble onto the white floor and pour red down the drain. The director placed the cold metal against my temple.

"Enjoy your new life," he said and pulled the trigger.

# Chapter 4 - The Gloam

I bolted upright, stifling the scream that caught in my throat; gasping for air as I tried to calm my racing heart. For a long moment, I took several deep breaths until my heart quit hammering. At some point during the night, my hair had fallen in my face, and I brushed it back to discover it slick with sweat.

"Godsdamnit, just what I needed to relive," I said as I stood up.

I must've passed out as I was on the floor, my empty decanter next to me on the stone. I picked it up and set it on the nightstand as the wind whispered outside, blowing a soft breeze along with morning birdsong. It was warming up outside, but that didn't quell the chill that had settled into my bones from the cold stone floor I'd used as a bed.

I grabbed the spare bottle I kept under the bed and refilled my decanter, trying to decide if I wanted to keep drinking. It was the only thing that banished my ghosts.

Losing Alistair brought up too many old wounds. *I've lost so much, yet I still keep losing the people closest to me.* Regardless if he would return to us, I was still angry and guilty as hell. It was my fault he was killed. He walked into the trap on his own, but I was the reason we faced down that dragon.

*Was it worth it?* I pulled up my character page in my Interface to look at my spoils of war.

*Character Name: Durandahl*

*Level: 100*

*Race: Human*

*Class: Blade Master*

*Reputation: Wanted Criminal*

*Bounty: 300 Gold*

*Stats (-)*

*Strength: 100*

*Strength Sub-Stats: 100*

*Constitution: 50*

*Constitution Sub-Stats: 0*

*Endurance: 50*

*Endurance Sub-Stats: 100*

*Agility: 100*

*Agility Sub-Stats: 300*

*Wisdom: 25*

*Wisdom Sub-Stats: 0*

*Luck: 75*

*Luck Sub-Stats: 75*

*Charisma: 25*

*Charisma Sub-Stats: 0*

*Sub-Stat List [+]*

So much gold and time spent on this. I'd put my wants ahead of the guild's needs and spent too much hunting that bastard. *Was my greed worth the price I forced upon the others?* I wasn't sure I wanted to know.

"Still, it was one hell of an adventure."

*I'm too in my head right now. I need a distraction.* My interface flicked to life in my eyes. The clock read nine in the morning. There shouldn't be anyone in the training room, and I'd developed a sudden need to stab something.

My walk to the training room was uneventful, only interrupted by a handful of maids and guards patrolling. I pushed open the oak door and went inside. Someone was already here, one of the twins. Evelyn. She was currently working her way through her kata on the sparsely padded mats that covered the floor.

"Good morning, Evelyn. Odd to see you here at this hour."

Her gaze turned my way for a moment, her golden eyes positively glowing. "Ah, hello, dear guild leader. Adam was making too much racket with his toys, so I needed some quiet. You?"

"Felt like punching something."

She nodded and returned to her practice. My hand-to-hand combat was rusty; there'd been a hint of awkwardness when I fought the pirates. So, I decided to drill the basic techniques to warm up. A few minutes in, Evelyn's voice startled me.

"Keep your left hand up. Also, your footwork slipped several times."

Evelyn had stopped training to watch my form. I nodded to her and fixed my deficiencies. "Thanks."

We slipped back into silence until Evelyn had finished her forms, and I'd warmed myself up nicely.

"Care to spar?" she asked, her full lips rising to smirk at me.

"Sure, getting my ass handed to me sounds like fun."

It was her turn to laugh. "Well, maybe if you weren't so big and clumsy, you might be able to hit me."

Her jibe didn't faze me. "I've hit you before."

"You've never beaten me, though," she said with a devious glint in her eyes.

"Maybe today's the day."

We settled opposite each other. Evelyn tied back her silver hair and cinched the belt tight on her charcoal gi before she settled into her stance.

Evelyn was small and lean, her entire body sharp and deadly like a blade. Her cheekbones were high and tight on her face, not an ounce of unnecessary fat on her frame. She shifted her balance side to side, her movements quick and agile. We nodded to one another, and before I'd finished moving my head, she was on me.

A predictable move for her. She aimed a roundhouse kick at my side, which I countered by lowering my guard, catching her kick on my shoulder. Such a high kick put her off balance, allowing me to grab her. I flung her into the center of the mats and rushed to press my advantage.

She recovered from the throw quickly and already had her hands up as I reached her. I threw a combination of punches, trying to break her guard. She absorbed them easily, but her foot slipped on one of the mats, and Evelyn lowered her guard to balance. Pressing my luck, I landed a solid hook to the side of her face.

She rocked back from the force of the strike, shaking it off. Grinning, she spat blood on the mat and changed her stance, switching styles. Before I could blink, she rushed me with an open palm strike. Air whistled past my ear as I ducked, right into her next attack. She pivoted and brought her leg up. I couldn't block it.

Agony rippled across my side along with a jarring crack as she broke two ribs. Before she could move, I cinched her leg to my side and lifted her off the ground. Using my other hand to grasp the collar of her gi, I slammed her onto the mats, knocking the breath from her. She gasped as I picked her up again.

Her legs locked around my waist as I picked her up. She arched her back, bending to plant her hands on the mat and used the momentum to throw me. My back slammed to the ground, doing my ribs no favors.

Evelyn slithered across my body to grip my throat, nearly suffocating me.

"I believe I am victorious." She spoke with absolute confidence, and there was nothing I could do to remove her hand.

I nodded at her, and she lessened the grip on my throat. However, she did not pull away entirely. The second my windpipe opened, I gasped for air. "Damn, you got me good with that kick."

Evelyn smiled at me, much in the way I imagine a cruel child who pulls the wings off a fly smiles as the fly tries to crawl away. I was the fly, and I wasn't going anywhere.

"I know. However, you did manage to surprise me a little with that hold, and that right hook was as solid of a punch as you're likely to ever land on me," she said, still holding that smile that chilled me to the bone.

Her gi had come loose during the fight; the pale flesh of her shoulder and collarbone peeked out at me from within her clothes. She caught my eyes, and her smile twisted into one of lasciviousness. She pulled at her belt to let her top slide down her arms.

While not the first time I'd seen her body, I still marveled at the beauty of her curves. Her breasts, small and firm, pale nipples erect as she reveled in my gaze. She shimmied her hips into my groin, leaning down to whisper in my ear. "You gave just as good in that fight, dear guild leader. How about you give it to me even harder now?"

I shook my head. "I'm not nearly drunk enough to handle you right now."

She leaned over to whisper in my ear. "We can always fix that, or you can just give in and take me here and now; you know you want to," she said, sliding her hand towards my pants.

*I shouldn't.* In the back of my mind, I knew where this led, but I wasn't in the best state at the moment. I wasn't in a good head space after reliving my past, and thinking about Sophia always tore at the fragmented remains of my soul. I needed some avenue of escape, and it presented itself as a hyper-sexual sociopath, staring down at me with bedroom eyes.

Evelyn leaned down to kiss me before biting at my lip and lowering her hands to the hem of my shirt. Honestly, I might have given in if she hadn't pressed her hands on my chest as she removed my shirt and brushed against my ribs. The pain I'd been ignoring flared to life, and I fought back a scream.

"Son of a bitch."

"What's wrong?" Evelyn asked, her face displaying curiosity rather than concern for my wellbeing.

"Think you broke a couple of ribs," I hissed.

A flash of understanding came over her. She rose in one fluid motion, sensing that playtime wouldn't be happening. "You should drink a health potion and get some rest. We'll pick this up another time," she said.

She swiftly bent down and retrieved her gi, turning toward the door. She slid her tunic back on, tying in neatly back into place and walked over to the entrance of the room.

"Have a good day, guild leader," she called, shutting the door behind her.

I just stared at the door for a moment in wonder at the situations I managed to get myself in. *As beautiful as she is, I should know better than to keep getting involved with her. I've gotten used to her, so I forget how utterly terrifying she can be.*

A message from Markos interrupted my thoughts.

**D.**

**Come down to the grotto. There's something you need to see.**

I sighed. *Odd, he usually gets uppity when I intrude on his work. Let's see what the hell is going on.* I made my way through the castle and to the main gate exited through the main gate, the only entrance or exit for Castle Gloom-Harbor. A strategic advantage to be sure, but a significant pain in the ass when I needed to get down to the cove. I nodded at the current NPC guard operating the gate.

*I should probably get to know the new guards at some point.* We'd lost a few during the last siege, and I hadn't gotten around to learning the names of the new NPCs. I was always a little weirded out by NPCs. *Technically they're not alive, but even after thirty years, I still find it hard to tell the difference between players and NPCs off the bat.*

The steps leading to the grotto were always damp and mossy from the spray of water that crashed and broke against the rocks. I climbed down carefully and rounded the bend to the cave itself.

Markos was waiting for me and not paying any attention. I nearly collided with him. I put my hand on his shoulders to steady him and ensure he didn't topple over into the cold water.

"Whoa there, bud," I said, taking my hands off him once I knew he wouldn't fall over.

Markos looked up from the ground, wiping the small bit of dirt and water from his white robes. He stared at me, but how he could see me through his thick, shaggy mop of brown hair covering half of his face was magic beyond anything I'd ever witnessed here.

Markos was a younger-looking man of rather average height and a paper-thin frame. A stiff breeze could cut him in half. It had been so long since I'd seen them, I couldn't quite remember the color of his eyes. I wanted to say blue, but I wasn't sure about it. He had a thin, angular face without a wisp of facial hair to complement his slight stature.

"Sorry, D, I didn't see you there," he said frantically, "I was just coming out to wait on you, though the fates ordained this fortuitous encounter."

I stifled the sigh I felt coming. "What's up? Your message was vague."

He motioned me to follow him instead of answering my question. "Come with me, quickly." He turned to walk deeper into the damp cavern. "This is something truly spectacular," he said, rushing ahead in the dark.

Unlike Markos, I took my time navigating the slick cave. One wrong slip and I'd end up in the drink, a prospect I didn't relish repeating ever again. There were torches sporadically placed to make sure we could see a vague outline of the cave and not much else.

As I walked further and further into the cave, the distance between the torches grew. As the pale orange light from the torches faded, I expected to be plunged into darkness. I wasn't, which surprised me. A faint blue glow came from the large cavern ahead of me. As I got closer, the lights grew brighter to where every detail of the rocky cave was outlined by the glow.

I knew what I was looking at, but what I was seeing made no sense. The medium-sized cave that had previously held our growing supply of mushrooms was still comprised of the small fungus. With a tiny difference, half of them were glowing. A soft blue light emitted from each of the mushroom caps, along with a rather pleasant aroma that made me lightheaded.

"I would cover your mouth and nose and try not to breathe in too deeply, if it pleases you," Markos spoke from somewhere in the cave.

Footsteps shuffled over the rocks just above me, and I found Markos with a large black cloth wrapped tightly around the lower half of his face.

He tossed me one, and I misjudged the feather-light material and wasn't able to grab the fabric on my first attempt but managed to snag it before it floated to the ground and got soaked in the water. I hastily tied the cloth around my head and cinched it tight. Almost immediately, the dizzying haze faded, and I could breathe better even with the damn cloth around my mouth and nose.

"What the hell is going on, Mark?" I asked him in a muffled breath, the cloth making speech infinitely more difficult.

He looked at me, and even with his entire face covered, I could imagine the way his face lit up as he spoke. "The fates have been kind enough to grant us a revelation." His voice held the slight tinge of a fanatic.

"Would the fates be kind enough to let me in on this revelation?" I asked him with barely suppressed exasperation.

Markos looked at me and sobered slightly from the internal reverie that went on in his head. A slight relaxation of his shoulders and the way he carried himself told me he had regained some of his facilities.

"Ah, right...of course, Duran," he said softly. He gestured to the surrounding mushrooms. "I was tinkering with the chemistry of our already-potent Gloom mushrooms. Most of the additions failed or created a somewhat toxic substance, but I played with some glow vine since, as it produces a mild hallucinogen as a defense system, I thought it would be neat to meld the two. After fiddling around with my *Botany* and *Alchemy* skills, I was able to combine them both.

"Behold!" He spoke with a flourish of his arms. "The Gloam, the same effects as Gloom mushrooms with an added, addictive hallucinatory effect."

I stopped and just stared at our newest creation. This would be an excellent source of additional income for us, and I just knew Miguel would be dying to get his grubby hands all over these.

"We will need to run a few tests on them," I told Markos. "To be on the safe side. I don't want to start selling these only to find out they kill people or make them go insane."

The last thing we needed was even more heat brought down on our heads. The Alliance already had it out for us; we wouldn't survive if the Merchants Guild joined the fray.

He nodded his head at me, probably understanding the need for safety better than I did. Markos being a healer first, burgeoning drug kingpin second.

"I agree with you. As you have experienced, this new strain of Gloom mushroom emits a rather dangerous spore that affects the mind. A nice side effect for a drug user, however, not so great for a drug maker. We will need to be careful not to breathe it in while cultivating them," Markos warned me.

His demonstration complete, Markos and I walked out of the narcotic-filled portion of the cave and back into the walkway that led outside. As soon as we got far enough away that we could no longer be affected by the mushrooms, Markos took off the makeshift gas mask, which told me I could as well. I was relieved at the cool air filling my lungs, and I shifted my gaze to where I looked at both Markos and the illuminated path so I wouldn't fall and bust my face.

"This new project is solid. After you give the green light, I'll get a message to Miguel to send a few men over to help package up the first shipment," I told him.

My mind currently worked on the best way to profit from our new resource. I saw stacks of gold in the guild's future. This new venture on top of the other deal I'd worked out with the suave crime lord would ensure a rather lucrative stream of income for us. It would mean we could take fewer contracts and maybe start working to pay off our bounties. *A pleasant daydream.* I made my way out of the cave and back towards the castle. The damp, spore-filled cave had left me in pressing need of a nice long bath.

But it would have to wait because as soon as I stepped out of the cave, Wilson's contact card lit up in my interface.

I clicked accept, and Wilson's light breathing filled my ear.

"What's up?" I asked.

"Guild meeting. Thirty minutes," he said abruptly and hung up.

*Great, just what I needed. Fuck it, let's get this over with.*

I went back up through the castle, only stopping to get a mug of ale, and I made it to the meeting in record time, which I shouldn't have bothered with because nobody else could be bothered to be punctual. *I could have had a bath and a change of clothes by now. Damn it all.*

In usual fashion, it took the entire thirty minutes for everyone to show up and five minutes after that to get down to business. Wilson called the meeting, so I deferred to him and let him go over what he needed to.

"All right, everyone. Settle down," he said as he stood from his chair to gaze around the room. "We have a few matters to discuss since it has been some time since our last official meeting."

"Let's hear it," I said.

"Right," he said, pulling a stack of papers from his inventory. "A few things to go over. Several contracts came in over the past few weeks, a couple escort jobs for Yllsaria, along with a bounty on one of the bandit kings, but I obviously turned that one down. And finally, a retrieval job. Some nobleman's estate was robbed by a thief not associated with the Thieves Guild, so naturally, both parties want the matter resolved and are willing to pay handsomely for it."

"All right, good call on turning down the bounty. Let's leave the bandit kings to their own devices," I said, taking a long pull of my ale. "What was taken?"

"Gold and other small items, but the noble only cared about some heirloom of his, a ruby-inlaid golden amulet that held sentimental value or some such nonsense."

I chuckled. "Nobles and their jewelry. Though, it's odd that someone is operating outside of the guild. Risky business, and suicidal. Reach out to your old Thieves Guild contacts and see what details you can learn about the robbery."

"Already on it," Wilson said with a wry smile.

"Of course, you are. Anything else?"

"Just a few more minor things. A representative from both Aldrust and Yllsaria stopped by about a week ago, both wishing to renew our trade agreements. I told them I would need your approval on those."

"Done. That's just more easy money in our pockets. Besides, we have to clear out any monster nest that pops up in our territory regardless—might as well earn some coin while we're at it. Is that it?"

"All I needed to discuss, at any rate."

I stood up, a headache already creeping up on me. "Well, that makes this the shortest meeting, ever."

Everyone laughed and began to rise from their seats and filed out of the room. I was about to head out myself when Wilson grabbed my arm.

"What is it?" I asked, turning to face him.

"When my contacts reach back out, I'd like to take the job personally."

"Don't see why not," I said with a shrug. "But why all of a sudden? I thought you got tired of fieldwork?"

He smiled, wrinkling his forehead and lighting up his storm-cast eyes. "What can I say, retirement has worn thin these past few years."

I clapped him on the shoulder, returning his smile. "Have at it. I can run the guild for a little while by myself."

"No, you can't," he said smugly.

"No, I can't," I said, laughing.

"Just don't burn the place down while I'm gone," he said as he walked past me and into the hall.

Chuckling, I followed him. "No promises. I do love a good fire."

Before I forgot, I pulled open my interface and opened the *Guild Quests* tab.

**Quest: Thief Taker**

**Recover Stolen Heirloom For Central Kingdom Nobleman**

**Type: Contracted**

**Difficulty: B**

**Reward: 4500 Exp**

Cycling through the guild roster, I selected Wilson's name.

**Assign Wilson**

**Yes/No**

*Yes.*

Wilson stopped, staring at his interface, and accepted the quest.

**Quest Accepted.**

**Exp Share: 75/25**

Since I'd hit max level, the experience didn't matter, but we'd get paid well for the quest, and that was good enough for me.

"Thanks," he said and vanished into the shadows, leaving me alone in the corridor.

*All right, time for that bath.*

Once I climbed to the third floor, I went to my room and straight to my bathroom. The same stone that comprised my room and the entirety of the castle met me as I shut the door. In the center of the room was a long basin filled with water. It resembled a small pool more than a bath, but I loved it. A mirror and sink sat in the corner, and held my toothbrush and shaving kit, while a shelf carved deep into the stone wall on the opposite end of the bath housed my soaps, shampoos, and washrags.

The only other items in the room were a towel rack and wicker laundry basket by the door. I stripped, tossed my dirty clothes into the basket, and climbed down into the bath. It was hot, but not quite as hot as the day before. *Fire stones are wearing thin. Need to get with Adam in a couple days to replace them.*

The reflection of the water shimmering along the stone-gray walls and ceiling gave the room a charming atmosphere, like an underwater cave deep beneath the earth. Rather than feeling claustrophobic, I was at peace. This was my favorite place inside the castle hands down, a place that was entirely mine.

I stared at my reflection in the mirror of the water. My appearance had changed slightly in the thirty years since coming to this world. I still looked exactly like I did when I was twenty, though, with a few exceptions. My time as a refugee had emaciated me, but years as a warrior had left me with lean muscle, and I'd grown my hair out in the past few years. My copper locks were tied back in a knot.

I undid the leather cord that held up my hair and ran my hands through the strands as they fell about my shoulders, trying to work out any tangles that had accrued since last night. I reached over to the stone shelf and picked up my hairbrush to gently brush my hair, a process that took time if done correctly.

Once my hair was brushed, I caught a glimpse of wiry hair and ran my fingers over my prominent jawline, as the heavy prickles of stubble threatened to blossom into a beard. I'd yet again neglected to shave. Glancing at the sink, I thought about grabbing my razor and just getting it over with, but I didn't feel like getting out of the bath. The heat from the water took away my will do anything else.

I sat under the water for almost an hour, my amber eyes staring back at me as I daydreamed. When my skin started to resemble that of a raisin and the heat from the water began to make me drowsy, I reluctantly climbed out of the bath and headed for the sublime comfort of my bed to catch up on my sleep.

# Chapter 5 - Under Siege

I awoke to someone banging on my door. An occurrence I wish I could say was a rarity for me. Our guild's idea of politeness was knocking half a second before entering, not exactly the easiest people to live with at times. From the rhythm of the knocks, I could tell at once who was outside, rapping at my chamber door.

Without waiting for an answer, the door swung open, and Wilson stepped through, looking somewhat disheveled. His dark leather armor was oiled and silent, but his face was a mess. A sight that immediately put me on alert. His gray hair was tousled by sleep, and his usually perfect beard hadn't been combed. Wilson was such a fanatic about his appearance that anything that made him disregard his morning routine was cause for concern.

"D," he called, as he caught sight of me, forgoing his usual polite greeting to get straight to the point, "Trouble on the home front."

"Oh, by the nine kings of Hell, not again." I rubbed at my temples, wincing as the lingering headache pulsed through my skull. His words could only mean one thing. *We're being invaded...again.* I nodded at him. "All right, understood."

We both knew the next move, and I hopped out of bed so I could change into more appropriate attire. Going into battle in my pajamas was a nightmare I'd stopped having after my first few months here.

"You don't need me to give you orders. You know the drill. Get everyone ready."

"Already done, before I came and woke you. I figured that would be your response."

Wilson's cheeky grin teased my back as he spoke. As much of the boring, stuck up, and general pain in my ass that he was, he was damn good at his job. I had to admit, I couldn't lead the guild half as well if he weren't here to back me up.

"Thank you, Wilson. Did the representative from Aldrust happen to drop off a package when they were here? Please say yes."

"Indeed, they did. You're going to have to tell me one of these days how you managed to convince the dwarves to forge you a set of shadowsteel armor?"

"It's a very long and painfully humiliating story that I'd rather not get into…besides, King Balthazar still refuses to let me live down the incident with the chicken."

I walked over to my wardrobe. Sitting on the lower shelf was a thick wooden box wrapped in canvas. I unwrapped it to find my armor whole and completely repaired.

Wilson snorted and tried to cover it with a cough. "In any case, the bill was fifteen thousand gold. I deducted the amount from your savings and sent the payment back with the representative. That's quite a hefty sum for simple repairs, Duran."

"Yeah, well. Thrayl promised he'd make me pay the next time I damaged his precious armor. It's just his way of getting me back. All right, get out there and see what you see. I want a report by the time I arrive."

"Will do," he said and departed, silent as a wraith. The emptiness in the room from his absence alerted me that he'd left.

*Fifteen thousand, Thrayl? Really? Oh, well. Should still have close to a hundred thousand left, more than plenty.* Not having the necessary information on who was attacking, I opted for overkill and donned the gear. I quickly changed into my shadowsteel armor by hitting the equip-all button on my interface.

The light metal settled comfortably around me as I equipped it. Shadowsteel had the look of lightweight plate, but rather than the blocky hunks of metal most adventurers strapped to themselves, my armor was a smooth, glossy black, which seemed to suck in light from any nearby sources. *Anyone can buy hunks of shadowsteel ore, but it takes a master dwarven craftsman to forge something this spectacular.*

Sliding it on, I knew it was worth whatever price Thrayl asked for. *It's almost as beautiful as Lachrymal's Heart, if not nearly so terrifying.* I shied away from thoughts about The Weeping God and its strange artifact. My one and only visit to witness it had left me running from the Iron Cathedral.

Thrayl had even taken my suggestion to heart and accented the trim of the umbrae armor with a splash of purple to reflect our guild's colors. The royal purple complemented the stark black nicely. As soon as I was sure there wasn't an issue with it, I exited the room in a rush, donning my sword as I left.

I enjoyed the familiar weight on my hip as I strolled through the hall. Even more so than my armor, my sword was the most expensive item I owned by far. Crafted by a good friend in the noble district in the Central Kingdom, my sword was made of shiversteel, a lightweight and incredibly sharp metal that could cut through nearly anything but dulled quite easily.

I wasn't into ostentatious or flashy gear like most players; my sword was simple and unadorned. Forged out of a single piece of metal, the hilt was plain, and the only thing added was a simple leather wrap for the handle so it wouldn't slip out of my grip.

Passing several maids shuffling about cleaning, I made my way to the ramparts. *Even when we were under attack, the duties of a maid never cease.* I nearly ran into Phillip as he was making his way to the ramparts. He was carrying a dozen bows, and he had probably several hundred arrows strapped to his back.

"Pardon me, Lord," he said, his face flushed in embarrassment.

I was more careful of myself as I hurried along so that I wouldn't run into any of the other people bustling about with their preparations. I reached the outermost wall that looked over the Rolling Hills and out to the vast plains.

Over half of our men-at-arms were standing by the gate. Our archers had received their bows from Phil and were waiting for me to give them orders, but I ignored the waiting expressions on their faces and concentrated on the field, taking stock of the situation. For all of two minutes, I just stared at the sea of troops currently marching towards our front gate.

Hundreds of troops were approaching, marching in a disorganized formation toward the castle. We'd never repelled a force this large before. I couldn't believe the Alliance would send this many men just for us.

Wilson walked up to me as I was gazing at the troops making their way towards us. He said nothing for a moment, just stared as I was doing before tilting his head toward me. "I stopped counting at four hundred. It's a little excessive."

"This is ridiculous. I'd thought they'd have given up after the last two times," I said.

"Securing our castle will secure them the trade rights for Aldrust and Yllsaria, but I can't see how it's worth this level of response."

"Doesn't matter, this is declaring war."

"What do you want to do, Duran?" Wilson asked.

The numbers were concerning, but not unduly so. I smiled; it would be a good fight. *We should be able to take the troops long before they breach the massive wooden gate. I hope.* Staring down at the ever-closing army made my blood boil, so I made a snap decision and hopped onto the lip of the wall.

"Cover me!" I yelled to our archers as I leapt over the ledge.

I didn't realize the soldiers had gotten as close as they had, so when I hopped down from the wall, I dropped onto the face of one of the invaders, who had the misfortune to be staring up at us when I jumped. He didn't even have time to cry out when I used his body to cushion my fall.

As I landed, I unsheathed my sword and plunged it into the man's broken body, ignoring his pained groans as my sword pierced his heart. I stepped off the corpse and looked over the battlefield while planning my next move.

Leaping down onto the grass had been a hasty decision but standing on the tower twiddling my thumbs was doing no good.

Of course, Wilson would have wanted to discuss a plan of attack before I ran off. If we had it his way, we'd be up on the walls staring at the massing troops until Armageddon, deliberating on the correct course of action. Sitting still was never in the cards for me, so I ran forward into battle. Arrows rained over the walls to pepper the arriving army, but I ignored them and focused on the ones in front of me.

The downside to this plan was that Wilson was going to bitch me out something fierce for being so reckless. I could already hear his lecture in my mind, his words droning on and on. *"You're the guild leader, we can't afford to have you run off half-cocked, and getting yourself killed."* His you-should-be-more-careful speech hadn't changed in all these years.

"Duran, you dumbass!" Wilson's exasperated voice shouted down at me as he poked his head over the ramparts.

I laughed. *I am so getting my ass chewed today!* Putting Wilson out of my mind, I charged into battle. A pair of soldiers rushed me, trying to claim glory ahead of the others, but their eagerness cost them.

My blade cut them down mid-swing, their cries of war dying in their throats as my sword danced between them.

I ran until I found a small portion of the army. A dozen or so men who'd broken off from the main force marching toward the front gate. They roared when they noticed me, but before they could reach me. I activated my auras.

My battle fatigue jumped as they activated. Two faint shimmers edged along my skin, one red and the other gold, before they sank into my flesh. *Aura of Speed* was like an injection of caffeine into my veins as my speed and agility increased by an order of magnitude, while *Aura of Might* toughened my defense and boosted my damage.

Using both in conjunction was a powerful move, and an incredibly risky one. As long as they were active, I was almost unbeatable, but as soon as they timed out, they'd max out my battle fatigue.

I strolled through the mass of bodies, men and women who stood ready to murder me. It wasn't even fair.

With my auras in play, they couldn't hold a candle to me, their movements slow to my eyes. Shields hefted and swords raised to cut me down—all fell short as I slaughtered scores of the invaders. They simply couldn't react fast enough to harm me. My blade slid across throats and pierced the hearts of dozens of men with the ease of a hot knife through butter.

These soldiers would've been adequate for guarding the Compass Kingdom, but they were far too low level to pose a serious threat to us. I guessed them to be level thirty or so, impressive for an NPC, but unless they had an ability to throw at me, they wouldn't be a threat.

A pang of guilt rose at killing them. They were following orders, most likely on behalf of the Alliance, who could never be bothered to get their hands dirty, preferring to hide behind their meat puppets. As distasteful as I found it, it wouldn't stop me. They chose to stand against us and would die for it.

Fighting them was nothing short of a cakewalk, but as easy as I found it, I didn't need to get cocky. Wilson's words echoed in my head, and I had to acknowledge that he was right. I needed to keep my guard up. There were over five hundred troops to contend with, more than we had ever faced at once before. Even if they were low leveled, I couldn't take them by myself. They would drown me in sheer numbers alone.

*Guess I'll need help.* I pulled up the guild chat in my interface. "Not saying I could use a hand down here, but where's the fun in sitting in the castle where it's safe?"

Everyone would already be geared up and ready to go. They knew me as well as I knew them and were just waiting on me to admit defeat and call for backup. Besides that, the twins would hate sitting this out and would already be chomping at the bit to join in.

"Standard siege tactics, everyone."

A torrent of affirmatives resounded in my ear, and I fought back a smile. *We may be the most raucous guild anytime else; however, when in battle, we have the efficiency of a well-oiled machine.* The gate slammed open, hitting the ground and sending a tremor rolling through the grass.

Within a minute after the gate came down, Gil's *War Cry* echoed out onto the battlefield. The effects of the ability caused my health and damage to increase when the shout reached me. The other side effect of the cry is that the small amount of battle fatigue I'd begun to feel washed away in an instant.

Having given the orders to the other members to the guild, I knew what my job was going to be. I was going headhunting for the leader of this invasion force. There was, without a doubt, either a high noble leading the men or a general of some standing, though if this was the Alliance, I knew they wouldn't risk losing one of the aristocrats or generals. They would contract out the job.

78

The other, more likely option was using a high-leveled player. To command an army of more than a few hundred, you had to have high levels in the *Military Commander* skill. Commanding this large a force would put their skill level above sixty. Which meant the player should be around level seventy to eighty—either that or they were the best leader the Alliance had.

I ran further from the castle and deeper into enemy lines. I spared no wasted effort, moved no more than necessary. Soldiers who were in my path fell beneath my blade, my sword stained crimson with the blood of many.

Most of the troops I left to die from their injuries. Every thrust or slash struck a fatal, if not immediate, wound. Several men outside my reach turned to follow me as I passed. Fast as the wind, I flew through the troops, scanning the plains for any sign of a commander, but I only found more soldiers. I dropped several more as I started up the grassy hills.

I rounded the hill and came upon a large white tent, surrounded by several guards. I surged forward, heedless of the soldiers in my path. Quite a few of the foolish men turned at my approach. I paid them little mind, and their heads rolled to the ground in my wake.

The tent was within a stone's throw of me, and the commander's bodyguards bolted up in alarm, moving to intercept me. Four of them advanced on me, while two others ran inside the tent to alert their master.

I slowed my speed, letting my momentum carry me within a few yards of the men. A small cloud of dust kicked up into the air as I stopped and faced my newest opponents.

They charged me together—a completely unfair and dishonorable tactic, which I immensely approved of. Two of the men were faster than the others and drew their swords as they closed the gap. One was a hand and a half longsword, not dissimilar to my own, while the other came at me with a heavy claymore.

I ducked the swing of LongSwordsman to parry Claymore's overhead cleave. Metal clashed as I angled his strike to let the overused momentum carry his blade into the dirt. With a dull thud, his sword sank deep into the earth, giving me a few seconds to focus on LongSwordsman while Claymore pulled his weapon free.

Wind whistled as Longsword's namesake sailed through the air towards me. I couldn't bring my steel up in time, so I passed it to my off-hand and caught the base of his sword on my vambraces. Pain radiated through me as the blade struck. My armor held easily, though the vibrations from the impact completely numbed my arm. His sword fell off-center; taking advantage, I slugged Longsword in the face.

His head snapped back as I shattered his prominent nose, delighting in the satisfying crunch of cartilage. He howled in pain and dropped his blade to clutch at his ruined face. My sword, awkward in my off-hand, cut deep into his neck. Blood poured as though a dam burst as I sliced through his artery, and he fell to the ground, grasping his spurting neck.

I hadn't paid enough attention to the rest of my opponents and allowed the other two members to catch up to us. Claymore retrieved his stuck sword and sauntered over to join his friends. His eyes held a gleam of superiority in them; he thought he had the upper hand here.

This battle could have ended in an instant with *Dance of the Immortal*, but I held off using any of my abilities. These chumps were an appetizer compared to the main course I had to look forward to, and I didn't need to waste my trump card.

Claymore turned to look at Goon One and Goon Two, I expected, to signal a combined assault on me. *Fool.* As soon as his eyes left mine, I rushed them, closing the distance in under a second and shoving my sword through the gap in the metal plates across Claymore's chest.

His look of overconfidence shattered to one of pain and despair. He was dead; his brain just hadn't registered it. Blood pooled out of his mouth as his lungs filled with blood. His death would not be a swift one. Claymore dropped his weapon and crumpled to the ground as I pulled my sword from his chest and turned to look at the goon squad.

Both of their faces held a mixture of rage and disbelief. To give them credit, few could move as fast as me, and in their shoes, I wouldn't have expected it either. Goon one bellowed in rage, pulling out a morningstar, while the only female goon took out a short sword and dagger.

Morningstar came at me, abandoning all reason. He flailed wildly as if swinging at a horde of invisible bees. Duel-Wielder, however, came at me slow and cautious, not willing to let any more surprises catch her off guard.

I dealt with Morningstar quickly. His unhinged swings left him vulnerable, and several wide swings later, his arms tired. I stepped forward, grabbed the handle of his weapon, and rammed the tip of my sword through his face.

He didn't react at all, dead instantly. Morningstar gurgled a death rattle as I pulled my blood and brain coated blade from his skull.

Duel-Wielder took the death of her comrade in stride, using it as an opportunity to use *Sneak Attack*.

She caught me off guard, but only for a moment. *Color me surprised. An NPC with an ability, that's rare. Must have been a member of the Thieves Guild, and a damn good one if they thought it a good investment to teach her Sneak Attack.*

I'd dueled against Wilson enough to know what the subtle rustle of wind behind me meant.

I rolled forward as her blades struck the ground where I'd been a split second before. As I landed out of my roll, I turned to face her, rightfully cautious now.

*An NPC with an ability is rare. An NPC with two is unheard of. I doubt she has any more tricks up her sleeve.*

I ducked her agile swipes, grounded my stance, and swept my leg out. I dislocated her knee with a sickening pop, which was followed by an ear-splitting shriek of agony.

Duel-wielder toppled to the ground, sobbing in pain and clutching her leg. Shards of her tibia stuck through her skin, and blood pooled beneath her fingers. I raised my sword to silence her and was mid-swing when a voice stopped me.

"Halt!"

I glanced at the person I assumed was the commander as they marched forward, with the remaining guards in tow. I got behind Duel-Wielder and placed the tip of my blade to her neck.

From first glance at the leader, I could tell it was a player rather than an NPC. They were clad in gleaming white plate mail, with a full-faced helm obscuring their features. A flowing scarlet cape billowed in the wind behind them as they approached.

Their armor was high tier and in exceptional condition. *Least my guess at their level was right.* I had no reason to believe this player was anything less than mid-seventies, and I would treat them with caution. A level seventy player who knew what they were doing could kill me if I was sloppy.

The commander stopped ten feet from me. The two remaining bodyguards fanned out and drew their weapons—a bow for one and another longsword for the second. I ignored the peons and focused on the actual threat in front of me.

"Who are you to give me orders?"

Their helmet scraped against their gorget as they turned their head to speak to me, "Please, don't mistake my words." The commander spoke with a more reasoned tone. "I did not mean to command, merely to request you lower your weapon from my friend's throat."

*Like hell!* They had me completely outnumbered, and the commander was bad news. My sword sliced into Duel-Wielder, drawing a thick heavy drip of blood down her neck.

"I don't think I'll be doing a damn thing you request of me."

The commander realized I meant business, and that I wouldn't be so easily swayed. They took off their helm. Long, scarlet locks flowed out and cascaded down past their chest. *A girl?*

She had stern, firmly set blue eyes that shimmered in the sunlight. Her face was thin with low cheekbones, and she had naturally red lips that were striking even from this distance.

*A shame, but woman or not, she came here to bring ruin to myself and my family. I'll destroy her for that.* Neither she nor any one of her men would receive mercy from me.

"Please," she begged, her eyes softening. "There is no need to harm her further. This is all a misunderstanding. Let her go, and we can parley in peace."

*Parley in peace?*

"You want to negotiate now!" I roared. "You march onto my lands and assault my family. You and your Alliance dogs tried to steal our home! And only once I've cut a bloody swath through your men and am staring you in the face, seconds away from slaughtering all of you, you decide to have peace talks!"

I laughed at her, cold and dark. It was a twisted, vile sound that did nothing to cool the rage in my heart.

"I don't think so," I said and slammed my sword through Duel-Wielder's throat.

Her scream drowned out the music my steel made as it sliced through her neck. Duel-Wielder gave one final rasp, as I pulled my sword free before toppling over and bleeding her life into the ground.

Any chance of peace died with the girl on the ground.

Bowman nocked an arrow, while Longsword Junior ran at me with his sword. I caught Bowman's arrow in the shoulder, but it pinged off my armor. I parried Junior's thrust and sliced a deep gash into his arm.

Bowman had already nocked a second arrow and prepared to fire. I didn't relish the idea of dodging arrows while simultaneously fighting off Junior. Prioritizing the archer, I ran at Bowman, trying to put some distance between Junior and me.

Before I could reach Bowman, a burning sensation sliced along my cheek. The hot rush of blood down my face told me how close I'd come to death. *Keep some battlefield awareness, idiot!* Being level one hundred would do nothing for me if an arrow struck my unprotected face.

I reached Bowman before he could nock another arrow and sliced through his bow. My sword cut through the wood and his leather armor, slicing a furrow across his chest. He fell backward, whimpering in pain as blood soaked the front of his armor. Bowman tried to back away, but I thrust my sword into his chest before he could move.

I yanked my sword free and left him for dead.

Junior closed the distance between us quickly, his sword sliced down towards my neck. I caught his strike on the edge of my blade; his inferior common-tier sword chipped as it landed. With a push kick, I sent him reeling back. Before he could recover, I thrust at him, keeping him from getting his balance and edging him toward my target.

With one last thrust, he backpedaled, right over the corpse of Duel-Wielder.

84

Junior fell to the ground and shrieked as he landed in his friend's warm blood. He tried to stand, but panic had taken hold, and he only caused himself to slip and fall right back down. I stepped forward and put him out of his misery; my sword pinned his body to his fallen friend. He struggled in the throes of death to free himself to no avail and died looking into the lifeless eyes of his comrade.

With his death, I'd killed all the commander's guards.

The commander knelt by the body of Duel-Wielder, oblivious to the deaths of the others. I could've killed her on the spot if I'd wanted, but that would've been too quick.

I knelt and stared into the broken gaze of my opponent. I held no remorse for my actions, nor the one I was about to commit.

She refused to look at me, and I lashed out. My fist slammed into her jaw, sending her to the dirt amid a cloud of dust. Her look of sadness turned to black hatred as she stood.

"Tell me your name," I demanded.

"My name is Elizabeth." She spoke through clenched teeth. The fury in her voice rivaled what was in my heart. "You will pay for what you've done, you monster!"

*Monster? I suppose I am.* I smiled. "That may be true, but you and yours are the ones to blame. I didn't ask for any of this."

I bowed low, keeping my eyes on her. "Well, Elizabeth, it's a pleasure to make your acquaintance. My name is Duran, and I challenge you to a duel."

# CHAPTER 6 - DANCE OF DEATH

As with most duels, ours started slow; only fools rushed headlong into one. I kept my distance, sizing up my opponent, while she did the same. Which surprised me. I half expected Elizabeth's rage to cloud her judgment as it had for her friends. I figured she would charge me with no plan of attack, but she impressed me by remaining calm.

I had my sword at the ready and could have attacked her before she'd even drawn hers, but I held off. I wanted to see how good of a fighter she was. Even with my history, I still loved duels. They were the ultimate test of skill.

She drew a gleaming one-handed sword; it bore a silver, sapphire-encrusted hilt. The large gemstone set in the pommel matched her eyes, and while beautiful, it was a piece of art rather than a weapon. To display such extravagance on a sword, a tool designed to kill, was bordering on the ridiculous. The length of the sword was also unusual. It was quite short, just above a shortsword but thicker than a longsword.

Elizabeth unstrapped a small kite shield from her back. I hadn't noticed it before; her cape had hidden it well. Having a shield explained her shorter weapon. It would allow the full operation of her blade while also being able to defend with herself.

The shield was a mixture of rich, dark wood with metal for its center. The tell-tell silver-white sheen coming from the metal told me it was good quality Aldrustian steel. Vastly cheaper than the dwarves' shadowsteel, but still more expensive than regular steel.

Neither of us had made an opening move yet, both of us playing it cautious. I thought I knew what kind of person Elizabeth was considering her choice of armaments and current profession, but it would have been reckless of me to charge in based on what I thought I knew.

I glanced at the timer for my auras in the bottom corner of my interface. I had a little over two minutes remaining before they timed out. Which meant I had to hurry.

I circled Elizabeth for a few moments longer, studying her stance and footwork, an often-overlooked aspect of a duel. Players tended to put faith in their abilities and didn't bother to practice proper form or technique. Even now, they didn't realize how unforgiving this world could be.

Elizabeth, however, had decent form. A bit too conforming for my tastes, but it wasn't awful. She followed the military-style close to the letter, and I detected hesitation in her movements when I suddenly shifted or moved in a way she didn't expect. A weakness I would use to my advantage later, but I kept circling, waiting for the opportune moment.

I found it a few moments later, when I decided to change the speed of my footwork. Elizabeth shifted to face me head-on and dropped her shield an inch off-center as she raised her steel. Giving me my opening. I lunged forward, activating *Twice Critical,* and thrust into the opportunity.

My sword struck the spot just above her heart and stopped cold. A semi-translucent silver outline appeared just off her skin and shattered like glass, cracking and falling to the ground before vanishing. *Damn, that's Full Defense, a passive ability in the defender class.* An automatic extra bit of armor that lasted until it absorbed too much damage.

Having been caught off guard, I quickly backed out of reach, though I was a half-second slow. Her sword pierced through my armor, scoring a shallow wound across my side.

*Damn! That was sloppy of me.*

Elizabeth impressed me yet again. She fought with clear skill, had the mind of a tactician, and was also talented enough to be given command over an army. If we'd met under any other circumstances, I'd have liked to offer her a place within our guild.

She was a member of the Alliance, just a puppet for them. A simple piece to move on a chessboard, but a piece of them nonetheless, and I refused ever to allow those bastards to get that close to us.

*Damn shame.*

Elizabeth having abilities from the defender class and sporting a heavy shield told me everything I needed to know about her fighting style. While I couldn't begin to guess at the others in her arsenal, she was a purely defensive fighter. Prone to reacting rather than making the first move. It would give me the upper hand while I dictated the pace of battle.

A flash in the corner of my vision told me I was out of time. *Sixty seconds left. If I'm going to end this fight, it needs to be now.*

I was reluctant to use so many abilities back to back, but I had little choice. If the timer wore down before I killed her, it wouldn't matter how many I kept in reserve. I activated *Holy Blade* in tandem with *Rush Strike*. My sword took on a golden hue as light spilled down its silver blade, and the scent of summer filled the air.

*No matter what defensive abilities she has, Holy Blade will negate them all.*

Time seemed to slow as *Rush Strike* kicked in, and the wind enhanced my movements; before she could blink, I was on her.

My golden blade speared straight through her shield and chest plate like they weren't even there, but there was resistance as my sword cut through tissue and bone. As the radiant light faded from my weapon, Elizabeth slumped over into me, my sword protruding from her back.

When I pulled my sword from her, she crumpled to the earth, blood spilling from her wound to soak into the dirt. A fit of coughs wracked her, and blood dripped slowly from her mouth.

My fury, having been satiated by my victory, left me feeling weary. I knelt by her on the ground. I'd done some awful things in the name of my guild, things I'd do again in a heartbeat, but they left a sour taste in my mouth. I wasn't sorry for my actions, but the weight of them settled around me.

"Just so you know, you fought well," I told her.

I was never one for disregarding my enemy's talent. She looked up at me with pain-filled eyes, but they were missing the hatred that had consumed them previously. She, too, seemed to find peace with her inner rage.

"If you and the Alliance hadn't been so greedy, this needless death could have been avoided," I said softly, my voice little more than a whisper on the wind.

Fire filled her eyes for a brief second. She reached up to grab the back of my head and pulled me down to whisper into my ear, "It's not what you think. You need to be careful…he's coming."

I didn't understand, so I leaned closer to her to ask her what she meant, but it was pointless. Elizabeth was dead, her glassy eyes staring absently into mine.

I never liked killing other players; taking decades of work from someone else over whatever petty reason presented itself didn't seem right. I'd still do it, but I never liked to.

Standing up, I wiped the small pool of blood she'd dripped on my legs. Which was the exact moment my auras timed out. Absolute bone-deep exhaustion filled me as my battle fatigue skyrocketed, and I couldn't control my body any longer. My legs buckled, and I crashed into the ground, motionless.

I stayed in that position for five minutes as my fatigue slowly returned to zero. When it finally receded completely, I shakily picked myself off the ground. *I'm lucky none of the soldiers I'd left alive stuck around. They likely fled back to the main force when I engaged Elizabeth and her guards.*

Elizabeth's body was gone, deleted from the world. Though her equipment was transported automatically to our loot room, since this was our territory and we were under siege.

*With Elizabeth dead, the rest of the troops will have lost all the buffs she provided them and will be even easier to kill.* The rest of the guild should be playing clean up duty right now. It'd been half an hour since I jumped down from the castle. There shouldn't be that many left.

I started my walk back towards the castle. In my aura-induced state, I hadn't realized how far I'd traveled from home. I was a good mile or so from Gloom-Harbor. Still incredibly weak from the battle fatigue, I couldn't have fought off a one-armed rabbitman in my current state.

The mile-long trek back to the fields was excruciating. Every step was shaky, and I thought I'd topple to the ground at any moment. I came around over the green hill that led to the front gate. The dark gray stone of the castle wavered and shrank under the glaring light of the sun peeked out from the white clouds.

It was a rather beautiful day for a massacre.

I stood staring over the fields of Gloom-Harbor; it was bloody in every sense of the word. The rancid tang of iron and rust coated my tongue and clung to the back of my throat with every breath.

I looked down at the troops left alive. I'd taken out dozens of the men myself, which still left a few hundred soldiers for the rest of the guild. There wasn't even half that number left; the Gloom Knights were running them ragged.

90

Gil took out four men with a single swing of his axe. They couldn't even get close to him. The ebony berserker was a sight to behold in battle.

Searching for the rest of the guild, I wanted to see how they were faring in the battle.

Harper was nowhere to be seen, but Yumiko was stationed on a nearby hill, dressed in her forest greens, firing arrow after arrow into the crowd. In ten seconds, she'd dropped at least fifteen men. It was damn impressive. Yumiko was undoubtedly a hand with the bow, but she didn't hold a candle to Harper. She kept firing, pulling caches of arrows from her inventory as she continuously ran dry.

Wilson seemed to materialize from the shadows, and wherever he appeared, someone died. He *Shadow-Walked* through nearly fifty men himself. I forgot that sometimes, behind his strict, rule-obsessed personality, lurked a truly terrifying man.

I didn't see Adam in the mass of bodies, but I saw several of his creatures meandering about, taking out men without a care in the world. He'd summoned a couple of bane wolves to herd the troops and lead them directly to a lava golem. It sloughed off pieces of its own skin and threw chunks of molten rock and lava on the men, boiling them alive.

Evelyn was around somewhere, I assumed. Though I never saw her, I'd found where she'd been. All I had to do was look for the biggest pile of corpses. There were at least a hundred bodies, dead in a disorganized circle. You could've filled a swimming pool with the blood she'd spilled today, and I chuckled at my dark joke. *A rare sight to see her let loose.*

The clang of a gong rang loudly through the battlefield, and I looked until I found the source. Several men took turns hammering their swords against Levi and Behemoth's greatshields and having absolutely no luck getting through. Levi and Behemoth stood back to back, fending off troops en masse; no one could get past those two with their massive shields. They truly epitomized the phrase "immovable objects."

All in all, the guild was kicking serious ass. I was half tempted to pull up a chair and relax my weary bones while watching the rest of the fight with a cold drink in my hand. *We've got this in the bag.* Chuckling to myself, I dragged myself back to the castle, considering I'd be nothing but a hindrance to the team if I even attempted to join in with how weak I was.

I kept the battlefield in the corner of my vision as I walked. After a few minutes, the majority of the troops were dead or dying. The last few stragglers would be picked off with minimal effort. I was proud of my family.

*Another victory for the Gloom Knights.*

I was about to send a congratulatory message to everyone, but fate had other plans. As if the gods themselves were listening to my inner thoughts and decided to punish me for my arrogance, I received a notification on my interface. I opened it up to find it was a message from Harper.

**Boss, we got problems, call me now!**

I immediately pulled up his contact card and sent a call request. He picked up the second I sent it.

"D, we got more trouble inbound."

"Elaborate. And while I'm at it, where the hell are you?"

He sighed. "It doesn't matter," he said in a hurry, his usually flippant attitude disappearing for a moment. "I count thirteen riders inbound from the east. They kept to the hills, so I only spotted them once they got to the plains. We have at most, ten minutes before they are in range."

"Son of a bitch!"

Thirteen people could only mean one thing: a rival guild was coming to join in on the siege.

A pit of fear filled my stomach in a way that a couple hundred NPCs couldn't manage. I'd been confident that we could repel the soldiers without much trouble, and I'd have bet my fight with the elite bodyguards and Elizabeth had been the most taxing, but combat with actual players was an entirely different beast.

A full guild terrified me.

"All right, Harper. Lie low. Work your way around them. Drop out of the siege party. You know what to do."

"Roger," he replied.

I dropped the call and immediately pulled up the guild chat, speaking aloud to the interface, which transferred my speech to text.

"Message to all members. We have what looks like another guild coming to fight. Harper counted thirteen riders, so it's a full guild. Ten minutes out, coming in fast. Heal what injuries you have, and if you need a recovery potion, take one. We'll worry about the consequences later. Prepare a defensive formation. I'm on my way."

Taking my own advice, I pulled out a recovery potion and chugged the contents. A crisp, minty flavor filled my mouth, washing out the lingering taste of battle from my throat. The drink went down smooth with only the barest hint of bite. However delicious it was as it went down, it wouldn't make up for the pain that would come later.

The rush that filled me was nearly indescribable, as Atlas would have felt if he'd stopped carrying the weight of the world.

All of the aches plaguing my body washed away instantly, and the timer for all my abilities lowered to zero and then faded from my vision, a new one appearing in their place.

I had three hours until the timer zeroed out, and potion sickness set in. It usually took an overdose of many different potions in a short period to cause it, but with how powerful recovery potion was, the cost had to be equally severe.

By the time I met up with the frontline a short jog later, I was back to my usual self. Everyone looked in peak condition, so I was sure more than a few had followed my example. *All right, time to form a plan.*

"Gil," I hollered.

He turned at my call. His bright green eyes lit up with humor at my approach, and he smiled widely at me, despite the situation, I couldn't help but return his infectious grin; it was hard not to smile around him.

"Fancy seeing you here, D," he responded as I walked up. After the obligatory fist bump between us, we got down to business.

"How bad is it?" I asked him, looking at growing silhouettes in the distance.

"Not good, but it's also not as bad as it seems," Gil said. "Everyone else was pretty conservative with their abilities during the fight with the soldiers, so most of us aren't nearly as bad off as you." He gave me a knowing look. "You're going to regret that recovery potion when this is over."

I laughed but couldn't deny it; he knew me inside and out and didn't even have to ask if I wiped myself out fighting. "Most definitely, but we've all dealt with potion sickness before. It's godsdamned miserable but survivable."

"True enough," Gil said. "So, what's the plan of attack?"

I paced back and forth for a moment, kicking up a small cloud of dust as I worked through the rest of my thoughts.

We'd faced other guilds in the past, but those had been organized duels, either in a small group or one-on-one fights. They were meant to settle disputes, not wipe us out entirely. We'd never had an all-out free-for-all with the entire guild before, and with one seat empty and Alistair gone, we were outnumbered. *I can't know how this is going to play out, but anything I come up with is going to have to be simple. Once the fight starts, everything is going to go to hell anyway.*

"Stay on the defensive till we figure out our enemy's weaknesses and then goad them to waste their abilities. Don't let any of them overwhelm us, and take them down one by one," I told him.

Gil thought on my words for a moment, rubbing the back of his bald head as he tried to add any other ideas. "Yeah, that sounds like the best plan we've got," Gil agreed. "I can't see a way to improve it without knowing more. If we don't jump the gun on anything, we should be able to handle it."

After our words, Gil went and walked over to Levi and Behemoth. Since both of them as our tanks would be handling the brunt of our defenses, Gil would want to hash out the tiny details with them. I left him to his strategizing and went to talk with the rest of the team.

I didn't want to risk any one of my friend's lives if I could help it. That made talking to Adam and Markos priority one. Since Markos was back at the castle, I went to find Adam. He was standing with Evelyn, talking amongst themselves.

"Adam," I said as I walked over to him, realizing that I'd inadvertently interrupted whatever Evelyn had been telling him. "Sorry, Evelyn," I said quickly as anger crossed her eyes, but it faded, and she inclined her head, letting me know I was forgiven.

"What do you need?" Adam asked.

"You have any tricks up your sleeves?" I asked. "I don't want to take any risks here."

Adam was quiet for a moment, staring off into space before turning and giving me a small smile.

"Oh, yeah, I have a new creation that I just made and have been dying to test out. Also have a few smaller beasts that I caught recently," Adam said with a wild look in his golden eyes. He was lost in thinking about his babies.

As similar as the pair looked, Adam was different to his sister in nearly every capacity, kind and funny where Evelyn was cold and calculating. I considered Adam a steadfast friend. *Though they're both batshit crazy in their own twisted way, at least Adam doesn't leave my ribs broken.*

As our unofficial engineer, summoner, and beast tamer, if it could be crafted, hatched, summoned, or tamed, Adam was master of them all.

I left Evelyn to her own devices since she didn't need any input on how to kick ass. Besides, as my still-sore ribs could attest, anything other than the most basic of conversations with her tended to go south quickly.

*Need to talk to Mark.* Pulling up my interface and selecting the map, Markos's name appeared at the castle gates. He was making his way toward us, and I decided to meet him halfway, jogging up the hill as he came into view.

"Ah, how kind of fate to ordain this chance encounter, Duran," Markos spoke, slightly out of breath from his run. "I needed to speak with you when I arrived at the field of battle."

"Wouldn't want to inconvenience fate any further," I said, letting him catch his breath before speaking again.

"Makenna wanted me to pass these along," he said, pulling out several small vials of dark liquid.

I picked one up carefully before inspecting it. Knowing Makenna, she could have brewed any manner of potent poisons. Reading the description told me the contents—crater snake venom—I shuddered. *I don't even want to know how she obtained this.*

"I'm guessing she picked these up on her recent outing to the ruins of Machine City?"

"More than likely, though she is far braver than I to tempt the fates so," Markos said, eyeing the brackish liquid sloshing in the vials.

Harvesting the venom from them was incredibly dangerous, though knowing Makenna, she'd probably had a blast doing it. I also wouldn't put it past her to have kept a few of the snakes as pets in her room. *I'll need to talk to her about that.*

"Remind me to give her my thanks, though I'm guessing she's sitting this one out?"

"Ah, yes. Yes, she is. Her talents, like mine, are not suited for open combat."

"Figured," I said. *Damn, that puts us even more outnumbered, but what was I expecting?* "Anyway, stay out of the fight and focus on healing, got it?"

He nodded, though I didn't know how much registered past the constant funhouse party in his head. I bid farewell to the quirky mage and went to where Yumiko was setting up. She seemed to be deciding on what bow to use for the coming fight, having several laid out in neat rows. I tapped her on the shoulder, and she jumped, stifling a squeak before she whirled around to glare at me.

"Godsdamnit, D, you scared the hell out of me!" she said.

Usually soft-spoken, Yumiko could have a mouth dirtier than any sailor when she was frightened or angry.

Her small stature was also in complete contrast to her mouth. She was petite with gorgeous olive skin that had paled sharply recently, and she had a cute, oval face with lips the color of cherry blossoms. Yumiko kept her long black hair tied back into a ponytail to stay out of her face while in battle, which showcased her newest feature: her bright crimson eyes.

"What do you want, you sneaky bastard?" she grumbled.

"Hey, now, don't be like that. Especially since I've come bearing gifts."

I tossed her the bottle of venom. She caught it one-handed, not even glancing at it before glaring at me.

"The fuck is this?"

"Well, if you would stop cursing me and read it, maybe you'd find out."

She harrumphed and looked down at the little glass bottle for a moment. I knew she'd found out what it was when she visibly paled, quite a trick for her. "Wh-what the hell? Where the fuck did you get this? And why the hell are you just tossing it around so casually, you clumsy shit?" she yelled her questions in rapid succession.

"Consider it a gift from Makenna."

Her stare could wilt flowers from fifty paces. "Well, no shit, it's from her. Who the fuck else would be willing to get close to those creepy-ass things? What I want to know is what the fuck do you expect me to do with— oh, I get it," she said. Her eyes lit up as she comprehended my plan. The glint in her eye turned diabolical. "An arrow poisoned with crater venom, that'll ruin someone's day, all right."

I smiled, tossing her the last couple of vials. "Several somebodies, I'm hoping. You have fun with those."

I walked off, leaving her to her preparations, and glanced at the incoming guild. They were close. Maybe two minutes out now. It was time to get in position.

We had nine of us against thirteen since Markos and Makenna would be sitting out of the actual fighting. Which left us outnumbered in terms of sheer numbers. Our abilities and levels, however, would bridge the gap and even the playing field quite nicely, especially since we wouldn't be fighting fair in the slightest.

I received a ping on my interface. It was Harper, letting me know he had reached his flanking position. With that, we were as ready as we could have been. All that was left was our skill in battle and a little luck.

I smiled at my friends, my family, as we stood side by side and went to war.

# CHAPTER 7 - WAR IS THE ANSWER

The enemy advanced quickly, pushing their mounts hard. Multiple hues of brown to gray told me that the horses were regular mounts: no rainbow unicorns or the four horses of the apocalypse heading our way.

When they were within the range of Yumiko's arrows, she pinged me, and I sent back two pings in rapid succession, letting her know to hold off. The enemy didn't seem to be reaching for their weapons just yet, so I let them approach. *Suits me just fine if they want to talk first. Gives me time to better prepare our ambush.*

As the thirteen players arrived, they slowed to a stop a few dozen yards from us and dismounted their horses, fanning out in an attack formation not unlike our own. From their weapons and armor, they held a decent mix of roles. I counted four warrior types and two archers, though one wielded a crossbow, which was unusual.

They also had two tanks, two rogues, and two mages, but I couldn't tell what elemental aptitude they'd chosen. That left one guild member who I couldn't place. He seemed to be the leader, and he bore the appearance of a king, with heavy golden armor that bore a familiar crest.

The Order of the Dawn.

I sighed. *Of course, it would be them.* Our paths had never officially crossed, but they held a reputation nearly as famous as ours was infamous.

Their leader walked out in front of the formation. His name was Richard, and he was as pompous as they came. Sporting blond hair that draped down his shoulders, it matched his armor almost too well. His ice-blue eyes held both contempt and superiority in them, and his high cheeks and pointed chin gave his face the resemblance of an arrowhead. Richard's smile held a bitterness that matched his eyes perfectly.

He stood half a dozen yards from us and looked each one of us up and down before speaking, "Ah, the renowned Gloom Knights. I would say it's a pleasure to make your acquaintance, but why sully my mouth with a lie." His smile twisting with cruelty.

While everyone else focused on the bastard's face, I watched his hands. His fingers twitched as he looked over at us, counting. I could easily tell what he was thinking. He was going to be overconfident since he outnumbered us.

"Seems you are missing a few of your retinue...what, they see us coming and run off?" Richard asked with a loud, forced laugh that caused the rest of his guild to chuckle meekly in response.

I smiled darkly at his ridiculous performance. "They had other, more pressing matters to handle and couldn't be bothered."

His grin grew wider. "Ah, truly, that is a shame. I had hoped to round you all up at once and look at what you're doing. Making us work extra hard to catch you, wicked deviants."

*Are they here bounty hunting?* That didn't make sense. The Alliance didn't hire mercenaries, preferring to rely on their soldiers, and they especially didn't contract bounties to player guilds. The Compass Kingdom left such work to the Adventurers Guild.

If the Alliance was attempting to take our castle from us, having the Order arrive at the same time as the troops didn't fit. *The Order shouldn't even be in the same company as the Alliance. Something else is going on here.*

"Who the fuck hired you to bring us in?"

"My, my. The mouth on this one. Poor Durandahl. You don't need to worry your head about these things; you'll soon be parting with it," Richard said.

I scowled as he said my full name. "Why don't you and your friends ride on out of here, and we all forget this misunderstanding ever happened?"

Richard's grin deepened. "Why would I do that when I have you right where I want you?" His gaze shifted, becoming something malicious and cruel. "Now, why don't we dispense with these trivialities and get down to business?"

He spoke to all of us next.

"You can all surrender quietly, or I can kill most of you. I was only hired to bring back two of you alive. Every one of you has kill orders placed on your heads, so we get paid regardless if you're dead or alive. It doesn't matter to me."

It was my turn to laugh. "You think we would ever surrender to the likes of you? Think again, jackass."

He shook his head, clearly displeased with my answer. I sent a mental ping to both Harper and Yumiko. It was time.

"I'll admit, Durandahl. That was the answer I expected of you. Too stupid to take my most generous offer. I'm going to enjoy killing you, but I'd have spared your friends' lives if you had cooperated."

"You and your guild can go to hell!" I yelled at him. "Gloom Knights, to war!"

Several things happened at once. Gil activated a couple of his abilities to start the fight off on a literal high note. His thundering *War Cry* rang out as if emphasizing my own battle cry, followed closely by a higher-pitched scream. Gil's *Stun Shout*.

The members of the Dawn took on the appearance of statues frozen in motion. Both rogues were unaffected by the shout and disappeared in a puff of smoke. I figured they would be able to break the stun lock, and tried to keep track of them, but lost them in the thick cloud.

Harper and Yumiko, as soon as they heard my call to war, leapt out of their respective hiding spots and fired into the now frozen crowd. The smoke and tightly massed bodies made scoring head shots nearly impossible, so they didn't even try for them, going for the easier body shots.

Yumiko used her venom-coated arrows to take out a few key targets, putting one in each of the mages. While not instantly fatal, the toxins would soon get to work, wreaking havoc on their organs. She tried to take out one of the rogues, but the arrow buried itself into the grass by the startled rogue's feet.

Harper activated *Black Sun Arrow*. An ominous black glow pulsed off his bow as he raised it skyward. He released his arrow with a satisfying twang. As the shaft reached a certain height, it lost all its momentum and hung in the sky for the briefest second before changing course and flying back towards the earth. Just before the arrow hit the ground, it burst into hundreds of smaller arrows to pepper the helpless guild.

The small razor-sharp flechettes formed a cloud of hornets and indiscriminately pierced flesh and armor as they descended. Still afflicted by Gil's shouts, the players couldn't even cry out in pain. A hundred minuscule rivers of blood flowed from torn flesh to pool into a small lake at the feet of the guild.

Harper's attack landed with brutal efficiency. *Bleeding will raise their fatigue, hopefully enough to stop them from using a few abilities.*

By the time Harper and Yumiko finished their opening move, the effects of *Stun Shout* wore off, and the Dawn shook off our opening sneak attack. We'd surprised and panicked them, but they were professionals and quickly recovered, attempting to regroup in a defensive formation. We didn't give them the chance.

103

Having used up the poison arrows, Yumiko followed Harper's lead. She took the gloves off and chained *Tempest Shot* with *Multiply*.

The salty scent of the ocean filled the air as she drew back her bow and released her arrow. It took on a pale blue ethereal light as it flew through the air, ice forming in its wake. When it reached the halfway point between us and the Dawn, *Multiply* took hold, and six identical copies of *Tempest Shot* struck home with the fury of Poseidon.

Ice rose in great sheets to tear into the guild. The jagged icicles ripped through the mages' cloth and the light leather armor of the archers with ease. The ice steamed as warm blood poured down it like an ocean adding to the rapidly growing lake of blood.

While painful, the attack wasn't as debilitating as I'd hoped. *Tempest Shot*, if you got lucky, could spear through weaker armored players with ease, but we hadn't managed a lucky kill.

The added blood loss only helped, though, and it was time for the frontline to go to work. Our archers gave us an opening, and by the nine kings of Hell, we were going to take it.

I rushed forward across the field, blades of grass trampled underfoot as we charged ahead. Gil and Evelyn nipped at my heels. I was faster than Gil by far, but Evelyn could outpace me at every turn. With her watching me, I let my pride cloud my judgment and decided to make a big splash for my opening move.

I activated *Dance of the Immortal.*

Immediately, the world came to a standstill. My vision was awash with a score of every hue of gray. Everyone froze in place, it seemed, but not exactly—their movements were painfully slow. So slow that I could barely tell they'd moved at all.

I leapt into action. Leaving my comrades frozen behind me. As I reached the forefront of the Dawn's formation, I had two of the warriors and an archer to deal with.

My sword slid into the heart of my first foe with ease. The warrior was a dark skinned, well-built man with long dreadlocks, his handsome face set in a scowl as he bared his teeth at the rest of my frozen guild. My blade sliced through his leather armor and pierced his heart. With *Dance* active, he couldn't even cry out as my sword slid through his chest.

When I withdrew my blade, a shock of crimson followed. It was the only drop of color in the gray world. He would bleed out quickly when *Dance* ended, so I turned my attention to the others.

My next opponent was the second warrior in the group. A heavily muscled man with a shaved head, except for a braided ponytail that stretched down his back. His wide-set eyes lit up with delight, a man whose purpose was on the battlefield. He wore heavy plate mail, but it looked worn from use and not well maintained. Dozens of tiny nicks and dents marred the surface.

I didn't waste time trying to pierce through his dense metal plating. I slid my blade through his neck. Too-bright blood welled as I cut through his flesh, scoring a heavy, bloody gash.

Only the archer was left. As I got close, I found a thin girl underneath the leather hood. Her hair had come loose from her ponytail, drifting about in wind that no longer blew. I slit her throat and plunged my sword through her heart.

Having dealt with the forefront of the formation, I ran over to the next closest member.

It was one of their tanks; the man was clad in dark steel plate mail, in sharp contrast to the leader's glittering gold armor. His entire head was covered in a jagged helmet, revealing nothing more than a pair of deep recessed eyes. In his hands, he hefted a giant shield and looked to be mid-charge, one of his legs hovering just off the ground. I was half a second from plunging my sword through the large man's armpit, the only exposed flesh I could find, when the gray world stuttered and flashed.

The world changed back to color for a split second as a warning. *Damn it, I'm out of time.* At this point, I did the stupidest thing I could've and got greedy. My sword was raised mid-thrust when *Dance of the Immortal* wore off.

The three players I'd killed dropped to the ground, lifeless, blood bursting like a geyser to pour over the earth. My battle fatigue nearly maxed, and I stumbled as exhaustion set in. My sword was a hundred pounds heavier in my hand, and I tripped over my feet and stumbled to the ground. *Get up!* I thought and rose to my feet, directly into the massive fist of the man I'd been about to kill.

I looked up at the exact wrong moment, as a giant, plated fist slammed into my face, shattering my nose and jaw. It broke and unhinged from my skull along with several of my teeth, which rattled around my ruined mouth. Blood poured from a thousand cuts in my mouth and ran through my torn lips, pouring like a faucet from my nose. My conscious waned, but I didn't pass out. Even if I wished I had.

The tank lifted me off the ground. I half stared through my swollen eyes at the man in the dark plated armor—the man who would be my executioner. My sword slipped from my unresponsive fingers. My mind was muddled, incoherent thoughts swirled around, and I forgot where I was.

I subconsciously slipped back in time, and was on a whole different battlefield.

106

Lonny stood over me, his glittering gold sword bit into my neck as he looked down at me with unbridled hatred, tears streaming down his face. My own sword shattered to pieces; I'd been beaten.

I wasn't fast enough, and this was deserved. I'd let my carelessness run rampant for far too long. *This is my punishment for letting Sophia die. I deserve this.* I faced my death with as much bravado as I could muster, spitting a mouthful of broken teeth and blood straight into the face of the man who'd been my best friend.

Then I blinked and came back to my senses. I wasn't fighting with Lonny anymore, though I was still about to die.

Rage shone in the eyes of the darkplate warrior as he wiped the blood from his helm with one hand, while still holding me aloft with the other. He raised back his fist to finish me off, and I had no doubt he would succeed. His mammoth hands would shatter my skull like glass if it connected, but it never did.

Leaves rustled in the wind, and I laughed until I coughed blood as Wilson *Shadow-Walked* behind my would-be killer. His twin daggers tore through the weak spots of the giant's armor. He gurgled and choked as blood filled his lungs. The man dropped me to the ground and fumbled for the knives in his back, dying before reaching them.

Wilson picked me up with a grunt and *Shadow-Walked* back to our side of the battlefield.

It was my first time experiencing the Realm of Shade, and it was like being submerged underwater on a moonlit night. Everything was hazy and distorted, my blood too loud in my ears, its roar drowning out everything but an insidious whisper next to my ear, begging me to stay. It was a very unsettling experience. Wilson had always told me he enjoyed the peace of the place, but I didn't share his sentiment. Soon enough, we were out of that strange place, and the world made sense again.

The sky looked incredibly blue to my eyes, and a flash of Markos's robes told me I was well away from the battle. Wilson tossed me like a sack of potatoes on the grass next to Markos.

"Ow," I tried to say, though it came out more like a strangled, raspy groan.

"Don't be a baby," Wilson scolded as he handed me back my sword.

I was grateful for that, but his words made me angry. I wanted to give him a scathing retort, but my head tingled, and the words in my head got jumbled together. "Shut u—" is all I managed before I heaved blood, vomit, and pieces of my shattered teeth all over the ground.

"Oh, stars above. What happened to him?" Markos asked.

"Our glorious leader decided to show off and nearly got himself killed for the trouble," Wilson said with bitterness in his voice.

I was going to hear about this later, hopefully after my ears stopped ringing.

I couldn't see anything by the time Markos got around to healing me. My eyes had swollen shut, but I could hear just fine as Markos chanted in Script. The guttural, fricative words rolled from his throat as he carefully built his spell.

He took his time to maximize the efficacy of the healing magic, and a bright warmth spread through my body that got increasingly hotter as it reached the damaged portions of my face. My skin itched like fire ants had burrowed under my skin and stung me relentlessly as my bones reset themselves, and my teeth regrew in my skull.

In under half a minute, my injuries were healed, and the pain disappeared entirely. I sat up off the ground and dusted myself off.

Having been taken out of direct combat for a few minutes, my battle fatigue had lowered enough to where I felt comfortable going into battle again. I looked around for Wilson, but Markos and I were the only ones around. Wilson had disappeared, likely run off to join the fighting, and Markos was zoning out, sipping on a small vial of mana potion, but when I went to head back to the battlefield, he put his hand out to stop me.

"Whoa, there, my friend. You shouldn't be heading back into battle. The fates spared you once. Best not to tempt them a second time today."

I shrugged off his hand. I was angry. Not at Markos, at myself. I'd been stupid, an idiotic child, showing off in front of my friends only to make a fool of myself. I had to fix it.

Markos sighed into his hand. He knew he couldn't talk me out of it, so he didn't even try. "Good luck, D," he whispered to my back.

I ran back to the front of the battlefield, which had devolved into pure and utter chaos. Using *Dance* at least had a positive effect on the battle. I'd taken out three members by myself, and with Wilson killing the tank, we'd evened the playing field nicely.

Gil and Behemoth were side by side, attacking and defending against two members of the Order. It seemed neither party was gaining ground; every time one of them would go for the kill, the other would step in. They weren't landing any quick kills, but there was damage being dealt. The enemy warrior bled heavily from a gash in his sword-arm as he hefted a large saber and swung at Gil.

Behemoth brought his shield up to block Saber's attack, sending his sword rebounding off the metal with a clang, which allowed Gil to bring his battleaxe 'round to slice Saber in half.

As Gill heaved his mighty axe, the other member of the Dawn brought their much smaller shield in to deflect Gil's attack. His smaller shield glowed green, and Gil couldn't stop his swing in time.

Gil's axe collided with the buckler, and *Repel* activated, sending Gil's axe flying out of his hand. Saber danced forward and sliced a deep groove down Gil's chest before Behemoth could defend him.

Behemoth kept Gil safe while he retrieved his axe, and it looked like the gash was just a flesh wound.

The pace of the battle changed when a bolt from a crossbow slammed Behemoth. It glowed and shimmered translucent as it passed through his massive shield, and *Phase Shot* took him in the shoulder. It would have hit his heart if he hadn't been moving at the time it struck. He was thrown back from the force and lost hold of his shield.

Saber rushed in to press his advantage given to him by Crossbow, gunning for Gil. I wasn't going to let that happen.

I activated my auras simultaneously for the second time today and rushed in to save my best friend. My body was a thousand times lighter when my auras kicked in; it was a temporary high, but right now, I could take on the world.

Saber swung his sword to take Gil's life, but I caught it on my cross-guard with the barest moment to spare. Surprise rose on Saber's face. So focused on Gil, he'd been oblivious to my approach, and he snarled wordlessly when I denied his kill.

Binding with Saber wasn't an ideal situation, not with Gil injured and still in Crossbow's range. While Saber and I had our swords locked, I kneed him in the stomach, and Saber doubled over in pain as the air fled his lungs. Wasting no time, I brought my sword up and took Saber's head off in one swing.

It passed through the air where Saber had been standing, shattering the illusion I hadn't known was there. Saber reappeared a few feet away in a haze, smiling.

"Missed me," he taunted, and with a whisper, spoke an incantation.

A small purple Script circle appeared in his hand and vanished in an instant. He charged us, but before he could take a step, six identical copies of Saber appeared. All grinning wickedly.

*Shit, he's a battlemage!* Saber was using illusion magic. *Mirror, Mirror,* a spell that could create copies of the castor, who were able to interact with the real world. Meaning we didn't have one opponent to deal with. We had seven.

Two of them countered Gil, while the other five came after me. I backed out of reach and danced between several sword thrusts. Something I knew I couldn't keep up. They backed me into a corner, and I was too slow to stop a couple of stabs slicing through my armor. One on my shoulder, the other across my ribs. Neither deep, but I was running out of time.

I activated *Aura of the Antimage* to level the playing field once more. It bubbled effervescent on my skin, invisible to everyone but me and rolled off, expanding in a circle fifteen feet in all directions. With a small but audible pop, every bit of magic in the area dissolved, leaving only one very confused Saber to deal with.

I rushed in before he could react and severed his head. The second time around was much more permanent. Blood fountained out from his stump as Saber's lifeless head rolled around in the grass. Unfortunately, Gil was right in the path of the spray and was coated in the hot, syrupy mess.

Gil's face was unreadable as I pulled him to his feet. He reached down and ripped into Saber's clothes, creating a makeshift towel and neatly cleaning the blood from his face. He growled and spat several times.

"Sorry," I said sheepishly.

Though I knew that didn't make up for the impromptu shower of gore I'd subjected him to.

Gil grinned at me with his blood-stained teeth and went to respond, but we'd made a colossal mistake on the battlefield. Never stand still.

A sledgehammer smashed into me. Intense pressure hit me in the back, right over my heart. The bolt flung me to the ground, with several bruised ribs. My shadowsteel armor splintered under Crossbow's *Hammer Bolt,* but it hadn't broken through.

My life had been spared twice today.

My armor was tough, but I didn't want to chance it again. I rose to my feet and took off at a dead sprint through the grassy plains towards the main force of the Dawn, passing by several of my guild in the process.

Evelyn and Richard were going head to head, but even from a glance, Evelyn was toying with them, only using the barest bit of effort to fend off Richard. He tried and failed to activate his abilities against her. That pompous bastard even had his other tank with him, but he would need more firepower than that if he wanted to take her down.

I left Evelyn to her fun and went hunting for the bitch who put a bolt through my armor.

She was lining up a shot that would have taken Levi through the chest. Levi was currently guarding Gil with Behemoth, making sure Gil was back up to fighting shape.

Levi engaged with the last warrior, who had discarded his ruined buckler and was currently wielding his longsword with both hands, trying to hack his way through Levi's shield. So focused on his fight, Levi would never see the bolt coming.

With a burst of speed, I slashed at the wooden crossbow, and splintered it with a heavy crack, severing the tightly wound string. Crossbow jumped back from my next thrust, which would have taken her through the chest. She cursed at me for breaking her weapon and pulled a small dagger from her belt, running at me wildly, screaming unintelligible words as she did so.

It was clear to me that she'd never faced a situation where she'd lost her primary weapon. Her stabs and half-formed slashes with the dagger were clumsy.

As Crossbow struck once more with the knife, I maneuvered around it and stepped into her space, catching her hand by the wrist and breaking it with a twist.

She screamed and tried to punch me in an attempt to free herself. I caught her weak punch on the chin, wincing when she glanced off my jawbone. I shrugged it off and pivoted on my feet. Clutching her arm with both hands, I used my back as a fulcrum to throw her over my shoulder and to the ground. She gasped as all air forced out of her lungs and struggled to catch her breath.

With her crossbow, she was a fiend, but she hadn't mastered even the basics of hand-to-hand combat. I knelt before she could take another breath and clamped my hand over her mouth and nose, effectively cutting off her airflow. My sword would be clumsy for the task at hand, so I blindly reached behind me, never taking my gaze off the panicked young girl who struggled in vain against my grasp. It was useless; she didn't have the *Strength* to break my grip.

I found the object I needed in the dirt, and after some clumsy pawing, I had Crossbow's dagger in my hand. Her eyes widened in fear as I brought it into her view. She struggled in a fit of desperation, like an animal caught in a trap, willing to do anything to survive.

I slammed it home under her chin, and the light fled from her eyes.

I stood and glanced around; one look at the battlefield, and I was impressed. We'd taken down half of their number without losing any of our own.

An explosion blasted into the ground next to Levi, sending clods spraying haphazardly all around us. Levi went flying after trying to deflect the *Fireshot* with his shield. He landed with a sickening thud some fifteen feet away. Behemoth was unhurt and still in the same position where *Fireshot* had landed. He'd activated *Barrier*, a bright red dome was all around him, as the fire around the *Barrier* died, the color changed from bright cherry to a dull crimson, and finally a clear translucent glass.

Markos and Gil rushed to check on Levi. I didn't know what condition he was in, but I knew he wasn't dead, one look at the guild tab told me that much.

With the safety of my friend in good hands, I wanted to find the mage responsible. The crater venom should have taken both out of commission, and it hadn't.

Weakened as they were, I still should have killed them myself before focusing on anyone else.

Mages were the most versatile players on Nexus. As such, they were always the first targeted during a fight. It's for that reason I kept Markos off the front lines. His cloth robes would do little to protect his life. Putting the mages out of my thoughts after they were struck with the poison was a grievous mistake.

The fire mage regrouped with the remaining forces of the Order of the Dawn on a nearby hill. They were down to one warrior, a rogue, the two poisoned mages, and Richard. I glanced around for the last tank that had been fighting Evelyn. I found his twisted, broken body, nothing more than so much meat and blood now.

Richard and his group formed a defensive line to try and recover from the battle. *Everyone's battle fatigue must be high.* The only reason I could even stand right now is because of my auras. Once drained, that would be it for me. I knew that the others would be in similar straits. We'd been fighting for what felt like hours, and if it went on much longer, we would all collapse from the fatigue long before we could kill each other.

Richard looked a little worse for wear; he had a deep gash over his left eye that streamed blood down his face, and his right arm hung limply by his side. He pulled out a health potion from his inventory and went to drink it, but before he could, an arrow sailed through the air and shattered the potion. Bright red liquid rained to the floor, and Richard shouted in alarm.

I followed the trajectory of the arrow to find Harper grinning like a madman while looking as smug as he could. Even I had to admit that it was a great shot, with perfect timing. It figured. *Harper's going to boast about that for weeks.*

Richard, having been denied his chance to heal, was furious. By the looks on the faces of his mages, I doubted they were in any shape to provide healing. Both had ashen faces, dripping sweat. It looked like the venom was doing its job, albeit much slower than we needed it to. From the looks on their faces, they could tell they were dying.

The two mages huddled together, speaking in hushed tones; they seemed to reach an agreement and stumbled over to Richard. After a brief conversation, Richard's face grew solemn. He patted both mages on the shoulders, and they marched forward down the steep hill towards the grassland where we resided. I didn't like this, not one bit. *They're up to something.*

As the pair of mages reached the foothill, they stopped. They were about two dozen feet from us. *Damn, out of range from my Rush Strike.* This would've been over in an instant, but they could easily build a quick *Fireshot* and snap it off at me before I reached them, and I didn't like my chances of surviving an explosion at such a close distance.

Both mages unstopped mana potions and raised them to drink. Harper tried his trick shot once again, but Richard was prepared for it this time. In the blink of an eye, Harper fired one arrow, loaded up another one, and released that one as well. Harper's arrows sailed through the air to their intended targets and were cut down mid-flight.

Richard raised his sword, and the air in front of it rippled and distorted. In rapid succession, he slashed his blade through the air twice as each strike finished. An arc of pure energy shot forth from the tip of the sword. The two jagged waves met Harper's arrows and destroyed them. Only ash remained. They continued after taking care of the arrows as they crashed into the ground grass burst alight, and the blades of plasma burned deep furrows into the dirt.

*Hyper Slash.* The ability could only be stopped by magic or hero-tier weapons and armor. Anything lower and they would burn straight through it. Even my sword might suffer some burn damage if I tried to parry them.

Our attempt to stop the mages from recovering their mana failed, and they greedily downed the contents. Some of the pallor of disappeared from their faces, and they looked a little healthier, if for only a moment. The venom still wreaked havoc on them, eating their bodies from the inside. They were still just dead men walking.

*Dead men walking.* That errant thought struck a chord through me. They knew they were dying, and nothing would save them.

"Son of a bitch!"

*They're going to kamikaze us. Try and drag as many of us down with them as they could when they died.* The two mages joined one hand together and raised their palms towards us. Two bright neon lights erupted from their hands. With each passing second, the lights grew more vivid and more detailed. Soon a pattern emerged as they chanted.

Each mage built half of the design in their hands. The design resembled an intricate pentagram split in half, each side with swirling letters forming, dissolving and reforming. Each time it did so, the pattern grew more elaborate. I couldn't read or speak Script, but I'd seen this spellwork once before.

*Nova Wave.* Cataclysm class magic, also known as mutually assured destruction. It was the atomic bomb of Nexus, and required two mages of level fifty or higher. To perform. As a secondary requirement to cast, it cost the lives of both mages. Once complete, it would send a wave of pure kinetic energy forth, destroying everything in its path.

It was so powerful that not even antimagic could dissipate it. My *Aura of the Antimage* would be useless here. Even Evelyn would find herself powerless against such devastation.

I turned to look back at my guild. Recognition shone across a few faces, but some didn't know what to make of it.

"*Nova Wave!* How the hell do we stop it?"

Harper and Yumiko tried to pick off the mages. They let loose arrow after arrow at them, but every time the arrows got close, the magic absorbed them. The spell kept building. I even attempted to run in and use *Rush Strike* anyway, to see if I could do anything, but as soon as I got close to the mages, I was flung back by a wave of turbulent energy. I landed painfully and retreated to our defensive line.

"We can't," Markos shouted.

*Yeah, I know.* I dropped my sword, succumbing to the inevitable, my heart heavy. Our teleportation scrolls wouldn't work. We didn't have the time. We only had seconds left. I spared one last look at my friends who'd stood beside me for a decade now. *It was a damn good run while it lasted. I'll see you guys when we respawn.*

Adam shouted at me from the back of the line. He made his way toward me and reached out to grab me by the shoulder, shoving me out of the way before tossing a pitch-black crystal onto the field. It stopped about halfway between our two groups.

As *Nova Wave* reached its completion, the two now giant halves of the spell formed into one. The design stopped shifting and competed itself, glowing a bright red. Then all at once, the color melted into black.

The spell was cast.

Blinding white light emerged from the mages as their spell consumed them. The blistering wave of light reached a critical point in its brightness and imploded in on itself, coiling into a tight ball of pure energy before releasing a massive explosion. The heat lapped at my skin as the *Nova Wave* unleashed its power. It shook the world to its core, and oblivion itself descended upon us.

# CHAPTER 8 - NOVA WAVE

The top layer of earth tore itself from the ground in the onslaught of blinding hellfire, chunks of dirt and grass swallowed whole as the *Nova Wave* destroyed everything in its path.

I grabbed Adam and flung us both down the hill, knowing damn well we were going to die, but bracing myself anyway in hopes of surviving. As the pure white light rushed ever closer, I shut my eyes tight and waited for the end.

But death never came.

When my skin and bones weren't reduced to dust, I risked a peek and gaped at an incredible sight. In the middle of the once-grassy field, now nothing more than scorched earth, stood a void golem.

*What? What's it doing here? How did it even get here?*

Adam was lying next to me in the dirt, grinning from ear to ear, the widest smile I'd ever seen on him before. The slight maniacal shine running wild in his eyes told me he wasn't entirely behind the wheel anymore.

"Did you summon it?"

"You like it?" Adam asked in a sing-song voice.

I gaped like an idiot, my mind not comprehending the literal tear in the fabric of reality which was the void golem. "What the—how the—how?" I spluttered, my eyes glued to the scene in front of me.

The void golem was a humanoid fragment of the void, manifested in our world—a vessel for the eternal darkness where nothing could survive. An unthinking construct to be controlled. I'd heard about them, but never met anyone who'd seen one, let alone summoned one of the damned things.

The *Nova Wave* slammed into the golem at full force and was eaten entirely; a minuscule black hole in the center of its chest devoured everything. The blast of pure kinetic energy rolled over the void golem and was sucked down unto the depths of the abyss. The void was all-consuming, and it greedily polished off its meal. A few seconds later, nothing remained of the suicidal mages or the *Nova Wave*.

Further up on the last patch of grass left on the hill, stood Richard and the final three members of his broken guild. They stared slack-jawed at the void golem as the wind picked up. A cool breeze raced over the hills but died as it reached the golem, unraveling into nothingness.

Richard was the first to break out his stupor and ordered the rest of his men forward, despite the monster in front of them. The last remnants of his guild stared down at us with fear dripping from their faces, most of them rethinking their leader's death march. One of them, however, decided to play the hero.

Their last warrior charged with a barbaric *yawp*, his longsword raised as he ran. A faint shimmer encompassed him as he activated an aura. Though I couldn't tell the specific one used, I doubted anything would be effective against the golem.

Before he stepped off the hill, his blade glowed cherry white, bursting into flames. The faint acrid tang of burning metal drifted towards us, but I caught only a whiff before it too was swallowed into the depths.

Longsword was using *Volcanic Thrust,* and he swiftly buried his sword into the golem. His sword hissed, and a brief cloud of steam enveloped them as he rammed the sword into the void. Grinning in triumph, Longsword pulled his blade free from the within the darkness. Every inch of the blade was gone, devoured to the last shard, his hilt and nothing more was the only part that remained untouched by the golem.

Panic bulged out of his eyes as he realized he wouldn't be able to deal any damage to it. Longsword backed away from the golem, or he tried to. He backpedaled continuously, going nowhere, slowly being drawn toward the golem, inching ever closer to his death.

Struggling brought him no escape, and he screamed as fear robbed him of all reason. He pushed his hand in front of him as if to stop himself from falling in. When his hand touched the abyss a moment later, it was eaten. Peeled, layer by layer to the bone as Longsword cried in misery. When the flesh was entirely picked clean, the bones cracked and fractured. Within half a second, his left hand was dust.

The void, having tasted the sweet meat of mortals, was ravenous for more. Longsword's arm was pulled in next to repeat the same process. His entire body, eaten. Bite by delicious bite.

He was torn asunder only to be swallowed by the gaping black maw— first his arm, then his legs when he tried to kick the golem.

With his remaining hand, he flailed about, trying to grab hold of anything to save himself. He dug his fingers deep into the smoldering earth, carving deep grooves in the ground as he was dragged deeper into the dark. The bones in his hand snapped from the effort of trying to save himself.

His face ripped free from his head, his skull, the yellowed ivory too bright next to the darkness. Then it too crumbled and was gone. The only thing remaining was his arm and twisted, mangled hand. Then nothing remained of the man at all.

All of this took place in seconds, and when it was over. Adam ordered the golem to march up the hill. As it lumbered slowly forwards, Richard's bravado fled, and he and the one remaining member of his guild scrambled to get away from the monster chasing them.

They didn't get far. While the Order stood transfixed on the death of their comrade, Wilson *Shadow-Walked* behind them and laid all manner of traps for them to stumble into to.

The last rogue noticed the trap and jumped away in time to save herself. Richard, however, had succumbed to his fear and ran headlong into the snare. With a loud snap, a long thread of black wire coiled up to bind Richard, stopping him from moving and sending him to the ground.

But the rogue, a thin, masked woman with the grace of a dancer, maneuvered away from the rest of the traps—right to where Evelyn waited. So fast, I couldn't even see her move, Evelyn wrapped herself around the rogue, like a snake constricting its prey.

Evelyn tore the black silk mask free from the rogue's face to reveal a shock of pink hair. She had short hair, styled in a pixie cut. The brightness was highlighted even more by the sharp contrast between the blacks and grays of her outfit.

Pinky struggled in Evelyn's iron grip. Having already been disarmed of her weapons, she was effectively powerless against Evelyn. In a last-ditch attempt, she attempted to use her abilities to escape.

She activated *Slip*, which would have allowed her to break free of Evelyn like she wasn't even there. Would've worked too, if she had been facing anyone else, but as she was fighting Evelyn, *Slip* fizzled out like a firecracker in a thunderstorm.

Neither magic nor abilities would be of any use against Evelyn. She took you down to your bare minimum combat ability and then beat you with experience.

Evelyn uncoiled from Pinky and held her aloft by her throat, watching her struggle and squirm with unhinged delight. After a few moments of letting Pinky fight, Evelyn grew bored with playing with the rogue and crushed her throat.

Pinky gurgled, clutching at her shattered windpipe before choking her last breath. Evelyn tossed the woman's corpse aside like trash and glided back over to us, all with a positively wicked smile on her face, winking at me.

I let out an involuntary shudder and walked up the hill toward Richard's prone form. I steered well clear of the void golem and glanced back to Adam, who walked a slower pace than me.

"Hey, Adam. I think the danger has passed. Is it possible to get rid of tall, dark, and all-consuming here?"

He chuckled, and I noticed his eyes had returned to normal, which was a positive sign. Adam could lose himself for days at a time, forgoing sleep and food when he was working on something.

"Yeah, just give me a second."

He stared off into space, which meant he was going through his interface, his hand scrolling through invisible screens. After a second or two, the brief crack of shattered glass filled the air as the void golem shrank back into its crystal housing. The onyx crystal flew to Adam's outstretched hand and disappeared as he placed it in his inventory.

"Abby will need lots of downtime before I can summon her again," Adam said.

"Abby?"

He nodded. "I couldn't think of any name that rhymed with void, so I decided on Abby."

I wracked my brain. "Short for Abyss, I'm guessing?"

"Ding, ding, ding. Give the man a prize!"

"Oh, oh. What's my prize?" I asked sarcastically.

Adam pretended to think for a moment as we reached the top of the hill.

"I've got it!" Adam said. His voice filled with just as much snark as mine. "How about an overbearing blond asshat, tied up with nowhere to go," he said, pointing down to Richard, who was looking at us with pure, unadulterated hatred in his eyes.

"Oh, Adam, it's perfect. How did you know this is just what I wanted?" I asked, my voice dripping false saccharine.

I stared down at Richard, whose emotions were plain to understand. His eyes were filled with hatred and depravity, telling me all the things he wanted to do with my corpse.

I kicked him in the head. That was my mother his eyes were talking about.

*What to do with him?* I mused while pacing, kicking dust every so often into Richard's face. *It's the little things in life.* I finally decided on the age-old classic—torture for information, then slit his obnoxious throat.

I picked him up into a kneeling position and peeled the tight wire from his mouth so he could speak. His immediate response was to spit in my face and curse me like a dog. I calmly wiped my face clean and smiled. If he wanted to play games, then I'd be happy to oblige. I grasped the side of his face almost in the same way you would do to a loved one, but what I was about to do was anything but loving.

I placed my thumbs just under his bright blue eyes. Richard deserved to suffer, but I was feeling merciful. *There's been enough pain and suffering today; I don't need to cause any more unless I must.*

"Tell me who hired you?"

"Fuck you!" Richard spat.

My anger flared, but I calmed myself. "I'll give you one more chance to answer. Who. Hired. You?"

"Fuck you!"

*So be it—only chance you'll get from me.*

124

With a grimace, I dug my thumbs sharply into both eye sockets. He screamed as blood and vitreous fluid oozed out of his sockets to coat my hand with a mixture of clear gel and bright red blood.

He kept on wailing as he twisted and struggled against his bonds, but struggling would get him nowhere. I'd yet to meet someone who could escape Wilson's traps. Within a few minutes, his screams died down, and his breathing became less ragged as his hollowed sockets stared blindly at me.

I brought a healing potion from my inventory and poured the contents down his throat, letting his eyes reconstruct themselves. After a couple of moments, his eyes were whole again, which meant Richard was back to glaring hatred.

My thumbs went to his eyes once more. His blood still lingered, staining my fingers red. "Ready for round two?" I asked.

"F-f-f-fuck y-you."

*Very well.* And so, I retook his eyes, over and over again. Giving him less and less time to recover. His voice grew hoarse as he tore his vocal cords from screaming, eventually devolving into low guttural moans and grunts. The health potion focused on his eyes and never fully healed his voice, and after the sixth time I took his eyes, I finally broke him.

Richard was shaking, mumbling nonsense in a hoarse whisper. One look at his face told me he'd had enough. I was merciful and let the potion fully heal him this time. When it finished, I placed my thumb one last time under his eye, reminding him of the cost of lying to me.

"Tell me, who gave you the job?"

"I-it w-w-was a m-man."

"What was his name?"

He shook his head, drool slipping from his mouth. "Can't s-s-say, he'll k-k-kill me."

"What do you think I'll do?"

He kept shaking, refusing me.

"Tell me!" I shouted and slugged him, breaking his nose. Blood poured down his shining armor. I screamed and kept hitting him. "Tell me! Tell me! Tell me!"

"Stop," he spat through broken teeth. "I'll talk."

He caught his breath, and I eased off him. He coughed and spat a gob of blood and teeth on the grass. Richard sighed and whimpered, squirming under the bindings. "His name is M—"

His voice cut off suddenly. Richard tried to speak, but no words would come. He screamed wordlessly, looking around in terror, searching for something that wasn't there. Then he started to choke.

He freaked and railed against the ropes that bound him, his eyes pleading with me to save him. I watched as Richard slowly choked to death while not making a single sound. His eyes rolled back into his head, and he stopped struggling. He died a slow, painful death. Unable to even cry out, as if his vocal cords were removed.

Richard was dead, his eyes staring glassily at something not meant for mortals. *What the hell!*

"What the actual hell just happened?"

I looked around frantically, trying to see if someone was nearby hiding behind an invisibility potion or illusion spell, but there was nothing. Nothing I could see at any rate.

*Godsdamn it!* I slammed my fist into the grass. *He had been so close to answering me!* Now we had only an incomplete gurgle for a name and the fact he was male. *Not much to go on at all.* A sigh escaped my lips. Nothing I could do about it. *Can't wring answers from a dead man.*

This complicated matters to a frustrating degree. I wanted answers, but I'd have to go about it the hard way. *I'm sure some of our underworld contacts could help out.* I thought, but that was a problem for future Duran; present Duran needed a shower and a nap. My battle fatigue was back at zero, but when my potion sickness kicked in, I'd be bedridden for a while.

"D!" a voice shouted from down the hill.

I turned around to find myself alone on the hill. Everyone else must have left when I started working on Richard.

"What?"

"Slight issue here," Wilson yelled back.

The silence stretched for a moment before I gestured for him to continue.

"Unless I am miscounting here, we are missing one guild member."

*Who did we miss?* I did my own count to confirm. Wilson was correct. Minus the two mages and Longsword, who had all been devoured by the void golem, that left us with twelve members. *Someone was missing. Who had run off or hidden?*

I received my answer a moment later. A whisper sounded as someone *Shadow-Walked* behind me. It was one of the rogues. I turned slowly, too slowly. Pain erupted from my side as the rogue struck, ramming his dagger through my ribs, missing my heart by a fraction of an inch.

My lifeblood pooled from my armor as I backed away from him and drew my sword. My health dropped low into the yellow as I bled my life onto the ground at an alarming rate.

The rogue was quick and got in under my guard before I could stop him and ripped out his knife, still stuck in me.

I couldn't breathe. The pain stole every ounce of oxygen from me, and I staggered, turning, and gave the rogue the opening he needed to strike.

He took it, rushing me with his dagger.

Sucking in a quick breath, I lowered my center of gravity, put most of my weight on my back foot, and lashed out with the strongest side kick, I'd ever performed.

My kick took the rogue in the chest. Like he'd run headlong into a wall, all his momentum stopped as I drove the air from his lungs. Not wasting my opening, I stomped on his knife hand, shattering his wrist, and plunged my blade into his heart.

Rogue coughed as blood ran from his stained lips. "You and yours are doomed. You can't stop what's coming next. Once he has set his sights on something, he gets what he wants…" he trailed off as death took him.

*Who's coming?* I thought as I stumbled, my injuries finally caught up with me, and I crashed to the dirt as my blood loss took hold.

Coming close to death always brought my thoughts around to my family. Flashes of those happy days before the Night-Fall, before the apocalypse, ran through my head.

We didn't have much, but we always had enough, though Mom and Dad usually worked early and stayed late on weekdays. It fell to me to make sure Micah was taken care of and up for school in the morning.

Micah and I had been inseparable in those days, despite him being eight years younger than me. We spent pretty much all of our time together. He became the mascot for our group of friends, who loved him almost as much as I did. He was a hyper kid, but it was never annoying. He talked so fast sometimes that it was hard to follow, but it was adorable. Micah was my best friend in the world. And I failed him. I failed all of them.

"Run! Go now!" my mother screamed, brandishing a revolver, aiming at the ghoul devouring what remained of our father.

It was a creature from my worst nightmares. Humanoid, but wrong. It crawled on all fours, its too- pale, thick, leathery body hunched over my Dad as it tore into his body and sucked long strips of flesh down its gullet.

I gripped Micah's hand as hard as I could, ignoring his pained protests. The ghoul was focused on its meal, ignoring my mother for now, which changed as she opened fire. The first shot took it in the neck, burrowing in its dense flesh. Shockingly white blood dripped down its pallid skin like a glass of spilled milk.

Three more shots in rapid succession did little damage. A few more spurts of blood, nothing more. It opened its wide, angular face and let out a pained shriek that sent waves of fear through our minds. Mother stood steady and fired twice, finally hitting the thing's head. One bullet took its jaw off, spilling hundreds of small, needlepoint silver teeth to the ground. The final shot went through its eye. White blood splattered in the air, and the ghoul dropped to the ground. Dead.

My mother stood still, in shock, pulling the trigger again and again. *Click, click, click.* Both of us moved to go to her and run from our home, our sanctuary that had been corrupted. As I stepped on the hardwood, my footsteps echoed in the quiet house. A high-pitched growl came from the kitchen, and a second ghoul stalked around the corner, its ice-blue eyes dripping with hunger.

Micah cried out with fear, and that broke the spell on us. Mom turned to us and nearly tackled us out of the doorway. We fell back off the porch and hit the gravel driveway hard. I stumbled up faster than Micah, while Mom stood in the doorway frantically attempting to reload.

The ghoul savored the hunt, inching forward a step at a time. Just as mom grabbed a handful of bullets from her pocket, it howled. The suddenness caused her to flinch, sending half a dozen rounds clattering to the floor like drops of rain.

Mom tossed the empty handgun at the thing in desperation, it went wide, bouncing off the wall. She hurriedly shut the door as the ghoul lunged, smashing into the door with a crack. The wood tore like cardboard, but it held. She threw her shoulder against it and screamed at us to run. I yanked Micah's hand, and we took off into the night.

With a howl of rage, the ghoul shredded the remains of our door, and I looked back to see my mother lying on the porch amid broken planks of wood as the ghoul opened its mouth wide, thousands of needles glistened as it bit into my mother, her blood spraying in the air to coat what remained of our doorway. I swallowed my bile and pulled Micah along even faster.

We didn't get very far.

Voices too loud next to me brought me out of the memory. "Shit, get him a potion quick!" someone shouted.

The voice was low and deep. *Must be Gil.* My body wasn't responding anymore; I was cold, and my fingers wouldn't work properly. Someone turned me over into the sun's blinding light. I closed my eyes to shield myself and couldn't find the strength to open them again.

# CHAPTER 9 - UNEXPECTED GUEST

I awoke with a headache. If you could call the blinding pain that was currently using my head for sword practice as such. From the warm light streaming through the open window, I could tell it was late afternoon, at least. Though I couldn't know if I'd been unconscious for a few hours or a few days.

The events of the day raced through my mind. I sat up swiftly, which did nothing but add to my misery. Nausea, cold chills, and the most mind-numbing headache possible formed the basis for my current state of being. I tried to get out of bed, but the thin bedsheet got tangled around my legs, and I fell onto the floor with a dull thud.

After five agonizing minutes of my face kissing stone, I tried to sit up again, this time much slower. I was in the infirmary. However, none of our medical staff were present, which was unusual. *It must be dinner time.*

With none of our admittedly cute nurses to scold me for what I was about to do, I went over to the medicine cabinet, opened it, and took out a cloth bag of cure powder. With a large pinch, double or triple the recommended dose, I went over to the large granite sink on the far wall, past the small row of pristine white cots.

Searching through the alchemy bench led me to my prize, and I grabbed a large glass beaker and poured it full of whiskey. I downed the cure powder with a grimace, followed with a hefty swig of liquor.

The sharp bite of the alcohol did little to mask the chalky and bitter powder. I gulped down the rest of my drink and poured another, it would help keep the headache at bay. While not remotely curing me of the potion sickness, my homemade remedy would help me manage the pain enough to bear moving.

I opened the wooden door that led to the hallway and stepped outside, nearly running into one of the maids.

"Pardon me, sir."

I smiled at her. "Its fine, Ruby."

She curtsied and walked around me, immediately focusing on her cleaning duties.

My interface told me it was just past five-thirty in the evening, so everyone would be dining. I walked out toward the main hall. Bright red rugs and golden tapestries accented the cool tones of the dark stone walls and ceiling with torch sconces placed between the fabric. The bright colors gave the castle a warm and comfortable atmosphere.

I hadn't the heart to change the color scheme from the previous owners. The Gloom Knights' guild colors were black and purple, but one glance at the gray stone, and I'd known that those colors wouldn't work.

I'd planned to head up to my room immediately, but a deep rumbling from my stomach brought food to the forefront of my thoughts. I stopped by the kitchen, not even trying to find a place to sit in the dining hall. I grabbed a plate full of chicken and pork, scarfing it down and finishing my beaker of whiskey.

With my belly no longer screaming in protest, I went to check the loot room.

There were a hundred other things I'd rather do than sort through the spoils of war, but Wilson would bitch at me in the morning if I didn't do it tonight.

As I stepped into the basement, I was met with an ostentatious display. The entire lower level of the castle housed our loot room. A heavy metal door dominated the hallway. It was made of reinforced Aldrustian steel and looked like an old-world bank vault—and it could only be opened by a unique key. While the door itself was impressive and expensive, it was nothing compared to the floor guardians.

Whenever I visited, I couldn't help but appreciate the two massive creations on either side of the vault. Next to the door were two giant figures. Crystalline golems. Both standing nearly ten feet tall, crafted out of enchanted sapphires, they'd cost a fortune to create but were made almost unbreakable by white magic—both hefted greatswords in their outstretched hands.

*Adam outdid himself with these two.* I walked to the door without incident, but anyone deemed a threat by the golems would find themselves reduced to a bloody paste.

The vault door swung open without a sound as I unlocked it and stepped through, pulling the door closed behind me. The room wasn't large by any means, but we'd made the best use of the tight space as possible. Along all four walls were individually labeled chests for specific types of items, from gold to weapons and even magical ingredients, all neatly organized and stored away—courtesy of Wilson.

The center of the room was nearly bare except for a large crimson rug and a solid brass table. Upon which lay an inordinate amount of gold and items, enough that they spilled over the table and onto the carpet.

I whistled appreciatively. *Not bad, not bad at all.* The gold was piled high, at least forty thousand coins stacked in chaotic disarray, which was more than enough to pay the guild well for a few weeks. The coin was nice, but it troubled me deeply. Either the money came from the soldiers or the Order of the Dawn, and I didn't think Richard would be stupid enough to go into battle with this much coin in his guild's possession. Though the Alliance didn't pay their soldiers nearly this well. Most only earned a hundred gold a year—a pittance.

This much gold presented a serious problem. I wanted to pin this attack on the Alliance. The backstabbing, political machinations of the Compass Kingdom were nothing new. We could handle them easily enough, but this money hinted at someone else being behind this. *A new player on the board could mean trouble for us, especially if we don't know their identity.*

Much as I wanted it to be the Alliance, my gut told me otherwise. Too many things didn't add up, but all the years of bad blood between our two groups didn't let me rule them out entirely. Regardless of whether it was our old enemies or a new threat, I didn't care. They'd provoked us, brought war to our home, and they would pay for that. I'd make sure of it.

The guild would need to be convened, and a plan of action discussed, but right now, I had to sort through this mess.

Without even counting it, I stored the pile of gold in its respective chests. Wilson would make sure each member was paid equally, so I left the unenviable task to him and started sorting through the items, hoping to find a new piece of gear I could use.

Other guild leaders took advantage of their position and took all the best equipment for themselves; I restrained myself to one item, usually a weapon.

But at once, I could see that there wasn't anything that could outdo my current sword. Hero-tier was the best for a reason. Several high-tier and even a few hero-tier weapons were scattered throughout, but I skipped over all the others that littered the ground. Richard's armor caught my attention. It was top quality but far too flashy for my tastes. *Still worth a hundred thousand gold, at least.* Everything here was of exceptional quality and would either make great new gear for the guild or fetch a high price from the Merchants Guild.

However, there was one item among the lot that was out of place. Hidden among the random assortment of gear sat a small green crystal. It was well worn, and upon closer inspection, the crystal itself wasn't green. It looked to be made from obsidian glass. The green coloring came from the whirling green smoke that twisted and writhed inside it.

It looked similar to the crystal Adam used to summon the void golem, but it wasn't a summoning crystal that I could tell—the material was different. It was something the like of which I'd never seen before. There were small chips and nicks in the crystal, but the majority was whole.

It was an oddity, so much so that I immediately picked it up. It was small enough to fit comfortably in my hand and was warm to the touch. As soon as my hands wrapped around it, there was a tiny pinprick of pain and when I turned it over, a minuscule sliver of my blood smeared the obsidian. Using my interface, I pulled up its stat screen.

**Prison of the Hive Queen: Increases luck permanently by twenty.**

**Trapped inside a Void crystal by black magic ages past. The Hive Queen commands all races of the Hive. However, the method of releasing the queen has been lost to time. Now, this item is little more than a lucky charm.**

*Some strange flavor text, but no way am I passing up a stat boost.* While Luck didn't play heavily into my build, finding an item that automatically increased it by twenty was unprecedented. *I'd rather use this than spend my money at the stat trainers. Fucking highway robbery for a couple points increase.*

I took the crystal and stored the rest of the gear in the chests and was about to head upstairs when a thought struck me. *If the others find out about this crystal, they'll mob me for it.* Adam and Wilson especially would salivate over the possibility of twenty extra points in *Luck* since it factored so heavily into their classes.

Removing it from my inventory, it pulsed with warmth, and the texture of the crystal in my hands was strangely smooth, despite the nicks. As I brought it closer to my face, I smelled hints of pine and cedar wood, with a note of something bitter lurking underneath. *Brimstone perhaps?*

A notification popped into my vision.

**Use Item Yes/No**
*Yes.*
**Luck Increased by 20!**

As I waved the screen away, the crystal grew noticeably hotter in my hand, pleasant at first, then becoming scorching with each passing second. Half a minute later and I couldn't hold onto it any longer.

Before it burned me, I tossed it into the center of the room, expecting it to hit the floor. However, it hovered just off the ground.

The crystal glowed like a lump of red-hot coal in a fire and steamed. Fractures appeared along the small gem, releasing tendrils of green smoke, which drifted lackadaisically to the floor. It shattered with a sharp crack and burst into a thousand rainbow-colored shards, pouring out a cloud of the same noxious smog.

I knelt as the emerald wisps filled the room and stung my eyes, coughing as the scent of the forest filled my nose. As the smoke dissipated, I thought it was over, but the whiff of brimstone grew stronger, and a thin tendril of pitch-black murk trailed out of the broke shards.

It twisted and curled as if in anger and moved like it had a mind of its own. The obsidian mist drifted toward me and I was too stunned to react as it covered my face, and the acrid scent burned in my nostrils. I was forced to inhale as it suffocated me, and the burning sensation went away, replaced by frigid ice that settled over my heart.

The black smoke was gone, but I wasn't alone any longer, a new presence settled in the room.

*What the hell? It should be impossible for another person to be here once the vault shut.* Nothing but the key in my pocket could open it, and teleportation was impossible, except to a gate. As the smoke cleared from the room, I received a better look at the creature who had appeared before me.

It was a person, but not a person. They gazed up at me, silent and expectant.

It looked like a girl, but she wasn't human. That much was obvious. Small in stature, maybe a hair or two above five feet, with a cute, cherubic face and thick, wavy dark blonde hair that fell in chaos to her shoulders.

Her ears were long—longer than even the elves, extending four or five inches past her face. While unusual, I'd met a few elves, so I wasn't bothered by them, and I'd have called her an elf, if not for her eyes.

She looked up at me with eyes that were far larger than any humans. They weren't the eyes of any creature I'd seen on Nexus before. Neither the elves nor the dwarves had eyes like these. It was as if they were made from solid obsidian—a pure, glossy black.

As I looked closer, I found they weren't as solid as I thought. Dozens of miniature hexagons refracted in the dim light as she looked at me. *Her eyes are compounded, like an insect. What is she?* These were the eyes of a creature entirely alien to me, deep and unfathomable.

Terror gripped my heart as I realized who she was. There was only one answer, and I shouldn't have dismissed what the text read so quickly.

For my petty greed, I could have just doomed the entire guild.

My heart pounded in my ears, and I mustered up the courage to speak. "Are you the Hive Queen?"

She looked at me and cocked her head to the side, as if not comprehending what I'd said. Her eyes were unfocused as she stared at me, as if she'd been jostled out of deep sleep and hadn't fully woken up yet.

*Damn it, the one time I wish I'd leveled up the Detection skill. I can't see her level.* Even if I couldn't tell it, she had to have one. Everyone did, even NPCs.

I didn't want to startle her, in case she lashed out in pure reflex, so I backed away a few feet and knelt, silent while she composed herself. Her mouth moved like she was trying to speak, open and closed, but no words would come. When she opened again, a flash of white startled me. Instead of four canines, she possessed eight, side by side on both rows of teeth.

"Whhhee," she started to speak. Her words came out thick and mumbled.

She stopped and shook her head. Trying to be polite, I pulled a waterskin from my inventory and handed it to her. She looked at it and back at me, just staring. I sighed and uncapped it, taking a small sip and pouring some on the stone.

"It's just water."

The girl comprehended and held out her hand. I scooted closer on the stone and offered her the skin. She took it from my hand, but her fingers brushed against mine as she did, and it was like a jolt of static shock zapped my hand.

I pulled back, my face growing hot for some reason. *Her fingers were soft, and very warm.*

She drank deeply, polishing off the entire thing. When it was dry, she wiped her mouth with the back of her hand and gave it back with a nod of thanks.

"Where...where am I?"

With the dryness of her mouth gone, she had a lovely voice. Soft, yet rich and lilting. It drew me in automatically, and I had to stop myself from inching closer. She looked around in confusion, her eyes going wide at the unfamiliarity.

"Easy now, are you all right?"

At the sound of my voice, she turned to stare at me again, her rigid posture relaxing when she looked at me.

"Ah, it's you," she smiled, flashing her sharp teeth. "This place is strange and unfamiliar to me. Do you know where I am?"

I nodded, holding up my hands. "You're safe and in my castle, which resides in the heart of the Isle of Nexus."

She hummed under her breath. "Nexus. A human word. I take it to be your name for the island?"

"It is, has it not always been called Nexus?"

She shook her head. "In the time of my people, it was known as Telae."

"Your people?" I asked.

"Yes, the Hive."

"So, are you the Hive Queen?" I asked again.

She flinched at the title, and a look of great sadness fell over her. She chuckled, but it was hollow and bitter.

"I suppose I am," she said, sighing.

Despair filled her voice; it seeped out with every word and movement, and I was afraid to know the reason. I had so many other questions, more than enough to occupy me.

The girl looked up at me, and she seemed to pull herself out of her sadness. "Tell me, what is the year?"

*Ah, hell. She's not going to like my answer.* "It's Tuesday, the fifteenth of July."

She harrumphed. "More human words. What is the year?"

"The twenty-ninth year."

"I don't understand."

"Sorry about that," I said sheepishly. "It's the best I can do. All I can tell you is how long it's been since we arrived here."

"That isn't helpful. Surely you must have a record of history, of time, yes?" she asked, uncoiling herself to sit cross-legged on the floor.

Her gray clothing was torn and threadbare, showing off too much of her pale flesh. Her once-cotton pants had been torn to her thighs, leaving most of her legs bare.

"Unfortunately, not. There isn't much in the way of history here. Plenty of books on magic or monsters, but very little regarding history. What we do have is a few stories and word of mouth."

I'd never paid attention to what little history we had in this world since there wasn't an accurate reference for time and recorded events. I had more important things to focus on, and besides, most of the history of this world were stories carried by the dwarves and the elves whose lives measured in the centuries. Though all of it was mired in hearsay and conjecture—and getting an elf to open up to you was about as easy as fighting a manticore with just your fists.

My answer hadn't pleased her, and she frowned slightly. "Your lacking frame of time aside, I feel like it has been centuries since I was sealed away, maybe longer."

She held her hand out in front of her; fingers splayed out. For a time, nothing happened. Her face grew sterner, and more scrunched as she concentrated on her hand. It was as if she were focusing her entire being on that one task.

Slowly, ever so slowly, the air changed. It started with a faint whiff of pine needles and wood rot. Not unpleasant by itself, but as the smell intensified, dark green smoke dribbled out from each of her fingertips, mixing and slipping aimlessly to the floor.

Then as abrupt as it appeared, it stopped and what remained slowly dissipated into the cracks in the stone. I was stunned by the display, at the verdant mist as it swirled and broke when it touched the ground, but I looked up to see tears of frustration in her eyes. They slid down her cheeks as she fought back a scream.

"Weak. I'm weak, even more so now."

"Why are you weak? And what was that just now? I've never seen anything like it."

She barked a sarcastic laugh. It twisted her beautiful voice into something dark and ugly. "Behold my power. Nothing more than a few drops of magic, that's all I'm able to muster. All that time imprisoned has stunted my growth even further, it seems."

*Wait, hold up. That was what?* "Did you just use magic?" I asked.

She jerked her head, nodding, as she ground her teeth.

"How did you just do that?"

That got her attention, enough to snap her out of her anger. She looked up, confused. "What do you mean?"

"You said you just used magic?"

"Pathetic, right?"

"What?" I shook my head. "Never mind. How did you use magic without Script?"

She cocked her head to the side again, much in the way a dog does at something it doesn't understand. "What's that?"

"The language of magic. You can't cast spells without it."

*There has to be some form of tangibility to magic. You can't cast magic without a Script circle or incantation.* She still held a look of confusion on her face at my words.

She leaned over on all fours and crawled toward me. She moved lazily, but it was sudden enough that she was nearly in my face before I realized what was going on. It startled me, and I went to back up, but my balance was wrong, and I ended up falling on my ass.

It seemed personal space didn't mean anything to her, as she kept going forward, our faces were close enough that I could count the number of hexagons in her large eyes. Her eyes lit up at my unease, and she laughed softly. Her laugh was bright and musical; it filled the room and brushed against my skin like a physical touch, sending goosebumps up my arm. It was soothing to hear, like an old, favorite piece of music I hadn't listened to in years.

As the laughter faded, she smiled once more at me. "Really, Duran, don't be absurd. I am not one of the lesser races. Magic is in my very blood."

*Odd, so she doesn't use Script to cast…but, maybe that strange smoke acts as the catalyst for her magic. There has—*

"Hold up! You just said my name!"

I hadn't told her my name, and she hadn't told me hers. *How the hell does she know it?* I backed up, suddenly realizing that I knew nothing about this girl, and she was inches from me. I'd let my guard down, something I never did, but I didn't get far as my back hit one of the wooden chests that lined the room a few seconds later.

She didn't move closer right away, staying a respectful distance apart, still on all fours, looking at me strangely. "You seem wary of me, why?"

"You just said my fucking name!"

"Of course," she said.

142

"How did you know it?"

She was tired of maintaining her distance as she crawled towards me. Refusing to answer my question, which sent me into panic mode. I tried to back away on pure instinct, but I was pinned by the chest, and she covered the short distance in a second.

She was close again. Too close.

"You told me...or rather, your soul did."

*What now?* It was such a ridiculous statement that it took me out of the situation. I forgot to be cautious of this girl; she'd certainly grabbed my attention. *What the hell does that even mean?*

"Would you care to explain that last part?"

She knelt between my legs, sitting back to rest on her heels. Still closer than I liked, but her hands folded around her slight chest.

She'd sensed my frantic emotional state and was attempting to appear as non-threatening as possible. Her calmness was contagious, and it helped to ease some of my abject panic, but the question still hung in the air. Once I'd calmed myself to her satisfaction, she spoke.

"I'm sorry, that was probably a bad way to put that. You humans hold such high value on that word, but what I meant was I simply got a glimpse at you when you first touched my prison; your memories, your actions, the things that make you who you are. They're what form your soul."

"Yeah, that's not creepy in the slightest," I said and couldn't keep the bitterness from my voice "And what did my soul tell you?"

*Nothing good, I expect. I've done too many horrible things to be good anymore. I'm nothing but the last gasping breath of a dead man.*

I was dead; my mind just hadn't caught up yet.

Her features softened, holding sorrow and pity for my sake. Here was someone who'd spent centuries locked away, and she was concerned for me. I wasn't worth her compassion.

Even still, she smiled at me, and it was a kind smile. Placing a hand on my own, she gave mine a quick squeeze. It didn't jolt me this time, but it was still so warm. "I saw your pain. The guilt and anguish that tears at you every single day. It was just a glimpse, but I saw many of the awful things you've done, and the good."

"There's nothing good about me," I spat. "Not anymore."

She held my hand tighter, and the heat radiating from it grew even hotter, taking away the chill of the cold stone underneath me. "I don't think that's true, not really. Your cruelty is logical in a way. Past the brutality is a kind man who cares deeply for his friends. Everything you do is for them."

"You're wrong," I snapped.

"I'm not, and I think deep down, you know that."

A part of me was furious. Furious at her for seeing my innermost being. The monster I'd become. Though another part of me was elated at her words. Whether I wanted her to see my true self or not, she had. *Seen my soul laid bare…and she's not running away.*

The girl lowered her eyes from me and blushed. "It's the reason why I've chosen you to be my master."

*Wait, run that by me again.* "I'm sorry, would you mind repeating that?"

She frowned, and it was kind of adorable, almost like pouting. "I'd rather not. You heard what I said, and it's embarrassing enough already."

I shook my head, standing up, using the chest behind me as a chair. The wood creaked as my weight settled. "I'm nobody's master. Not going to happen."

144

Her frown deepened, turning to a scowl. "Believe me, I'm not thrilled about the thought of selling myself into slavery either, but I don't have a choice."

*Hell, no! I'm no slaver. Not going to happen!* Unlike the Alliance, I'd never held with the practice. Even though it was the single most profitable business on the Isle of Nexus, I never took part. Humans were illegal to enslave, but the other races, the elves, and dwarves, along with the rabbitmen and wolfmen, were fair game in the eyes of the Merchants Guild.

*And the Alliance wonders why tensions between the kingdoms are so high.*

"I'm not going to be your master, so forget it," I said and stood up from the chest.

I walked past the girl, who kept her gaze at my back as I went over to the vault door, taking the key out of my pocket in the process. I turned back to her.

"Look, I don't know anything about you, but you've obviously lived a rough life. If you want, you can stay here. We have more than enough room. Or, if you want to leave, I'll give you whatever you need, and you can go and find your people, wherever they might be."

I placed the key in the lock and twisted. She stood up from the floor to look at me with steel in her gaze. "That's kind of you to offer, but irrelevant. If you don't accept the pact, then I will die."

My hand froze halfway from pulling out the key. "Godsdamn it," I muttered. *Of course, it wasn't going to be that simple. She's probably lying, anyway.*

I took the key out, leaving the door unlocked and sighed. *Damn it.* "All right, I'll bite. Why will you die if I don't accept?"

Her face darkened, holding such conflicting emotions. Rage, sadness, and misery all ran through her eyes, while venom dripped from every word. "I wasn't sealed away for nearly a millennium for my own benefit. I was cursed.

145

Sentenced to the void by black magic, but that wasn't a good enough punishment, it seems, as I'm also bound to whoever I choose to free me."

*She chooses her master, so that means she could have been freed before now.* "Why stay imprisoned if you could have been free?"

She scoffed at me. "It's exceedingly rare for anyone to touch the crystal, as it requires a tear in the void to allow me to escape that wretched place. You are only the eighth person to hold it since I was sealed away."

"Seven others, so surely one of them would have been better than me."

A harsh bark of laughter echoed from her lips. "How wrong you are. You may think yourself a monster, but your actions have nothing on them. Tainted souls, all of them. Murderers, betrayers, thieves, and rapists. Those who would have used and discarded me without a second's hesitation."

She crossed the room to stand before me, the top of her head barely reaching my chest, and she was forced to stand on her tiptoes to reach my cheek. Her hand was like fire on my face, a few degrees away from burning me, but I didn't mind the pain.

She smiled at me, a truly genuine smile, with respect in her eyes. "You are the first person in a thousand years that wouldn't have abused me. You are worthy of being my master, as distasteful as we both find the prospect."

I sighed, being the best out of thieves and killers wasn't much to boast about—I'd been both of those at one point or another—but I'd already resigned myself to fate. I didn't want to be her master, but nothing she told me reeked of deception.

She wasn't lying, or if she was, she was better at it than anyone I'd ever seen. Either way, I wasn't willing to risk her death by saying no.

"Fine. I hate it, but I'll do it."

A bittersweet smile flickered as I spoke. "I need you to say it."

"Say what?"

146

"That you accept me."

I grumbled at her, which cause a snort of laughter. "I...I accept you."

The moment I uttered those words, a bitter chill rose from my chest to squeeze my heart and freeze my blood. As if a hand made from pure ice was trying to crush my heart. After a second and a lifetime, the hand released me, and I fell to my knees, trying to catch my breath, clutching at my chest, where the frost lingered still.

I looked up to see her in similar straits; she wore a pained expression as she stumbled, trying to keep from falling over.

"By the nine kings of Hell, what was that?"

She gasped, trying to speak. "The accepting of the pact. It should fade in a few moments...hopefully."

After that, the strain was too much for her, and she toppled over. I was clumsy in the catch, just managing to grab her before her head cracked against the stone. On instinct, I cradled her against me and fell on my shoulder, knocking the side of my head on the table in the process. After the fall, I managed to scoot up to lean against the brass table leg.

The girl was still in my arms, eyes shut, breathing deeply. I let her rest. Besides, she was deceptively heavy. For a girl who looked like she weighed little more than a hundred pounds, she had some heft.

A good portion of her skin was uncovered from her threadbare clothes, and her legs were smooth and looked soft. Curiosity got the better of me, and I poked her leg. It was just as I thought and as heated as her hands, but below the softness of her skin, lay something firm, much harder than any muscle should ever be.

"Hmm." *There's more to her than meets the eye; it feels like armor beneath her skin, but how?*

My question would have to wait, as I found her looking up at me with a peculiar expression on her face. My hand still very much on her thigh. I jerked away, flushed with embarrassment. "Ah, I'm sorry, I shouldn't have done that."

"I don't mind. Your hand feels nice, and you are my master now. You can touch me as much as you want."

*Nope! Nope! Nope!* I pulled away from her, she seemed to have regained enough of her strength to sit up by herself, so I hurried out from under her and slid a couple of feet away. "Let's get one thing straight, what I did, I did to save your life—nothing more, nothing less. I am not, nor will I ever be your master. So don't call me that."

She beamed at me. "Excellent! I knew you were the right choice." She stood up from the floor, still a little shaky, using the lip of the table to balance herself.

"Wait, was that a test?"

She slid me a wink. "Maybe."

The girl found her balance and moved away from the table, stretching languidly, her arms outstretched and back arched. "Oh, by the void, that feels amazing. You have no idea how good it feels to be able to feel my body again after all this time. Now, let's try this again."

She concentrated, bringing her hands in front of her, focusing on her fingers. Once more, green smoke dripped to the ground, bringing more scents from the forest. Slowly, second by second, it grew from a trickle to a stream. Still small, but enough that she smiled.

"I can feel them. They recognize me and are excited."

"You lost me, who are you talking about?" I asked.

"My little ones, all the descendants of the Hive."

Suddenly a veritable horde of insects and spiders came crawling out of the stone—hundreds of all kinds of creepy crawlies with too many legs and eyes. Spiders and ants, with a few centipedes and cockroaches thrown in the mix for good measure. The slithered and swarmed from beneath the stone to scurry towards their queen. The Hive Queen.

"Fuck me!' I screamed, jumping back and scrambling on top of the table to get out of the way of the swarm.

Absolute terror pierced my heart, and I couldn't breathe, could barely think. All I wanted was to flee from the room and never return. The creatures scuttled over the stone and rug to crawl over her feet and up her legs.

She wore the brightest smile I'd seen on her yet. She loved them, keeling down to let them run up and down her arms as if they were adorable little things instead of my worst nightmares. I was about to run, for I couldn't stand to be there for another second when she looked at me and smiled.

"Trust me."

I was about to tell her to fuck off, but the look in her eyes stopped me. It was pure radiant joy. Those two words calmed my phobia enough that I just sat cross-legged on the table while she played. She kept going for several minutes until she started to look a bit ragged and worn out.

She still wore her smile, but her hands trembled and her breathing deepened, sweat started to bead and drip down her neck. *Mana depletion. She's running on fumes.*

"Hey, you're about to collapse. Stop the spell."

She looked up, suddenly realizing the truth of my words. She nodded, and the smoke faded from her hands. As it disappeared, so too did the insects.

They scurried off, back to their homes in the dark.

After a couple more seconds, only the two of us remained in the room. As soon as the flow of mana stopped, she sagged, exhausted. I thought she was about to collapse again, but she held up her hand.

"I'm fine, just give me a minute."

She leaned over the table, her breath coming in great gulps. The table supported her easily, but her arms still shook from fatigue. I pulled out a mana potion and offered it to her.

"Thank you," she mumbled and took a few tentative sips until her strength returned. When she knew it wouldn't come back up, she finished off the bottle, and a little color returned to her cheeks. She stood up from the table, managing to support herself and chuckled. "That was foolish of me."

"Yeah, it was," I agreed, "But more importantly, what kind of magic was that? What are you?"

She looked up at me with a small, very sad smile. "I'm an entomancer, the last of my kind."

# CHAPTER 10 - STRANGER THINGS

*An entomancer? I've no idea what that is.* I'd never heard the term on Nexus before, but it nagged in the back of my head, echoing around my empty skull and on the tip of my tongue. *Maybe from one of those old games Micah always played.* I cursed under my breath at the half-remembered thought, abandoning my pride enough to ask.

"I've never heard of one of your kind before."

For a brief moment, as I gazed into her eyes, I could feel her sadness, could feel that bottomless pit of despair that welled up inside me. It was so deep and lonely that I couldn't breathe; her grief suffocating under the weight of it all, then she blinked, and the moment passed.

"Has it truly been so long that we've been forgotten?" she sighed. "Maybe it's for the best. A fitting punishment for the crimes we committed."

"What crimes?" I asked, leaning back against the table, pulling at the short hairs on my chin.

History had never been important to me, but even I would have remembered if someone had mentioned a race of insectoid demi-humans living on Nexus. *I've never even heard of the Hive or entomancers or met anyone else who talked about them. Must be a reason for it…or a good story if nothing else.*

I gave her my full attention, but the entomancer girl next to me was hesitant to speak, shifting on the spot, trying to work out something in her head. "Cat got your tongue?" I asked.

She looked up, startled. "That's disgusting. Why would you ever let a cat hold your tongue?"

I couldn't help but laugh at her. "It's just an expression. All I meant was that you seem to have a lot on your mind."

"I do, and it's not that I mind telling you, it's just…it's just a very long story."

"Well, then I won't push you to tell me," I said, hopping onto the table. "What *do* you want to talk about then?"

"Doesn't matter, just something else, sorry," she said and started to poke around the room, kneeling and opening chests at random to peer inside. She opened one filled with gold, running her fingers over the numerous coins, picking them up and letting them spill out of her fingers.

I did have one question I wanted to know; it'd been burning in my mind since I met her, more so than the plethora of others I had, at least. "What's your name?"

She stopped playing with the gold and turned, staring at me, but not answering.

"You do have one, right?" I hedged.

She smirked at me, but her eyes darkened. "You had to ask a complicated question."

"I didn't realize it was."

"I used to have one, but I can't remember what it was."

"How'd that happen?" I asked.

"Another long story," she replied with a bitter chuckle. "But I suppose I do owe you something for saving me. I guess I should start with my mother, the true queen of the Hive. She…she wasn't a good person, as painful as that is to admit. The day she became queen, everything changed. She took the throne by her strength alone, deposing the former king by force. And no one could stop her."

"Why?"

"I don't know, but one day we were a normal enough family, and the next, my mother was the ruler of the entire kingdom," she said, coming to lean against the table next to me. "Our society valued status and power above all else, but the power my mother received changed her, or maybe she was always that way, and I just never noticed."

She hopped up on the table and lay back, staring at the stone ceiling above us for a minute. Her eyes held an emotion I couldn't place, but it wasn't a happy one.

"I loved my parents, but my family was a fine example of everything that was wrong with my people. My father only cared about advancing his station, and he couldn't have been happier when my mother became queen, though it was short-lived. My father…he died shortly after my mother became queen."

"I'm sorry," I said, absentmindedly placing my hand on her shoulder.

"Thank you," she said, placing her hand on my own. It had grown hotter, but I made no move to remove it. "Though after his death, and as awful as it is to say, some semblance of the mother I knew returned to me. I was so happy to have her back that I ignored what was happening around me."

Her fingers clutched at my hand, curling around my fingers to wind in between them. She held my hand the way a lover does, and my heart skipped. I pulled back on reflex, and she looked up, a little confused.

"Sorry," I said, but offered no explanation.

"It's okay. I just feel comfortable around you."

"Right." I coughed. "So, this story is leading to why you lost your name?"

She inclined her head. "I have to explain what led to it, or it won't make any sense. Our people kept to themselves for the most part. We stayed secure in our home, the Nymirian Forest, but my mother began to expand, using our army to push well past our borders and toward Aldrust."

*Nymirian Forest? Never heard of it. Only thing next to Aldrust is the Badlands, nothing but sand and nightmares out there.* I leaned back on the table, though worn, the sharp scent of brass was evident as I traced my finger over the nicks and scratches in the metal. "I'm guessing Aldrust didn't take too kindly to that," I said.

"That they didn't, even though the majority of their kingdom is underground, they still owned the land above and pushed back hard. A few drops of blood were all it took for our kingdoms to go to war. But the races of the Hive were far stronger than the dwarves."

"There are other races?" I asked, interrupting her.

She frowned at me. "Yes, there are...were five, including entomancers, but this will go much faster if you'd stop interrupting," she said, grumbling.

"Sorry, I'm only human."

Her frown thawed a bit. "It's okay, I just don't like remembering all of this. It still hurts."

I knew that pain only too well, and I felt a twinge of guilt at basically making her tell me. "Look, you don't have to continue—"

"Its fine, Duran. I'm almost to the end anyway."

She shifted on the table, drawing her knees to her chest and resting her head on them. "When the war broke out, we had the upper hand, but eventually, we dragged Yllsaria into it as well. The elves and the dwarves banded together to defeat us. And they did."

"They won the war?"

"Just barely, but yes. We'd exhausted ourselves and lost nearly all our forces. We'd brought the world to the brink of annihilation, and because of that, they demanded the eradication of our entire species.

"We couldn't stop them from burning our forest to the ground and slaughtering us to the last. My mother took me and fled. We ran to the sacked city of Iryn, thinking it would be safe, but the dwarves quickly found us."

"What happened after that?"

"We were punished. For instigating the war, my mother received the worst punishment possible: she was erased. Using black magic, everything she was, her entire being, was struck from the annals of time. It's because of that I can't remember what she looked like, what she sounded like. I don't even remember her name."

"Is that why you can't remember your own name?"

She nodded, her obsidian eyes downcast as she stared at her bare feet before standing from the table. "My mother named me, and because it came from her, it too was erased. The only reason I still exist at all is that I'm not just a creation of my mother. The only thing my father was ever good for…and you already know my punishment. To be sealed away and bound as a slave to whoever freed me."

Her eyes held such pain and loneliness as she walked away from me that I couldn't stand it. Something in me reacted to that ocean of misery, and my body moved on its own. I jumped down from the table, crossed the room, and wrapped my arms around her.

The heat from her body was scalding, but I put it out of mind. She froze at first, going stiff as a board for a full minute, before relaxing and returning my hug. I could tell she was trying to remain strong, but before long, she started to cry softly, fighting her tears.

"It's okay," I said, hugging her tighter.

At that, she broke down and started sobbing. Clutching at me, her fingers dug into my back, taking handfuls of my shirt as she cried into my chest. Crying away a millennium worth of terrible memories while I just stood there and let her.

It felt like the most natural thing in the world, and that petrified me. *Why am I going so far for this girl?* I kept people at arm's length for a reason and never

155

let anyone get this close to me. Even my guildmates, who I loved as family, never really got that close to me. *So why? Why her? Why now?*

I had no answer as I stared down at the top of her head. A strange urge came over me, and I ran my fingers through her dirty blonde hair; it was soft as silk and dense enough that I'd need a machete to get through her thick locks.

The top of her scalp was just as heated as the rest of her, if not even more so, and my fingers burned as I stroked her head. The pain was uncomfortable, but I ignored it. *Maybe the heat will burn some sense into me.* I didn't know whether me playing with her hair was doing anything, but she never told me to stop, so I kept at it as she sobbed.

She cried until she had nothing left, no more tears to cry. At some point, it seemed she'd cried herself to sleep. Her breathing deepened, yet she still clung to me. My foot had fallen asleep from standing in one spot for so long, so I tried to peel her from me, but she was stronger than she looked and wasn't budging.

I didn't want to wake her, so I settled for lowering to the ground and leaning against the table leg. While not the most comfortable I'd ever been, the rug was plush, and her body heat was more than hot enough to banish the chill from the room. I didn't mean to fall asleep there, but the lingering effects of potion sickness left me very tired, and her warmth lulled me into a deep sleep.

\*\*\*

It was pitch black when I woke; I couldn't see a thing. The events of the day sped through my mind in a flash as I sat up, my head pounding with a migraine. The familiar silk told me I was in my bedroom, in my bed. My sheets bunched around me as I sat up and turned on the lamp. As my eyes adjusted to the light, I found I was alone in the room. *How did I get here? Was all that just a dream? No. It was much too real.*

I climbed out of bed and went out to the hallway. The flickering lights of numerous torches greeted me as I shut the door. Wilson had been waiting for me, hiding in the shadows cast by the torchlight. He was dressed in his usual attire, tailored black pants and an elegant black vest over his pristine white tunic with the sleeves rolled up. Numerous small tattoos ran up his arms, which was odd as he usually kept them covered. He crossed his arms and leaned back against the wall, his steel gaze boring holes into me as I exited the room.

"Wilson?"

He nodded to me, no trace of humor in his eyes. "Duran," he responded.

"What are you doing skulking about at this hour?"

"Waiting for you. Would you care to explain the demi-human we found with you in the loot room?"

I froze at his words, my mouth going dry. "Where is she?"

"In the dungeon, naturally."

"What?"

Wilson looked at me, confusion in his eyes. "What else was I supposed to do? When I couldn't find you in the med ward, or your room, Gil and I searched the castle for you. Only to find you unconscious in the loot room with an unfamiliar demi."

I gnashed my teeth, fighting the urge to lash out at him. *Wilson is my friend, why am I so emotional for a girl I don't even know.*

"Take me to her."

"Of course," he said, turning on his heels and heading down the stairs. We walked in cadence down the winding steps.

157

"So, where did she come from?"

"Um, she was imprisoned in a crystal. I found it amid the items from the siege. The item offered an instant boost to my stats, so I used it. The crystal shattered, and she appeared."

He scratched at his beard, lost in thought as our footsteps echoed down the stairs. "I've never heard of such a thing before."

"Believe me, I was just as surprised. I don't quite know what to make of her, either."

"Well, it's an easy enough fix. Send her on her way and be done with it," he said, casting his gaze at me.

"Can't do that."

He turned to look at me. "And why not?"

I tugged at my ponytail, hesitant to speak. "Because she kind of belongs to me now."

Wilson's eyes nearly bulged out of his skull. The vein in his forehead pulsed as his face reddened.

"What?" he shouted, almost walking into the door that led to the second floor.

I didn't respond, merely opened the door and made my way down to the first floor in silence, while Wilson followed after me, chewing things over and calming from his outburst.

"We don't keep slaves, Duran. That was one of the rules you set in place when we founded the Guild."

"You think I'm happy about it? I didn't exactly have a choice in the matter."

He held the door to the first floor open for me, and we made a sharp right and down another long hallway till we reached the entrance to the basement. "We always have a choice, D."

"She would have died otherwise. She told me she was cursed."

He scoffed. "And you just believed her? You've always been reckless, but never stupid."

I didn't have an answer for him. The situation was confusing as hell. Even if I tried to explain things, I had no clue what was going on, let alone a way to describe it properly.

I just accepted everything she'd told me out of hand, without doubting her for a second. *Wilson's right. I've never been this naive before.* But as we walked down the damp steps to the dungeon, I knew without a doubt that what she'd told me was the truth. *Those tears were real. She couldn't fake that.* And I also refused to believe anyone would willingly bind themselves into slavery.

"She's given me no reason not to trust her, so until she does, I'll take her at her word."

Wilson just sighed and shook his head. To be fair, I couldn't blame him for his skepticism—it'd kept us alive in the past, so I couldn't hold it against him. But he wasn't the one in the room with her. He didn't hear her story.

We walked down even more steps, the air growing colder and the cleanliness worsening as we walked to the deepest level of the castle, stopping at a large iron door. The metal door to the dungeon was rusted with age and damp with moss. This level of the castle was underneath Lake Gloom, and the moisture sunk into the stone along with our lungs with every breath. Mold and rot.

The iron wailed as we shoved the door open, entering the room. There were four cells in the small room, two on either side of the walls. While the room itself was in disrepair, Gil periodically forged new iron bars and gates for the cells whenever they rusted. It had been some months since the last time, and the iron was looking worse for wear, reminding me that we would need to replace them soon.

There was only one occupant in the room. She huddled on the mildew stained cot in the corner of the first cell; her knees pushed to her chest, and her arms hugging them while her large black eyes stared straight ahead, vacant and unblinking. Not looking at anything.

*Back in prison, so soon after escaping.* She didn't so much as stir as we entered and walked over to her. Wilson stood by the gate, looking at her with distrust.

"Open the door," I commanded.

Her eyes went wide at my voice. She shot up from the cot and stared at me with nothing short of hope in them. "Duran! I wasn't sure you'd come back."

I gave her a reassuring smile. "I'll have you out in a second."

"I advise against this D. We should leave her here till we determine if she can be trusted."

"Do it."

"D—"

"Now, Wilson."

He whirled on me, fire in his eyes. "For once in your life, would you please listen to me? You gave me the job for a fucking reason!" His shoulders slumped over as the heat left his face. "You're one of my oldest friends. We can't afford another loss right now, and I don't want you to end up like Alistair."

He had to go there; he knew I felt responsible for Alistair's death. I sighed. Any other time and I'd have listened to him. Much as he thought I didn't, I never shirked his advice, but I didn't always take it, either. He was right about the girl, but I wasn't about to leave her here to rot.

"The door."

He rubbed his eyes but didn't fight me, pulling the key from within the pocket of his vest. I wasn't budging, and he knew it, but that didn't stop him from trying one last time to get me to see his reason. "You don't even know this girl's name, and you're still going against me?"

My migraine worsened. Blood, too loud in my ears, my head heavy, a phantom itch in the back of my mind. I snatched the key from his hands. "Her name is Eris."

I unlocked the door, it swung open to rattle against the iron bars. She rushed out in a flash and ran over to me, wrapping her arm around mine.

Giving me a smile of gratitude, she turned to Wilson. "I know you have no reason to trust me, but I hope to prove you wrong about me."

Wilson's frown deepened, his crow's feet sharp against his gray eyes as he furrowed his brow and gave her a curt nod. "Doesn't seem like my opinion matters regardless."

He walked past us out of the room, only stopping long enough to say one last thing.

"Guild meeting, tomorrow morning, nine o'clock."

His footsteps thumped sharply against the stone as he stormed out.

I leaned on the cell. "Best give him a minute. I don't want to run into him again tonight, not while he's still upset."

"That's probably wise. He doesn't like me," she said, leaning against me. "So…Eris, huh?"

My face flushed, and I grinned down at her. "Yeah, sorry. It just came to me."

She hummed to herself for a few seconds. The beginnings of a song I'd never heard before, but it was soothing. "Eris, Eris. I like it."

"I'm glad," I said, and we stood there for a few more minutes in comfortable silence, though even with her next to me, the cold and damp was working its way into my lungs, and I was ready to leave. "All right, I think that's enough waiting. Let's head up."

Eris nodded. "Yes, let's. I can't stand this place."

We exited the basement and headed up to the bedrooms on the third floor. Eris trailed behind me, staring at the decorations on the walls as we wound through the halls. We didn't run into anyone else out at this time of night, so it made the trip up the floors quick.

I walked past my room as we exited the stairs and to the very end of the hallway. We had a few unused rooms that were designated guest rooms, even though we never actually had guests over.

The door was unlocked, so I opened it and motioned her inside. "There's a small bath in the far corner of the room with hot water, and there should be plenty of clean clothes in the dresser. The restroom is down the hall, and if anyone challenges you, give them the phrase: 'to the king who walks in shadow,' and no one will bother you."

"Okay…"

"I'm in the first door before you reach the stairs. Just come get me if you need anything," I said and turned, leaving.

Before I got out of the room, I turned back and wished her a good night.

"Night," she said and shut the door.

Back in my room, the oil in the lantern had nearly burned out, so I doused it, refilled it, and lit it again. Before I went to bed, I washed my face and brushed my teeth, barely managing to stumble out of my shirt before I crashed onto the bed and passed out.

It seemed I was going to continue to be denied a decent night's sleep as I was awoken by intense heat. It was sweltering in the room, and I was sweating bullets. The light from the lantern was out, but it was out of my reach, forcing me to get up and light it. I went to throw the comforter off me, but it was at the edge of the bed. *Why is it so hot?*

I found my answer when I moved to sit up. Scorching arms were wrapped around my neck. I tilted my head to find Eris asleep next to me, nearly nuzzling into my throat. Her hair fell across her face and smelled faintly of peppermint and lavender. She'd also discarded her ragged clothes in favor of a cream-colored cotton shirt. It fell past her hips, which was good, as she wasn't wearing pants.

*The hell is she in here for?* I sat up as gingerly as I could, just managing to pry her loose. She sighed and hugged my pillow close to her as she tossed in her sleep. It was too hot in the room even though the window was open, the wind whistling softly outside. I got out of bed and poured a glass of whiskey, walking out to the balcony. The sun had yet to rise, and the moon hung fat in the sky.

I opened my interface to glance at the time. Just past four in the morning. I took a sip of my drink and stared at the moon. *What a day*, I thought and wished my neat whiskey was on the rocks.

*Tomorrow is going to be just as long, though.* I still had so much to do when the sun rose. The guild needed to know what my would-be assassin had told me, and we had to discuss a plan. *Someone is after us, and we need to understand why.*

*A quick trip to the Compass Kingdom should give us all the information we need. With how expansive our network of informants is, one of them should know something.* Evelyn and Wilson paid them well enough. *Might have to rely on Evelyn this time. I doubt Wilson has forgiven me quite yet.*

I was interrupted from my thoughts by a swish of cloth. Turning, I found Eris behind me, rubbing the sleep from her eyes. She looked at me with one eye closed and the other half open. I took another sip while she roused herself enough to speak, though it came out thick and heavy with sleep.

"Morning," she said.

I grunted back a non-reply. Finishing my drink in one large gulp and savoring the fire that drenched my throat, I went back and poured another glass before returning to the balcony. "Mind telling me what you're doing in my room?"

She mumbled something, but it was drowned out by the wind. "What was that?" I asked.

"Um," she said and fumbled with her hands, picking at her nails. "I…didn't want to be alone. The room was far too empty and dark, even with the oil lamp. It reminded me of being back in the void."

*Oh. I didn't think about that. I wouldn't want to be alone in her shoes either.*

"All right, that's fine, I guess. You can stay here tonight."

"Thank you." Eris smiled and walked back inside. When I didn't follow her immediately, she poked her head out to stare at me.

"All right, all right. I'm coming," I grumbled and downed my nearly full drink, heading inside out of the wind.

She'd already crawled into bed. I placed my glass back next to the decanter and settled on the bed, laying on my side, facing the wall. Eris scooted close to me, her body heat seeping into my back. *I hope I get used to the heat, or I'm going to be miserable.*

Eris placed a hand on my arm and curled up on the pillow next to me. I wasn't entirely comfortable with how close she was, but it wasn't worth mentioning.

I tried to fall back asleep, but I was all too aware of how close she was to me. It'd been years since I'd slept in the same bed with a woman. The occasional drunken one-night stand with Evelyn didn't count. She never lingered, always going back to her own room when we finished.

Eris was…different.

164

I shifted, rolling onto my back, careful not to brush against her. *I mean, she's beautiful, but that's beside the point. She's essentially a slave, and that isn't okay.* However, she seemed fine with invading my personal space, because as soon as I turned over, she came even closer, propping her head onto my chest. Her cheek burning against my heart. I shut my eyes and willed myself asleep to no avail. I groaned softly and stared at the top of the bed.

"Can't sleep?"

Eris was awake, staring at me. Her compounded eyes reflecting my face a hundred times. "Just a bit."

She crawled toward me, draping half of her body over me and laying her chin on her hands. "Because of me?"

"Sorry, I'm not used to sleeping with someone else in bed with me."

"It's a new experience for me as well, but after so many years alone, it's wonderful. Thank you for suffering for my sake."

I cracked a smile. "I wouldn't call it suffering exactly."

She leaned up and kissed me, nothing more than a quick peck, but her warm lips lingered on mine for just a second. "Still, thank you."

Her lips were soft, and like a jolt of electricity and a sleeping draught rolled into one. "Yeah, anything for you." *Why did I just say that? And why do I really want her to kiss me again?*

Eris looked up at me. "Anything?"

"I don't like the look in your eye. What do you want?"

"Nothing much, well, nothing much to you, but it would mean a lot to me—" she started to ramble.

"Look, just tell me what it is, and if it's within reason, I'll agree," I said.

"Well, I know you're not happy with being my master, and I'm not happy with it either, I mean, you're not going to take advantage of me, but I still don't like it—"

"Which is why I'm going to find a way to break the curse on you and free us both from this."

Eris smiled. "That's what I expected you to say, but it's an impossibility. As far as I'm aware, nothing can dispel the curse…except maybe one of the divine, but I'm not sure."

"And asking anything of the gods is a terrible idea," I replied.

"I agree. The Morrigan would be the god to ask, but she won't help. My goddess enjoys the chaos of mortals."

"So that leaves us screwed."

Eris eyed me, shifting on her hands, the heat from her body soaking into my bare chest. "Not exactly. There is one way, not a cure for the curse, and it wouldn't get rid of the master-servant bond, but it would lessen it."

*Still dancing around the topic, I don't like this. Where is she going?* I motioned for her to continue, waiting to hear her plan.

"Well…we could…bond together."

"Bond?"

"It's what entomancers call our pairings. We bind ourselves together through magic."

"Are you asking me to marry you?"

Eris cocked her head, this time at an angle no human head could manage. "I don't know what that means."

"It's when two humans who love each other, vow to spend the rest of their lives together."

Her eyes glinted even in the darkness. "That's more or less what bonding is, though my people rarely did it for love. So, yes. I guess I am asking you to marry me."

I shook my head. *No, I can't. I couldn't then, and I can't now.* Even if it would help her, I couldn't agree to her request. Anything else, and I'd have been okay with, but not that.

*I'd be a poor partner. I can't protect anyone. Not Micah or Sophia; they deserved better, and so does Eris.*

"No, I can't. I'm sorry," I said, or well, it's what I attempted to say. What actually came out of my mouth was. "Yes, if that's what you want."

*What the hell? What just happened?* Another headache pulsed in my head, bringing a wave of nausea over me. My stomach was in knots, and my mouth tasted metallic, like copper. *What's going on with me?*

Those weren't my words. Something had twisted them. My first thought was to blame Eris, but one look assured me that it wasn't her. She was very conflicted, her eyes held happiness that I'd said yes, but I don't think she was happy about being bonded. I tried to take back my words, but I couldn't.

"Is that not what you wanted to hear?" I asked, instead.

"Yes, and no. This would help the both of us, I think, but I've seemed to fall into the same pit as the rest of my race. Bonding myself away for power, rather than love. I'm no different."

I sat up, pushing my back to the headboard. The wood was cool and soothing after being so close to Eris. I wasn't happy being forced to bond with her, but the more I tried to fight, the worse my headache became.

Something or someone was forcing me down this path. Pushing me into a role and making it clear that pain waited for me if I kept refusing.

*I want to fight, to rail and scream with all my might, but what good would it do? And at the end of it, I don't think I have a choice here.* The thought turned my stomach, but looking at her...*Maybe I don't mind so much? If it's her?*

"Well, if it helps you, then what does it matter?"

She smiled sadly. "You're right, but still...I thought I'd be different."

"So how does this work? Is there a ceremony or what?"

Eris nodded. "Well, typically, there is. It usually needs to be held by the monarch of the Hive, but that's me, so I think it can work."

"Then, let's get started."

Her hands pushed on my chest as she sat up. I brought my legs in to allow her room to sit. Eris sat on her knees and seemed lost in thought, humming to herself. I waited patiently for her to sort through her thoughts.

She sat still for a few minutes, eyes closed until she finished. Eris rolled her shoulders and neck side to side and back and forth.

"Where'd you go?" I asked.

"Sorry, I was sorting through the Hive Mind. Trying to recall the ceremony for bonding."

"Hive Mind?"

"It's hard to explain, as I doubt you have a frame of reference for it. It's like an archive of sorts, filled with memories, spells, and history, all scattered around and in complete chaos. It takes time to navigate, and I barely have the strength to manage it."

"Did you find what you needed?"

"I did, and it was buried deep, as if it didn't want to be found. But I know what I have to do."

"What do you need from me?"

"Your blood."

"Come again?"

I backed away without thinking about it, while Eris just giggled.

"It's not as bad as it seems." She held out a hand. "Don't be a child about it and come here."

Though I was hesitant, I let her take my hand and pull me toward her. She pulled me close to her and crawled into my lap.

168

"What are you doing?"

"Trust me."

"Why should I do that?"

"Because I will never abuse it. I promise."

I didn't want to trust her. Everything I'd gone through in this life and before told me that putting my trust in anyone would only lead to disappointment. But staring into her eyes as they pleaded with me, I could only nod.

Eris placed her hands on my shoulders and opened her mouth wide. Far too wide. Her tongue flicked out to lick her lips, and it was long, nearly double the length of a humans. She bent over my neck and ran her tongue over my neck.

Her hot breath was sweet to my nose, and her tongue was strong. The muscle sent pressure through my flesh as she licked to and fro. Her saliva sunk into my skin and sent a tingly, numbing sensation through me. It wasn't entirely unpleasant; however, my tone changed as she drew back for a second.

Eris's canines had elongated. All eight of them looked wicked sharp and menacing.

I gulped, and she winked at me.

"Again, trust me."

My words fled me, and my heart sped up as Eris bent low and sank her teeth into my neck.

# CHAPTER 11 - UNTIL ETERNITY

I expected to be wracked with pain, but there was nothing but slight pressure as she bit through my skin to lap at my blood and shredded flesh. She slurped loudly as she ate even deeper into me, allowing more blood to flow, but not a single drop spilled from her mouth.

After a few seconds of tensing up, I relaxed as the roughness and heat of her tongue danced over my neck. Eris straddled atop me, pushing me to the bed. Only a comfortable pillow saved me from banging my head on the wooden headboard.

Some minutes later, the blood loss caught up to me, and my vision swam with spots. Just as I was about to speak up, she finished with one last flick of her tongue and sat up. She wore the look of a glutton, lazy contentment glazed her eyes.

A slight drop of blood welled at the corner of her mouth. It should have been disgusting, but while macabre, I found it kind of cute. Like cherry syrup.

"You have some there," I said, pointing at her mouth. With a grin, she ran her tongue over her lips, licking up the final drop.

"That was fantastic."

*Even if it had been painless, my neck must be a mess right now. I'll need a health potion and quick before I scar.* I ran my fingers over what surely must be my ruined throat, but it was whole and perfect, nothing out of place. *Did her saliva heal me?*

I smiled down at her. "Glad you enjoyed your meal, little vampire."

She scowled at me. "I am not one of the nocturnals. Do not call me such."

"Sorry," I apologized but wore a smirk. "Not a fan of vampires?"

"They're nothing but savages masquerading as high society, and their blood magic is revolting."

"But you both feed on blood?"

Eris poked my chest. "We are not even close to the same. While I gain a few nutrients from blood, it's not my primary food source. And at least when I feed, I don't kill anyone."

I ran my fingers through my beard, a few wiry hairs poked at me. "So, you can't use blood magic, and you don't subsist off the blood. What's the point, then?"

"When an entomancer consumes blood, we get a glimpse of the life of whoever's blood we drink. We enter a dreamscape called the Mnemosyne. It's a powerful and very intimate thing for my kind and acts as a sign of trust. As such, it's used in many of our ceremonies and rituals."

I froze, barely hearing the rest of her sentence. "What did you see from my blood?"

Her face held sadness and pity; I knew I wasn't going to like her answer. "I saw a strange place, strange buildings and machines, all broken and empty. I saw you and your brother…"

She left her words hanging as if she were afraid to continue. I didn't want to hear anymore, knowing precisely what memory she saw. It was already playing through my mind.

The ghoul was occupied devouring what remained of our mother, leaving the two of us alone. Quick as I could, I raced over to Micah and yanked him by the arm. He was sobbing and half frantic with fear, but I pulled him along as fast as our feet could carry us. The gravel road crunched with every step, announcing our presence to anything nearby. I ignored it and ran, trying to outrun the monsters.

Half a mile later, we reached the main road; broken glass littered the streets from dozens of wrecked and looted vehicles, while busted out streetlights loomed overhead. We ran to the nearest car and huddled behind it, leaning against the shredded remains of the tire to catch our breath. I pulled Micah into me, trying to get him to stop crying, but he was scared out of his mind and wouldn't stop shaking, so I held him close and let him cry while my heart rate settled.

A high-pitched screech came from ahead of us, sending my pulse back into a frenzy. One of them was close. I laid down flat, the rough concrete scraping into my palms as I looked towards the front of the car. The ghoul was a dozen yards in front of me, low to the ground.

Its pale, angular face was upturned, sniffing the air. It was only then that I noticed a wetness dripping down my arm. A thin line of blood snaked from my bicep down to my hand, a tear in my shirt told me I'd snagged my arm on something.

My heart froze in my chest. The ghoul could smell the fresh blood. It knew we were here and was taking its time hunting us. Micah was unaware of this, still crying into his hands, but I knew it was only a matter of time, and I had to make a move. Sitting here would get us both killed.

I was the one injured, and it would follow my scent. I had to get away from Micah, or he would die along with me.

"Micah, listen to me," I said, shaking him to get his attention. "There's a ghoul up ahead."

He looked up at me with tears streaming down his face. "Sammy, I'm scared."

I brushed his hair back the way Mom always did with us. "I know you are. I am too. But I need you to be brave for me right now, can you do that?"

He gave me the barest half nod. "I'll try."

172

"Good. Now when I give you the signal, I'm going to jump out and lead the ghoul away from here, and when I do, I want you to run as fast as you can. Go straight ahead. In about two miles, there's a camp. Hide somewhere close and wait until sunrise."

"Don't leave me!" Micah sobbed.

"No choice, bud, I'm bleeding. It's already got my scent, so I can't get away," I hugged him tight, one last time. "All right, get ready."

I released him and crept around the car. The ghoul was closer now, maybe fifteen feet away. *If I time this wrong, I'm dead.* A few shards of taillight littered the ground beside me, and I snatched them up, ignoring the pain as they sliced into my skin, and tossed them in front of me. They scattered in the air, turning the moonlight into a bloody kaleidoscope and pinged off a row of cars in front of me.

The ghoul turned its head at the sound, and I took off at a dead sprint hollering at the top of my lungs, waiting for it to chase me. I made it to the other side of the road before I realized the ghoul wasn't coming after me.

I stopped and turned back to see it in the same position, not moving a muscle. It's neon blue eyes glowed bright as it stared at me, opening its mouth wide. Thousands upon thousands of sliver needles formed a grim smile, and I realized I'd been played.

Two more ghouls dropped down from one of the buildings nearby. Right next to Micah. He hadn't moved from the car, and they were right on top of him.

"Micah, run!" I yelled and ran as fast as I could, trying to reach him before they did.

I didn't make it.

One of them lunged at Micah as he ran. He threw himself to the side, almost dodging it…almost.

173

The ghoul wrapped its teeth around his arm, taking it clean off in one bite. Blood fountained from his stump, but his eyes glazed, he was in shock, I could tell he didn't even feel it. He fell to his knees and looked straight at me.

"Sammy—"

The other ghouls swarmed him.

The last sight of my brother was him staring at me with tears in his eyes. Waiting for me to save him.

Micah died, waiting for me to save him.

I didn't remember the next few minutes. My mind refused to process anything. When I came back to myself, I ran—ran as fast as I could, away from my dead family—trying to outrun my failures. I ran until I couldn't anymore.

My body wouldn't respond to me, and I crashed to the asphalt, lying amid the dead and ruined city, waiting for it to be my turn.

How I didn't die right there is a mystery. I lay in that street for hours, as night waned and the sun rose over the burned-out skyscrapers. When the sun reached the road, I knew it was safe for me to move, but I couldn't. I lay there as the sun continued to bake overhead, burning what exposed skin I had. I let it, and I welcomed the pain, the burning concrete, and my bone-dry lips and mouth.

If the ghouls wouldn't take my life, then the beating sun would. I stayed there, waiting for my life to end so that I could be with my family.

Fate had other plans, as I eventually heard footsteps approaching me. I ignored them, hoping they would leave me to my end. They didn't and crept closer and closer. Eventually, they stood over me, shielding me from the sun for the first time in hours.

"Another poor soul. Decent pair of shoes, though. Strip him, and let's move on. We're burning daylight."

I was roughly turned over, and the harsh light of the sun blinded me, forcing me to cover my eyes.

"By the abandoned god. He's alive. Quick, get him some water," someone said.

Another set of rapidly approaching feet. A canteen of water was brought to my lips, and soothing water dripped, which I drank greedily.

"Easy there, don't drink too much too fast."

I opened my eyes to stare at an unfamiliar face. It was a girl with a kind smile who grinned even wider when I opened my eyes. "Heya there, I'm Sophia. Nice to meet you!"

She was the first person who showed kindness to me, and that kindness never wavered. She was too kind for that broken world, and she was too kind for this world as well. *And I let her die.*

I didn't want to think about that anymore, didn't want to remember them. It only brought pain. Eris didn't mean to throw open that door, but she had, and it was always hard to close it again.

*Whiskey. I need whiskey.* I didn't even bother with the tumbler this time, preferring to drink straight from the decanter. Several large gulps of the amber liquor brought me back to myself, and I slammed the glass on the nightstand much harder than I meant.

I turned my back to Eris while I got my emotions under control. I didn't want her to see my tears or hear me sob, so I wept in silence for my long-dead family.

She was supportive. She knew I was crying, but she didn't pry, just wrapped her hands around my waist and placed her cheek on my back and let me.

Her presence helped tremendously and let me get my feelings in order much faster than usual. I wiped away my tears with the back of my hand. "Thank you," I said, my voice hoarse and rough.

"Of course. I'm sorry for bringing it up. I should've known better."

"It's fine," I said, brushing off her concern. *I don't want to think about them anymore. I need a distraction. Any distraction.* "The first part of bonding was drinking my blood, what's next?"

"The opposite, actually. As I have tasted of you, you must now taste of me."

*What? Do I have to drink her blood?* She stepped off the bed and came round to face me, pushing in between my legs. "I have to drink your blood?" I asked.

She nodded. "You have to taste me."

*Taste her? An odd way to phrase that…but it doesn't specifically say I have to drink her blood, just to taste her. Would saliva count?* "I'm not comfortable drinking your blood, would your spit count as me tasting you?" I asked.

"Hmm. It's always been sharing blood, so I don't know if it will work. I'm not opposed to sharing blood with you. I trust you, but your saliva is different than mine, it would be excruciating if you bit me, so I'm open to suggestions."

"Right, no magic spit to heal bite wounds for us humans."

Even though it was my idea, I still didn't like it, and my stomach tied itself into knots. *It beats ripping a chunk of flesh from her, but gods, I don't really want to do this.* But it was only a half-truth, part of me was excited about the prospect, like a need that demanded to be filled. I leaned down, our faces mere inches from each other, and Eris grinned as I approached. "Oh, so that's your plan."

"Sorry, if this makes you uncomfor—"

Before I could finish, she kissed me. Eris wrapped her hand around the base of my neck, pulling me into her. Parting her lips slightly as she pressed them against mine, she ran her tongue across my mouth, searching for an opening. I obliged, letting her in for her tongue to dance with mine.

Her breath was hot and sweet. It drew me in like a moth to the flame, and I couldn't pull away. I didn't want to.

Eris pressed even harder with her mouth and body, bringing herself fully into my embrace. I placed my hands under her thighs and lifted her to me, she drew her legs around my waist and supported herself with her hands around my neck.

We fell back against the bed but did not break our kiss. She ran her fingers through my hair, dislodging my hairband when she dug into my locks. The tips of her fingers burned like candles on my scalp, but it was a good pain. It brought me closer to her.

A new heat blossomed in my chest, slow at first but it grew as we kissed. It became as hot as a raging inferno before settling comfortably. When the heat faded away, I knew that we'd bonded. I knew it in the far reaches of my mind and the depths of my soul. We belonged to one another now.

Both master and slave at the same time.

We had completed the bonding, yet we did not break away from each other. She must have felt the same thing as I, but she kept kissing me, continuously running her tongue through my mouth.

*I'm enjoying it, but we should stop.* Easier said, as I kept getting drawn back to her mouth and its sweetness.

With great force of will, I managed to pry myself loose. She tried to keep going, brushing her lips across mine once more, but I pulled back, panting and trying to catch my breath. Eris nuzzled my forehead with hers, breathing just as heavily as I was. Her eyes were filled with lust, clearly asking why I'd stopped.

"By the void, that was amazing," she breathed.

"I agree, but that got heated way too fast."

She ran her hand over my cheek and through my hair. "Is that a bad thing?"

*Is it? Yes. No…I don't know.* "This is all just happening so fast. Give me a minute," I said and moved to stand up.

Eris climbed off me, rolling over on the bed to lay on the mass of pillows piled in disorganized chaos, propping herself up with a smile and a nod. The stone floor was cold as I climbed down, but I barely felt it, flushed with the heat of her embrace.

I padded over to the bathroom, shutting the door firmly behind me. Steam rose in currents from the bath, but I ignored it for a second and went to brush my teeth and comb my hair back. The familiarity of the routine helped calm me and gave me something to focus on while I sorted out my thoughts.

*I feel strange, but good.* The heat had faded from my chest, leaving only the shard of ice still burrowed into my heart. It pulsed even now, bringing a chill into my bones. I thought about heading back into the bedroom, but I wasn't ready to face her yet. I stripped and lowered myself into the bath. *Odd, it's gotten even colder, the fire stone can't have degraded that fast. Need to talk to Adam in the morning.*

I waded over the stone shelving and kept busying myself with getting clean, even taking the time to wash my hair. As I rinsed the suds out, I realized what I was doing. I wanted to be clean before I saw Eris again.

*Maybe I do know how I feel about her? We just met, but I've never met anyone like her before.* Yes, I was attracted to her, but that wasn't enough to justify the lengths I'd gone to for her. *Here I am, essentially married to her. Something I swore I'd never do, especially after Sophia. So what's going on with me? What force pushed me down this path?*

It wasn't Eris herself—that much I was certain—but no other answers presented themselves to me, and at this point, I was stalling. I was as clean as I'd ever be, so with some trepidation, I climbed out of the bath, snagging a towel by the door and tying it around my waist before exiting.

Eris was lounging in the same spot as when I'd left her. She tilted her head when she heard the door open, her ears twitched slightly and she smiled. "You smell nice, like cherries and sweet cream."

"You can thank Yumiko for that. She enjoys making soaps and the like."

I opened the top drawer of my wardrobe and picked out a pair of black cotton pants and a royal blue tunic with a deep v collar, not my usual taste, but it was a gift from Gil, and it'd do for sleepwear. I was conscious of her eyes on me as I changed but tried my best to ignore them. My hair was still wet and dripped water down my neck, so I dried it roughly before crawling into bed.

Almost immediately, Eris shifted, coming over to rest beside me, linking her arm through mine and cuddling into me. "Not that I mind, but you seem too comfortable around me, given that we just met."

She chuckled softly in my ear. "I guess it must seem that way to you, but I've seen your soul, remember? I know exactly what kind of man you are. Your soul can't lie or deceive, and I've tasted of your life, seen for myself the lengths you are willing to go to for those you love. And you keep proving yourself to me, you haven't taken advantage of me, even when I've given you ample opportunity. You've impressed me."

I turned away from her. "I'm just me...and who I am isn't good."

Eris crawled over me and took my chin in her hands, forcing me to look at her. "You are, my bonded. Your memories didn't tell me the reason why you tear yourself asunder, but you're in pain, such tremendous pain. You don't have to be anymore; we are one now. Let me shoulder some of your burdens," she said and leaned down to kiss me with abandon.

As if she could erase my despair with her lips alone. They burned me, but not near enough to burn away the past. The fires of hell wouldn't be enough.

Her kiss was enough to bring me out of myself, and I returned it for a time, but soon enough, we broke apart, both acknowledging the closure of the kiss.

She sighed with contentment and laid on my chest. *Maybe I could get used to this. I've been so cut off from everyone that I've forgotten how nice this feels.* I traced my fingers through her hair and over her ears. They were softer than I imagined, and Eris quivered under my touch. *Sensitive, huh?*

I put a little more pressure on them and massaged a little harder. She squirmed and let out a squeak, which made me want to laugh, but she didn't stop me. The more I kept it up, the more she shuddered, clutching at the hem of her tunic.

Her breathing deepened, and she moaned. It slipped from her lips, and she looked up at me with a flushed face and desire in her eyes. *Uh-oh, not what I meant to happen.* I'd been having fun and didn't realize the effect it was having on her. I stopped touching her and withdrew my hand quickly.

Eris leaned back, propping her arms behind her to support her weight, still straddling me. When she shifted, her tunic bunched around her hips, giving me a brief glimpse and making it painfully apparent she wasn't wearing underwear.

I looked away, but she'd caught my gaze, and my burning face betrayed me. She grinned at me, a devious little smirk that set her eyes smoldering. "See something you like?"

"Not on purpose."

Eris raised her shirt even more, pushing up past her stomach, just under her breasts. The porcelain skin of her abdomen seemed smooth and soft, but there were hints of primal muscle as she shifted. And I knew something more than muscle lurked underneath.

She watched my eyes as I forced myself not to stare and grinned wide. "You can look, I don't mind."

"I'm good for now, thanks."

She chuckled and lowered her shirt back down, covering herself once more. "Humans are such strange creatures. You get flustered over the most mundane of things."

"I don't think casual disrobing is that mundane."

"To you maybe, but not for entomancers. Since we can share so much more of ourselves than just our bodies, physical intimacy is commonplace for my kind," she said, crawling up to me and kissed my cheek, her lips like tiny flames on my skin. "Besides, you are my bonded. We belong to each other, bound together for now until eternity."

Eris looked at me with want in her eyes, her hands slipping under my shirt to caress my chest. Her fingers burned, but it was pleasant. She took one of my hands and placed it on her waist. Her skin was as soft as it looked, but pressing in, more unusual material resided just beneath.

Without thinking, I traversed across her waist and stomach, marveling at the softness of her skin and the hardness as I pressed deeper. She tensed each time I touched her, growing more and more heated. Eris moaned and dug her fingertips into my chest, the pain bringing me back into the moment.

She pushed her hips deep into my groin, feeling my burgeoning hardness and grinning down at me. In a flash, Eris removed her shirt; It fell off the bed, and Eris stood nude before my eyes.

Her skin was perfect—not a single scar, or hair for that matter. Barring the hair on her head and her eyebrows and eyelashes, she was completely hairless.

Her breasts drew my gaze. They were small, yet firm and perky, her light brown nipples were fully erect as she watched me. "Do you like them?" she asked. For the first time, there was uncertainty in her voice. "I know they're small an—"

"They're perfect," I assured her.

Her face lit up. She smiled her thanks and took one of my hands to cup her breast. Heat radiated from her as her flesh yielded under my fingers, bringing the beat of her heart into my palm. I was tempted by her beauty and lustful eyes, but I stopped myself and pulled away.

"Not tonight," I said with a shake of my head.

"Why not? Isn't it normal for humans to mate after they bond?"

"Normal, yes. Though this is anything but, and I'm not comfortable sleeping with someone I've just met."

Eris sighed with disappointment but nodded and slid off me to rest beside me. "Maybe that's best. For entomancers sharing blood, is much more personal than mere sex, but that's not true for humans. I understand your hesitation, but it'll happen eventually, so I can be patient."

I chuckled. "You seem certain of that."

"You are my bonded. We are drawn to one another, until eternity, and even though you did it to help me, I don't want this to be solely for the sake of convenience. I want..." she said but trailed off.

"Want what?"

182

She shook her head, coming to lay her head on my chest. "Doesn't matter, it's not important."

Eris quieted after that, and I settled down to get some rest. I slept for what felt like seconds before I awoke again.

*What was that?*

Something had awoken me and set my skin on pins and needles. I scanned the room for intruders, but there was no one in the room besides Eris and myself. Turning to check on her, I found her awake and staring at me.

Eris opened her mouth to speak, but the voice that rose from her lips wasn't the voice of Eris. It was lifeless and robotic as if something were speaking through her.

"Human. Durandahl. You who have cast aside your identity, I name you once more. Sampson Acre."

My blood froze in my veins, and my head ached as if it were about to burst. I went to speak, but my voice caught, and I choked. "H-how do you know that name? Who are you?"

"I am the beginning and the end. The serpent which devours itself."

"I don't know what that means!"

"Irrelevant and inconsequential. My time is short. I must do what I came here to. You have interwoven yourself into events much greater than yourself. It couldn't be helped, but you will not survive as you are now."

"What the fuck are you talking about?"

She didn't respond immediately, shifting to sit up and stare around the room before looking back at me. "You were not the intended choice, but you met the qualifications, and she has chosen you. My influence is limited now."

*Hold up! Is this who's been manipulating me?*

Not-Eris nodded at my unvoiced thoughts. Giving me conformation. "Yes, when chosen, I could not interfere, and you were unwilling to cooperate. My actions were necessary."

Before I knew it, I was in her face, my finger jammed in between her chest as my face burned with anger. "So, you're who's been fucking with my emotions, making me feel this way?"

"Incorrect," she said with a shake of her head. "Once perhaps, but no longer. I lack the power to influence your emotions. I can only push you along the desired path, but I cannot affect your mental state."

I had so many more questions, my head pounded with agony, but she held a finger up to my lips, silencing me. "My time is up. I would apologize for this and ask a favor. Do not hold this vessel accountable for her actions. She knows not what she does."

With those words, Not-Eris slumped over, and the otherworldly presence faded. "Eris?" I asked.

Her head bolted up at the sound. She stared at me, but she wasn't looking at me. It wasn't the same force that had taken her a second ago, but she still wasn't herself.

"You belong to me," Eris spoke with a tone that commanded obedience, the tone of a monarch, and I could not go against her. Her words echoed in my very soul. The shard of ice within my chest bellowed in rage and wrapped its frozen fingers around me, refusing to relinquish its control.

Eris opened her mouth wide, far too wide. Her canines had elongated again and dripped a vile emerald liquid. Out of her mouth spilled green smoke and scents of the forest, so quick that I couldn't stop her, she latched onto my neck, sinking her teeth into my flesh.

Pain the likes of which I'd never experienced floored me. *Oh, by the nine kings of Hell, it hurts.* Like my veins were being pumped full of powdered glass, it shredded through every inch of me. For an eternity I suffered, the agony so intense I couldn't even cry out.

A wisp of green smoke entered my bloodstream. It slithered through my body, bringing a burning pain with it as it crept toward my heart.

The magic that had control knew it too, and it was furious. It lashed out, digging its frost-ridden fingers into my heart, nearly stopping it from beating.

The new smoke smothered itself over my heart and wormed its way through every crevice it could find to pump my heart full of its viridescent tendrils. I screamed as smoke and ice shattered my heart as they waged war.

A clash of wills battled for supremacy. The two opposing sides colliding over and over again as they fought. My heart fell to pieces, obliterated to a pulp while the two sides fought over the scraps. The smoke was stronger, but the black magic was crafty and elusive. It never allowed itself to be pinned down long enough and would strike back with precision and savagery.

They became too much for me to bear, and my body began shutting down. My heart no longer beat, and I was dying. I couldn't even muster the strength to scream.

The dual magics collided one last time, but this time they didn't separate, not entirely. They absorbed one another, each one still fighting for control, but neither side could best the other. With one final tug, they tried to separate, but failed and became one.

Something grew from them, something greater than the sum of the two halves.

This new magic settled over what little remained of my heart and thrived.

Stretching out, it gathered each broken shred of my heart and began rebuilding it, forming a brand-new core for me. One that wasn't entirely mine any longer.

A process that topped my personal best in terms of pain. My torment didn't increase, nor did it fade. Not by one iota. At some point, my mind couldn't handle it anymore, and I shut down, falling into blissful unconsciousness.

# CHAPTER 12 - HIVE KNIGHT

Though it wasn't the way I'd planned, I slept deeply, and my whole body was stiff when I awoke. My nerves were shot from the pain I'd endured, and my skin was hypersensitive; goosebumps welled from the gentle breeze blowing through the curtains.

I wanted nothing more than to go back to sleep, but I had to get up. The clock in my interface read almost eight in the morning. *Ugh, last thing I want to deal with is a fucking meeting.*

Panic set in when I noticed Eris wasn't in bed next to me, but it settled the moment the door to the bathroom opened.

Her hair was damp, and she was wearing one of my gray cotton tunics; it was several sizes too big and came down to mid-thigh on her. It would have been an adorable look, if not for one thing. Her face held an emotion I couldn't place.

She seemed more reserved now, like there was a wall between us. *She knows what she did last night.*

Eris went over to the edge of the bed and sat down the furthest she could away from me and still be on the bed, refusing to look at me. Instead, she stared down at her hands, fidgeting absentmindedly with the hem of the shirt. *She feels responsible for whatever the hell that was.*

"What happened last night?" I asked.

She gave me a look filled with sadness and confusion. "I...I don't know," she finally spoke, looking back at the ground. "I was awake and aware, but I couldn't speak or control my actions."

I moved closer to her on the bed and placed my hand on her thigh, squeezing. "Obviously, I know it wasn't your fault, but I still need to know what happened."

She took my hand in hers, still not looking at me. "I changed you, in a way I don't fully understand."

I remembered the utter misery she'd unwittingly submitted me to. *That kind of pain worries me deeply.* It was by far the worst experience I'd had since coming here. And whatever had taken Eris over wouldn't have inflicted that upon me for no reason. *I've interjected myself into a much bigger game, it seems. That's what Not-Eris told me anyway.*

She leaned over and touched a finger to my temple, closing her eyes. An indescribable rush of something washed over me, and an itch formed in the back of my mind. "Do you feel that in your head?" Eris asked.

I nodded in response.

"That's me. I can feel your consciousness within me."

*What? Is she in my head? Eris, can you hear me?* I didn't receive an answer, so I had to voice my concerns. "Can you read my thoughts?" I asked with trepidation.

"No. I can feel a general sense of your emotional state, but right now, it's weak, and your emotions seem to be all over the place."

I ran a hand through my hair. *It's better than having her read my mind, I guess.* But I still didn't like it. My mind was my sanctuary, and I didn't like the thought of it being invaded, even a little. *Doubt I can do anything about it right now, though. Better table that for the time and focus on the elephant in the room.* The question I wasn't sure I wanted the answer to.

"You said you changed me. How so?"

Her face held a look of pained discomfort. "I am not sure how," she whispered. "But I don't think you're entirely human anymore."

Fear, anger, panic, and a slew of other emotions hit me like a sledgehammer. I couldn't speak, and cold panic chilled me to the bone. I shakily pulled up my notifications to find an ocean of them waiting for me.

*Warning! Outside interference detected!*

*Warning! Forceful race change in progress...*

*Warning! Forceful class change in progress...*

*Warning! Abnormal brain-wave spike detected!*

*Warning! Brain-wave activity exceeding danger threshold!*

*Warning! Inducing mild coma to repair damage!*

*Alert: All mental faculties within acceptable parameters.*

*Alert: Anti-cheating program in effect.*

*Alert: Outside interference logged.*

*Alert: Level reset due to cheating.*

*Alert: Hidden quest "One of Us" accepted.*

*Alert: "One of Us" completed.*

I read them all in rapid succession and pulled up my character screen.

*Character Name: Durandahl*

*Level: 1*

*Race: Hybrid (Hive)*

*Class: Hive Knight*

*Reputation: Wanted Criminal*

*Bounty: 300 Gold*

*Stats (-)*

*Strength: 0 (10)*

*Constitution: 0 (10)*

*Endurance: 0 (10)*

*Agility: 0 (10)*

*Wisdom: 0 (10)*

*Luck: 0 (30)*

*Charisma: 0 (10)*

*Sub-Stats Not Available*

I stared at my screen for the longest time. In less than a day, I'd lost everything. *My levels, my abilities, my stats. All of it's gone. I'm a level one player again.* Though with several significant changes.

Hybrid was something completely new. Only three races were available to players. Human, vampire, and werewolf. That was it. Hybrid was something I'd never come across before.

A sudden thought came over me, and I bolted out of bed and into the bathroom, running over to the mirror and analyzing my features.

I looked like my usual self and heaved a sigh of relief. Changing race usually involved some characteristics of your appearance changing. Vampires got the pale skin and blood-red eyes, werewolves sometimes increased in muscle mass and took on more animalistic attributes.

I turned to head back into the bedroom when my ears caught my eye.

They'd elongated. Not to the degree Eris's were, but longer than any humans. *I look more like an elf now.*

After inspecting my newest feature, I washed my face. The cool water helped to abate my chaotic emotional state. *I guess I don't mind the ears so much, though I won't look entirely human to anyone who looks closely.* I didn't look like an elf—too much facial hair and rugged features—plus, I didn't have the correct bone structure. *I just hope the tips won't stand out when my hair is tied back.*

Eris hadn't moved one inch from her spot on the bed. I went over and knelt to look her in the eye. Her dark gaze sat unblinking, waiting for my judgment of her.

I wanted to be angry, wanted to scream, and break things. I should've been furious at what had been done to me...but I wasn't. *It's not her fault. It's whatever entity took over her body, and I will have my recompense for what they took from me.*

"I'm not angry at you," I said.

Immediately all the tension in her melted away, and she wrapped her hands around my neck, nuzzling against me. "You promise?"

"I promise."

We sat beside each other in comfortable silence after that, my left-hand tracing over her hand and up her arm in ambient boredom while I sorted through my new class.

When I pulled it up for the first time, I couldn't stop my rage and guilt boiling up again. Years spent chasing down every scrap of a lead to reach blade master. *All of that work gone. Alistair lost his life helping me, and what do I have to show for his sacrifice? Nothing.* I'd lost nearly all of my abilities.

*Holy Blade* was gone, along with *Aura of Might*. That was a devastating blow. I couldn't get those back, not after what I'd done to acquire them. My *aura* and abilities from the rogue class had also been taken. *I'm ruined. Without those auras, my build is useless.* I could still raise my base speed to the point where I could be faster than most any other warrior, but without my auras, it was pointless.

By some miracle of the gods, I still held possession of *Dance of the Immortal*. It seemed I'd kept every ability not directly tied to a class. *Dance*, as well as *Aura of the Antimage*, were universal abilities. *Twice Critical* was still in my list as well since it was one of the starter abilities available to everyone, but it was next to useless without my speed. *I just need to remove it.*

*Delete Ability: Twice Critical?*

*Yes/No*

*Yes.*

As it stood, I was effectively crippled. I'd lost eight of my abilities. *This new class better be fucking worth it.* I opened the Hive Knight class tree and was greeted with the general overview and description.

**Only the strongest and most loyal are allowed to serve as handpicked honor guards to the Monarch of the Hive. As such, they are expected to give their lives for the Hive Kingdom. Rejoice, Hive Knight! For you have been chosen.**

**All Main Stats receive a bonus (+10) when in proximity (Thirty Feet) of the Monarch of the Hive.**

**All Main Stats receive a penalty (-20) when further than one hundred feet of the Monarch of the Hive.**

**You are now soul bound to the Monarch of the Hive.**

Reading through the flavor text didn't tell me anything specific except for the fact that if Eris died, my life would be dragged down right along with hers. While disconcerting, I didn't plan on letting anything get close enough to her to try. *She's mine!*

I shook my head. *Where did that thought come from?* My heart was beating fast, and anger flared up in my chest. *The hell is going on?* I didn't have an answer to that, but I was letting myself get distracted from the task at hand.

Since I was level one again, I could only use one of the abilities I still had left to me. I chose *Dance*, and immediately *Aura of the Antimage* grayed out.

Being level one terrified me for a solid minute until I took a second look at the notifications I'd received.

*What the hell's a hidden quest?* I'd never heard of such a thing, but I wasn't going to curse my good fortune. Though I scratched my head at the influx of new and crazy information, feeling like I'd stumbled into something dangerous.

*The game world isn't behaving as it should be, and that worries me.* Though I didn't have any way to qualm the uneasy feeling in my gut. *Par for the fucking course there. I've no clue about anything anymore.* And regardless of if it should be or not, I'd completed the quest, which gave me an honestly mind-boggling amount of Exp.

**Quest: One of Us Completed!**
**Become a member of the Hive**
**Reward: 100,000 Exp!**

A hundred thousand Exp would push me past level forty easily, which would give me access to aura again and two additional abilities from my new class. I could've gotten rid of them in place of whatever new abilities I'd gained access to, but I immediately discounted it.

*With my level in the forties, I can only have four abilities, and both Dance and Aura are too powerful to let go. They're still my aces up my sleeve.*

**Level: 1**
**Exp: 100/100**
**Level Up Available!**

When I accepted the quest reward, I was immediately rewarded with a string of level-up notifications. I advanced to level forty-four and made it almost a fourth of the way to level forty-five. Which meant I had four hundred and forty stat points to allocate, and once each stat had at least twenty-five points, I could access the sub-stat list.

Though I was torn on my build. I couldn't go back to the same layout as before. Blade master wasn't an option anymore. Besides, I had a feeling whatever had caused this change wouldn't let me just switch classes.

Eris had fallen asleep while I was fiddling with my interface, and I wasn't yet ready to wake her. She shifted when I stood from the bed, turning over and clutching one of my pillows to her chest. A strand of her hair fell across her face, and I brushed it past her ear. *She's cute when she's sleeping.*

I started pacing the room, lost in thought. *What to do? What to do?*

I'd been the textbook definition of a glass cannon previously. While at full strength with my auras, I'd argue I was one of the strongest players on Nexus, but take away my abilities and I could only handle a few hits before I redlined.

*Can't go back to that, not when I have to stick close to Eris.* I thought briefly about being a tank but quickly discarded that idea. *Playing the punching bag isn't my style.* I wanted to keep my speed and damage up, but maybe I would add a bit more health and defense. Become more of a well-rounded swordsman this time.

Satisfied that I had at least a vague outline of my build, I opened the Hive Knight's abilities list.

### First Tier List
### Aura of the Arachnid
### Poison Blade

*Exoskeleton*

*Chitin Shield*

*Hive Guard*

I could only pick two, and I knew *Poison Blade* was a must. It added a constant effect to my weapon. A permanent twenty-five percent of additional damage to my attacks and gave the damage over time poisoned effect.

I'd never seen a skill like it. Normally, assassins and rogues would have to apply poison to every attack individually. Having an ability that just added that effect was tremendous. *Wilson and Makenna would lose their minds over this.*

After I had one skill picked out, I had to deliberate over which other one I would choose. *Aura of the Arachnid* was a must pick, though one I would save for when I was stronger. It would be able to take the place of a few *auras* I had lost, since it boosted verticality, movement speed, and attack damage.

I was leaning towards *Exoskeleton*. It was a passive ability, like *Poison Blade*, and they were rare. Usually saved for the final tier class abilities. *Exoskeleton* was also a defensive ability. It permanently increased my base defense. The flavor text was a little weird, though.

**Assimilate with the Hive, imbue yourself with hard chitin to become harder to kill.**

It was between *Exoskeleton* and *Chitin Shield*. Both were similar; *Chitin Shield* created a small shield of hard chitin on my off-hand. It'd be handy to have a shield that I could deploy at will, but I held off for now.

I decided on *Poison Blade* and *Exoskeleton*. *Having both will put a significant strain on my tiny mana pool. I'll need to add a few points to Wisdom to offset the cost.* The last thing I wanted was to be at constant risk for mana depletion.

I accepted my new abilities and a tingle ran up my spin. My skin itched, which quickly grew into a burning sensation. I yelped at the pain before I could stop myself. Then quick as it came, it dissipated. I looked down at my arms and legs. They didn't appear any different, though when I ran my hands up to my shoulders, there was a hardness just below the skin. *Guess that explains how strange Eris's body felt when I touched her.*

With my abilities sorted out, I had to allocate my stats.

Since I was keeping my speed high, I decided to continue being a damage dealer. Though I would change my health and defense to be a bit sturdier, I wouldn't be as fast or strong as I used to be, but I would be a good bit more durable. After I had placed my stats where I wanted them, my new character build looked a lot better.

*Strength: 75 (85)*

*Strength Sub-Stats (-)*

*Attack Damage: 25*

*Constitution: 75 (85)*

*Constitution Sub-Stats (-)*

*Health: 25*

*Health Regen: 25*

*Endurance: 75 (85)*

*Endurance Sub-Stats (-)*

*Battle Fatigue: 10*

*Battle Fatigue Regen: 10*

*Agility: 50 (60)*

*Agility Sub-Stats (-)*

*Attack Speed: 15*

*Movement Speed: 10*

*Wisdom: 25 (35)*

*Wisdom Sub-Stats (-)*

*Mana: 20*

*Luck: 0 (30)*

*Charisma: 0 (10)*

*Not exactly min/maxing, but even if I've never had much use for them, I don't like having zeros on the board. Still, it should keep me alive for the time being.* My go-to strategy was to always increase the main stats first before working through the comprehensive sub stats. Having most of my stat points in my main attributes was a better bet before I started specializing with sub stats.

For every point added to a main attribute, it increased by a single percent. Having one hundred in *Strength* would give a hundred percent increase to my strength. The main sub stat I focused on in *Strength* was *Attack Damage*. For every point in a sub stat, it increased by half a percent. And having a hundred in both *Strength* and *Attack Damage* would give a hundred and fifty percent increase to my damage.

Of course, that wasn't the end of things. A hundred other factors played into it as well. So just having high stats wasn't enough to succeed. Weapons and armor, abilities and magic, potions and auras—all of it had to be accounted for as well. And the biggest factor of all was pure skill.

A far-too-often overlooked factor for most people.

*Our stats are only multipliers, nothing more.* Hard work and training mattered because you couldn't multiply from nothing. A weakling who could only lift twenty pounds wouldn't find much benefit in having a hundred in *Strength*.

197

*Character Name: Durandahl*
*Race: Hybrid (Hive)*
*Class: Hive Knight*
*Level: 44*
*Exp: 1000/4400*

After I finished dealing with my stats, I glanced at the time. It was nearly nine, and I had a meeting to get to.

Eris was awake and staring at me with a sleepy expression when I closed my interface and looked over to her.

"Good morning," I said, smiling.

"Morning." She yawned, stretching her arms in the air. "How long was I asleep for?"

"Not long, maybe half an hour or so. I didn't want to wake you up while I was fiddling with my new class."

"That's okay. I needed a nap anyway. I'm still shaking off the aftereffects of the void."

"What do you mean?"

"Spending so much time there drained much of my strength away. I'm considerably weaker now. Not that I was that strong, to begin with."

I leaned over and pulled her to her feet. "Well, don't worry about it. I'll keep you safe."

She stood up on the tips of her toes to kiss me and beamed at me. "Thank you. That means a lot to me."

"I mean, it's not like I have a choice. We're bound together body and soul, apparently."

Her smile faltered at my words. "Right."

198

*Ah, hell.* "Look, I didn't mean it that way. We're married now, or bonded or whatever. And even with the extenuating circumstances, it still means something to me. But this is all so sudden and new to me. Just give me some time to process things, okay?"

But my words did little to brighten her mood. *She wants this to be more than just necessity; she wants an actual relationship.*

I ran my hand through her hair. Her body heat had already dried most of the water, but there was still a little dampness as I brushed my fingers across her scalp. *She wants something I don't know if I can give.*

Whatever entity had forced me into bonding with her seemed to be gone for the time being. I wasn't happy about being bound with Eris against my will, but if we were going to be together going forward, maybe I could at least give her chance. *She seems like an easy person to fall in love with. Not right away, but maybe…maybe I can at least try.*

"I can't make myself fall in love right off the bat, but I can promise you that I will at least give it a chance."

Her smile returned; It lit up her eyes and made them sparkle. "I'll hold you to that," she told me, clutching me tightly to emphasize her point.

I grinned at her and set her down. "All right, let's get dressed and call a meeting."

The guildhall had the largest door in the castle. Eris stopped just before we went in to admire the carvings in the wood, running her fingers over the wood. "It's beautiful."

"Thank you," I said as I pushed open the door.

Ten pairs of eyes stared at us when we entered. "Look who finally decided to join us," Gil bellowed, as Eris and I walked in.

"I see you brought the demi with you. Eris, right?" Wilson asked softly as I sat down.

"What was I supposed to do, leave her by herself?" I hissed at him.

He grunted and didn't answer. Since both seats next to me were occupied, Eris settled for leaning up against the side of the chair next to me.

"There's a seat right over there," I told her, pointing at the seat next to Markos, the only other empty chair beside Alistair's.

Eris leaned over to whisper in my ear. "I'd rather not sit alone next to strangers. I'm fine where I'm at."

Gil, having heard her, despite the hushed tone, immediately chuckled and held out his hand to Eris. "Hello there, miss. I'm Gilgamesh, but you can call me Gil," he said with his deep voice.

She took his hand, which engulfed her own, and returned his smile. "It's nice to meet you, Gil. I'm Eris."

"A pleasure. So, since Duran is being so inconsiderate to our esteemed guest, would you like my seat?"

Eris held up her hands and stammered a bit. "No, I couldn't, but that's kind of you to offer. Really, I'm fine."

Gil, being the kindhearted person he was, stood up and wouldn't take no for an answer. "I insist, no way can I let you just stand ther—"

I grabbed Eris by the waist and brought her closer to me. "If it will stop this conversation, you can sit in my lap."

She grinned at me but did as I said and plopped down on my leg and curled around me, leaning her head against my chest.

"That works too," Gil said before devolving into a fit of laughter.

Which, of course, made most of the others join in and laugh at my expense. A chorus of chuckles and snickers filled the air for a moment. Though not everyone joined in. Evelyn seemed particularly interested in Eris.

"Who is this strange creature you have brought into our hall, dear guild leader?' Evelyn asked me with a peculiar expression on her face.

I coughed loudly to clear my throat. "Everyone, this is Eris." I paused for a moment before continuing. "She is—"

I was interrupted by Harper and his loud, obnoxious voice. "She's the weird demi-human with the freaky eyes Wilson found with you in the loot room yesterday."

"Thank you, Harper," I said to him with clenched teeth. "If we could refrain from such rude comments toward our guest in the future, I would consider it a personal favor."

Harper opened his mouth again.

"And if we can't, Harper—" I put fury on the edge of his name. "—I would be more than happy to settle things with a duel."

Harper shut his mouth quickly after that. At close range, Harper was next to useless, and he knew he couldn't win against me, even weakened as I was now. I'd still bet on me in that fight.

"Now back onto business," I said as I dismissed Harper. "There has been—"

Gil's booming voice interrupted me. "I have a very important question."

I nodded at him to continue.

"Why isn't she wearing pants?" Gil asked, before descending into even more raucous laughter.

I facepalmed as the rest of the guild joined in again with the laughter. I let them get it out of their system. As they died down, Eris chimed in with her musical voice.

"I don't like wearing them, so I don't," she said, as if that solved everything.

The guild cracked up again at her words.

"Did you wear that to sleep in?" Evelyn asked with a mischievous smile.

"Of course not. I don't wear clothes to bed."

Gil fell over from laughing, and a few wolf whistles echoed around the room. Evelyn looked a little...dare I say jealous? *Or maybe just possessive, that's more her style.* Wilson leaned over to whisper to me. "Don't you think that it was a bad idea to let her sleep naked in your room...given your 'Unique circumstances?'"

He made a good point; it was out of character for me, and he knew it, but he didn't know every facet of mine and Eris's relationship. *Let's keep it that way. I barely know what to make of it myself. The others wouldn't understand.* Thankfully, Eris had my back on that one.

"Why is that strange?" she asked in a too-loud voice. "Is it normally strange for husband and wife to sleep together?" she asked Wilson, before turning to me. "I did get the names right, didn't I?"

"Yep, you did great," I groaned.

Dead silence reigned for all of two seconds before literally everyone started asking questions all at once.

"Oh, look, a lovely wall right over there to bash my head against," I muttered to myself.

In between waiting for the roar to die down, and contemplating the angle needed to do the maximum amount of damage to the wall with my face. Eris tugged on my arm.

I looked down as she stared up at me with her big obsidian eyes, and ignoring everyone else in the room, I leaned down and kissed the top of her head, promptly tuning out everyone else in the room but her.

Eris was warm against my chest, and while the room wasn't freezing, without a fireplace, it was a little cool. Eris took the chill away instantly.

*Getting used to this wouldn't be the worst thing in the world.* A few moments of me ignoring everyone later, the room got quiet again.

"All right, you mongrels!" I yelled at them. "Settle down. Now. Yes…I guess Eris and I are married… Sort of. Kind of…look, it's hard to explain, and I don't feel like going over the details. So, let's just all accept it and move on. Trust me, you'll have much better questions in a few minutes."

Gil just laughed and clapped me on the shoulder. "Hey, no worries, I'm just happy you've got a lady in your life. A less homicidal lady, in any case," he said with a whisper, glancing over at Evelyn.

"Thanks, Gil. Now I didn't call everyone here to gossip like schoolgirls. There are two serious matters to discuss."

Everyone quieted up and listened to me—instant silence. *We're the worst, except when it comes to business.*

"First and most important is the recent attacks on Gloom-Harbor." Taking stock of the room, I continued. "This last raid was the worst we've experienced yet, over five hundred troops and a full guild to siege one castle. We were incredibly fortunate to win without taking casualties."

Wilson spoke up, "The Alliance has gone too far this time. It was a declaration of war on us."

"Except I don't think this was the Alliance, not this time," I replied.

Wilson and Gil both looked confused. "Please elaborate," Wilson said.

"Look at the evidence. We have a small fortune in gold down in the basement. Since when has the Alliance ever paid their soldiers so well? There's enough gold to pay every soldier they sent for ten years of service."

Wilson thought about that statement, and I knew he would see the logic there. I added to my debate. "Not to mention the guild we fought. The Order of the Dawn were hardcore mercenaries, just like us. And I know exactly how much we charge for our services. Hiring mercs isn't cheap. Besides, the Alliance doesn't contract out bounties, plain, and simple."

"Then, who?" Adam asked, chiming in.

"I don't know. When I fought the would-be assassin, he told me that someone was coming for us and that we wouldn't be able to stop them."

Everyone paused for a moment, letting what I'd said sink in.

"That…is disconcerting news," Wilson mused. "If not the Compass Kingdom, that means it's someone new. We should've had forewarning regardless. It seems like we are being kept out of the loop."

*He's got a point. We should have had some warning about this.* We paid a lot of money to be kept abreast of any important news. Either our contacts hadn't heard anything, or they were being paid off to keep us in the dark. Neither option a good one.

I turned to Wilson and asked him, "Do you think you could talk to any of your old Thieves Guild members, see if they heard anything?"

He ran his fingers through his beard, stroking his well-groomed silver hairs in thought. "I could try, but I doubt I'd get much from them, and since I'm unable to enter the city anymore, it would be a costly venture to try and arrange a meeting."

I wracked my brain, trying to come up with a solution. "Evelyn, do you think any of your networks could be of use here?"

She looked up from her interface to answer me. "Oh, absolutely, though like Shadow, I can't exactly go strolling through Compass Kingdom right now."

"Shit, I forgot the Assassins Guild still has that hit out on you."

"Indeed, though I'm not worried about my safety. They've tried to kill me dozens of times now, but anyone seen with me would be a target, and most of my contacts are cowards who wouldn't risk it."

At this point, Eris piped up. "You all seem to make friends well."

Everyone laughed, and Makenna spoke. "We all have bounties on our heads. It's just a way of life for us," she said softly.

I was always surprised by Makenna. With her long red hair tied in pigtails and a swatch of freckles dotting her cheeks, she looked like everyone's favorite kid sister. But she was one of the deadliest assassins on Nexus. She flashed her emerald eyes to Eris for a second before turning back to the thick leather-bound tome in her hands.

"You're all criminals?" Eris's eyes looked to each member of the guild before finally looking up at me.

"Hey, don't lump me in with the rest of this rabble, I'm no criminal."

Levi snapped back at my words. "Oh, yeah? What about when you pretended to join the Church of the Penitent Whisper, to become a paladin?" he asked me.

"Hey, technically, I didn't commit any crimes," I told the big brute.

Wilson, of course, took the opportunity to add his two cents. "Well, you did pledge an oath of service to the church and the Alliance, only to immediately ditch after you got your hands on the paladin class," he said.

"That would make me an oath breaker, not a criminal," I replied to him.

"Well, what about that guard you knocked unconscious, trying to escape, hm?" he said with a smug nod of his head.

"One assault charge, c'mon that doesn't count. The bounty was like, what, three hundred gold? That's peanuts." I said, clearly in denial.

Everyone started chuckling at me. Levi and Wilson held up their hands in mock surrender. "Okay, fine, you win," Wilson said, "Though my point was that out of all the members here, you have the best chance of walking through the five kingdoms unmolested. As long as you stay out of Cardinal Square, that is," he said with a laugh.

*It looks like I have no choice in the matter.* "Okay, fine. I'll go and check things out in the capital. See what I can dig up," I told everyone. "I'll head out first thing in the morning. I shouldn't be gone more than a day or two."

Eris tugged on my sleeve and gave me a look that said in no uncertain terms would I be leaving without her.

"Sorry, what I meant to say was that *we* will be leaving first thing in the morning. We have the spare teleportation scrolls on hand right, Wilson?" I asked the stony-faced guild treasurer.

"Of course, we do, but D…." he said, then trailed off.

I just stared at him. "Yeah. What?" I asked, confused.

"Aren't you forgetting something?"

I didn't comprehend what he was asking me. *What have I forgotten?* Eris shifted in my lap, and the movement made me glance at her. The realization hit me like a ton of bricks.

"Oh, son of a bitch," I lamented.

"Ah, there goes the little hamster wheel turning," Adam quipped.

Gil and Levi fell over laughing at that. Even Makenna and Yumiko chuckled at my expense.

"Eris is an NPC."

"Indeed, she is. Albeit, like one I've never seen before, but an NPC regardless," Wilson stated.

I sighed into my hands. "NPCs can't use teleportation," I groaned, "Which means that if Eris is coming with me, we have to travel by mounts."

"What's an NPC?" Eris asked.

"Well, the technical term is non-player character, but that won't mean anything to you. NPCs are most of the people here. Most of the humans and every single one of the other races. Anyone other than one of us players."

206

"Oh," she said and leaned against my chest. "I knew that, then. I had just never heard the term before."

*Wait, does she know she isn't real? No, that's impossible; NPCs have never shown any sign of self-awareness before.* "Eris, could you explain how you know the difference between us?"

"Um, I can try, though it's strange. I don't know how I know that we're different, but I do. And it's not just in species, but I recognize that you were summoned from a different world by the gods of this world, even though no one has ever told me. I just know it."

Wilson spoke up, echoing the train of thought going through my mind. "I guess the governing AI would need some way to explain our presence here, but it is odd that this is the first time an NPC is speaking about it."

"It's probably an unconscious bit of knowledge placed by Edn—the AI when they create an NPC. And I don't know about the rest of you, but I don't exactly go around having deep conversations with NPCs." Evelyn spoke up from whatever she was looking at on her interface to chime in.

"She's right, though," I said, looking down at Eris. "Eris is the first NPC I've ever really talked to beyond polite conversation. But surely someone out there has spent more time with them than we have."

"Perhaps, but I fear we have gotten off-topic. We'll have plenty of time for philosophical debate once we're no longer under threat of attack. So, I'm assuming that Eris is adamant about traveling with you?"

It would take ten minutes to reach the Compass Kingdom using a scroll. Traveling by mount would take at least a week. I leaned over to speak to Eris. "Are you sure I can't convince you to stay here while I make a quick trip to the capital?"

She shook her head. "Not a chance, my bonded. Wherever you go, I follow."

I could see immediately that I wasn't going to have a shot in hell at convincing her otherwise, "Okay, you win. We shall go together," I told her.

She just smiled wide at me, showing off her sharp teeth. I went to address the room. "Now that we have the first order of business taken care of. I have a more personal issue to announce." I paused. *How am I going to say this?*

I tried to find the right way to say it and came out wanting. "Ah, hell. I guess I don't have a good way to say this, so I'll just put it bluntly. I'm not entirely human anymore."

It took me about five minutes to get them to stop laughing. Well, most of them, anyway. Adam and Evelyn seemed to take me at my word, at least.

After the laughter had died down to a dull roar, I pulled my hair back and let them all get a good look at my newest feature. It got quiet fast after that. They could all see the elongation and pointedness of my ears. Rationalization dawned on their faces, as they tried and failed to come up with a logical explanation as to why I was suddenly different. I saved them the trouble.

"I am now a hybrid. What that means, I haven't figured out yet. Though it seems I am half human and half Hive, which, according to Eris, were several races of insectoid demi-humans that thrived in this world before we ever came here."

"Okay, sure. You're now a hybrid, got it, great. We've seen other things just as strange, and you have the ears to back up your claims, so I have no choice in accepting what you're saying," Wilson said. "The better question is, how did this happen? Is it because of Eris?"

"Yes…and no. It's complicated."

Wilson got quiet for a second, his face turning several unflattering shades of red and purple, and his veins stretched tight. He was trying very hard not to scream at me. He blew out a heavy breath and placed his palms on the table, trying to calm down. "I told you to be careful, D. And look what happens. I told you she couldn't be trusted."

"Hey, don't blame Eris for this. It wasn't her fault."

He wasn't convinced but backed off. Which I was thankful for. *Any more and we might have come to blows, but he's just looking out for me.*

"Now let's get back on topic. Yes, I am now a hybrid, but that's not the only new change with me. I also received a new class, and on top of that, my level was reset," I immediately held up my hand to stop the onslaught of questions I knew would be coming. At this rate, we would never get through the meeting.

"I will tell you a little about my class, but not everything. As we all know, sharing information like that is generally considered a faux-pas. My class is called Hive Knight, and as far as I can tell, it's unique," I said, before telling them about receiving the hidden quest and jumping back up to level forty-four.

After hearing this, a few had concerns about Eris and me going alone to Central—and right in the middle of Alliance territory. I shared their concerns; it freaked me out that I was so low leveled and with a strange and unfamiliar class to boot. *Godsdamn it! It's not fucking fair! I lost everything...but what else can I do? Getting furious won't solve anything, won't get what I lost back. Man up, Duran, and deal with it.*

I dissuaded them from having someone else accompany us. "I hate to admit it, but I have the best chance of getting in and out without incident. You know, barring me getting caught and strung up by the church."

The debate went back and forth for around fifteen minutes before we settled the matter.

"Okay, no more arguing. I'm going."

"While we are all here, I have a few guild matters we need to discuss," Wilson said, standing from his chair.

"Yeah, yeah," I said, standing with Eris from my seat. "I approve whatever, go team."

"Duran!" Wilson shouted at my back.

I waved him off and left the guildhall with Wilson cursing my name. I needed food and a lot more sleep. I took care of the first when we went by the kitchen. Eris and I devoured a whole chicken and then we went upstairs for some quiet time so I could catch up on my sleep.

# Chapter 13 - On the Road

I'd wanted to get an early start in the morning and get on the road quickly, but circumstances had other plans.

Said circumstance was currently drifting lackadaisically on her back in the bath.

"The heat is wonderful; it's working out tension I didn't even know I had."

"Glad you're enjoying," I said. *You better be—I had to turn the heat up to nearly boiling to get it to a comfortable temperature for you.*

I'd been hesitant to step into the water, but it wasn't unpleasant when I found the courage. It was a comfortable heat. *Guess my new race came with a few perks. Though Eris still feels hot to the touch, odd.*

Eris took her time enjoying the bath with me while I cleaned myself in a mechanical fashion, trying desperately not to let my eyes linger over her body. She didn't care one bit about being naked in front of me, but it was incredibly distracting.

After we were clean, I ran my fingers over the rough, copper stubble that framed my jawline, finally caving and deciding to shave my beard. When I got back into the water after grabbing my razor, Eris asked what I was doing.

"Shaving, finally getting rid of my beard."

She ran her fingers through the stiff hairs. Her hand was admittedly nice as she brushed over my cheek. "I like it on you. It's a good look."

I didn't really enjoy having a beard, but Eris liked it. So, we compromised, and I left it alone.

"What did Gil say to you this morning? He sounded upset."

I chuckled. "That's just because I woke him up early and he's not a morning person. But I needed his help. Because of all the recent changes, none of my regular gear will work."

"So, is he letting you borrow some from him?"

"Something like that."

When we finished in the bath, I got dressed and handed Eris a shirt to wear in the interim, but to my surprise, she'd already dressed.

She was wearing a chocolate skirt, which on anyone with longer legs would've been considered indecent. On Eris, it was perfect, barely hinting at her pale thighs.

The skirt was complemented by a juniper tunic and was only a hair or so big on her, with a slight V shape in the collar that was meant to flaunt substantial cleavage. Eris's chest was petite, so this feature was wasted. *Such is the fate of the small-breasted.*

She'd acquired a pair of well-worn leather traveling boots that came to mid-calf on her, but her face looked unhappy as she stared down at them. To finish off the ensemble, she wore a small brown cloak with a hood that would hide her unique features well enough. *She looks adorable.*

"You look stunning," I told her honestly. She smiled happily at that, glad that I approved of her outfit. "Where'd you get those clothes, though?"

"They were lying on the ground by the door. There was a small note with my name on it," she said as she handed me the note.

I didn't recognize the handwriting, but that wasn't exactly shocking. *When was the last time I hand wrote anything?*

It was either Yumiko, Makenna, or Evelyn, but I immediately discounted Evelyn. She was never kind to anyone without cause. And I'd never seen Yumiko in anything other than pants, which left Makenna. *Need to thank her, next I see her. That was incredibly thoughtful.* Especially since I should've realized all Eris had to wear was my oversized tunics and cotton shirts.

"Well, it doesn't matter, though you do look lovely. Now let's head down to the forge. I don't want to keep Gil waiting. He gets impatient quickly."

She held out her hand and said. "Well, then let's not keep him waiting, Sam."

Cold ice gripped my heart, a chill that had nothing to do with the magic inside me. "Don't call me that...please."

"Why?"

"Because that man died a very long time ago."

She walked over to me, hugging me. "You're lying to yourself, my bonded. Sampson Acre is alive and well, just buried under a lot of pain. You can't hide him from me, not when I can see right through you."

I pulled away and headed out into the hall. "Let's go," I said tersely.

The walk to the forge was quiet. Eris was downcast, and it didn't take some strange magic to know that I'd hurt her feelings. But I wasn't going to apologize; I'd worked too damn hard to bury who I'd been to let it all unravel now.

Opening the metal door to the forge, we stepped inside. The blistering heat assaulted me along with the stench of burning wood and metal.

Racks of weapons lined the stone wall as I turned the corner and went into the workshop. Gil sat bent over his anvil, working on what looked like a chestplate. He was completely absorbed in his work, and I wasn't about to disturb him.

*Haven't been here in a while, wonder what's new?* In the far corner of the room was a gigantic black battle-axe. It was crude, roughly shaped from a solid piece of metal, but for some reason, it called to me. I wanted to wield it, and I walked over to it, bending to pick it up.

Something whistled through the air just before pain smacked me in the side of the head. A lump of metal dropped to the dirt floor next to me.

"Ow! What the fuck, Gil?"

"Don't touch," he said and turned back to his work.

"Fine," I grumbled, rubbing the side of my head.

Eris had been smart and took a seat on the metal benches that lined the back wall. I followed suit and settled in while Gil plied his craft.

"Hey!" Gil shouted in my ear while shaking me. "Get up and try on the armor so I can go back to bed."

I jolted upright, waking Eris in the process. "Sorry, I didn't mean to fall asleep," I said, wiping a strand of drool that slipped from the corner of my lip.

Gil grunted a non-reply and shuffled over to let me get a look at what he'd made.

It was perfect.

The base was studded leather; dozens of little studs were sewn into the armor around the vital areas that weren't covered by plate metal, the collar, hips, and groin. They were grouped as tightly as possible to help disperse the impact of blunt weapons and deflect a slice or thrust from a blade. The leather was a vibrant azure, and the steel studs reminded me of scales. The inclusion of the studs acted like scale mail to add an extra layer of protection while keeping my movements unhindered, but the separation of the studs would mean they wouldn't jostle and clank as I moved.

Heavy plate mail was added on the chest and back with leather-backed metal pauldrons for the shoulders. The legs had thick leather greaves that stopped just before my ankles.

214

To top everything off, Gil had accented the collar of the armor with the silver and black fur of a bane wolf, which surpassed even the size of the already monstrous dire wolves.

This was a masterfully crafted set of medium armor built for movement and to take a beating.

"Gil, you shouldn't have," I told him. "You used the leather from the storm dragon, didn't you?"

He shrugged. "Yeah, well, it does me no good if you go off and get yourself killed because you can't stay away from trouble." He turned and gave me a fierce look. "You'll be paying me back for that leather. It was damn near priceless, as you well know."

I raised my hands in surrender. "Of course."

His features softened. "I know, I'm just giving you a hard time because I need sleep. Or better yet, coffee. Ye gods, what I would give for just a sip."

I nodded in agreement. We shook hands, and he pulled me in for a quick hug. "You be safe out there, D."

He walked over to Eris and knelt to look at her, even though he still towered over her.

"Don't think I forgot about you, little miss," he said as he presented her with a light breastplate and a set of matching vambraces. "It's not much, since I had to spend most of the time on the idiot's armor, but it should fit you well enough and keep you alive if you run into trouble."

Eris smiled wide as she equipped her new armor. It took a little help to get her into it, but in no time we had succeeded. Her traveling cloak concealed her armor entirely. She spun around, getting a feel for the added weight.

Satisfied, she wrapped her arms around Gil's giant neck and placed a kiss on his cheek.

"Thank you, Gil," she said, as she clung around his neck. It took nearly both of her arms to wrap around the giant berserker.

He blushed scarlet and mumbled, "It's no trouble, don't mention it."

At the sight of Eris holding on so tightly to my best friend, something dark uncoiled itself from my heart. Ice-cold hands tore into my chest, and a pitch-black rage welled up inside me as Eris hugged him and pressed her lips to his cheek.

*How dare he put his filthy hands on her!*

*"Kill him for touching what's rightfully yours. Make him suffer,"* a smoky, sibilant voice demanded from inside of me.

I unconsciously reached for my sword before I could stop myself. I shook my head, trying to dislodge the voice that was inside me. *Gil is my friend, not my enemy. What the hell am I thinking?*

The feeling came and went in a flash; it receded when logic told me what I was feeling was wrong. It happened so quickly that neither of them noticed. *What is wrong with me?*

I turned away from the pair of them and went outside to get some air and ready our supplies and my horse.

As I exited the stifling workshop, I breathed in deeply, letting the chilly morning air cool the lingering presence of rage within me. After a moment or two, normalcy reasserted itself, and I went to organize our packs.

Our supplies were rather simple. Just two identical sets of the standard adventurer's kit. A camping set, one hundred feet of rope, dry rations and water, flint and steel, a torch, and ten health and mana potions.

I added some personal additions to the kit. A set of burglar's tools that were a gift from Wilson—I wasn't anywhere close to his skill at lock picking, but I managed well enough. I also threw in a few vials of poison and some smoke bombs in case we needed to make a rapid getaway. I also carried my wood carving tools, for when I would inevitably get bored on the trip. It would give me something to do with my hands. And, of course, my large travel flask of whiskey.

After packing everything and storing it all in my inventory, I went to ready my horse.

As I slipped through the wooden doors, the stench gave me pause. A mixture of manure and the pungent odor of animals combined with the smell of damp hay, which always lingered no matter how often we changed the straw.

There were only five animals in the stables, as most of us used teleportation to get around. Before the hunt for the dragon, it had been months since I had ridden my mount.

She stood in the back. Even among the admittedly impressive array of animals we had acquired over the years, I held a special place in my heart for my horse.

Lacuna was a massive warhorse, taller than even Gil and just as long. She was the perfect shade of midnight with a coal-black mane. Her coat was immaculately groomed. Adam made sure to take excellent care of all the animals or creations under his care. The only spot of color on her was the whites of her eyes.

She perked up immediately at my approach; I ran my hands along her snout as she nuzzled into me. I unlatched the gate and guided her gently out of the pen and outside, stopping to grab all the gear I would need and quickly saddled her. My saddle was the exact shade of her coat, and I thought it suited her well.

Eris was waiting outside on a bench. She was leaning on the side of the wall and looked like she was about to fall asleep.

After I had finished, I walked Lacuna over to meet Eris and to make sure Lacuna wouldn't react poorly to having a new person riding her. Eris lit up at the sight of the large horse and shook the sleep from her face in an instant as she hopped over to greet the horse.

Eris was comically tiny compared to Lacuna, who would put even a Clydesdale to shame with her size. Eris gently reached out to pet the flank of the horse. Lacuna huffed for a moment at Eris's touch, but she grew accustomed to it quickly as she walked over and ran her fingers through Lacuna's mane.

Satisfied that both the girls would get along, I climbed up, only to realize there was an issue. Eris wouldn't have a chance in hell of climbing up by herself, as she was coming to realize as she looked at the stirrups with a contemplative expression.

I reached down and offered her my hand, telling her where to place her feet and guided her on how to mount a horse properly. We had some small difficulties, but I managed to get her there.

Once we had settled on the large horse, we set off out of the keep as the gate thumped to the dirt. Dawn broke over the hills but hadn't yet fully decided if it wanted to keep going. The fog was still rolling in, and the grass was slick with dew.

Eris stared in awe and took big heaping gulps of the fresh air that the breeze brought in. I'd never been a morning person, but even I had to admit the pure calm that came with the very early mornings was worth the trouble.

"It's been so very long since I have felt the fresh air and sunshine on my skin," Eris said in wonderment. "I'd forgotten what this feeling was like."

Her head darted back and forth to catch a glimpse of every single speck of landscape she could. We rode that way for a long time, a couple of hours spent in silence, letting Eris enjoy the sights and sounds of nature. Past the green grassy plains surrounding our territory to the Rolling Hills immediately beyond Castle Gloom-Harbor.

There were no towns within a day of us, and we were just over five hundred miles from the outskirts of the East Kingdom. It would take us around a week to reach the East Kingdom of the Compass Kingdom and another ten to twelve hours once we were in the East Kingdom to enter the Central Kingdom.

A few hours later, after we'd traveled about fifteen miles, Eris had absorbed enough of the scenery. She stretched herself out, arms extending and arching her back. Which was a pretty impressive feat considering we were on horseback. She sighed as she fully stretched herself out, and more dark green smoke came trailing down her hands and through her fingers.

Sharp scents of wood and fauna flooded my senses, and Lacuna spooked slightly at the new smells that appeared without a source.

"Much better," Eris said as the smoke slowly dissipated.

"What'd you do?" I asked her.

I had seen her magic twice now, and neither time was what I would consider a pleasant experience.

"I'm working on building up my magic again. I'm useless right now with how weak I've become. I'm trying to reconnect to my little ones." She smiled and leaned back into my chest. "It's going to take time, but we've got nothing but time, right?"

Her tone was light, but there was unease in it like she was afraid she could blink, and I'd disappear. I leaned down and kissed the top of her head. "Right. I'm not going anywhere."

We rode for hours, simply enjoying the journey and each other's company. We had a lot to talk about; there was so much that I wanted to know about her and her about me. Even with her seeing fragments of my life, there were still plenty of gaps, including my first life here.

Eris was surprised to hear that this wasn't my first life in this world, turning and looking at me strangely. "You've died before?"

I nodded. "Twice, actually, but yes. This is my second life here."

"What happened?"

Flashes of memories flooded through my mind, things I didn't want to remember. The four of us, me, Sophia, Mika, and Lonny. *So many good memories, ruined now. Because of me.*

The man who'd been like a brother to me raised his sword, the one just yesterday he'd been bragging about, its ruby-inlaid golden hilt branched out at the crossguard. The quillons formed a stalwart golden cross as the silver blade whipped toward my head.

"Lonny, stop!" I yelled as I stepped back.

I was too slow as Lonny flicked his wrist and sent the blade across my chest. Scarlet danced on the tip of his sword, and my blood splattered across the earth.

Before I could register the wound, Lonny charged me, his steel heater shield glowing with a soft yellow light. Four different swords crossed together over a rising sun, the emblem I'd once found so much pride in, grew in brightness as his ability took hold.

I braced, preparing for his *Shield Bash*.

He barreled into me, knocking the wind out of me and snapping my left arm like pine wood. I flew back and hit the ground hard, my health bar dropping to mid yellow.

Tears dripped down Lonny's face. He was handsome, with strong cheekbones, a rugged chin sprouting the beginnings of stubble, and short chestnut hair. It was thick and curled randomly, giving his face a hint of youthfulness that didn't belong with his eyes. His caramel eyes that once held so much laughter in them now held grief and hatred.

I stood, ignoring the aching pain spreading up my left arm and focused on my target. Lonny was skilled at close quarters, even better than me, and since we both fought with swords. It put me at a disadvantage up close.

*Damn him!* I lunged, activating *Blade Shift*. Like a mirage, my sword faded translucent and was quickly joined by three copies, all writhing and shifting like an illusion.

Lonny knew what the ability did, but he couldn't guard against it entirely. I wormed through his defense to jam my sword through the opening.

It stopped just shy of his armor, the silver outline shimmering to life and cracking under my blow. His *Full Defense* held under my attack, and I backed away as he turned and swiped at me.

Lonny's sword was poised to bite into my neck, but I activated *Flash Step* and was out of reach as his blade passed through empty air.

Any other time and Lonny would have grinned that he'd managed to get me to waste my most powerful ability, but not this time. I couldn't read anything beyond the rage in his eyes.

I circled him, knowing I had one good sucker punch left in me. As Lonny turned, I danced in. Activating *Swordfeint*, I vanished, as a copy of myself appeared in my place. I thrust; my blade angled towards Lonny's exposed neck.

*Scatter Pulse* hit me like a bulldozer. An invisible force shattered my blade and lifted me off the ground. Lonny struck with the side of his shield, bashing me across the temple and opening a deep cut across my scalp.

I blacked out, coming to with Lonny standing over me, void of any mercy. I had only one ability left to me, and I used it. *Phantom* copied Lonny's sword exactly and materialized in my hand, an ethereal shimmer cascading down its length.

My final thrust was weak, lacking any force, and Lonny easily parried it and sliced through my wrist, severing my flexor tendons that led to my hand, stopping me from holding my sword.

When the illusionary blade hit the ground, *Phantom* ended, and the sword faded from existence.

My own sword was shattered, and I couldn't stop Lonny from raising his blade to me. The cold metal bit into my neck, and Lonny, with tears streaming from his hate-filled eyes, took my life.

I sighed, shaking myself out of the past. I held Eris close, her heat helping to ground me in the present.

"It's a long story…I failed someone very close to me, and after they died, everything fell apart. The blame fell on my shoulders, and I was killed in a duel by someone who'd once been a friend."

Eris squeezed my hand. "I'm sorry."

"It's fine," I lied. "It was a long time ago."

*I'm still so wrapped up in the past that I can't see the future. Sophia's dead. No matter how much I wish I could take it back, I can't. Maybe it's time to move on.*

"What was your guild called?" Eris asked.

"The four of us were the Swords of Legend. When we founded the guild, we all took the names of holy swords. I was Durandal, the sword of Roland the Paladin. The others were Mika, Takamikazuchi, and Lonny, Ascalon, the sword of Saint George."

We rode a minute or so in silence. The only other sounds were the chirping of the birds and Lacuna's hooves treading through the dirt. I waited to see if she would drop this topic of conversation, but Eris wasn't stupid. She realized I'd omitted one member. "You left someone out. Who?"

222

I didn't want to answer, but not explaining would lead to more questions.

"Her sword was Mistilteinn, but we just called her Sophia," I whispered.

Eris noticed my change in mood, picking up on my hesitation. "You cared for her, didn't you?"

I nodded. "She was my best friend. I loved her…just not nearly enough."

Thankfully, Eris didn't pry any further. She was inside my head, and I knew she felt my misery. She let the topic drop, though she pulled my hands to her waist and held them tight.

We rode that way until I pulled myself out of my head. I had questions of my own, and they seemed like a good distraction.

"Tell me more about the Hive. You mentioned other races besides entomancers, what were they?"

"There were four other races. The mantearians and apocritans, which formed the bulk of our labor force, and the warrior clans, the arachne and scorpius."

"Are they still around?"

Eris shrugged her shoulders, and her head hung low. "I don't know. They were resilient and strong, all of them…but a thousand years is a long time. Anything is possible, I suppose."

"What about you?" I asked, changing the subject. "What was your childhood like?"

She turned around and smiled, but it was an empty smile, full of longing and regret. "It was…lonely. Even before my mother became queen, I was kept like a bird in a cage. I wasn't allowed to choose my friends. My father only let me associate with children of a respected dynasty."

"Your father treated you like property?"

"Yes. I was a valuable piece for him. Too valuable to let spoil, so even when I was allowed to associate with other children, it was all under the guise of finding a suitable candidate for bonding. Before my mother became queen, I was to be bonded with a nobleman's son. The family wasn't high in the upper echelon, but it would have secured my father's place in the upper nobility."

Eris spoke in a concise, mechanical fashion. Laying out the facts as if they had no meaning, but there was a deep pain in her eyes as she spoke. Her hands trembled as she finished speaking, breaking her façade.

Fury caught in my chest, raising a heat that put even Eris to shame. Hatred for a man who'd been dead a thousand years flowed out of me, and I gripped Lacuna's reins tight enough to hurt.

Eris caught my expression, and her face softened; a tear spilled down her cheek. She could feel emotions, and she smiled at me. "Thank you for getting angry for my sake, but it was the way of life for my kind. Our society existed on favors bought and sold. It was straightforward and brutally efficient."

"To treat a person like property to barter with is disgusting but treating your own daughter like a slave is unthinkable."

"You're probably right. He was my father, and I hated him, but I also loved him," she said, sighing.

I laughed. It was sudden, and I didn't mean to. Eris whirled around, looking a bit shocked.

"I'm sorry. I'm not laughing at you, I swear."

"I know, but you don't laugh much. It's nice to hear. What made you laugh?"

I slowed Lacuna to a trot. She was strong, but we'd been switching from walking to cantering off and on all day, and we'd covered a good bit of ground already. Lacuna deserved a rest. The grassy plains around us rose to thick forest, and the burning sunlight fell to spotted twilight.

"What you said reminded me of my own dad. He was a hard man to love, but he did his best to raise Micah and me. For being father and son, we were like night and day. We had nothing in common and fought over the littlest of things. But at the end of the day, I loved him, and even if we couldn't communicate, I knew he loved me too."

"I saw the love he had for you. He gave his life for you and your brother, your mother as well. Your family loved you immensely."

I hung my head. Letting the weight of what she'd said settle around me. *She's absolutely right. They loved me and trusted me to save Micah, and I couldn't even do that. I betrayed their trust.*

We rode for another few hours, talking briefly, but both of us had too many weighted memories rattling around our heads to continue a long conversation. As the light waned through the trees. We came through the small forest to an expanse of plains ten miles wide. A deep stretch of forest lay beyond them, but it was as good spot as any to stop and find a place to make camp.

I didn't want to camp out on the open plains, not with the deep forest so close. Bandits used the forests as natural hideouts, and I didn't want to give them an easy target. So, we pushed on until we came to a copse of thick trees amid the green fields. An oasis of dense trees to hide ourselves, and as we entered the thicket, I found a decent spot to make camp.

After hopping down from Lacuna, I set to work taking care of her and feeding her. Afterward she started to meander around. She never strayed far, so I wasn't worried about her, and instead set about making camp. Eris sat on the dirt as if it were the most natural thing in the world and helped dig a fire pit. Clearing the rocks and leaves away, and then while I set about erecting the tent, she went to forage some kindling. *Good thing I had the foresight to bring a two-person tent in my bag. Though hers is still available if she wants to sleep apart, but I doubt it.*

I'd just finished with the tents when Eris returned, carrying a decent sized bundle of sticks in her arms. She deposited them by the hole she'd dug and sat back on the ground. Closing her eyes and letting more magic drip from her fingers. I watched for a second before turning back to my duties. I piled the pit with sticks and got a nice fire going.

That done, I stretched out and got comfortable, taking off my armor and stowing it away, and I set to the task of preparing dinner. We hadn't eaten anything all day, and I was ravenous.

I set the small pot down and poured a generous amount of water in to boil. I'd decided to make a light stew, though we had only dried meat and potatoes to make up the bulk of it. I added a dried beef stock cube along with a liberal amount of powdered garlic and pepper and let it all simmer.

Once the food was done, we tucked in and made short work of the meager stew.

Finished, I leaned back with a satisfied sigh, staring up at the stars while the fire cracked and curled in front of me. Eris came over and sat beside me, leaning over and laying her head on my shoulder.

We stargazed for a time while our food settled, but before long, I was too tired to keep my eyes open, and we called it a night and headed for bed.

In the morning, we packed up camp and set off. I wanted to push past most of the wildlands if I could, but after two days hard riding, I gave in to defeat and started looking for places to camp.

An hour later, I'd picked out a pretty good spot, nestled in a clearing just off the main road, and was about to climb off Lacuna when Eris turned around and put her hand on my wrist.

"What's up?" I asked.

226

She didn't speak right away, tilting her head towards the blowing wind and sniffed. Her ears twitched, responding to a sound I couldn't hear. I was about to speak again when she held a finger to my lips and shushed me.

"There's a pack of dire wolves nearby. Five of them and they're out hunting. They haven't noticed us yet, but I don't like how close they are."

*Shit. One or two would be no problem, but five is a challenge.* Dire wolves ranked just under bane wolves in terms of size and savagery, and the average level for one was about fifty. I didn't want to put Eris or Lacuna at risk, but I also didn't like them hanging around our campsite.

"All right. I'm going to go deal with them. Eris, stay with Lacuna and get our camp ready," I said and dropped our packs from my inventory.

"Let me go with you!" Eris pleaded.

"Hell, no. I'm not putting you or Lacuna at risk. I can handle them, but not if I'm playing babysitter."

Eris shook her head and looked like she wanted to argue, but I didn't give her the chance.

"Please, for me?" I asked.

She huffed and pouted but acquiesced.

I took off at a sprint, not bothering to even attempt stealth. The dire wolves would sniff me out long before they caught sight of me, and nothing I could do would prevent that, so I didn't even try. Howls in the distance told me they'd spotted me, and I drew my sword.

A slight hiss alerted me to a bubbling purple liquid falling down the length of my sword. *Poison Blade.*

*Time to test my new skills.*

Two dire wolves jumped me before I'd even made it out of the woods, each of them the size of two full-grown men, with gorgeous, shimmering gray fur. Their paws were as big as my head with thick claws that would rend my flesh asunder if I let them get close.

Their sharp blue eyes regarded me with caution as their hackles raised. The pair lowered to the ground, growling as they circled me.

*Too slow!* I burst to the right as the closest took a step. Caught off guard by the suddenness of its quarries advance, it couldn't skirt away in time. My blade scored a gash from neck to chest. Its vicious jaws snapped in retaliation, but I danced out of reach.

First blood went to me, but it wasn't as deep as I'd wanted. And now it was two against one. I backed to the tree line, putting some obstacles in front of me as the beasts charged.

The trees divided them, and I used that to my advantage. Grabbing a low-hanging branch as the unbloodied wolf leapt at me, my feet sailed just over its snout as it jumped. I pushed off the branch as it sailed past. I gripped the hilt of my sword in both hands and drove it as deep as I could in between the wolf's shoulder blades.

Poison splashed across its fur and deep into its veins, but it was useless; my thrust had punctured its heart. It toppled to the ground as it bled out what little life it had.

Claws whistled next to me as the injured wolf attacked. It pounced on me, forcing me to relinquish my sword still stuck in the first's carcass. I landed hard on the ground, my head hitting dead flesh and crimson stained fur. Blood tickled my hair and the back of my neck.

I put my arm up to keep it at bay, but it wrapped its powerful jaws around my forearm and bit down. Aldrustian steel was top-notch steel, but it couldn't match the pounds per square inch force of its bite. The metal bent and crumpled, but it held off the initial attack and allowed me to reach overhead and pull my sword free from the carcass of the beast.

As the dire wolf reared back for a second bite, I rammed the tip of my blade through its mouth and out the back of its head.

It slumped against my sword, and several hundred pounds of dead weight came crashing towards me. I scrambled back and out of the way as it hit the ground.

*That was close.*

Standing up, I checked myself over for wounds and found myself whole and relatively unscathed. *The vambrace is still usable, but it took a knock.* The thick metal had jagged teeth marks sunk into it, but there weren't any tears or holes.

I quickly looted the fur, eyes, and claws from both creatures and left the meat to other scavengers. *Two down, three to go.*

Half an hour later, the remaining three were dead, and I was beyond exhausted. I sagged to the ground and fought back the urge to fall asleep where I sat. As I waited for my battle fatigue to lower back to zero, I cleaned the blood off my sword and armor. I'd only taken a few more light nicks and scrapes during the fight.

When my heart rate cooled, I stood and began the walk back to camp, cursing my bad luck. *Five dire wolves and not a single core between them. It's what I get for not putting any points in Luck. Even with the bonus, without any stats in loot drops, I'm going to lose out.*

I took off my armor and let the heat of the fire dry the pouring sweat from my chest and neck. Eris had set up her tent separate from mine and was already in bed. She peeked her head out when I returned.

"I'm glad you're all right," she said and went back in.

*Guess she's still pissed.* I ate some bread and drank some water but was too tired to eat more. When my belly wasn't gurgling anymore, I pulled up my interface to look at the notifications.

*Combat Results*
*Five Downed (Dire Wolves): 5000 Exp!*
*Total Exp Gain: 5000 Exp!*
*Level: 44*
*Exp: 4400/4400*
*Level up!*
*10 stat points available!*
*Level: 45*
*Exp: 1600/4500*

*Well, that's quite a bit of Exp for just some dire wolves. Last time I fought them, they only gave me four hundred apiece. Odd.*

I added five points to *Strength* and *Constitution,* bringing both to eighty, nighty-five with my boost from being close to Eris, but I didn't want to rely on an outside force to increase my power, not when it could be taken away. As I closed out my Interface, I pulled out my flask of whiskey and a glass along with a small frost stone. Dropping it into the glass, I filled it and waited for the liquid to chill before taking a sip.

It was perfect.

The stars were pretty, twinkling high above my head, and I wasn't quite ready to sleep, so I stargazed while I drank.

Eventually, I turned in and fell asleep, only to be woken by Eris when she crept into my tent sometime later.

With a mumbled, "I couldn't sleep," she lay down beside me and wrapped her arm around my chest and was asleep almost instantly.

# CHAPTER 14 - INN OF ILL REPUTE

After a few fitful hours of sleep, I awoke to the sounds of the forest. The same thing that'd kept me up, snapping me out of sleep with every crack of wood or howling beast, now unleashed a chorus of songbirds to chase the last vestiges of sleep from me.

I sat up and found that Eris wasn't asleep beside me. The wind rustled the flap to the tent, bringing the scent of roasting meat and carrying the sizzle of grease in a pan. I pulled on my linen trousers and a clean gray shirt and exited the tent.

Leaving, I found a very picturesque scene waiting. Eris, wearing one of my tunics, too large on her petite frame, was cooking a modest breakfast over the fire, humming to herself as she worked.

I sat by the opening to the tent and watched her for a time. She hadn't noticed me, and it was charming to see her be herself. I knew how she behaved around me wasn't an act, but she was too focused on me at times.

I wanted to see her when she was alone. She was unbearably adorable as she worked, bobbing back and forth, humming along to an unfamiliar song while she cooked. I couldn't help but smile at her natural energy. After a couple more minutes of cooking, it seemed the meal was done. She turned to call out to me.

"Sam, breakfast," she said, turning and seeing me watching her. Her mouth broke into a smile when she noticed. "Ah, good morning. How long have you been there?"

The familiar hurt rose at hearing my old name. "I wish you wouldn't call me that."

She smiled sadly and nodded. "I know, but it's your name. Duran is just a mask, a false name to hide behind. Its not who you are."

Eris wasn't wrong, but it was still hard to hear. "Duran is the name I chose. Sam is the name I left behind too many years ago."

She left the food alone and came to sit beside me. "I understand, and if it's truly what you want, I won't call you it again, but I think you should give Sampson Acre another chance, my bonded."

I didn't want to, too many things came with the name, but I couldn't find a defense beyond I just didn't want to hear it again, and that wasn't good enough.

"If it makes you happy, then I guess it doesn't matter. Call me whatever you like. Maybe it'll make up for the fact I hurt your feelings last night."

The smile fell from her face for a second. "About that, I'm sorry for overreacting. I know you were just protecting me."

"I was, still, I'm sorry for upsetting you," I said, kissing her gently. "What's for breakfast?" I asked when we pulled apart.

"A bit of bacon, with half a loaf of bread."

It smelled delicious, and after the inadequate food last night, I was ravenous.

"Let's eat."

"I'm beyond starving," Eris agreed and handed me a plate before grabbing her own.

My rumbling stomach was only too happy to indulge. We sat side by side as we ate, never going too long without brushing up against one another. We couldn't help but find the littlest of excuses to touch each other. I wiped a smidge of grease from the corner of Eris's mouth, and her response was to stick my whole finger in her mouth and lick it clean.

After we ate breakfast, Eris helped me pack up the camp and get Lacuna situated. As I was stowing our supplies in my inventory, I had a thought and pulled out a small pouch of fifty gold and tossed it to Eris.

"Here, catch."

She was busy petting Lacuna and didn't hear me, but I'd already thrown it, and it was sailing towards her head.

"Eris!"

Without turning, she plucked the pouch out of the air a second before it hit her. She stopped playing with Lacuna and stared at the bag. "What's this?"

"Money, in case there's anything you want to buy when we get into town."

"That's sweet of you," she said and tossed the money back at me. "But I don't need it."

"Why not?"

"I don't see the need for it. The Hive never used it. We bartered and sold favors for things we needed. I don't know what use I'd have for it."

"Very well," I said, stowing it back in my inventory. "But it's yours if you want it. Times have changed, and we use money for things we want. You'll need some when we get to the capital."

*I'll see if I can't spoil her a bit when we get there. She definitely needs her own clothes.*

*Speaking of spoiling.* I put the gold away and pulled out a brush for Lacuna and proceeded to spend the next hour or so brushing her coat while praising what a good girl she'd been.

Lacuna was a smart horse, and I believed she could understand at least the meaning behind my words, if not the words themselves. Her eyes were bright and happy as I brushed her down. Once her coat and mane had been brushed thoroughly. We climbed into the saddle and continued onward through the forest.

A few hours in the saddle and we started passing signs of rural civilization. The rough dirt road we'd been traveling on became smoother as we reached an area with a lot of foot traffic. A few other travelers, merchants, and adventurers kept cropping up—some on horseback like us and others in large wagons with armed escorts.

Wealthy merchants always hired guards to protect their cargo on trips like these. Bandits and highwaymen were commonplace on these backroads, and I had Eris cover her face with her hood. While I doubted anyone would recognize what she was, Eris still was exotic enough to stand out easily. I didn't want anyone looking too closely at her, so she kept her hood up whenever other people were nearby.

As the day passed by, there were even more signs of activity. Albeit not the kind I was hoping.

We passed several splintered wrecks of wagons that had been looted. Not an uncommon sight, but what was unusual were the bodies. Most of them were human, simple merchants who happened to be in the wrong place at the wrong time. But there were also a couple of demi-humans in the mix. *Rabbitmen? What are they doing so far from the Pale Everlands?*

They were unmistakably rabbitmen. Their long, gray ears gave them away. Both were male, with lean, functional muscle and bloodied cotton tunics. Multiple stab wounds and lacerations covered them from several different weapons along with four or five large holes that had punctured their chests. *Some type of curved blade did that, but what kind of weapon made those holes?*

Eris tugged on my shirt. Her eyes wide with concern. "We need to stop and help them; they might be alive."

I ignored her, and sped Lacuna to a full gallop, racing as fast as I could away from there. Eris looked shocked at me—and more than that, hurt—that I would so callously abandon people in need. I had to explain things quickly to get her to calm down.

"It was more than likely a trap."

She cocked her head to the side. "What do you mean?"

234

"That's a common trap used by bandits: rob a caravan, butcher the merchants, and lie in wait for a good Samaritan to pass by and try to help. Then rob and murder them. Rinse and repeat."

She was quiet for a few minutes, absorbing what I'd told her. "Did you ever do anything like that?" she asked, barely more than a whisper.

*Ah, guess I shouldn't be surprised she saw that part of my life.* I let out a breath through my nose and nodded. "Yeah, quite a few times, but it wasn't my clan's go-to," I said.

"Why?"

"It's not good business. The bandit empress didn't like us drawing so much attention to ourselves; butchering merchants was a good way to bring the wrath of the Merchants Guild down on top of us. So we usually stuck to less bloodthirsty methods, but we didn't let the opportunity slip by if it presented itself."

She wasn't happy with my answer, but I wasn't going to feel bad about my past. I'd done some truly awful things to innocents, but that was behind me. I'd put my bandit ways to bed a long time ago.

"I wasn't in a good place after Lonny…after I died, and I took my anger out on a lot of people who didn't deserve it. It doesn't make what I did right, but I can't go back and change what happened."

She nodded and gave my fingers a light squeeze. "I know. Even though I witnessed it for myself, I find it hard to reconcile that side of you. You're a killer, but almost always, you have a good reason for it. But those deaths were for nothing but selfish reasons, and that's not who you are."

She lapsed into silence after that, letting the past weigh heavy in my heart. *Damn it all to hell. Life isn't so black and white, Eris. People have just as much capacity for evil as for good, and I'm no exception. It's what I tried to tell you before. I'm not a good person. Not anymore.*

Whatever I wanted to say faded into nothingness as the silence stretched on. It seemed she'd said her piece and was content to leave it at that, but there was no absolution; she understood and accepted it, but she couldn't condone it.

As we rode, I kept a lookout for more traps or potential ambush sites, but thankfully we didn't encounter any as we made our way through the many forested trails. Night came quickly, and before I knew it, it was time to make camp.

We stopped at a graveled trail that led to a small encampment. There was no one else around, but it was a frequent enough stop for travelers that someone had taken the time to set up a semi-permanent campsite.

There weren't any tents, but there were plenty of places to set them up and a rough granite circle built for a fire pit. With holes drilled in for cast iron poles to hang a caldron or grate.

Once I pulled out the camp supplies, Eris set about getting the cookware situated while I handled the tent. Once the tent was set up, I went looking for firewood and grabbed an armload of twigs and small logs.

The fire pit was cleaned out and ready to go when I came back. I set the logs on the ground next to Eris. "There's a small stream past the woods a ways. I'm going to go and see if I can't catch a fish or two," I said.

She stood up, brushing the loose dirt from her knees. "I'll come with you."

"No, get the fire ready," I said, holding up a hand. "I won't be long."

Before she could argue, I set off, walking through the thicket of trees and brush toward the stream. *Last I remember, a good spot is just before the stream bends and widens.* I reached the spot after ten minutes of walking and looked around for what I needed. *C'mon, they always leave them by the tree line—ah, there we go.* I found the spears left behind by the last fisherman. It was a tradition to leave a spear for the next person to use since most travelers didn't carry one with them.

I took off my armor and boots, stowing them in my inventory, and waded into the water. It was chilling, and the running water was enough that it splashed up to my calves on occasion and riddled me with goosebumps. I endured and waited for a fish to swim by. Minute by minute, I acclimated to the water and waited for the perfect fish.

Fishing was the excuse I used, but I really just wanted to get away from Eris for a minute. She seemed to be fine with how the conversation ended, but I wanted some time to myself to work out my thoughts. We'd been glued together practically since we met, and only once she shoved my past in my face did I get apprehensive about being around her. *Godsdamn it, what am I supposed to do?*

*She knew about my past or at least part of it, knew who I was before she chose me, so why now is she getting hung up on what I did a decade ago?*

*Or is she?*

*She didn't berate me on my past at all, she just told me she knew, and she didn't approve. Maybe I'm the one that's hung up about it.*

Heat and shame crept up towards my face and settled in my cheeks. *She's the first person who's ever called me on it, and that's why it's getting under my skin.*

I wasn't sorry about my past. I knew it was wrong, and what I did was awful; I felt guilty at getting called out by her, but I wasn't sorry for the things I'd done.

*Maybe that's why she brought it up, to force me to confront that side of me?*

Lost in thought, I almost let a large catfish swim by. On reflex, I thrust with my spear, and two of the three points caught the fish. I pulled it up as it flopped around, spraying me in the face with even more cold water before dying.

I climbed out of the water and pulled the fish free. Setting the spear back where I found it, I headed back to camp, where Eris was sitting, staring at the fire. Her ears twitched as I approached, but she didn't turn around. Instead she drew her knees to her chest and pulled her arms around her.

Taking the fish to the fire, I ignored Eris for a moment, taking a roll of cloth from my inventory and proceeding to clean and fillet the catfish. Eris stole a few glances my way while I worked that I caught out of the corner of my eye. And she shuffled over on the ground to watch what I was doing.

She placed her hand on my bicep as she leaned over to watch my hands. "Do you mind if I watch?" she asked, her voice hesitant.

It was the first thing she'd said to me in a while, so I nodded. "Of course."

Eris kept her hand on my arm throughout the process, and I wasn't going to say anything that could cause her to remove it.

When I'd cleaned the fish, I salted it and sprinkled a bit of lemon pepper seasoning on it and cooked it until it was perfect. After dicing a few potatoes, I sautéed them using the leftover fat and oil from cooking the fish.

We ate, and when it was finished, we just sat there, letting the tension hang over us. When it reached the point where I'd have relished letting her insects crawl over me again rather than sit in the abhorrent silence for another single second, she finally spoke up.

"Are you angry with me?" she asked, her voice faltering.

"No, of course not. I'm just not sure what to say, what I *can* say, that'll fix the silence between us."

Eris smiled, a tilt of her lips threatening a grin before she crawled over to me. "Then we don't have to say anything if we don't want to."

She kissed me softly, a single kiss that held our lips together as she rested her forehead against mine. It washed the tension from my shoulders instantly, and I reveled in her touch. She took away my apprehension and replaced it with understanding. She leaned back, her hand on my cheek as she gazed at me with her graphite eyes.

"I knew the kind of man you were from the moment we met. I've seen for myself some of the lives you've taken without remorse, and I accepted you anyway. I accepted that part of you, because I think I can see you better than you can see yourself. And I want to know the man you've hidden away beneath your rage and self-loathing. Even if that man can be rude at times, I know you don't mean it." Eris stood up, kissed me on the forehead and took my hand, pulling me up with ease despite my reluctance. "Now, let's get to bed. We have a long day ahead of us tomorrow."

We set out early the next morning, just before the sun rose over the horizon. Eris shook me awake, and we groggily packed up and got on the road. By my guess, we were only a few more days out from the East Kingdom.

A few hours later, we came to the end of the wilderness. As we broke through the trees, we stumbled across our first real signs of civilization in a few days.

There was a small town that had cropped up since the last time I'd passed this way. It was nothing more than several large grain farms and a cattle ranch, along with a few shops and a tavern, but after the endless trees and plains over the last few days, to my eyes, it was a regular metropolis.

Forgoing anything else, I made a beeline to the tavern, which also doubled as an inn, but I was more concerned with the variety of ale they served than the beds. Long days in the saddle had worked up a thirst, and the whiskey I'd brought hadn't lasted half as long as I thought it would.

As we rode closer to the tavern, I made out the name on the hanging sign jutting out next to the door.

The Inn of Ill Repute. *A strange name, but I don't get any bad omens.*

It was a charming two-story building made of sturdy, freshly sawn wooden logs, with darkened windows that refused to let in light and a thick, slate stone roof. A glance behind the bar told me where the wood had come from. Dozens of tree stumps lay dotted next to the forest. The inn had a cozy, homey atmosphere, and the scents of the smoke rising from the cobblestone chimney hinted at delicious food.

I was salivating at the thought of a proper meal. Not that I hadn't enjoyed the meal last night, but fish had never been my favorite. I was hoping they had fresh boar. *I would kill for a boar steak with freshly steamed potatoes.*

We dismounted Lacuna and I stabled her in the small, clean building next to the inn. As I opened the large oak door, darkness assaulted me along with the smell of meat that combined with the sweet, slightly stale scent of alcohol in the air. I kept Eris close to me as we walked in. She had her hood up, and her face pressed into my ribs.

The inside of the inn was dark, though torches lined the walls, and a roaring fireplace provided heat to combat the chill from the stone flooring and ample lighting. Several patrons were seated at the various wooden tables, eating and drinking their fill. They seemed to be a mixture of farmhands and laborers. The East Kingdom was renowned for its farming and grain harvesting, so it made sense why the patrons were mostly farmers.

What didn't make sense were the splattering of adventurers around. Several hardy men and women clad in armor of various types and weapons strapped to their belts sat around drinking their fill and talking in hushed whispers.

Ignoring the curious glances that came our way, we walked over to the bar, a huge slab of oak freshly stained that had yet to be worn down and soaked through by thousands of spilled drinks. There was a man stationed behind the bar who was, of course, cleaning a mug with a washrag when we approached.

He was a tall man with broad shoulders, heavyset with muscle, but with a nice layer of fat over them. The hem of his dark tunic and leather apron stopped mid-bicep and showcased his arms, which were corded with muscle and bore numerous scars that descended to his hands and fingers.

His hair was a rich chocolate, longer than mine. It fell well past his shoulders. A magnificent beard covered the lower half of his face, and he wore an eyepatch over his left eye. His right was one of startling green; it shone like a gem when the light from the fire reflected in his iris. He bore numerous laugh lines around his eyes and wore a constant smirk across his lips.

I liked the man immediately, and I'd have bet my entire purse of gold that he was a former adventurer or soldier.

He smiled widely as we approached, showing off white teeth, giving me the standard once over that all adventurers give one another, glancing over my gear and weapons, trying to discern my intentions. I passed his test, it seemed, as he offered me his hand.

His hand engulfed mine, and he pumped his arm vigorously. His smile was as infectious as Eris's, and I couldn't help but grin back at the giant bear.

"Howdy, there. Good to meetcha!" he said, "Name's Rufio, but everyone calls me Ruff."

"Hi, there. I'm Duran."

Ruff glanced down at Eris, who was still sticking close to me. He smiled at the sight of Eris peeking out of her hood, though her eyes were still covered. "And who is this little lady?"

"I'm Eris. It's nice to meet you," she said. Her voice, while soft, was strong and clear.

*She's not afraid of humans. She's hiding because I asked her to. Can't help it, though. Don't want to attract attention.* Ruff chuckled deeply, amused by her antics and melodious voice.

"What can I do for you two lovebirds?" he asked.

I withdrew one of the smaller pouches of gold and slid two gold coins across the bar. "A room for the night, preferably one with a bath if you have it, and a meal."

He glanced at the two gold coins. It was far more money than a room, and a meal should ever cost. At most, it should be a fistful of copper, but being a former adventurer himself, Ruff knew what the extra money was for, and he swept the two coins into his pocket with a nod. He pulled out a small key cast in bronze and handed it to me.

"Upstairs, first door on the left. Our cook is just about to start on dinner if you don't mind waiting, or we have some bread and cheese to tide you over," Ruff said.

I shook my head. "Waiting is perfectly fine with us."

I looked down at Eris. I tapped her on the head to get her attention. Her compound eyes gazed up at me. "Why don't you run upstairs and get a bath? The food should be ready once you're finished."

"You don't want to join me?"

I chuckled and shook my head. "As appealing as that sounds, I'll stick down here and keep an eye on things."

Eris nodded her head and took the key from me, making sure to keep her head covered, and walked up the creaking wooden steps to the second floor. I watched her open the door and go inside, then turned to find a good table. The best one was in the center of the room next to the fire. I'd have preferred my back to a wall, *but beggars can't be choosy. Rather keep an eye on her. I can take care of myself.*

I caught Ruff's attention and mimed taking a drink. Ruff nodded his head and held his arms to the side, raising and lowering them, respectively, like balancing a scale, asking how strong I wanted my drink. I raised my arm, telling him to make it strong. He nodded and grinned wide. Most adventurers liked our drinks strong.

He went over to a large cask and poured a frothy mug of ale with a strong head to it. Ice formed on the mug as he poured. *Ice magic? Using frost stones to keep the casks cold, but they don't come cheap.* He brought over the cup and set it down with a heavy hand. Some of the ale sloshed over the side and ran down the glass like the world's tastiest volcano.

"Keep em' coming, Ruff."

He barked a laugh in acknowledgment and went back to the bar and tending to his other patrons. I raised the mug to my lips and took a generous swig. The ale was sweet and delicious, with a strong underbite of the booze. It was wonderful.

I drained the rest of the glass in an instant. Ruff had expected this and was already on his way with another mug. *An ideal bartender.*

"Go easier on the next few. They have a stronger bite than you'd think," Ruff said.

I nodded to him, though I didn't plan on heeding his advice; I had a pretty strong tolerance. I'd frequented enough of these establishments over the years that my *Drinking Skill* was nearly maxed. *Couple more levels, and I'll unlock the final ability—no more hangovers for me.*

I was thankful that whatever force sent me back to level one had spared my skills. They hadn't changed. The hundreds of little skills like *Woodworking* or *Cooking* I'd picked up over the years were irreplaceable, and it would have been a pain to level them up again.

When I drained the second glass, Ruff gave me a warning look as he brought the next round. I slowed my consumption by a little, or I'd be shirtless dancing on the table in no time.

The minutes went by quickly, the drone of the other patrons mixed with the subtle music that a lone lute player was producing, which made me very sleepy. I hadn't had the best night's sleep of my life last night, and the table looked very inviting.

About the time that my tiredness was about to out-weigh my hunger, the door of our room opened and out walked Eris. She'd discarded most of her traveling clothes and had opted for one of my long-sleeved tunics again— my favorite burgundy one. Like with most of my shirts, it came well past her thighs and looked really good on her. She'd also kept her thin cloak and had it wrapped around her shoulders and head.

She made her way down the stairs, garnering many more looks than when she had gone up them the first time.

The creaking stairs drew everyone's attention first; Eris's legs are what kept them. The men—and a few women—eyed her hungrily as she bounced down the stairs. Oblivious to the looks the other patrons were giving her, Eris smiled at me and came over to the table. She pulled out one of the wooden chairs next to me, sitting in the chair and laying her head on my shoulder. The scent of an unfamiliar soap drifted from her damp hair. *Strawberry and coconut.*

Just as she got settled, our dinner was ready. The cook brought out our meals from a room that I could only assume to be the kitchen. He was a thin man with dark hair and gray eyes. He set our food down with a comment to enjoy and left, back to his domain.

Our food was a stew. It was venison and had a strong aroma as the steam wafted past me, though what had me salivating were the roasted potatoes and carrots. After a few days of trail rations and game, a proper meal was tantalizing.

We ate our fill and then some. Eris seemed to have a fondness for venison, as she kept eying the chunks of meat in my bowl and grinned when I spooned some into hers. When our meals were finished, Ruff came by and cleared our table. He set down another mug of ale and walked away, whistling a jaunty tune. I picked up the ale and was about to take a sip when Eris asked what it was.

"It's ale."

"You seem to like it. Can I try it?" she asked.

"I dunno, I might have to card you; you don't look old enough," I joked, knowing she wouldn't get it, but snickering anyway.

"Sam," she pouted. "I don't understand anything you just said, but technically I'm over a thousand years old. I think I can handle a drink."

"Fair enough. I was just teasing you." I handed her the mug, and she took a huge gulp of it as I had. I was about to warn her about the strength and bitterness of the booze, but she drained the glass instantly. Wiping her mouth with the back of her sleeve.

I pulled out another gold coin and motioned Ruff over. As the godsend that he was, he had witnessed Eris down the ale and brought two fresh mugs. I slid him the extra gold. He took it, although with some protest as the ale we drank wasn't worth a whole gold coin.

"Consider it a tip. Besides, the rate we're going, we are likely to drink your entire stock."

"Oh, I wouldn't worry about that. I am well prepared. I couldn't show my face around here if I ever ran out of booze. My customers would have my head," Ruff said as he walked away.

I laughed a little too loudly. The ale had already affected my mood, making me boisterous and cheerful. I was an overly affectionate drunk, and I was sure Eris would take full advantage of my inebriation. Though, from the looks of Eris, the alcohol was having an even stronger impact on her. Her face was beet red, and she stared at me hazily. Hiccupping slightly, she burst into a fit of giggles.

Eris leaned heavily into me and tried to pull me into a kiss. I didn't put up much fight. It was sloppy, and her mouth tasted of ale, which I didn't mind so much. But when she tried to get handsy, I put a stop to it. *Not in public.* The devious glint in her eyes spoke to me, promising so many things. Eris leaned over and whispered into my ear.

"Why don't we head upstairs and get you cleaned up?"

My libido perked up at her lascivious whispering, but I still wasn't sure about taking her up on her offer just yet. However, we did need to get some sleep, and I was about to take both of us to bed for the evening when the door to the inn slammed open.

# Chapter 15 - The Hand That Holds Time In Its Palm

It was sudden enough that it sent my flight or fight reflexes screaming. My buzz faded away in seconds as four people walked in. They swaggered through the door like they owned the place, cocky and utterly full of themselves.

I calmed myself and went back to my drink, watching them out of the corner of my eye. They were adventurers—that much was clear, but I couldn't tell anything beyond that. The one who walked in first seemed to be the leader of the merry band.

He was handsome, though there was a falseness about it, as if he were wearing a mask. He had short auburn hair, styled precisely, and muted brown eyes. His features were elegant but not feminine. Long, yet symmetrical.

*He probably has women swooning over him all the time.* He sported medium plate mail polished to a shine and an ostentatious silver scimitar encrusted with gemstones.

The three members that followed seemed much tamer in comparison. All tall and with good looks, but not nearly as so over the top as their leaders. All male and each wearing a slightly different style of armor, but each bore the same crest—a guild logo of some sort—a hand gripping a barbed hourglass.

*The hand that holds time in its palm.*

The door slammed shut hard enough to rattle the windows, and I was about to finish my drink and take the now clearly drunk Eris upstairs when the leader opened his big mouth.

"Hey, old man. How about a round for me and the boys?" he called to Ruff as they strutted over to the only other empty table available, the one coincidentally next to ours.

I barked out a laugh. It slipped out before I could stop it. Leader and his goons turned to glare at me. Their noses upturned like they thought they were better than me.

"Something I said funny to you, friend?" Leader asked, stressing the word, making it clear that he didn't actually consider us friends. That broke my heart.

I turned to face him, Eris was now hugging me, whispering incoherently. *Giving her that much alcohol probably wasn't my best idea.*

"Calling Ruff old is like the pot calling the kettle black, don't you think? We're all old men these days, friend, even if we don't look it," I told him as I drained the last of my ale.

He chuckled at that, and his glare softened, even if it didn't fade completely. "Yeah. Suppose you're right about that," he said. "Maybe that was a little rude of me."

He glanced over his shoulder to call out to Ruff.

"Hey, Ruff, let me buy this man here a drink. In fact, next round for everyone is on me!"

A cheer rang out across the tavern. Everyone then tuned out the antics of our new arrivals—buying a round usually also bought you a considerable amount of goodwill with the patrons.

The leader brought out a silver and flicked it to Ruff, who caught it deftly while balancing a tray of ale in one hand. He set the party's drinks down first, then walked over and handed me mine.

I thanked him and then turned to the group. "Thanks for the drink, friend."

Leader shook his head and laughed. "Enough of that. Name's Darren."

I couldn't help but laugh. "That'll be easy to remember then. My name's Duran."

Darren laughed along with me. "That *will* be easy to remember," he said as he unequipped his armor for equally flashy evening wear that didn't belong in a bar.

He motioned to his group. "That's Mikhail, Wolf, and Slip," he said, pointing at his group.

Mikhail was shorter than Darren by a hair. Wearing heavy studded leather armor, he had light brown hair shaved close to his scalp, deep-set eyes, and a broad chin. He wielded a halberd, which was smart outdoors but a poor indoor weapon.

Wolf was an enigma to me. Long, raven-black hair tied into a ponytail. He had narrow eyes and gaunt features, like a starving animal, along with a calm grace about himself. Rather thin but lithe, and he bore no weapons which put me on edge since it made him either a mage or a monk. His leather armor spoke to the monk class, but he didn't have a caestus or gauntlets. *I don't like that I can't classify him. That annoys the hell out of me.*

The final member of the party was the rogue of the bunch. Light blonde hair and even lighter blue eyes. A black cloth mask covered half his face, and he bore an array of knives scattered throughout his black leather armor and had a bow strapped to his back. *A split class archer/rogue. A dangerous combination, but a tricky one to pull off.*

I was intrigued by his name. "Why do they call you Slip?" I asked.

"Because I can slip in and out before anyone knows I'm there," Slip said boisterously.

The group roared with laughter as if that was the first time they had ever heard the joke. I joined in with a chuckle. *It was kind of funny.*

Eris jolted up and took hold of my mug, trying to get another sip of ale. Her flushed faces and jerky movements told me she was teetering on the edge, and I took the glass from her. She frowned at me when I cut her off. "I think you've had enough for now," I told her with a smile.

She stopped frowning at me, still wearing a pout, but her eyes told me she wasn't upset. Our little encounter did not go unnoticed by Darren, who perked up when he realized Eris was sitting next to me. Darren's eyes traveled down Eris's frame to stare longingly at her pale thighs and legs.

"And who might this delicious-looking thing be?" Darren asked with lust in his mouth.

Eris chose that moment to drunkenly shoot up from her seat and loudly proclaim to Darren's party. "Hi, I'm Eris!"

When Eris stood up so suddenly, her hood fell from her head, revealing her compounded eyes and long ears.

Darren sucked in a breath at the sight of her, not from fear. No, his gasp came from a much darker place. The sound of their leader inhaling caught the rest of the group's attention. They all looked up to see Eris, bold as you can be, without a care in the world.

"She—she's a demi-human," Darren said.

I quickly grabbed Eris and pulled her to her seat, amid a torrent of slurred protests, pulling her hood back over her, and went back to facing Darren.

"Yes, she is. Is that a problem?" I asked with steel in my voice.

Darren quickly shook his head. His eyes held nearly unrestrained excitement in them. "No...no, not at all. Not at all."

Darren smiled wide at me, a wicked, devious thing, which sent shivers to crawl over my skin like ants.

He leaned over to whisper to me. "How much?"

I stared him down. "Excuse me?"

250

"Do you know how rare demi-humans are?" Darren asked, "I've seen plenty over the years, but never one like her."

Darren was practically leaning over me at this point.

"I'll give you ten thousand gold for her right now."

He was right about one thing. Demi-humans were rare, and nobles paid handsomely for them. Actual fortunes for rabbitmen and wolfmen, not to mention the fae. His offer was enough to set a commoner up for life. It was nothing to me. *No amount of money would be enough to hand her over.*

I scoffed at him. "So, you're slavers?"

If he was willing to shell out that much gold for her, I bet he had a client who paid well for demis like Eris. *No way he would drop that much coin just for a lay.* Though Eris was unique, I could see why he was so desperate.

It was Darren's turn to scoff. "I wouldn't call us slavers; we're simply merchants who specialize in select merchandise," he equivocated.

"So...slavers."

He slammed his fist on the table, knocking over one of the empty glasses of ale and sloshing the nearly full one. I quickly glanced around the room. The rest of the patrons were painfully oblivious to the exchange between Darren and me. Even Ruff was busy pretending to wash a glass, though I saw him glance our way.

"Look, my employer pays handsomely for rare creatures and artifacts. I know he would pay whatever you wanted for her. So why don't we be gentlemen about this and work out a deal."

"No. She's not for sale. Not now, not ever, and you've ruined what was a pleasant evening, so we're leaving."

I stood up, just as Darren lunged forward and grabbed the collar of my shirt, anger clear across his face. Here was a man not used to being denied.

"I refuse to walk away from this, not when we could make enough money to live like kings in the Noble District. So, hand her over before I lose my temper."

"Bad move."

Before he could blink, I took hold of his arm that was currently gripping my shirt, stopping him from going anywhere. I pulled him off balance, grabbed the empty mug of ale from the table, and smashed it into his face.

Shards of glass and blood flew into the air, raining down to fill the cracks in the flagstone floor. The glass shredded half of Darren's face, but I was just getting started. The magic inside me oozed out of my heart to stain my fury while my vision filled with swirling shadows.

Letting go of Darren's arm, I kneed him in the groin hard enough that he doubled over. Taking his bloodstained face in my hands, I slammed it onto the corner of the heavy wooden table, cracking the wood and sending the table to the ground.

Darren slid off the table onto the floor, his face leaving a trail of blood on the wood. He hit the stone with a soft thud and groaned.

His three cohorts decided to stand up from their table and join in the fight. Their eyes glared daggers at me, staring in disbelief that I had taken out their boss so quickly. They moved as one to intercept me.

*Perfect.*

As soon as they moved from their chairs, I kicked the table at them hard enough that the thick wood splintered in two. The shattered pieces hit them like a freight train, taking their legs out from under them.

With them out of the fight for a second, I turned my attention back to Darren, who was still lying in a slowly growing pool of his own blood. The wounds I'd dealt were painful and very messy, but he wasn't out of commission yet.

I reached down, taking hold of his right arm, his sword arm, and twisted. His bones cracked and shattered under my fingers, and I savored the sound his bones made as I broke them into little pieces. Broken and jagged edges tore through his thin skin to reveal bone and yellowed marrow. Blood streamed down his arm to join the pool on the floor.

*Good thing he's unconscious. Otherwise, he'd be screaming bloody murder right now.*

With Darren out of the fight, and the threat of a sword in the back removed. I focused on the others. Who were just now painfully picking themselves off the floor. They stared in horror at what I'd done. Darren's hand twisted at an impossible angle and spurting blood like a fountain.

"You monster!" Mikhail shouted and rushed me.

*"Fool."*

In the close confines of the bar, the three of them could have surrounded me easily. Mikhail had obviously never been in a bar fight before as he unstrapped his halberd from his back. In such confined space, his weapon would be a hindrance at best and fatal at worst.

Mikhail crouched into his fighting stance, which because of the length of his weapon, cut Wolf and Slip off from reaching me. I didn't want to fight the halberd emptyhanded, and my sword was in my inventory, so I cast my eyes around the room and quickly settled on my prize.

Stepping back, my heel connected with the lip of the fireplace and ignoring the heat, I grabbed the iron poker Ruff had left in the center of the fire.

It seared into my palm, but I bit down on the pain and yanked it free amid a shower of smoke and embers. The sharp tip glowed cherry red, and waves of heat rose off it as I shifted into a fencing stance. *Damn, I'm awful with a rapier, and the poker is a poor facsimile, but it'll have to do.*

Though, since the poker wasn't considered a martial weapon, it wouldn't affect my battle fatigue. And since I was unarmed facing an armed opponent, I was at a significant advantage.

Mikhail opened with a straight thrust, aimed at my heart. I sidestepped and parried with the poker, charring a line down the length of his wooden shaft. A quick lunge forward, and I stabbed the searing tip of the poker into Mikhail's right hand.

The acrid tinge of sizzling flesh filled my nose, and I fought down the urge to gag. Mikhail howled in pain and let go of his weapon on reflex. I took hold of it as soon as he released it and jabbed the butt of the halberd into his gut, taking the wind out of him.

He doubled over in pain and I tossed the halberd aside. It slid across the floor to rest under the table of a couple of farmers too busy watching the show to notice.

Disarmed and in pain, Mikhail stood up, only to have a red-hot poker whip across his face. He stumbled back and fell on his ass, at which point Slip tried to intervene, but I saw him go for his dagger and changed my grip on the poker and threw it like a spear. My aim was off, and instead of hitting his hand, I nailed him in the thigh.

It cut through his flesh with ease and stuck in the bone. He screamed in pain as the burning metal cauterized the wound with the poker still entrenched inside him. Slip dropped to the floor and clutched at his leg while trying to go for a health potion.

"Wait your fucking turn," I growled.

Mikhail wasn't looking so hot. I'd seared a deep groove across his face with the poker and taken out one of his eyes in the process. One of his hands clutched at his ruined face while the other came up and swung at me. I slipped his punch and caught him on the chin with an uppercut, slamming him back to crash into a table.

The couple who were eating dinner at the time, shrieked and stood up quickly before running away, shouting their heads off.

Mikhail cursed in Old Russian as he stood up, the translator in my interface flashing what he said across my vision. *Well, fuck you, too.*

He was bloody and enraged and snarled as he charged me, disregarding any kind of form or technique. His wild swings went wide of me as I ducked and stepped back before snapping a low side kick to his knee, dislocating it as he put most of his weight on it attempting to grab me. With an ear-splitting shriek of pain, he collapsed to the stone, and I curb stomped his face, shattering through the cartilage in his nose and sending blood spilling out to stain his lips and slither down his chin.

He was broken and bleeding, but he was still conscious, and he tried to shakily stand back up. At this point, even I knew he'd had enough, but my anger was too strong, and I wanted to keep hurting him.

*"More, hurt him more!"*

Before he could stand, I kicked his head, catching him just below his cheek and dislocating his jaw with a twisted pop. Mikhail somehow stumbled to his feet and swung wide. I caught his hook, dazed him with a jab, and flung him over my shoulder.

Mikhail hit the ground headfirst, smashing the base of his skull on the stone, cracking loudly as he landed, blood smeared the floor from a deep gash on the base of his head.

My anger still wasn't satiated, and I wanted to kill him. I raised my foot to shatter his skull.

"Stop!" a frantic voice shouted.

I turned to see Wolf, arms raised in a non-threatening manner, trying to keep me from killing his dim-witted friend.

"Why should I?" I growled at him, my vision thick and dark with shadows. I wanted to keep hurting. I wanted to kill them all for what they were planning on doing to my queen.

Wolf gestured around the room, at the broken and bleeding bodies of Darren and Mikhail. Slip had managed to pull the poker from his leg and downed half a health potion before climbing to his feet. Both walked toward me, and both had their hands raised. They knew who the strongest one here was.

"You don't need to continue this. You've won, there is no need to hurt them any further."

I pointed at them and roared, "You fuckers are the ones who started this."

Wolf shook his head as he motioned to the ragged body of Darren.

"No, he is the one that started this foolishness, and Mikhail got dragged into it trying to defend Darren. They both paid the price for their actions tonight. Let it end here."

I didn't want it to end. I wanted to keep fighting. To keep causing pain and suffering to those who had sought to subjugate and harm Eris. They would suffer agonizing deaths.

"No, I'll end this here and now!"

Both moved into their combat stances, and I was a second away from charging them when Eris grabbed my arm. Her eyes were hazy and unfocused, but there were tears in them, and that stopped me cold.

"Stop this, Duran. Please, let them go."

"They're our enemies, and they need to die," I said through gritted teeth.

"For me, please," she begged, tugging on my arm.

256

I didn't want to listen, but I wasn't acting in my right mind. My anger was so intense and overwhelming that it hurt, and I wanted to hurt in return. One look at Eris, and it was plain that she could tell how I was feeling and that she was trying to save me from myself. Her concern for me bled through my darkness, if only a little, but it was enough.

Now that I wasn't in combat anymore, the twisted magic's hold lessened enough to allow Eris's words to reach me, to let me regain a small piece of myself.

"Fine. Take them, and never let me see your faces again."

Wolf nodded his head, and he and Slip went and retrieved their unconscious and dripping comrades off the blood-soaked floor. Slip poured the rest of the health potion down Mikhail's gullet and dragged the men out of the inn and into the night, shutting the door with a heavy thud.

I sat back into my chair and tried to let the anger fade completely. *I need a drink.*

"Hey Ruff, can I get another ale?"

***

Eris passed out in the chair after the fight. *She was right to stop me, but she's also too soft. That's going to bite us in the ass, I just know it.*

If Darren and his cronies weren't already a threat before the fight, they were now. Letting them go was a foolish move. But Eris couldn't handle my brutality, and I wasn't going to kill them in front of her while she wept and begged me not to.

As I drained the last of my ale and waited on Ruff to bring another, I glanced at the notifications tab in my interface to see that I had several of them waiting for me.

*Combat Results*

*Three Downed (Human): 4500 Exp*

*Mercy Penalty: -1500 Exp*

*Total Exp Gain: 3000*

*Level: 45*

*Exp: 4500/4500*

*Level Up!*

*10 Stat Points Available!*

*Level: 46*

*Exp: 100/4600*

The notifications stunned me. I'd never seen so much Exp awarded for a simple bar fight before, let alone one that hadn't even ended in death. *Never seen the system grant Exp without killing something before…never seen a mercy penalty either, so this is all new territory.*

The mercy penalty scared me. It felt like something was pushing me to be more violent and ruthless—that and the strange magic that was ever-present in my heart. *I'm being molded for something. Whatever took over Eris and made me this way has plans for me, but what can I do about it?*

Even with the mercy penalty, I'd still earned a considerable chunk of experience. *Joke's on them. That was still far more Exp than I should have earned for such a fight.* I was okay with the system taking a little off the top. I came out ahead, regardless.

Ruff was busy dealing with another patron at the bar, so I walked over and waited till the farmer left with a tray of drinks. Ruff nodded at me as I approached.

"What can I do for you, Duran?"

258

I reached into my coin purse and pulled out another two gold coins. I slid them across the bar—much to Ruff's confusion. His eyes asked why I was giving him more money.

"For the damages and another ale," I said with a grin.

He shook his head and pushed the coins back towards me. "No need. You've already paid your insurance."

"Yeah, but I didn't think I would actually get into a fight. Consider the money a stupidity tax on my part."

Ruff laughed deeply at that, but still tried to give the money back.

"You can either keep the money, or it's staying on your bar, but I'm not taking it back."

"Stubborn, aren't ya?" Ruff asked.

"To a fault."

He took the money and poured me another ale. I drained it before moving and went to grab Eris and head off to our room. I gently picked her up from the chair she was snoring in. She woke up for a moment when I lifted her out of the chair, even in her drunken state, she smiled at me and kissed my neck as I held her in my arms, my brutality moments before already forgotten in her eyes.

I made sure to hold her tightly as I climbed the wooden stairs, but fumbled trying to get the key in the lock only to find out that Eris had never locked the door after she had taken a bath.

Pushing the door closed behind me, I found the room quaint and exceptionally clean. The dark wooden walls were fresh with wood stain, and the bed was new; the gray sheets were clean. The room felt fake; that's how new it was. I hadn't asked, but I doubted the inn was more than a month old.

The window was larger than average, and the panes of glass seemed cheap and easy to replace. I unlatched the casement window and pushed it open, letting the soft breeze in almost immediately. I sat there staring out of the window for a few minutes, watching the sleeping town. It was just after eight at night, but most farmers were up at the crack of dawn. I ducked my head to go back inside when I noticed a large pile of hay underneath the window.

Chuckling, I went back in. Ruff it seemed, had prepared for all eventualities, and it was comforting to have an easy escape route in case I needed it.

I left Eris snoring softly on the bed and went to take a bath. After I was squeaky clean, I patted myself dry with one of the fluffiest towels I'd ever seen and tied my hair up. Throwing on a clean shirt, I crawled into bed next to Eris, who wasn't as asleep as I'd thought because she immediately wrapped herself around my body and pressed her lips to mine.

She kissed me hungrily and with abandon but was still completely drunk; her eyes were utterly unfocused as she clumsily fumbled to undress. She managed to get her burgundy tunic stuck halfway over her face, baring her naked body to me in the process.

The sight of her struggling to remove her clothes was probably one of the cutest things I'd ever seen in my life, and I couldn't help but burst out laughing. Eris wailed in frustration, and at that point, I couldn't let her continue her losing battle against her greatest enemy: clothing.

I placed my arm on her bare waist to calm her, and then I helped get her shirt the rest of the way over her head. When Eris could see again, she gave me a look of such adoration that it made my heart hurt.

Completely nude, she flung her arms around me in delight. At this point, my libido was gone, and our first time wasn't going to be while she was drunk out of her mind. I just wrapped my arms around her and held her tight as

260

she tried to get frisky with me, but I didn't let go of her enough to do much damage.

After a few frustrating attempts, she got the hint and settled into my arms, cuddling into me and kissing my cheek.

"I love you, Sam," she said as she drifted to sleep.

My throat tightened as I tried to speak but couldn't. Couldn't say the words on the tip of my tongue.

"…me too."

I awoke when the early morning light hit my face, and I blinked my watery eyes open, pushing myself out of reach of the sun's unrelenting gaze before settling into the sublime comfort of the darkness. I leaned my head back onto the pillow and found Eris beside me, sleeping deeply.

She was cute while she slept, and I had no intention of waking her yet, so I lay there, enjoying the comforting weight of her beside me. This was the first time I'd woken up before her, and it was nice to relax in bed for a few moments. I checked the time. It was just after seven in the morning. We had the time to enjoy this for a few minutes. We still had a little ways to go before we reached the East Kingdom, but we were close.

I lay in bed, enjoying the simplicity of the act for about half an hour before necessity forced me to get up. I went into the bathroom and relieved my screaming bladder, only to have my stomach demand attention. It growled as I washed my hands.

I called out to Eris, as I walked back into the bedroom. "Wake up, sleepy."

Her ears twitched at my voice, but the only response I received was a loud groan. As she forced her eyes open, they were bloodshot, which on a normal person would be fine after a night spent drinking, but with her obsidian eyes, it was a strange sight—small tendrils of green shot through her compound eyes.

She looked at me, then blinked her eyes several times, fighting off the remnants of sleep.

"Can I go back to bed?" she asked.

Her stomach rumbled at the same time as mine did. I smiled cheekily at her.

"'Fraid not. C'mon, love. Let's get breakfast."

Eris groaned once more and flung the thin sheet off her body and hopped out of bed. She lumbered over to give me a quick good morning kiss as she went to the bathroom to splash water on her face and fix her bedhead, which was nearly impossible with her thick, unruly hair. As she walked out of the bathroom, I handed her a fresh shirt, a light sapphire color with long sleeves. *At this rate, she's going to leave me shirtless.*

"Put this on, you exhibitionist. Don't want to give the other patrons a show, do we?"

"It doesn't bother me that much, besides, your human clothing is suffocating. I'd rather feel the breeze on my bare skin," she said, but still wore the shirt. I didn't even bother trying for underwear or pants. *That's a fight I'm not going to win.*

She walked in front of me down to the bar. Even at this ungodly hour of the morning, there were still patrons drinking. I thought about grabbing an ale myself, but food first. The scent of freshly baking bread came from the kitchen and whetted my appetite.

Ruff was still handling the bar, though I noticed he'd changed out of the shirt he'd been wearing last night. He now had a crisp, white long-sleeved one that was sure to be stained a hundred times by the time the day was over.

"Morning," he called out sharply as we waded our way down the stairs.

We both responded, though, with far less enthusiasm. Ruff had cleaned up the wreckage from the night before, and a new table sat in the place the old one had been. You would almost think a fight hadn't occurred last night, except for a small divot in the stone floor from where the table had cracked it.

We sat down at the table, and Eris pretty much slumped over to use the table as a pillow. *Entomancer hangovers are as bad as humans', it seems.*

Ruff was a gift from the drunken gods as he brought two plates of food, heaped with bacon and eggs, with a side of the fresh bread I smelled. He also sat down an ale for me and a strange brownish-green concoction in front of Eris.

"Uh, Ruff, what the hell is that?"

"Ruff's rough and tough hangover elixir! Guaranteed to cure all ailments!" he said with all the charisma of a snake oil salesman. I doubted the efficacy of such a claim, preferring the age-old hair of the dog cure myself, but Eris was in bad shape.

I slid the noxious beverage over to her and pretty much had to force it down her throat as she was half asleep.

"Not so hard, be gentle," she mumbled.

I rolled my eyes and kept forcing her to take sips until the drink was gone. I sat back in my chair when it was over and started in on my own cure. When the ale was gone, I tucked into the food. It was cooked perfectly, and I savored every bite. Eris only managed a few nibbles, but she was looking batter by the time I'd finished.

When breakfast was over, and Eris standing on her own. It was time to hit the road. I went to thank Ruff for his hospitality and bid him farewell.

I turned to leave when Ruff grabbed my arm. "You be careful now, ya hear? I don't know who or what that girl is, but it's clear she's something special. You take care of her now."

I nodded to the perceptive barkeep. "With my life."

My answer rang with the truth of my conviction, and Ruff smiled before wishing us both well. Ruff was good people.

I said my goodbyes, and with one last glance at the spot where I'd nearly killed Mikhail, we left the Inn of Ill Repute.

# Chapter 16 - Can't Run From Your Problems

Outside in the too-bright light, the prints of dozens of feet painted the dirt streets, telling a story on the ground. Most of the villagers were simple farmers, and they were already off to the fields for a day of backbreaking labor.

I helped Eris on top of Lacuna and quickly fed the horse an apple or two before leading her out of the stable. As we walked past some of the shops, I decided to stock up on a few more supplies, leaving Eris nodding off in the saddle, and went into the small general store, procuring another week's worth of supplies and a few odds and ends.

While Eris slept off her hangover, I pushed Lacuna to the outskirts of the village. A few hours passed in silence until we entered another stretch of forest. The trails branched in three directions, but I stayed on the center line and urged Lacuna to a gallop.

Eris woke up just after midday. Her eyes had lost the eerie glow to them, and they were back to her usual hue of inky darkness.

"Remind me to take it easier next time," she said while stifling a yawn.

I leaned down a placed a kiss on her head. "No promises, you're a hilarious drunk," I said with a grin.

She turned around with a frown, but it melted to a smile when she saw my face. I kept going for a few more minutes until we were out of a particularly overgrown section of forest. We stopped to eat lunch in a small recessed area that formed a natural semicircle where no trees or grass grew. We sat down on a dead log that had fallen over and been worn down to a rough bench.

I wasn't starving since I was still full from breakfast, but Eris had only managed a few bites, and I could hear her stomach rumbling for nearly half an hour before we stopped. With the supplies I purchased, I made us a couple of trail sandwiches, and Eris scarfed hers down while I picked over mine, my stomach in knots about the fight last night, and my anger.

From the looks Eris kept shooting my way, I could tell she wanted to talk about something, and odds were it was about what happened last night. After about three minutes of her eating and not saying something, I put my half-eaten sandwich down and looked over to her.

"All right, c'mon. Let me have it," I said.

"Let you have what?"

"You want to talk about last night, so let's have it. Go ahead, yell at me."

She put down the remains of her food and came over to sit by me. Her umbra eyes held concern in them. "I'm not angry at you, Sam. I'm worried."

"Well, don't be. I'm fine," I lied.

I wasn't fine. And I knew it. I didn't disagree with any of my actions last night, and I still thought Darren and his cronies needed to die, but the viciousness in my heart that pushed me along wasn't my own. It wasn't the first brutal act I'd committed, and it wouldn't be the last, but it was the first that I took pleasure in, and that scared the living hell out of me. *I enjoyed feeling their bones break, reveled in their screams. I've done horrible things before, but the pure perverse enjoyment I felt, wasn't me. It's whatever is in my heart now.*

I held my face in my hands and ran my fingers through my hair, unsure of what to say. Eris, though, she saw through me instantly and placed her hand on my back, rubbing gently between my shoulder blades. The heat from her hands was lovely, and before I knew it, she'd calmed me down considerably.

"Thanks," I said.

266

Eris nodded. "I'm here for you, my bonded. For now, until eternity. That was the promise we made to each other."

I wanted to open up to her, but I didn't know how to say what I was feeling. The darkness in my heart was what was influencing me, but I thought I'd sound crazy if I told her, so I didn't say anything. Her touch was enough to keep whatever evil was in my heart at bay, and I was content with that.

Eris knew me well and knew what I needed right then, that no amount of talking or words would solve the issue, so she didn't say anything, letting her touch say more than her words ever could.

That I was accepted.

She scooted over to me on the tree, and before I could say anything, she came and straddled me, sitting on my lap and pressing herself against me. Eris brought her mouth to mine and kissed me softly, trailing little kisses all around my mouth like a flitting butterfly. Each of her kisses drew me into her, and I wrapped my arms around her before I knew what I was doing.

My hand traveled to her face to cup her cheek, and I returned her kisses with one of my own, long and slow, savoring the way her mouth molded around my own. After staying locked in our kiss, her tongue snaked out of her mouth to probe my lips, searching for an opening. To which I acquiesced.

Eris's tongue was long and strong; she explored my mouth with enthusiasm, intertwining our tongues to dance in bliss. She dug her hands into my back before running them through my hair, knocking loose my hair tie to fall by the wayside while she pushed me down against the log.

She ground against my groin, tempting my burgeoning hardness with the sway of her hips. Her hands dripped down my body to the hem of my shirt as she slipped under my clothes to caress my bare chest. My shirt was halfway off my body, so I finished the job, sitting up and removing my shirt in a flash before turning back to her.

As eager as Eris was to explore my body, I was of a similar mind. Eris had no problem with baring herself to me, and it had been difficult to restrain myself when she constantly tested my resolve. I finally gave myself to the living hurricane that was my partner.

My hands gripped her waist as I marveled over the muscle of her stomach as I trailed my way to her chest. Eris shuddered as I reached her breasts, cupping them gently while her nipples stiffened at my touch. I rolled my thumbs over them as Eris grew more heated, letting a soft moan slip from between her lips.

Her shirt was getting in the way, so she yanked it off in haste, tearing the weak fabric as it drifted to the dirt, already forgotten in the heat of the moment. Nude, I let my eyes drink in her form, uninhibited by my past reservations. Her breasts fit in my palms as if made for them, and with each pass of my fingers, I was rewarded with another unstifled moan.

Taking charge, Eris gripped the back of my neck and drew my face toward her chest. I took the hint and kissed both of her breasts before taking one of her nipples into my mouth. The heat of my mouth sent tremors through her as I flicked my tongue around. I took her nipple between my teeth and bit down lightly, drawing a loud cry as Eris clenched around me.

She'd had enough of my foreplay and shoved me against the tree. The rough bark and uneven protrusions dug into my back, but I hardly noticed, so consumed with Eris's radiance. Her eyes swam with desire, and she quickly grabbed my pants and ripped them down, exposing my manhood to her.

My pants were in tatters around my ankles, and I shoved them out of the way as Eris lowered her hips to my shaft, pressing her wetness against me.

268

Her opening was burning and slick with lust. She tensed with the slightest movement, her breath coming in short bursts as her face flushed red. Eris shimmed her hips back and forth, moaning with each pass before working up the nerve and slipping down, taking me inside of her.

Eris squirmed in pain for a moment before slowly shifting her hips up and down, increasing in rhythm. A few attempts and several long moments later, her discomfort faded to rapture. Her opening was hot and tight as she worked her hips, sending waves of pleasure through me. Eris was inexperienced but had good instincts and after only a few clumsy moments, she found her rhythm.

As her moments increased, so too did her volume. Eris cried out in pleasure each time her hips slammed down. She built her tempo into her cadence of moans, each one melding into an orchestra of passion.

Eris enjoyed being on top, but after a while, I decided to take charge and change positions. We went from the tree to the ground. Loose dirt stuck to us as I thrust into her, cupping her face and staring into her wholly inhuman eyes as we made love.

After what felt like a minute and an hour, we'd both built up to our crescendo. Eris's nails tore into my back as we reached our peak. As she hit her climax, she gripped my shoulders tight and forced me as deep as I could go inside of her, crying out to the void as she came.

I reached my own limit, and my low groan melded with her cries of delectation.

Panting and utterly spent, I held Eris close as we both rode the high. I held her and lay there as a breeze rolled through the trees.

We'd made a mess of things, and flailing around on the ground hadn't helped one bit. Eris rolled over on top of me, dirt clinging to the side of her chest and along her hips leading to her backside. Giving me a look of utter contentment, she leaned down and kissed me softly, before trailing her lips toward my ear.

"I'll admit, that was worth waiting for," she said with a grin.

I ran my hand through her hair as she laid back on my chest. "Yeah, it was…really nice. I haven't felt like this in a very long time."

"Like what?" she asked as she lifted her head.

"Content."

Eris smiled wide at me and nuzzled into my neck. "I feel the same, Sam. Before you, there was only darkness. I never expected to find happiness in the person who I was to be bound to, but I have, and it means the world to me."

I didn't say anything else, for no other words needed to be said. I just held her as we lay on the ground, neither one of us wanting to move. A few minutes passed before necessity forced our hand.

"Ugh," I said, leaning up. "I need a bath. Strike that, *we* need a bath."

Eris looked at her body and mine, both covered with dirt and dried sweat. "I agree. Let's find a place to wash up."

If memory served me, there should've been a river around the area somewhere. I pulled up my map in my interface, switching to local view to scan the terrain, but there wasn't one within the mile, so my map didn't detect it, and the world map wasn't detailed enough to show a river that small.

"Damn, I know there's a river nearby, but my map isn't showing me where."

Eris perked up at that. "Oh, I can help with that," she said, as her hands poured out small trails of smoke before they were whisked away by the wind.

She concentrated intensely; her eyes scrunched tightly closed. More and more of her magic bled from her fingers, drifting around us in the soft breeze and filling my nose with sharp tones of the forest. Less than a minute later, she stopped the flow of magic before it exhausted her.

"There's a river not far from here," she said, pointing in the direction we needed to go. I quickly climbed into a pair of cotton trousers and tied Lacuna to a tree. She wouldn't run off, but I still didn't want to take any chances. *If it's not far, I'd rather leave Lacuna here.*

Eris wound her fingers through mine, and we set off, though it quickly became apparent that her judgment of distance was a little skewed, as it took us nearly twenty minutes to reach the river. After the hike under the blazing heat of the sun, sweat dripped into my eyes, and my chest and back were stinging under the intensity of the sun's rays. Pushing past the brush, the sight of freshwater was almost euphoric.

The river rushed past like it was late for a meeting, and the strength of the current worried me. *Long as we don't stray too far, I doubt it'll be an issue.* After warning Eris of the current, I hurriedly climbed down the bank.

Eris seemed content to enjoy the sights of the river from the embankment; her eyes lit up with wonder as the river raced by. "It's so pretty here, isn't it, Sam?"

"Yes, it is lovely, though it pales in comparison to you."

She beamed at my compliment, reaching out to wind her fingers through mine. "I much prefer this side of you. It suits you better."

I laughed. "That may be true, but as I've said numerous times, I'm not a good person. This world isn't kind to good people, and I won't apologize for my behavior, even if you don't agree with it."

The river was too inviting, so I stepped out of my pants and climbed down the embankment and waded out into the swirling waters. Eris huffed at my back.

"That's not what I was getting at, Sam. I promise. I, too, know just how unforgiving this world can be, but I was just saying the sweet and charming side of you is nice to see, and I'd like to see it more often. Dark and brooding doesn't fit your handsome face."

I turned back and moved deeper into the water. *Sweet and charming? Eh, I guess I have been nicer to Eris than I've been to anyone in years. She deserves someone nice, though, so maybe I can make more of an effort in that regard.* I stopped when the water reached the bottom of my chest, careful of the current, but it still wasn't strong enough to drag me anywhere.

Pulling out a bar of soap and a washrag from my inventory, I proceeded to take my time cleaning the sweat and grime that had accumulated, along with the added dirt from the forest floor. By the time I had finished washing my body and rinsing off, a splash from the riverbank told me that Eris had joined me in the water.

Small suds and soap bubbles drifted down the river. Eris sighed in contentment as the water ran over her. She was much shorter than I was and resorted to nearly submerging herself as she swam over to reach me. Not wanting her to get swept away by the river, I reached out and took her hand, pulling her into me. She wrapped her legs around my waist, fearing the current.

The water swept away all but the most tenacious of dirt, so I held on to her as I took my washcloth and helped clean the rest of the grime off her.

Once she was squeaky clean, I went to store the washcloth and soap back in my inventory, but Eris stopped me. She took hold of my hand and guided it back to her breast. She gazed at me with intent and would not let me pull my hand away.

"See, look how sweet you're being Even after sharing one another's bodies, you're still treating my flesh with respect. I am yours, body, and soul. As you are mine. You can touch me as much as you want."

I leaned down and kissed her. "Honestly, I don't know what you see in a failure like me."

She took my chin in her hands and lifted my head, forcing me to look at her. "You are not a failure; I don't believe that for a moment. You may have failed, but that doesn't make you a failure."

"Oh, but I am. I couldn't protect the people I cared about the most, and they're dead because of me."

"You can say that as much as you want, but you can't convince me. I've seen much of your life, both in this world and in yours. I know how much you cared for your family, I know the pain Micah's death brought, but that isn't solely what haunts you, my bonded. I could not see any of the life you led before this one, so I don't know what the cause is, but it goes beyond the death of your brother, doesn't it?"

I nodded, not trusting myself to speak.

She stopped my busy work and kissed me on the cheek as she hugged me. "Tell me."

I hung my head and couldn't look at her. I knew I would see compassion and acceptance in her eyes, and I didn't deserve either. I deserved to be nothing more than shattered and rotting bones beside my brother. *Micah deserved better, and so did Sophia. If I had stayed by Micah's side, she would have never met me and would still be alive.*

We didn't speak for a long time after that moment. I just listened to the water as it swept past us. Eris stroked my cheek while I fought within myself, trying and failing once again to come to terms with the monsters of my past.

Since I'd met Eris, my past had been shoved into my face, over and over again. I just kept pushing it down and running, running from the pain that had been with me for thirty years. Eris wanted me to forgive myself, deep down I knew I wanted that, but I couldn't...not yet.

Forgiving myself would mean letting go of the last remnants of Micah and Sophia.

Eris caressed my cheek, sensing the change in me. The warmth of her hand brought a pain that seared into me; I felt the tears brimming in my eyes, but I wiped them away. I'd shed enough recently, and it wasn't helping anything. For the first time, I welcomed the magic within my heart; it chilled the brimming emotions that threatened to spill over.

I'd had enough of the water. It didn't hold the same appeal as when we'd arrived. I waded out of and threw on my pants. Eris had neglected to bring any clothes, though she didn't seem to mind being naked. It wasn't like mosquitoes would bite her; they wouldn't dare drink the blood of their queen. They didn't bother me much either, but they buzzed next to my ears enough times that I knew they didn't treat the Hive Knight with nearly as much respect as the queen.

The walk back to camp was a quiet one. Eris knew how I was feeling and knew that she couldn't force me to shed the shackles of my past, but she held my hand firmly, letting me know she wasn't going anywhere.

Knowing I would open up when I was ready.

We finally reached the small wooded area where we had stopped for lunch. In our absence, a band of insects had swarmed to our discarded lunches and were delighting in the food. I wanted to burn them alive, but Eris happily watched them while I readied Lacuna.

Eris got dressed in the skirt Makenna had provided for her, but it seemed she was vehemently averse to wearing shoes, so I stowed them in my inventory along with the armor Gil had given her. She donned one of my shirts, an emerald one this time, and one of my last truly clean shirts, along with her traveling skirt and cloak. The brown and greens played nicely off each other.

When she was dressed, she walked over and hugged me. "Just know that I'll accept whatever's in your past. And I'll be here to talk when you're ready to open up."

I smiled into her hair. It smelled like my soap: cherries and cream. *Even if I can't fix myself, I can at least be there for her.* I could be the immovable rock to which she tethered herself. She needed me in her life just as much as I think I needed her. I wasn't ready to accept her when we met, couldn't have known what she would come to mean to me, but I couldn't run from the truth any longer.

I cared for her, cared for her more than I dared to admit.

Smiling, I kissed her damp hair and held my lips there, enjoying her presence. *I'd like to stay here a bit longer, but I have promises to keep, and miles to go before I sleep.*

"C'mon, love. We're burning daylight."

# Chapter 17 - Outlier Farmstead

Over the next day, Eris and I rode our way to the edge of the Compass Kingdom. Long before we ever spied the towering white walls that encircled the five kingdoms, we came across the outlier farms.

Too many farmers grew tired of the taxes and regulations of the Merchants Guild and the lax nature of the five kings when it came to hearing their plights. So one by one, the disgruntled citizens left the safety of Alliance and set up shop in the untended fields far enough away from the hands of the guild.

Though the farmsteads were small in stature, their fields stretched for miles as we wound our way over the dirt road towards the East Kingdom. I thought the farmers both brave and stupid for their decisions. Living under the thumb of the guild was far from pleasant, but it offered protection too. Here, away from the walls and patrols of the Alliance, the farmers were subject to bandit raids and thefts.

*The Merchants Guild is the lesser of two evils. Better the devils you know.* Still, it was none of my business; far be it for me to meddle in the affairs of the guild.

I guided Lacuna over a thin dirt road next to a large field of barley. The ocean of amber twisted in the wind, bringing the wonderful aroma blowing our way. Eris giggled as a few loose stalks drifted past, tickling her exposed skin.

Her laugh invigorated me, and I drew her closer to my chest as we passed the numerous fields and the workers who raised their hands in greeting as we rode by. Eris couldn't help but wave back, and as long as she kept her head covered, I didn't care if she socialized to her heart's content.

I slowed down as we rode next to a farmer coming from the field. The man wore stained trousers and a once-white linen shirt, but it had long since seen its prime, though a wide-brimmed straw hat covered his face in shadow.

"Howdy, there," he said as he raised his hand in greeting.

He was an elderly man, worn down by the sun. His deeply tanned skin drooped like melted candle wax, but his eyes were bright, filled with warmth and humor.

"Hello," Eris replied happily.

He smirked at the sight of me with my hands around Eris's waist. "Aren't you a sight for sore eyes? It's good to see young love in these troubling times."

"What do you mean?" I asked.

"Ah, where are my manners? My name is Oscar," he said with a smile and a shake of his head. "And don't mind me, jus' ignore the ramblings of an old man."

"Duran."

"I'm Eris!"

I looked around, really looked instead of just a cursory glance. Plumes of gray smoke rose from the chimneys of dozens of farmsteads, but one trail of smoke was black and low like it had been burning for a while.

"Trouble with bandits?"

"Always, but that's nothing new. Mos' of the time, they take our 'tithes' and leave, but they've grown bolder over the years. The bandit kings are running wild without that empress of theirs to keep 'em in line."

"Could always pack up and head back to the East Kingdom," I said with a shrug.

"Bah," Oscar said, and spat onto the ground. "Bunch of fuckin' thieves and snakes, the lot of 'em."

Oscar looked up, realized Eris was there and what he'd said and reddened.

"Ah, my apologies, miss," he said with a sheepish grin. "Pardon this farmer's uncouth mouth."

"No worries, Oscar. You should hear this one. Could curdle milk with his filthy mouth alone," she said, smiling while ribbing me lightly with her elbow.

He laughed. "I was just about to head home for some lunch. It gets lonely out here, would you two care to join me?"

I shook my head. "Thank you for the offer, but we've really got places to—"

"I've got a fresh batch of beer that just finished brewing. Homemade," he interrupted, prodding me with a long stalk of wheat he picked off the ground.

"We'd love to join you for lunch," I said, relenting.

We followed Oscar up to his home, a single-story oak longhouse with a thick thatch roof, just dampened. *It has been a hot summer. Wonder how common brush fires are out here?* As soon as we entered the home, Oscar busied himself tidying up the place, opening the bay windows that looked out over the field and trying to make the house presentable for guests.

It wasn't a sty, far from it, but it was clear Oscar hadn't been expecting company. "Pardon the mess, friends. I haven' had guests in quite a while."

"That's quite alright, Oscar. Thank you for the hospitality; you have a lovely home," Eris said.

Oscar motioned for us to sit at the table, pulling our chairs out for us and heading to the kitchen. I sat down and leaned back against the wall, Eris had the view of the lovely fields while I had an eye on the door and the kitchen. She poked me under the table with her finger, smiling at me.

"You *can* relax, you know," she said, wiggling her finger to let a single drop of her magic spill out. "There isn't anyone around us except for Oscar."

I leaned over and kissed her forehead. "I'd rather be safe than sorry."

"I know, love."

Oscar came back less than a minute later with three tall glasses filled to the brim with beer. "I hope you enjoy," he said as he sat them down in front of us. "I usually make extra and sell what I can't drink to the neighbors, but I made this cask special, so I hope you like it."

I took a deep pull, draining half of it in a few gulps. It was a little hoppy, but it went down smooth, and I found myself draining the glass before I knew it. Eris, on the other hand, played it much more cautious this time around, only sipping at the beer, though from the way she licked her lips, I'd say she enjoyed the taste.

Oscar looked at me and laughed. "Finally, another man who can drink his beer," he said, pushing his untouched beer my way. "I'll go fetch us another couple mugs."

He returned shortly with even more beer and kept happily plying us with drink. I slowed my consumption considerably, after the first two, despite being tempted with delicious beer. Oscar seemed genuinely happy to have people enjoy the work he put into his hobby, but as much as I wanted to stay and keep drinking, we needed to reach the East Kingdom before dusk.

After we dined on a light meal of chicken and steamed vegetables, we helped clear the table and said our goodbyes.

"Thank you for the meal, and the booze," I said.

"Ah…I'm jus' glad you enjoyed it. Makes meh old heart happy."

He looked like he wanted to say something else, but he just smiled, thanked us for stopping by and wished us a safe journey.

We hopped on Lacuna and set off down through the farms. Eris hadn't drunk nearly as much as I had, but her face was a little red, and she seemed to be in fine spirits.

"That was lovely," she said, reaching for my hand.

"Yeah, it was nice to relax for a moment. Beer was damn good, too."

"It was tasty, reminded me a bit of banlin."

"Banlin?"

"It was a ceremonial drink for my people, only brewed during the celestial harvest. It was my favorite time of the year, since I could go out and meet other people without my parents watching over me. I loved banlin, though the children were never allowed alcohol. It was still delicious without it."

"Color me intrigued. What do you say we figure out how to make it ourselves? Do you know what goes in it?"

Eris perked up at that, turning around to smile at me. "I don't remember, but I bet I can find the answer in the Hive Mind if I look hard enough."

We passed the last of the farms and were back into open fields. With the last of the farms fading behind us, the dirt road widened, and I spurred Lacuna faster, pushing her to a trot. "I still know very little of your people, so why don't we try to change that when we get back to Gloom-Harbor?"

"I'd like that."

We continued onward, talking intermittently. Eris had few truly fond memories of her childhood, so we couldn't really talk about her past without inadvertently hitting a nerve, and my past was equally as damaged, so we talked about other things, stupid things like the names of trees and plants we passed.

Eris had extensive knowledge of fauna, and she lit up every time I asked her to name off an obscure plant.

I kept my eyes open for any sign of bandit activity since Oscar told us they'd been in the area, but I never saw any sign of them. By the time, the white walls of the Compass Kingdom came into view, I grew lax on my vigilance.

*We're five miles from an Alliance patrol route. We'll be fine.*

We were close to Grange, the hub of all things farming and one of the busiest towns in the area around the Compass Kingdom. More of a city than a town, as several thousand residents lived there permanently, and thousands more worked in the fields that surrounded the area.

Eris had been using her magic off and on all day, working to build up her strength and control. I'd long since gotten used to the strange scent it produced, and what little smoke dribbled out was quickly swept away by the wind, so I forgot she was even using it until she spoke up.

"How much farther till we reach the town?" she asked as we were about to enter a dense thicket of trees.

"Less than half an hour, why?"

She turned back to face me, holding a look of mild curiosity.

"Oh, I was just wondering. Do people normally come this far out of town?"

"It's possible, I guess. Why do you ask?"

She pointed at the group of trees coming up. "There are people behind the trees, about ten of them, they're just standing around like they're waiting for something."

I processed her words quickly, going through the possible options, and coming up with only one answer. *Ambush!*

"Shit!"

My instincts screamed at me, and I flung Eris off Lacuna a split second before an arrow pierced my chest, right where Eris's head had been moments before. I fell from Lacuna and crashed painfully to the dirt.

A familiar voice screamed from the tree line. A voice that made me seethe with rage.

"You fucking moron! You almost hit the merchandise!" Darren raged.

*So, the slaver returns for round two, and he brought more of his disgusting friends with him.* All ten of the slavers strolled out of the trees, as cocksure as can be, and with good reason. Ten against one wasn't so much a fight as it would be a slaughter. My slaughter.

It wasn't time to abandon all hope, though. *I still have a few tricks up my sleeve, and as long as I draw breath, they won't lay one a single filthy finger on my queen!*

I looked down at the arrow, amazed I was still alive. *The archer is skilled. I shouldn't have walked away from that.* The arrow had gone through my chestplate and the studded leather with ease. *What stopped it? I should be dead.* It was then that a strange liquid poured from my wound. It wasn't my blood—it was black. *Chitin!*

The chitin molded itself over my wound, pushing out the arrowhead and tiny slivers of wood and steel that had shaved off. It hardened over my skin and even filled the hole in my armor. Quick as I could, I leapt to my feet and drew my sword.

Darren gaped as I stood up from the ground, having assumed I was dead. Too bad for him. *It seems I'm much more difficult to kill these days.* I hated to admit it, but even as a level one hundred Blade Master, I wouldn't have survived that arrow.

"You fucking missed!" Darren screamed at Slip. My would-be killer. "Quickly, shoot him again!"

Slip nocked another arrow in the blink of an eye and fired. The arrow took me in the chest, almost in the same spot as the first. *He's a damn good shot, but even with his abilities, his arrows can't pierce chitin.* I flicked the shaft of the arrow off my armor and marched onto the field of battle.

"Eris, stay back. Let me handle this!" I yelled.

But she refused to listen to me, running from behind Lacuna to join me. "No! Never again will I sit back and leave you to fight alone. I won't do it!"

*Damn it, Eris!* "I can't protect you and fight at the same time!"

She shook her head. "No. I can help."

*She's never been in a fight before. Even with her magic, she's a liability.*

*"The queen is to be protected at all costs, knight."*

The voice rose up from my heart to whisper in my ear. It had spoken before, but this was the first time it had addressed me. My inner darkness terrified me, but I didn't have time to worry about my growing insanity. I had to fight.

*I know that, but she won't listen to me. She's too fucking stubborn to sit this out!*

*"Allow me to try?"* my Darkness asked, waiting for permission.

*Have at it.*

My heart froze solid, and the ice traversed itself to my head, filling my brain with its frigid touch. I wasn't in control anymore, and my mouth opened on its own to speak.

"My queen, you shouldn't be here. This is our fight."

Eris looked at me, shocked. The voice that rose from my lips was mine, but it was twisted, sibilant—the voice of the Hive Knight.

She quickly shook away her surprise. "I am queen, my knight. Sam is my bonded, and I will not let him go into battle alone. You will obey me."

*"Foolish queen!"* It hissed to me, but we couldn't go against her orders. My Darkness released its hold on me and retreated inside my heart, the ice faded away, and a burning heat flowed through my veins—the power of the Hive.

"All right, but do as I say, promise me that!"

She nodded, and I tossed her the hunting knife on my belt. "Leave the main force to me and back me up with your magic. Use the knife if anyone gets close."

"Got it!"

Because of our argument, we'd allowed the enemy to close the distance between us, and I had to put Eris out of mind and focus on the battle, or I would find my corpse cooling on the dirt before I knew it.

Darren and his group stayed behind while his peons flocked to us. Three of them rushed me, while the others held back and prevented us from escaping. They each wore light armor, black leather with minimal protection. Each also bore the same crest as their leaders.

A drip from my sword told me *Poison Blade* kicked in. *I hope the poison will even the playing field a bit. Even with Eris backing me, we're heavily outnumbered.*

Spurred on and their numbers making them overconfident, three of the men attacked at the same time. From a glance at their swords, I estimated them to be at least level forty. *A challenge.*

My sword and armor were well above my level, but I was only working with four skills, and *Aura of the Antimage* wasn't going to do a whole lot of good here. *Dance of the Immortal* would easily even the playing field, but if I didn't time it exactly right, I'd end up maxing out my battle fatigue, and that would kill me just as quickly.

All three had swords, one was a falchion, one was a longsword, and the final looked like a Roman gladius.

284

Longsword swung at me while Falchion and Gladius circled. I ducked under the first swipe and cracked Longsword in the face, he held firm and fought down the pain, swiping at me again. I dodged the second swing and kicked Longsword's leg out from underneath him. He tumbled roughly to the ground.

Pain burned from my side. Gladius slipped underneath my guard while my back was turned and stabbed me. His sword still stuck in me, but it didn't get through my *Exoskeleton*. Falchion attempted to take advantage of the situation while my attention was focused on Gladius. His steps were heavy behind me, but I turned too slowly to intercept him.

Eris stepped in, taking his sword on her arm. She cried in pain as it split open her skin. Blood welled and ran like a river over her arm, but just beneath her skin was black chitin. She grimaced and fought back the pain. Green smoke poured from her fingers as she worked her magic.

While Eris kept Falchion busy, I dealt with Gladius and Longsword. Gladius was still clutching his namesake, so I brought my arm down sharply, breaking his wrist. Gladius dropped his weapon and clutched his broken hand. Longsword came in quick, thrusting with his blade. I parried it and sliced a thin line down his arm, splashing a stream of poison into his bloodstream.

A bloodcurdling scream echoed behind me. Hundreds of spiders had come at Eris's call and were crawling over her and Falchion. They jumped from Eris to Falchion and scuttled over every inch of bare flesh. He frantically tried to peel them off, but they scurried to his face and neck, sinking their fangs deep into his exposed skin and refusing to let go.

Falchion wasn't even trying to fight Eris anymore. He dropped his weapon to focus solely on the horde tearing at him. Dozens of rivulets of blood ran from his face and arms from the spider bites.

Eris clumsily gripped the knife in hand and stabbed Falchion while he was busy with the spiders. The blade lodged deep in his chest, and she pulled it out in a fountain of blood. *Nicked the heart, but not enough.*

Falchion was still standing, and panic-stricken, he lunged for Eris. He pinned her to the ground while making a hasty grab for his weapon. She cried out as she hit the grass.

I kicked Longsword in the groin and ran over to Eris, tackling Falchion to the ground. My sword fell from my hands in the tumble, so I gripped my hands together and brought them down sharply. Once, twice, and a final time, I slammed my fists into Falchion's throat, crushing his trachea and shattering his hyoid bone. He spasmed with each hit, clutching his obliterated neck and wheezed, trying to breathe. His last breath would never come, and I stood from him as he fought for one more gasp of air.

No one was coming to his rescue, and without a healing potion, he would soon expire. I grabbed my sword and the falchion, handing the latter to Eris as Longsword got off the ground.

"Keep behind your sword at all times and never let your opponent into your space," I told Eris as I focused on Longsword.

He wasn't looking so hot. The poison wreaked havoc on his insides, and the kick to groin had bruised more than his pride. Longsword snarled at me and picked up the gladius, a drop of my blood fell from the blade as he charged me.

Longsword by himself, wasn't a threat, even with the added weapon. I dodged his sword and parried the gladius. His footwork was sloppy, and his swings heavy. He thrust with the longsword while I pivoted on the balls of my feet. His attack passed by my ribs as I brought my sword down at the same time and severed his arm from his body.

Longsword howled in agony and dropped the gladius, backing away from me and fumbling at the satchel at his waist for a health potion. Unlike Falchion, he'd had some foresight. He uncapped it as I bent down and picked up the discarded gladius. As Longsword put the bottle to his lips, I flung the gladius at him. The sword took him in the chest, sinking hilt deep into his heart. Longsword dropped to the ground, the health potion spilling to mix with his blood.

I backed up a bit to stand with Eris, handing her a health potion from my inventory. "Take two little sips, no more," I said.

"Right."

With her slight injuries taken care of, I turned my attention to the rest of the group. Gladius had regrouped with the other three, who were playing gatekeepers. They'd watched two of their friends die so callously and hadn't even drawn their weapons. They sure as hell did when I moved to engage them.

"Eris, use your magic to keep them from surrounding us."

She nodded and moved back a few steps. "I'll do my best," she said a little breathlessly.

*I'm pushing her; even that little display a moment ago was enough to weaken her. She probably can't use much more.*

Gladius had healed his broken wrist and picked up a spare weapon. A dagger. He stayed behind the others, though, shaking, rightfully cautious of me. The other three were more than willing to fight in his stead. Two rushed ahead of the others, while the third went for Eris. He held a spear in his hands.

My first opponent wielded a massive cleaver straight from Hell's kitchen, which he attempted to chop me into bits, while the second was a flamberge, the winding blade whistling as it came for my head.

Flamberge was easy enough to deal with. His two-handed sword was too unwieldy and slow to hit me. Dodging was easy, but as soon as I stepped out of reach of Flamberge, Cleaver struck with frightening speed, slicing me twice in under a second. I tried to deal with Cleaver, but as soon as I turned my back, Flamberge struck, and I couldn't dodge.

*It worked with her, better fucking work for me!* Pain rolled through me as I caught the sword on my palm. My skin split, spilling fresh blood, and the impact made my arm rattle hard enough to shake me to my core, but the chitin held under the onslaught of his blade—dark black chitin formed over my hand, acting as a second skin for me.

I grabbed hold of the flamberge, and with my chitin-wrapped grip, squeezed as hard as I could. It held for a moment before cracking under my fingers, shattering and tumbling to the ground in pieces.

Flamberge just stared in fear at the broken tip of his weapon sticking out of my hand. I let go of his broken sword, ducked under Cleaver's swipe, and ran Flamberge through with my blade. Cleaver swiped at my head while my blade was sticking out of his friend, and I managed to move just in time. His wide blade sank deep into his dying friend's neck.

Thick, heavy blood sprayed into the air, coating us in rancid gore. I shut my mouth and stepped back as Flamberge dropped lifelessly to the ground, his head nearly sheared from his body. I spat on the ground, making sure none of his vile fluids landed on my tongue.

I returned to Cleaver. My sword was stuck in Flamberge's body, and Eris still had my knife, so I fought with my hands.

Cleaver was much less confident now that we'd taken down half of their number. While Gladius stared wide-eyed at our duel, and Spear fought Eris, Cleaver was more cautious.

A glance told me that Eris was holding her own. With the falchion raised, she knocked aside what attacks she could and moved when she couldn't parry them. Her movements were stiff and awkward, but she could move fast and was strong, so it allowed her to survive what attacks were coming her way. While Eris was his target, Spear had much bigger problems. Namely, the bugs.

Spiders, scorpions, and even ants were encroaching on him, dozens of them. He stomped the larger ones as they got closer, but every time his foot landed, a few managed to crawl up his leg. The spiders scurried towards his chest, while the scorpions jabbed their stingers into his legs over and over.

Spear screamed and frantically clawed at his pockets for an item while trying to knock the spiders off him. He pulled out a small gray stone, polished smooth with Script on it. A fire stone. He spoke the activation word and threw it at his feet.

Which was a fatal mistake.

Whether his terror had overridden his common sense or he just misjudged the throw, the fire stone landed just shy of his feet and exploded, sending a wave of pressure toward us, and a massive, roaring fire rose to consume everything in its path.

Spear meant to kill the bugs but was too close to the spell when it went off—fire engulfed him in a matter of seconds. He screamed as he burned before falling to his knees, clutching at his blackened and cracked skin. He died a second later as the fire devoured his entire body.

Eris picked herself off the ground. The fire hadn't done much damage to her; a singed shirt was the worst of it. Though she was about to give out, she stumbled and was struggling to stand. Her mana had reached its limits. She smiled at me to let me know she was okay, but it turned to fear as she shouted.

"Sam, behind you!"

I turned, just managing to get out of the way of Cleaver's swing. He swung again and again. I stepped out of the way of what I could, but he was fast, a few of his swings sliced thin grooves into my armor, one slice carved into my face, just below my cheek. Hot blood rushed down my face, but I ignored it and looked for an opening.

Cleaver was lightning fast and his weapon razor-sharp, but even with how light it was, he was tired from the numerous swings. His speed was still just as fast, but his technique slipped, allowing me to step close to him and kick him off balance. He fell to the ground, and I wasted no time in pinning his arm and breaking his nose with a jab. I snapped his wrist, took the cleaver from him, and buried it in his skull, splitting his face in two. Yellowed bone peeked out from behind his eyes as his skull cracked in half.

Five of the six were dead, leaving only the still stunned Gladius to deal with. Eris limped over to me, still holding the falchion and handed me back my knife. I secured it and went to grab my blood-soaked sword from Flamberge's body. It came away slippery, which washed away as *Poison Blade* activated, and toxins dripped down it.

I turned to Eris and smiled at her. "Not half bad for your first time."

"Really?" she asked, practically glowing, despite her exhaustion.

"Don't get a big ego. You still need training, but this conversation can wait. We still have threats to deal with."

I wasn't talking about Gladius. He was kneeling on the ground, shaking with fear. I thought he was frightened of me, of the fact that I had beaten his friends so quickly, but no. He was staring at Eris, trembling with fear, and muttering to himself.

He looked from her to me and scrambled on all fours over to me, clutching at my pant leg, begging me. "Please, please, please, don't let her near me. Please have mercy. I'll do anything, just keep her away."

I smiled a grim smile. "Don't worry. I won't let her have you."

Gladius broke into tears, misconstruing my meaning. He blubbered at me. "Thank you, thank you, thank you!"

"No problem."

While he stared at me with pure unadulterated hope in his eyes, I plunged my sword downward into his neck and twisted, killing him instantly. His lifeblood spilled to the earth as I pulled my sword free.

With those six dealt with and their blood sinking into the earth, I faced the four men who were the actual threats, except there were only three of them.

*Shit! Where's Slip?!*

The wind picked up, rustling leaves rolled by, and I knew what was coming. I turned and sliced my sword behind me, right where I expected Slip to *Shadow-Walk*, except my blade whistled through empty air.

*No! Damn it!* I wasn't the target.

Eris was.

Slip appeared in a haze and wrapped his arm around Eris, fading back into shadows before I even had a chance to cry out. A few seconds later, he reappeared at the tree line with the others, passing Eris to Mikhail, who raised his sword to her throat.

Darren held a look of confidence. He wasn't sure he could take me in a fight, so he took Eris to save his own skin as well as make a profit off her. Two birds, one stone. He grinned wide at me.

"Take one more step, and your little girlfriend's head rolls to the floor!"

*Fuck.*

# CHAPTER 18 - WHAT ARE YOU WILLING TO LOSE?

Darren looked me down, bursting with confidence.

"Now, how's this going to play out, hero? You going to set your weapon down like a good boy and walk away, or is Mikhail here going to paint the grass with her blood?"

*Shit! What can I do? No way can I make it there without Dance of the Immortal, and if I fuck up my timing, I'm dead, and they'll take her.*

My hand gripped my sword tight enough to hurt, and I tensed, ready to make my move, but Darren was faster.

"Uh-uh, I don't think so," he said, motioning to Mikhail, who drew his blade tight across Eris's throat. A thin line of blood snaked down her neck, causing her to squirm in pain while her entire body shook with mana depletion.

*Even if I can get her away, she's too weak to fight anymore.* Darren smiled as he watched me trying to figure out a solution and come up wanting.

"Don't even think about it. Now, you're pretty strong. I mean, godsdamn. You two took out six of my men like it was nothing, but I wouldn't do anything rash if I were you, you'll just end up dead."

*Damn it!* I seethed in rage, but I couldn't attack without a plan, and a glance at my battle fatigue told me that I didn't have it in me for another fight. It was high, nearing the top and slowly creeping down as we kept up our conversation. But it wouldn't drop fast enough.

*"Do you wish for power?"* my Darkness asked.

*Like hell, I'm going to answer you. Nothing good can come from a question like that.*

*"Do you not wish for your queen to be returned to you, sir knight?"*

*Obviously, but I'll do it my damn self, with no help from the devil whispering in my ear.*

"*Very well, knight. It's your life if she dies,*" it said, chuckling as it faded away.

I had a plan, but it all rode on timing, and with Mikhail holding Eris, her safety came before anything else.

My battle fatigue was high, but I had a way to deal with it and activated *Dance of the Immortal*. All color bled from the world, sending my vision into a wash of every hue of gray. I sprinted the distance as fast as I could, reaching the four men in two seconds. *Eight.*

I pulled Eris free from Mikhail's filthy hands and ran her away from the group. *Six.* When we were safe from them, I pulled a mana potion from my inventory and pressed it into Eris's arms, and then rushed back to the group, hoping to do some damage before time ran down. *Four.*

My naked sword found purchase in Mikhail's chest, skewering him through the heart before I removed it and severed his head. *Two.*

A flash of color told me my time was up. I took out one final potion from my inventory and filled my mouth with half the contents as I ran back to Eris. *One.* Time returned to normal. Mikhail's body sprayed blood like a burst pipe, showering Slip and Darren in his gore. My battle fatigue soared as it nearly maxed itself, and a timer appeared in the corner of my interface. Counting down from seventy-two hours.

I stumbled as the effects of *Dance* hit my system and swallowed the potion in my mouth. The recovery potion kicked in almost immediately. Only drinking half of it was a blessing and a curse. It lessened the aftereffects, but it was also half as effective, knocking down my battle fatigue, but not removing all of it and only taking twenty-four hours from *Dance's* cooldown.

*It'll do. Hopefully.* Eris looked to me and back at the men with surprise. "How did I get here?"

"No time. Drink the mana potion and get ready."

"Wha—oh." Looking down and seeing the blue vial in her hands, she quickly uncapped it and downed it. As her mana climbed, she steeled herself for battle. A swift breeze rolled through the trees, chilling the sweat dripping down my face and bringing the stench of blood to us, I choked back the scent and readied for Darren and his thugs.

My Darkness whispered to me from my heart. *"Not bad, knight. But you still have enemies. I could help you get rid of them in an instant."*

*Fuck off.*

I could handle them on my own. It was up to me to earn the title of Hive Knight now.

Slip recovered faster than the others, wiping the blood from his face and baring his bloody teeth in rage. He aimed and fired at me almost as a reflex. A bright green glow appeared around his bow, bringing a torrent of wind to the tip of his arrow. He'd activated *Whisper of the Wind* and fired. His arrow sped forward as if propelled by a hurricane, accelerating it so fast it was a blur as it raced toward me.

Trusting my instincts, I threw myself to the side, hoping I wasn't about to end up with a hole in my chest. My instincts were right, but I wasn't quick enough to dodge it altogether. It left a ragged tear through my left bicep, spilling blood down my arm.

As the pain roared up my arm, I looked down to see the arrow had torn through even my *Exoskeleton*. *Shit! He got through my Exoskeleton. Not good.* Something that didn't go unnoticed. Slip grinned darkly. "Looks like you bleed like the rest of us mortals, after all, freak!"

He dropped his bow and drew his twin daggers, rushing me while Wolf and Darren stayed behind, Darren because he was still cleaning blood off himself, but Wolf was watching the show with a calmness about him, which unnerved the hell out of me. *What is his deal?*

I had to tune him out as Slip attacked, focusing my attention on dodging the rapid strikes.

Slip was true to his namesake and was as fast as any high-leveled rogue I'd ever faced before. *Might even be on par with Wilson.* I'd spent hundreds of hours dueling Wilson, though all that practice was a double-edged blade. Capable of harming me just as easily as it could help me. Spending so much time fighting a single person meant I was tuned to how Wilson fought. *If I try and let muscle memory take over, I'll find myself with a few new holes.*

Our dance went over and over—dodge, dodge, parry, and counter. Slip was indeed quick, but I still held far more *Agility* than any ordinary warrior. That and my decades of training were the only things keeping me alive.

If Slip had any abilities he could use in direct combat, I'd have died within the first minute. *Good thing stealth skills are useless in a straight-up fight.* I kept my footwork light and mobile, not risking standing still for a second. The grass beneath our feet tore free from the ground as we trampled it over and over. Keeping Slip at bay meant I couldn't go on the offensive. We'd been dancing for only a minute now, and unless something changed, I was going to lose. Slip was too fast.

*I need to act now if I have any chance of surviving.*

I stopped moving, giving Slip an opening to attack me, and he did not disappoint. As soon as Slip thrust with his twin daggers, I moved into his space, putting myself off balance and doing pretty much everything Evelyn taught me not to when in close combat if you wanted to stay alive. *Here we go!*

It was a suicidal tactic; either I would get lucky, or Slip's knives would skewer me. His blades sailed towards my chest, I took one in the shoulder, and another stuck into my ribs. *Damn, that stings! Hopefully, he didn't nick anything vital.* I'd find out if my health bar plummeted.

Thankfully it hit low yellow and went no further. A large pool of blood formed at my feet, but I ignored the pain and brought my knee into his solar plexus, crushing the air from his lungs.

Slip doubled over, but remained standing, coughing a large amount of blood onto the grass. Bloody drool dripped from his mouth as he stood. *Must have caused some organ damage, maybe broke a couple of lower ribs.* I charged him before he could regain his composure, but pain from behind me brought me to my knees.

Without looking, I swept my leg out and caught my assailant on the shin, sending him tumbling to the ground. Wolf crashed into my vision, grinning a sick smile. Even though my kick should have fractured his leg, he rose with ease. Warmth poured down my back as I got to my feet. *What the hell did he hit me with?*

I received an answer a second later, as Wolf's hands were encased in ice. Each finger formed a long, deadly claw. *Frost Talon? So, Wolf is an ice mage, but why use that spell?* Fog rose off them and hissed as my blood ran down his fingers, staining them a sticky red. Most ice mages hated it since close combat wasn't their specialty. Whatever the reason, Wolf had turned a useless spell into a deadly style of fighting.

His eyes held a perverse glee at the sight. He grinned and let his true self out to play, bringing his hand up to lick my blood.

"The fuck are you doing?"

Wolf laughed, a sick, twisted laugh that revolted me. "Your blood tastes foul, human. Sickening," he spat, trying to remove the taste.

My back ached, throbbing with every pulse of blood that spilled from my open wounds, slipping down to coat my hand a warm red. I stood, and ice cracked sharply, letting more blood flow down my back. Wolf was on me as soon as I was able to stand, raking at me with his claws. I moved but was hurt; the loss of blood and the pain made me slow.

I blocked his next strike with my forearm, only to have Wolf claw it open. Four long gashes ripped apart my flesh, they were deep and should have been spurting blood, but they weren't. Ice formed inside the wounds, spreading out and covering my skin.

*Frostbite! Shit! Of course, he'd have that passive ability. Need to end this quick, longer we fight, the more it'll spread.* I ignored the rapidly growing shards of ice on my arm and turned my attention to Eris.

She was fighting a weakened Slip, who was still proving himself a challenge. Eris was on him enough that he couldn't go for a weapon, but her attacks were sloppy, and even coughing blood, Slip kept her at bay, but he was racked with a fit of coughs and only halfway blocked a punch from Eris. It slipped off his forearm and connected with his temple. His skull cracked and buckled from the impact, and Slip dropped to the ground like a stone, unconscious.

*By the nine kings of Hell, she's strong.* Eris stood over him, the victor of the fight, but Slip was still a threat and needed to die.

"Eris, kill him."

"Bu—"

"Do it!"

I had to focus on Wolf. He wasn't giving me an inch, moving around me like a ghost, trailing ethereal fog in his wake, slicing my body to pieces. It didn't matter that none of the hits were deep or if they hit a vital area. The frost damage was working its way over my body. Even now, my arm was turning black, and I couldn't feel my fingers.

*If he hits my right arm, I won't be able to hold my sword, and that'll be the end of me.* I was growing weaker by the second. The blood loss and frostbite sapped my remaining strength.

*Shit, shit, shit. I have to get rid of his magic, but what will happen if I use Aura of the Antimage? I have magic inside my heart now, can I survive it?*

My choice was taken from me as Wolf ducked under my weak swing and plunged his claws into my chest, and I couldn't hold back my screams.

I didn't have another option left; I activated *Aura of the Antimage,* and it pulsed along my skin, billowing out in a circle, shredding any magic within it. My heart stopped as the magic inside it dissolved, and I dropped to the ground in blinding agony, but I was still alive.

Antimagic was powerful, but even it couldn't rid me of my Darkness. It was very weak, but it still clung to me. I gasped as I figured out how to breathe again, clutching at my now-beating heart, trying to find the strength to stand.

Wolf stumbled back as his magic shattered, sending shards of ice cascading to the grass, melting in the midday sun. The effects of *Frostbite* faded along with his claws, and blood began to pour from a dozen lacerations in my skin. I uncorked a health potion and drank it down while Wolf recovered from having his magic destroyed.

My health bar climbed into the green, but my battle fatigue was already too high, and I only had a few minutes of fighting left in me. Movement from behind me caused me to turn. Eris came to stand beside me, her hand brushing my own. Slip's lifeless corpse lay a few yards away on the grass, his head snapped and nearly twisted around his body.

"Good job," I told her, pride in my voice.

She jerked her head in a curt nod, not looking at me, staring at Wolf. "The russet-haired one got away, though. He fled when I killed that man."

*Darren? Shit, where'd he go?* I spied a couple of horses in the tree line. There were only five, and one was missing. *Damn it, I didn't want him escaping.*

Wolf was looking at me with surprise, and his sadistic grin only deepened. He opened his mouth wide to showcase his teeth, each of them pointed and sharp.

"Well, well. I expected Darren to flee. He's always been a coward, but that spell wasn't nullification magic, that was antimagic. I didn't think it actually existed. Tell me, human. Who taught you that?"

"Fuck you!" *Like hell will I tell you shit. Besides, Evelyn would kill me if I ever gave her name to a stranger. Especially an enemy.*

Wolf laughed at me. "Fair enough, human, fair enough."

*Why does he keep calling me that? Never mind, Aura is going to time out in a few seconds, which means it'll take around half a minute for his mana to refill enough to use Frost Talon again if memory serves. Need to make that time count.* I looked at Eris. "How are you holding up?"

"I'm fine. My magic is low, but I can still fight."

"All right, back me up. He's incredibly dangerous, and you can't take him by yourself."

Wolf only laughed harder at my words, nearly doubling over from it. "Yes, both of you come to me, let me savor your flesh and marrow."

His laugh deepened, turning to a low growl as he bent over as if in pain. It wasn't until his bones began to crack that I realized the situation, and how utterly screwed we were.

"Eris, run."

The tone of my voice caused her to look at me with fear in her eyes. She tugged on my arm, "What's going on? There's two of u—"

"Go! Take Lacuna and get as far away as you can, now!" I shoved her off me and towards Lacuna. *I'm sorry, no use both of us dying here.* I attacked Wolf before he could finish his transformation. My sword split a gash across his face, which had elongated. Wolf only smiled, using the pain to fuel his shift.

His fist rocketed into my gut, sending me flying, I hit the ground a few feet away and rolled over and up onto my feet. Ignoring the massive amount of pain I was in, I prepared to rush him again, but it was too late.

He'd completely transformed.

Wolf, the man, was gone. In his place stood a massive barrel-chested werewolf. Easily eight feet of rippling muscles, with thick, wiry white fur covering his body. He stood on two legs, shaking off the remains of his armor and roared. Jagged yellowed teeth jutted out from his maw, and Wolf looked at me with hunger in his sickly green eyes.

"Yes, run, run as fast as you can. It makes the meat so much sweeter when it's filled with fear." He spoke with a harsh, guttural tongue.

My heart pounded too loud in my ears, and my skin went cold. It took all I had to muster the courage to move. Wolf lowered onto all fours and was on me before I could take a single step, charging into me and knocking me to the ground. Wolf placed one of his gigantic paws on my chest, pinning me in place. He was salivating, long strands of drool fell from his mouth as his fetid breath rolled over me.

My sword fell from my hands in the charge and lay mere inches away on the grass, just out of my reach. Wolf was savoring my fear, prolonging the kill. His vicious claws dug into me, tearing through my armor with ease and going through my skin and *Exoskeleton* like it was nothing.

I screamed, for I could do nothing else. I gave him what he wanted in spades, screaming till my voice tore and devolved into a ragged croak. All the while pushing away as much of the pain as I could, inching my way towards my hunting knife.

So focused on his own hunger, Wolf was oblivious as he lowered his teeth to my neck. Nicking my flesh and drawing blood, he lapped his sandpaper tongue over my neck. "Still foul, but blood is blood, and I will gorge myself on it before snapping your bones and drinking your marrow."

"Eat this, you furry bastard!"

I pulled my knife free and jammed it to the hilt in Wolf's eye. He howled in agony and rage, jumping off me and trying to shake the knife free from its lodging. Blood and vitreous fluid ran down his face and into his mouth as he kept screaming. I got up from the ground and made it two steps before my battle fatigue maxed out, and my entire body seized up.

*Shit! Not now, not now!* I yelled in rage, but I couldn't move my body anymore. I was helpless as Wolf rose on two legs and pulled the knife free from his face, it thudded into the dirt as he dropped it and stalked over to me, his face twisted in pain.

"I was going to make your death quick, but now you will suffer," Wolf stepped onto my leg and ever so slowly applied pressure until my leg snapped like a twig.

My screams turned to whimpers as shock set in. While under the effects of battle fatigue, I could do nothing but scream as he took his time breaking my bones. My health redlined, and with the blood steadily leaking from me, I wouldn't last much longer.

Wolf shot up as a blur rushed past, slamming into him and knocking him off me. It was Eris, but as I'd never seen her before. Covered head to toe in jagged black chitin, she attacked Wolf with savage fury.

Eris's eyes glowed with ethereal green light, and smoke trailed from her hands, as she hit Wolf over and over again in an unhinged frenzy, screaming at him. "Don't you touch him!"

Her strength was incredible, but even it couldn't overpower a werewolf. Wolf's fist caught her across the jaw and sent her to the dirt. She scrambled to her feet in a second and managed to get her hands up to block a second swing. Her chitin armor held under the blow, but even in wolf form, he was still an excellent fighter, and Eris couldn't measure up.

He grabbed her by the forearm and flung her to the ground. His sharp claws raked at her chest and face, only to glance off the chitin. They couldn't get through her carapace armor. Wolf roared in frustration and backed off Eris.

With a few growled words in Script, Wolf cast *Frost Talon* once more.

I stared, unable to do anything until my battle fatigue lowered, but I was seething. *A werewolf mage? How unfair is that?* Wolf slashed with his frost-coated talons. His previous speed was hampered by his massive size, and his white fur matted with blood and sweat as he continued his onslaught. Eris backed away and dodged what she could, her chitin armor granting her much better speed than before, but wolf managed to land several hits.

Slowly, her chitin chipped and cracked, with each landed hit, ice formed, and if it broke open, the ice would eat away at her flesh. Eris stopped retreating and ducked under Wolf's next attack, getting into his space and digging into his chest with her pointed claws. Wolf tried to pry her loose, but she held firm until he pulled her free with howls of pain, along with huge bloody chunks of flesh and fur stuck in her hands.

She clambered up to his back as he cried in pain and perched on his shoulders. Eris thrust toward his face and dug her pointed claws into Wolf's face, taking his eye with a fountain of blood.

Blind and in utter misery, Wolf reached above and tossed Eris off him. She landed on her back, hard, tearing up dirt and grass as she rolled. She stood and ran at the blind wolf, confident of her success now that he was sightless, but she was overconfident.

Eris attacked at Wolf's back, but faster than she could react, Wolf countered, kicking her in the chest and crumbling even more of her armor.

"Stupid bitch, you reek of the deep woods, and even if I can't see, I can still smell you. You can't escape me, and I will grind your bones to dust for taking my eye, you and the human."

She stood firm. "I won't let you lay another finger on him!" she shouted, her voice echoing with her truth.

Wolf sniffed the air, the breeze bringing the smell of Eris to him, he pinpointed her location and smiled. "Then die and nourish me with your blood!"

I blinked, and Wolf was gone, on Eris in seconds, rending her armor asunder with his frosted claws. His swipe took her across the face, shredding her chitin and slicing a deep groove across her cheek. Blood poured down the right side of her head but trickled to a stop as *Frostbite* took hold. *Godsdamn it! She's going to lose! Fucking get up and do something, or Eris is going to die!*

*"Now, do you desire my power?"*

*Yes, shit, just let me help her!*

*"Very well."*

**Warning! Forceful Activation of Hive Guard.**

Black ooze pooled out of my skin to cover me, and a pleasant warmth spread from within my chest. As the chitin faded back under my skin. I was whole and unblemished. My battle fatigue was at zero, and even my cooldowns had been lowered.

Eris continued her losing fight, not giving Wolf any ground, but she was fighting the clock, and each passing second pushed her closer to death. The fight had been going on only for a handful of minutes, but it felt like hours. Eris, in a desperate attempt, used the last of her fleeting magic and summoned a horde of red wasps.

They swarmed by the thousands to the Hive Queen, drifting above her head like a crimson cloud, waiting for orders.

"Kill him."

They obeyed, their buzzing intensified, forming into a droning battle cry as they attacked, twisting and turning like a corkscrew in midair, sailing towards Wolf. Who was blind to the oncoming horror, but the buzz was unmistakable, and Wolf brought his frozen hands up in an attempt to fend them off.

He swatted to and fro, freezing the very air as his hands passed through dozens of the creatures, killing them instantly, slaughtering scores of them at a time, but it was useless; they froze on his talons, sticking to them. Each time one died, another ten took its place.

Hundreds of the wasps made it past his swipes and crawled over his arms, stinging him, but they were doing minimal damage—his fur was too thick.

Eris was doing everything she could to remain standing, but *Frostbite* and her depleting mana were sapping what little strength remained. *Soon as Wolf dies, so too does his magic. I have to end this.* Eris and her insects had helped, but precious few remained, a hundred at most, and each passing second Wolf killed more and more of them.

I picked up my sword from the ground and waited for an opening. *Poison Blade* activated as I closed my hand over my weapon, slithering out to drench my steel.

I called out to Eris, "Go for the face!"

She nodded and raised a trembling hand, pouring what remained of her magic out in a final command. "Attack his head!"

The wasps followed her order, and all swarmed to Wolf's face, covering it entirely.

They crawled over his ruined eyes and into his nose and mouth, Wolf roared in rage, his maw snapped shut and he swallowed a dozen or more, but more just kept coming. Each time he tried to breathe, more wasps entered his mouth and stung him repeatedly, clogging his throat with their lifeless bodies. His entire focus was on the swarm, giving me my opening.

I ran, my sword raised as I charged the werewolf. I flew across the ground as fast as I could, but Wolf still heard me coming, some small part of his brain rational enough to turn towards the sound. He looked dead at me, baring his throat to me in the process. He swiped, but his hands were heavy with frozen wasps, and his swipes were easy to avoid.

My sword connected with his neck, and I put my entire strength behind the blade. Resistance met me, and for half a millisecond, I feared it wouldn't go through, but his thick sinew gave way under my sword. Slicing through his neck and drenching me in blood. I'd given him an opening, and he punched through my chest with an errant swing from his claws, puncturing a few organs, and knocked my blade from my hands, sending me to the dirt.

Wolf gurgled as his blood poured freely from his throat, his hands trying in vain to close the wound. He dropped to his knees and slumped to the grass as the rest of his blood ran from him.

*We...we did it...*

I was too exhausted to celebrate. Everything hurt, and with each passing second, my consciousness waned as the blood loss caught up with me. Eris looked over to me, her magic drained to the last drop, and her chitin armor flowed to retreat under her skin. Her entire body was covered in frost, and her skin was turning a sickly blue-black as necrosis set in. She gave me the barest hint of a smile before toppling over, slamming into the grass.

"Eris!" I ran to her and knelt, scooping her into my arms. The grass soft underneath me as I leaned her against my chest. "Eris, wake up!"

Her eyes fluttered open for a second, and I took her hand in mine. She managed one more smile. "Did we get him?"

I smiled back. "Yeah, we got him."

# Chapter 19 - The Serpent's Tail

Her head lolled to the side as she passed out. I shouted at her to wake up, but she was out.

"Eris!"

Nothing, not even a flicker of her eyelids. Blood ran in rivers from her face and body, bleeding from a dozen different locations, all while the after-effects of *Frostbite* ate away at her flesh. *Not good, need to heal her and fast before it permanently damages her.*

I pulled my pack from my inventory and laid Eris's head on it while uncapping a health potion and pressing the glass to her lips. But she wouldn't drink, the red liquid falling from her mouth to run down her chin.

*Fuck it.* I poured a good measure into my mouth and pressed my lips to hers, forcing them apart and letting the liquid drain down her throat. I repeated the action until the potion was empty, and her wounds had closed. Her skin restitched itself, and the frostbite faded into nothingness. Eris's breathing stabilized, and she slept deeply.

*Okay, now, to take care of myself.* I drank a health potion myself and waited for it to kick in. My body repaired itself, but not without a cost. I'd consumed too many potions in a short period, warranting potion sickness, but I'd gone beyond even that, overloading my system, and I was about to pay for it with interest.

**Warning! System Overload! Shutting down to repair the damage.**

Without any further warning, I fell into unconsciousness.

I awoke to pain, mind-numbing agony that sent waves of misery through my veins with every beat of my pulse. The minuscule light drifting in through the thick heavy curtains was enough to send spikes of pain into my retinas. *Fuck, I forgot how awful this was.* System overload sucked, but I was riding the tail end of it, and even it hurt like hell, I could move around normally now. I sat up, giving myself a once over. I was naked, but I didn't have any visible wounds. Pulling my last set of clean clothes from my inventory, I put on a short-sleeved black tunic and black linen pants.

Just the act of getting dressed hurt and fighting the urge to hurl, I swung my legs out of bed. As my feet hit the wooden floor, I had a thought. *Where the hell am I?* I didn't recognize the surroundings, but it seemed I was in a house. I could smell farmland through the open window and pushed back the curtain, flinching as bright light hit my face.

Blinking back tears, I tried once more to get my bearings. Outside was a field of barley, and I recognized the landscape. *Am I back at Oscar's? But how did I get here? Eris?!* The fight came back to me instantly, and I strode across the small room and flew through the door.

"Eris!"

Both she and Oscar were seated at the dining table, having a meal. Eris had her hood down, and her pointed ears and compound eyes were easily visible, and Oscar didn't seem to mind in the slightest.

While I was taking stock of the situation, Eris sucked in a sharp breath. "Sam!" Eris shouted, plowing into me and sending me flying to the ground.

I managed to croak out a pained "Ow," before my mouth was occupied. Her lips were scorching as she kissed me before pulling away a second later and wrapping me in a crushing hug.

"You wouldn't wake up, no matter what I tried. I couldn't get you to wake up," she blubbered into my chest, on the verge of tears.

308

I leaned over and brushed her hair back. "I'm fine, Eris, don't worry about me."

"Why didn't you wake up?"

"It was the price I had to pay. I overdid it and was punished for it."

She punched me weakly—well, to her—but it was hard enough to numb my arm.

"I was terrified. I woke up, and you were unconscious on the ground." She punched me again. "Don't ever do that again."

I chuckled. "I'll do my best." to which her response was to hug me tighter for a few more minutes. When she was satisfied with her hugging, she leaned back and kissed me on the cheek.

"I'm glad you're all right."

"Me too, but how did we get here?"

Eris sat up and stood, pulling me up along with her. After her outburst, she calmed down considerably, and we went to sit next to Oscar, who went and fetched a beer for me. I took it with a nod and turned to face Eris.

"When I woke up, I tried everything to get you to wake up, but you wouldn't, so I wanted to make camp and wait it out, but all the supplies were in your inventory, so I couldn't. I picked you up and put you on Lacuna and walked here. Oscar was gracious enough to let us stay while you recovered. You've been unconscious for over two days."

*Only two? That's actually pretty generous, considering the last time I overdid it, I was asleep for nearly a week.* I took a drink of beer and thought things through while I pulled up my interface. I had several combat notifications to deal with.

**Combat Results**
*7 Killed (Human): 10,500 Exp!*
*1 Downed: 1500 Exp!*

*Mercy Penalty: -500 Exp.*

*Total Exp Gain: 11,500 Exp!*

*Exp: 4600/4600*

*Level Up! (x2)*

*Exp: 2300/4800*

*Level 48*

*20 Skill Points Available*

*Damn, that's a ton of Exp. How unbalanced is this system? It's getting a little ridiculous. Though it looks like I didn't get any Exp for the men Eris killed. I wounded Slip, but Eris got the kill, so I only received an assist. Still worth it, and I can't really complain about the abundance of Exp. Wolf just about slaughtered us.*

The massive Exp seemed a worthwhile amount for what we'd gone through. *Two against a werewolf, and we won. The Guild will never believe it, though I bet Yumiko will get a kick out of it.*

I closed the notifications tab and allocated my new stat points, putting five of each into *Strength* and *Constitution,* bringing both up to ninety. A solid feat for a level forty-eight. While previously, I'd prioritized *Strength* and *Agility,* having my *Constitution* so high this early made me much more durable than most others my level. But most players wouldn't be so unbalanced in their stats.

With ten stat points remaining, I decided to add them to my *Strength* and *Constitution Sub-Stats.* I added five points to my *Attack Damage* and five to *Durability,* ensuring that I could continue to do both attacking and defending.

My *Exoskeleton* shifted under my skin as I confirmed my points. *Does increasing my Durability also affect the resistance of my chitin?* An exciting line of thought.

With my stats settled, that left one problem to deal with.

"How much, Oscar?"

He turned to me with confusion before smiling. "Oh, it's no trouble, friend. There's no need for payment."

"That wasn't what I was talking about," I said, sliding my knife free from its sheath. "How much did they pay you to set us up?"

Oscar paled, which was all the confirmation I needed for my theory. He stood from the chair and started stammering.

"What are you talking about, Duran?" he asked, tripping over his words.

"Sam?" Eris asked, her head tilted to the side.

I stuck the point of my knife into the wood of the table, causing both of them to flinch.

"We were ambushed just outside the Outlier Farms. Darren and his filth were waiting for us, so someone tipped them off. I'll ask one more time, Oscar. How much did they pay you?"

Oscar deflated, sighing into his hands, his face red with shame. "They didn't pay me nuthin'. The leader kidnapped my wife, told me to keep an eye out for a red-haired male and a young demi-human. I was told to stall you if I could, and he gave me a communication scroll to warn him. Please believe me, I had no choice."

From the look in his eyes to the timbre of his voice, I could tell he was speaking the truth, but it didn't matter. It didn't change what I had to do next.

"I do believe you, Oscar. I believe that you were only thinking of your wife and felt you had no choice, but you put me—and more importantly, Eris—in danger, and that's not something I can forgive."

Pulling the knife free from the table, I stood. Oscar panicked and fell backward out of his chair, landing in the kitchen. He scooted back in fear but hit the wooden counter a foot later.

"I'll make it quick, if it's any consolation," I told him.

I stepped into the kitchen and raised the blade to slash his throat when Eris stopped me. She grabbed my hand and pulled me off balance.

"Stop, Sam. I know he wronged us, but put yourself in his place. What would you have done?"

"I'd kill anyone who dared get in my way to get you back."

"Okay, but not everyone is as strong as you. I'm asking you to see reason. You don't have to kill him."

I knew I didn't have to kill him. He didn't have much choice in the matter, and realistically in his shoes, powerless against greater odds, I'd have made the exact same call. But it was a mistake to let enemies live.

Eris was pleading for Oscar's life, but all of this was her fault.

"None of this would have happened if you'd let me kill Darren and his fucking friends back at the inn," I said, jabbing a finger at her. "All of this happened because of your soft heart."

Eris reeled back like I'd slapped her. Hurt filled her eyes as they watered, brimming with tears. *Ah, hell.*

"You're right. I'm sorry," she said, pushing past me to rush outside.

"Fuck," I cursed, before turning to Oscar. "If you run, I'll hunt you to the ends of the earth and butcher you like a dog."

He nodded emphatically, but I was already heading for the door.

Outside, I frantically searched for her. I ran around the house and found her. Eris was sitting on a small stone fence that came waist-high, separating Oscar's backyard from the road. Her head was in her hands, and she was shaking, crying.

More than anything else, I felt like an utter jackass for making her cry. Just because I was right didn't give me the justification to shove it her face like I had. She was too consumed with her tears to hear me approach on the soft grass I knelt and wrapped my arms around her, placing my forehead in between her shoulders.

"I'm sorry."

She shook her head. "You're right, though. I let all this happen. You warned me, but I didn't listen."

"Doesn't make what I said okay, though, or what I was about to do to Oscar. I was furious that you got hurt, and I was going to kill him because he put you in danger, but you weren't wrong, I'd have done the same thing in his place."

Eris looked up and turned around, pulling my face to hers. Tears were still falling down her cheeks, but she curled into my neck, holding me tight. "I love you, Sam, but you can be so cold to others. Killing just to get rid of an obstacle isn't always the correct thing to do."

I cupped her cheek, rubbing away the streaks of tears with my thumb. "And sometimes it is, Eris. If I'd killed Darren, despite the darkness pushing my anger at the time, none of this would have happened. We nearly died because I let them live."

"I know, but it can't always be the first thing you jump to, especially for people like Oscar, okay? Promise me, that you'll try to consider other options in the future."

I sighed, pulling back from her, hopping over the fence to sit next to her. I didn't say anything for a few minutes, trying to work out my thoughts. The more I thought about it, the more I knew I could never keep that promise.

"I can't, Eris. I'll do what I think is best to keep us both safe. Even if that means I have to wade through an ocean of blood to do it."

Eris chuckled, smiling at me. "You're the most stubborn person I've ever met."

"Right back at you," I said, laughing.

"I'll just have to be your moral compass then. I'll keep you on track."

"One hell of a job, you sure you're up for it?" I teased.

"Of course, my bonded. There's no one better," Eris said, leaning over to kiss me.

Her lips, her soft and welcoming lips. Whatever lingering tension between us dissolved with that one kiss. We forgave each other, and nothing more needed to be said between us about it. When we pulled apart, I stood to go back inside and decide what I was going to do with Oscar, but Eris held my hand and refused to let go.

"What is it?"

"There's something we need to talk about," she said.

Her tone was worrisome, but after what we just talked about, I wasn't nervous. *Whatever it is, we'll deal with it together.*

"I should have figured it out much sooner, and for that I'm sorry. It's about the Aspect inside you."

"The what?"

"The voice, the entity that spoke during the fight."

"You called it the Aspect. What is it?"

Eris ran her hands through her hair, trying to find the right words. "It's…hard to explain," she said, before pausing again. "It's kind of like a spirit, but that's not quite right. The Aspect of the Hive is a guide for the Hive Knights. A collection of memories and bits of consciousness of all the previous bearers of the title."

"So, it's supposed to help the knights?" I asked.

"It's supposed to, yes, but yours is acting unusually. It's violent and malicious when it's supposed to be very peaceful."

I paced in the dirt, trying to process and come up with answers. *I knew the anger wasn't my own, but I really should have spoken up when it started talking to me.* We didn't have much time to sit around discussing this, but my curiosity and nervousness made this conversation critical. I wanted to find out why I'm the one that was different.

"Is it because I'm human?"

Eris shrugged her shoulders. "I honestly don't know. I was kept away from much of the internal politics of the regency when my mother ruled, so I don't know much. I'll have to consult the Hive Mind more to see what I can find. I looked through it while you were unconscious, and that's when I found a bit of memory concerning the Aspect, but it was very brief."

"Well, I guess I'll just deal with it like I have been. Despite the increased anger, it did help during the fight with Darren."

"But at what cost? Just be careful, Sam. I don't trust it."

I leaned over and kissed her hair. "Now, that I *can* promise you."

She stood up and held out her hand. "Let's go talk with Oscar. Just talk, okay?"

"We'll see."

Oscar was sitting at the table when we got back inside. Three empty glasses next to him told me he was drinking his way through his stock of beer, and if I were in his shoes, that be my final act as well. His fourth mug slammed down empty as I shut the door. Oscar looked up and down at his empty glass with a sigh.

"Can I have one more?"

"Long as you bring me one."

While Oscar fetched us more alcohol, I thought about what I wanted to do. Anger that had nothing to do with the Aspect bubbled to the surface. I wanted to end him solely because he'd betrayed me, but after listening to Eris, I couldn't kill him in good conscience anymore. It was only barely justifiable in the first place.

Oscar returned and handed me my beer, but I left it untouched on the table. "Tell me, Oscar. Where is your wife?"

"I don't know," he said, shaking his head. "All I know is I was told she was being kept safe in a house near the ambush site and that she'd be returned to me when it was all over."

"Hmm." *It's not much to go on at all, but we were a few miles away from both the Outlier Farms and Grange. So how many houses could be out that way? If Eris uses her magic to search the area, then I bet we could find it quickly.*

Oscar looked to me with hope in his eyes as he realized we might just help him. "Please, please, please, help find my wife."

On cue, a quest icon flared to life in my vision, telling me I had a quest available.

**Quest: Find Oscar's Wife**
**Type: Random**
**Difficulty: D**
**Reward: 350 Exp**

As I accepted the quest, I sighed in relief. *At last, something about the game world makes sense again. No ridiculous amount of experience for a menial quest.* I was starting to think the game had broken with how much it was doling out for experience, but this quest proved that the game world was just fine.

*Though, if the game is working as it should, why the hell am I gaining so much Exp for combat?*

"All right. We'll find your wife."

Oscar's face blossomed from hope to relief as he sunk to the floor. "Thank you, thank you!"

"Yeah, whatever. The Gloom Knights complete a quest no matter the cost, so I'll bring back your wife. I promise."

316

He looked up, registered what I'd said, and the color drained from his face. "The—the Gloom—oh by Whisper's lips."

I didn't bother responding. Eris and I quickly left Oscar's and went to search the area. As we climbed atop Lacuna, Eris chuckled. "I see what you meant when you said your guild was infamous. Poor Oscar was practically shaking."

I snickered. "Blow up one noble's manor, and suddenly we're degenerate criminals. Though it did help us with our reputation with the Merchants Guild after that, so it wasn't all bad."

We made it back to the field where we'd been ambushed in an hour, and after nearly three days, there was very little sign that we'd almost lost our lives. None of the dead men's gear or loot was still around. After twenty-four hours, it was deleted from the world, which was a shame, but nothing I could do about it now. *Damn, a few high-tier weapons and armor would have fetched decent coin in once of Central's markets. Oh, well.*

There wasn't a scrap of blood or anything left in the field; only the trampled and torn grass told we'd been there at all.

"All right, Eris, do your thing."

Eris nodded and spread her arms out, calling upon the magic within her. It came quickly, pooling in the palms of her hands and spilling over to fall to the ground. It took her a few minutes, but I assumed she'd found something when her eyes snapped opened and she canceled her spell.

"I might have found it."

"Figured it wouldn't take long, where is it?"

She pointed to the east, toward the forest. "Not far from here."

"Is that not far in Eris speak? Because last time I asked you for directions, we spent twenty minutes walking in the sun," I said with a cheeky grin.

317

She laughed, then playfully poked me in the chest. "It's like five minutes from here, love. Don't worry."

Following Eris's lead, I guided Lacuna through the forest to search for the safe house.

Eris was right this time, as it only took us a few minutes to find it, but if I wasn't searching for it and without her help, I'd have gone past it and never known it was there.

The safe house was a long, wooden cabin with a porch. It was meant to look worn down and abandoned, but the wood was of good quality, and the single-story cabin was too well built if you looked at it closely. Rotten wood and vegetation had been piled up around the house and roof to further disguise it from anyone who came near, but they couldn't hide it from Eris.

We climbed off Lacuna, and I drew my sword, *Poison Blade* activated and salivated to taste Darren's flesh. *He might still be here, or if he were smart, he'd be on the other side of the continent by now.*

The wooden steps leading to the porch didn't so much as creak as I ascended the three steps. *Further proof this wasn't some forgotten cabin in the woods.* Creeping to the door, I listened for any sounds inside but could hear nothing through the sounds of the forest.

"One person is inside, Sam. They're breathing slow. I can't hear anything else though, so be careful," Eris said, her ears twitching as she crouched beside me.

"You're amazing, you know that?"

She tried to hide her smile, but it broke wide on her face. "No, so keep telling me."

Getting back to business, I gripped my sword tight and tried the knob. It was locked.

"Damn, locked. But I don't see a keyhole?"

318

"What do we do?" she asked as we stood up.

"We do things my way," I said, planting my feet and kicking the door.

My foot connected just to the left of the doorknob, the weakest point on the door, and the lock broke under my strength. I went in first, surveying the area while Eris stood at my back, her hands already forming jagged claws as the chitin oozed out of her pores.

The space was clean, but there was disorganization everywhere. Papers, supplies, and clothing were strewn about at random, as if someone had rushed through in a hurry before leaving. I ignored the mess and checked the place over to make sure we wouldn't be ambushed again.

The kitchen told me nothing, neither did the bathroom, which left only the bedroom to deal with. I crept through the hallway and jiggled the knob, unlocked. Twisting it as quietly as I could, I readied myself and flung the door open.

Inside the room was a sparse room with a single queen bed on a hand-carved wooden frame, a nightstand next to it, and a full body mirror in the corner. A chair was at the foot of the bed, and sitting there, tied up, was our target.

Oscar's wife had probably been striking once when she was younger, but like her husband, the years of hard farm work had whittled her refined features and left precious little beauty in its wake. Her hair was long and thin; gray strands stuck to her sweat-stained face while her thin, pinched face held deep laugh lines and crow's feet.

Her yellow shirt and gray pants were ripped in a few places, and her breathing was labored. I rushed across the room and cut the ties that bound her. She toppled over immediately, but I caught her and carried her to the bed and pulled a skin of water from my inventory. Pressing it to her lips, I got her to drink a few mouthfuls.

I kept plying her with water until the skin was empty, and she opened her eyes. Her milky brown eyes stared into mine.

"Who…are you?" she asked.

"Your husband sent me to rescue you."

"Oscar? Is he all right?"

"He's fine. Can you stand?"

She nodded and rose weakly to sit up on the bed. Several days without food or water had taken their toll, but after a few days rest and some good food, I thought she'd be fine.

When I was sure she could stand on her own without falling over, I introduced her to Eris. She was taken aback by her appearance at first, but no one could fight against Eris's personality, and by the time she was ready to leave, they were laughing together.

"Eris, can you take her back to Oscar? I want to have a look around here."

She nodded. "Of course."

"Thank you," I said, kissing her quickly. "Keep your hood up and come back quickly."

Eris helped Oscar's wife to Lacuna and set off back to the farms. *All right, someone left in a hurry, so let's see if they left anything I can use to find out where Darren went.*

I had no proof, but Darren had bragged about his boss, someone who was incredibly wealthy and was buying up things of value. I had a hunch that they were connected to the attack on Gloom-Harbor. *The Order of the Dawn weren't cheap, and there can't be that many faceless people throwing around that kind of money. My gut is telling me they're connected.*

But despite my hunch, I couldn't find any evidence to support my theory. All of the papers I went through were nothing of import, just bills of sale for several slaves. Though the prices were a little high.

"Damn." *Nothing here. But it's a lead of sorts. Maybe throwing Darren's name around will scare up some info.*

I finished going through everything and sighed in defeat. Laying back on the bed, I waited for Eris to return. A blinking notification told me when she'd returned the kidnapped wife.

**Quest: Find Oscar's Wife**
**Completed!**
**Reward: 3500 Exp!**

*Wait, what?*

I could have sworn that it was only three hundred and fifty experience for the quest. Just to double-check I hadn't misread the quest, I pulled up my interface logs and went to the original quest. *Yep, it says three-fifty all right. What the actual fuck?*

I thought back to whatever presence took hold of Eris. *It said I wouldn't survive as I was. Is this its way of helping me?*

**Exp: 4800/4800**
**Level Up!**
**10 Stat points available.**
**Level: 49**
**Exp: 1000/4900**

I wasn't in the mood to deal with my stats, and I quickly assigned them to both *Strength and Constitution*, bringing them both to one hundred. My head was reeling from the implications of what I should have realized much sooner. *The only thing that can affect the world like this is the governing AI. The serpent which devours itself? Ouroboros.*

Why Ouroboros wanted to bend the rules of the game world to help me, I couldn't fathom, but I didn't like it one bit. *I don't have a clue, but guess I shouldn't complain. I'm leveling faster than anyone else ever has before, so why does it leave a pit in my stomach?*

Eris returned while I was grappling with myself, trying to make sense of everything and failing. I was missing too much information, and what little clues I did have weren't enough to make any headway. *Whatever, figure it out later when I have more info. There are other things I have to deal with right now.*

Eris walked in with a big smile, carrying two rabbits. "Hello, love. I brought dinner," she said, glowing with pride.

"Excellent, I'm starving."

I prepared the rabbits in the unused kitchen. This was a safe house of sorts, but the utensils in the kitchen were spotless, and the rather impressive spice rack was completely untouched. I grabbed some fresh logs from the woodpile just outside the house and got a fire going in the woodstove. Next came cleaning the rabbits.

Eris watched me as I carefully peeled the skin from the meat and removed the organs. The pair of rabbits were plump, and even if rabbit wasn't my favorite, they'd both make good meals.

"I'm impressed. I didn't know you could hunt."

"Well, it's not that impressive, unfortunately. I took control of a few of my little ones, and it was easy to find the rabbit den. After that, I used a few of my wandering spiders to sneak in and bite the rabbits."

I was still impressed. *Her magic really is incredible. Her only downfall is how weak she is right now. As soon as she gets stronger, she'll be amazing.*

Once the rabbits were cleaned. I discarded the offal and rubbed a blend of herbs into the meat before I threw them on the skillet to fry.

"Eris, could you peel the potatoes, please?"

"Of course," she said, beaming.

She got to work on the potatoes and veggies while I coated the cast iron skillet in a mixture of butter and animal fat. The grease popped as the pan heated up. Eris hummed while she worked, and even though there was plenty of room in the kitchen, she kept close enough that her arm rubbed against my own several times.

I cooked the meat and boiled the potatoes while I threw in the carrots, onions, and a half clove of garlic to the pan along with more butter and a dash of flour to make the roux. When it was done, I mashed the potatoes and poured the thick roux over them with a fried rabbit for each of us.

While I got the table ready, Eris went outside and brought back a wineskin half her size. She set it by the kitchen counter and went and retrieved two tankards in one of the cabinets.

"Oscar gave it to us after I brought Mira back to him."

"Well, all things considered, it was the least he could do."

She smacked my arm. "Don't be rude."

"The man helped set us up, yet I'm the rude one?"

Eris laughed and sat down next to me. "Of course, you are, love. Now let's eat. I'm famished."

Without waiting on me, Eris tucked in with vigor and devoured the food. Even if Oscar betrayed us, his beer was almost worth it, and I drank half my weight in it before my stomach begged me to slow down.

Halfway through dinner, I began to feel a little off. I chalked it up to the copious amount of alcohol I drank and slowed down, but the feeling persisted. By the time dinner was over, I was certain something was off; my breathing increased, and my face was hot.

"Um, Eris, I think something's wrong."

She looked over at me, noticed my flushed face, and stood up. "What's wrong?"

"I dunno, I kinda feel like I've been drugged."

My thoughts were sluggish, and I couldn't concentrate. *How did I get drugged, was it the food? No, I cooked everything myself. Wait a second. Eris brought the rabbits!*

"Eris, would the venom in the spiders be harmful?"

She shook her head. "Absolutely not. Entomancers are immune to—"

"I'm not an entomancer, Eris!"

"Uh-oh."

I stood up in a panic. I had a health potion in my hand when Eris started giggling. *What?*

"Why are you laughing?"

"Because you're not poisoned...well, you are, but it's not going to harm you."

"Explain!"

Eris walked over to me and put a hand on my shoulder, trying to calm me. "Entomancers are immune to all toxins, but the other races of the Hive weren't as adept at filtering them from their systems. Though venom and poison didn't harm them, it was discovered that it had a few unforeseen side effects."

"What side effects?"

She pointed at my waist and I looked down to see my manhood standing at full attention, straining against my pants. *Oh...that kind of side effect.*

"So, you're telling me that spider venom is an aphrodisiac?"

"If that word means that it increases a person's longing and desire, then yes."

*Great, she accidentally roofied me. Fantastic.*

"Well, what do we do about it?"

"I guess you could drink the potion and flush it from your system, or..." she said, leaving me hanging.

"Or?"

Eris slipped her hand down my pants to grip my erection while giving me a look of pure need.

*Oh...option two it is, then.*

# Chapter 20 - Mnemosyne

Her hand, along my length, sent waves of lust through me, and all I wanted was her. The venom amplified my need for her, but it was still my desire. I wanted her because I wanted her, and that was enough for me.

I lifted her into my arms and carried her to the bedroom. The hallway seemed miles long, but before I could blink, I was poised over the bed. Eris slipped free from my arms and slithered to rest on the plain gray comforter. She gripped my pants and pulled them down, exposing me to her fully. It was an inch from her face, and her eyes glinted as she blushed before trailing a finger down my shaft.

"You know, in the seven people that picked up my crystal, as I peered into their souls, quite a few had very similar experiences, and I've always wanted to try one of them."

With only the briefest of hesitation, she took me into her mouth.

Though inexperienced, she had good instincts as she worked, back and forth in a hypnotic rhythm. Eris's tongue explored my manhood with abandon. I shuddered as her powerful muscles slipped around me. She kept her momentum as she worked, bobbing her head back and forth as her mouth slipped around me. It only took a few minutes to work me to my peak.

I wasn't ready for that, and just before I couldn't contain myself, I pulled back, my shaft slipping from her lips with a subtle pop.

"By the nine kings of Hell, that was fantastic," I said, my breathing labored and tense.

Eris smiled at me, a dopey look on her face. "I can see now why people enjoy that; it was…interesting."

"Shall I return the favor?"

She cocked her head to the side. "Return the…oh, yes. I think I'd like that."

I bent low, settling on my knees as Eris leaned back and opened her legs, baring her opening. Moving my hands to the outside of her hips, I pulled her closer to me, and she scooted toward me with a soft squeak of surprise before blushing.

Instead of just diving in, I teased her. I wanted her to fully experience the moment, so I started slow. I moved my hands slowly around her thighs as I caressed her perfect skin. My fingertips slid close enough to her opening that the heat radiating from her licked at the tips of my fingers as Eris moaned under my touch.

I brought my mouth to her leg as I caressed down her smooth calf, pressing my lips to her skin just once before flicking my tongue out. Eris squirmed, running her hands through my hair as I reached the meat of her inner thigh and bit down gently.

She spasmed, clamping down around my head as she stifled her cries of pleasure. I slid kisses up her thigh as I inched toward her sex. I moved my mouth to her wetness and gave it a tentative lick.

Eris had a surprising flavor to her; it was unlike anything I'd ever tasted before. She tasted of the earth, of the deep forest. Pine and ash, along with wood rot and of something darker, of the creatures that dwelled long forgotten. It was sweet, earthy, and bitter at the same time, but it wasn't unpleasant.

My tongue brushed strokes of ardor in careful arcs as I licked her, probing deeper with each pass. I gripped her hips tight, and my fingernails dug into her flesh, but she only moaned and ran her hands through my hair. Quicker than I'd have liked, I worked her up to her own climax, but instead of stopping, I increased my rhythm, bringing her to the edge and tempting her over. Eris screamed out in ecstasy as she came, digging her fingers into my scalp and shaking with effort.

As she rode her crescendo, something changed within me. The venom still coursed through my system, but something stirred deep within my heart and flooded through my veins. It filled my head with ice and burned my loins. All I could think about was Eris, taking her as my own, and so I did.

Eris was still coming down, but I didn't give her any more time to recover. Picking her up in my arms, I wrapped her in my embrace and kissed her before pressing myself against her sex. Before I could move, she clenched around me, forcing me into her.

"Sam!"

She groaned in rapture as I thrust in and out, letting gravity press her entirely on my length each time. Her legs clung around my waist while her ankles came to rest at the back of my knees; each time she clenched around me, she locked her legs, sending my hips forward and my shaft deeper inside.

All that mattered was the need that demanded to be slaked, and I took her with the primal instincts of an animal.

When my arms began to tire, I used the burning to fuel my desire even further. I shifted, turning toward the nightstand, the burning candlelight sent shadows dancing over Eris's skin, lighting the beads of sweat that slipped down her neck to rest along her prominent collarbone.

I extinguished the flame between my fingers and knocked the candle to the floor, ripping the curtain from the window in the process. Soft moonlight bathed the room in an ethereal glow as I rested Eris on the nightstand and continued.

With each thrust, Eris elicited a different moan, and I was determined to hear them all by the time I was done. Everything else ceased to matter but her, but the connection we had with our flesh. There was no tenderness, only desire.

I pushed into her again and again, as furiously and intensely as my body would allow. I lost count of how many times Eris climaxed, but there was an ever-present need to reach one more. Eris never said a word in complaint, only moaned my name over and over as she lost herself in the sex.

We were so desperate for one another that we lost all reason. After the fifth climax, a new sound joined us, the ripping and breaking of wood. Eris tore deep chunks from the nightstand as she gripped it. The furniture was crafted of solid oak, and rather than see it as the frightening display of strength that it was, it only made me want to work harder.

I bent over, trailing my tongue from the peak of her breasts to the nape of her neck and opened my mouth, biting softly.

Eris shuddered and moaned, gripping my back with her fingers, digging into my flesh. Warm blood slipped down my back, but I didn't care.

The rest of the night was a blur; as we went on, more and more of my rationality faded away into pure hunger, and I lost control of myself. Through our bond, my need bled over to Eris and rolled her under along with me. Her eyes were bleary and unfocused as we abandoned all reason.

After that, I lost sense of time, and the only thing I cared about was Eris's flesh in my hands.

When I finally came back to myself, be it hours or centuries later, we both lay tangled together on the bed. The pillows and comforter strewn about on the floor, and we were filthy with sweat.

Eris was curled against my side, her hair a mess, but I was enamored with the nape of her neck as it fell to her spine and back. Her vertebrae pressed against her porcelain skin as she breathed in and out deeply. I placed my hand just above her ribs and slowly caressed toward her hips and backside, marveling at the perfection of her skin.

A flash of red on my bicep drew my attention. A thin droplet of blood snaked from my bicep to my shoulder and continued towards my neck. *Did I bite my lip in my sleep?*

It wasn't just on my arm, a thick drip of dried blood was on my chest as well. *What the hell?*

Looking myself over, I didn't have any injures, and it was then that I took in my surroundings. The gray sheets were stained red, a deep splotch of it under the two of us. I wasn't bleeding, so that left only one conclusion. Turing Eris on her back, I found the source of the blood.

Eris had heavy crimson stains down her chest, stemming from a vicious gash in her neck. The broken skin was ragged, and even moving her opened the wound, causing a fresh tendril of blood to mix with the sticky mess.

Eris had been bitten, and a chunk had been torn from her flesh.

Cold dread filled me as I swallowed, and the tang of iron filled my mouth.

I turned to the mirror in the far corner and looked at myself. Blood was caked around my mouth and lips. As soon as I saw it, my stomach couldn't take it and I scrambled off the bed, heaving too much blood and the remnants of last night's meal all over the wooden floors.

I heaved my guts out until nothing but bile remained. My throat was raw and burned with the acidic remains of my vomit, but before I could wash my mouth out and check on Eris, my vision swam.

My strength fled as darkness crept along the edges of my sight, and I fell to my knees and then to oblivion.

\*\*\*

I didn't dream, for it was much too vivid to ever be confused as such. It was more like an out of body experience than a dream; my body was lying on the floor of the safe house, but my mind was someplace else entirely.

I was in a void of darkness, I couldn't hear, couldn't speak, but I was aware. Flashes of memories ran through my mind, but they weren't mine. Places and things I knew I'd never seen before, but it didn't dawn on me what I was experiencing until the flashes slowed, settling on a scene that played out like a movie.

I found myself in a dwelling, the likes of which I'd never seen before. It reminded me of the houses the elves lived in, but the elves were a practical race, and the residence I found myself in reeked of affluent wealth.

It was as if the house had been carved from a tree, one so large it could fit the entirety of Castle Gloom-Harbor inside it and still have room left over. The furniture looked like it had been sprouted from the very wood itself and was so finely carved and detailed, it put my own woodworking skills to shame. I could have spent a hundred years perfecting my craft, and I could never hope to match the quality of even the lowest barstool in the kitchen.

A chandelier hung fifty feet overhead and slithered like roots coming alive and forming the pattern of a rose. Mana crystals were sunk into the roots and shone brilliant blue-white light down on the entire house.

Eris, a young version of Eris, perhaps four or five, sat at a table in the kitchen, eating. On the table was a plate of food, and a vase of fresh flowers, arranged in a beautiful display. Eris reached for her drink, a crystal cup of water, and accidentally bumped the vase with her hand. It tipped over with a silent crash and spilled water and flowers over the table as the porcelain vase broke into several large pieces.

Before she could even rise from her seat to clean up the mess, a man appeared. He was an older entomancer. Tall and handsome, with broad cheeks and a chiseled jaw. His light brown hair was long and pulled back out of his face in a ponytail. He was well built; the bulging veins in his arms were surrounded by pure, functional muscle. But what struck me most about his features were his eyes.

His eyes were a pale cobalt that shone in the light, while his irises were pure black. I didn't know who this man was, but I was immediately put off by his presence. He was most likely Eris's father, but he unsettled me in a way few could manage.

The man took one look at the mess, and rage clouded his face. He marched over to the table, yanked Eris out of her chair, and slapped her across the face.

She reeled from the shock, her face already reddening from the impact. Tears welled in her eyes as the man shouted wordlessly at her and pointed at the mess, the water from the vase spilling over the table to drip on the rich hardwood floor.

With a shove, he released Eris, and she crumpled to the floor, though still, she did not cry. Only when the man stormed off, and she was alone did she let the tears fall. Eris curled in on herself and sobbed.

Pure hatred filled me as the scene unfolded. I wanted nothing more than to scoop her in my arms and tell her everything would be all right, but I couldn't move, couldn't speak. I could only watch as she silently picked herself up and wiped the tears from her face.

The vision faded after that, the edge of my sight distorting and going black before a new memory unfolded in front of me.

I found myself in a well-lit room. The stone that comprised the room was white marble, perfectly smooth, and even. Lit torch sconces lined the walls as twilight streamed through open windows. From my viewpoint, I could see the tops of trees, thick and unending as far as the eye could see.

I returned my attention to the room, it was packed with entomancers. Every color of the rainbow was reflected in the eyes of the well-dressed men and women here.

They all stood lined up on either side of an empty throne—a few dozen or so at most. There was a thick white and gold rug that lined the floor, which stretched from the throne to the entrance of the room.

The dark wooden doors at the entrance of the room opened, and a team of warriors in heavy black plate marched in on either side of the door. Followed shortly after by a few important-looking men garbed in beautiful clothes. Though the style was unusual: green flowing tunics with most of the chest bared and dark mantling that draped about their shoulders.

As the next guest entered the room, all eyes were on her.

She was beautiful.

By every form of the word, she was beautiful.

Long silken hair cascaded down her back like a golden waterfall and fell behind her long ears. Her cheekbones were high on her face and were sharp enough that I expected her face to start bleeding. She had the face of someone who demanded much and received everything she asked for.

As with every other member of the entomancer race, the most captivating aspect of her visage was her insectoid eyes. The held a bottomless pit of black at the far edges fading to a beautiful golden yellow, before returning to pitch black for her irises. Her eyes held the same pattern as the stripes on a bumblebee. Though the woman walking toward the throne was far more dangerous than any bee. She held an air of power about her that chilled me to the bone.

I knew immediately who she was. Eris was reflected in her features, though where Eris was soft and kind, this woman was a knife. Sharp and deadly.

As she turned to gaze at the patrons who came to watch the coronation—for it was obvious that's what this was—her eyes for the barest moment flicked to gaze directly at me. A bolt of fear shot through me, and I withered under the intensity of her gaze.

Then her eyes left mine, and everything returned to normal. The fear drained out of me and left me weak. I turned around to find Eris's father directly behind me. We lined up almost perfectly. I realized, with a wave of sweeping relief that she hadn't been staring at me at all. She'd been staring through me at her husband, who was looking a little worse for wear since the previous time I had seen him.

His light brown hair was much longer than in the previous scene; it fell past his shoulders, looking lank and greasy, and his face was sunken as if he'd been starved. The look in his dulled blue eyes was vacant, and his once-beautiful clothes were little more than shredded and soiled rags.

He looked nothing short of a dead man walking. Empty and void of life or hope.

As Eris's mother reached the throne, she sat upon it in a dramatic, flowing fashion. Exaggerated motions portrayed not a self-assured monarch, but a pretender playing at being queen.

I'd met true monarchs; I knew what a ruler should look like, and this woman did not measure up. Her beauty was her weapon, and I could tell she was a master in her form of combat, but beauty alone wouldn't make her a ruler.

Once she had so elegantly arranged herself on the throne, she barked an order, and immediately, everyone knelt and bowed their heads. All except for her husband, the walking corpse, and for just a moment, some fire returned to his eyes.

He hefted his chin proudly and stared down his wife, whose face held cold and righteous fury toward her defiant husband. She barked out another command, and everyone raised their heads. She then motioned for one of her aides, a spindly man with long features. He approached her nervously and bowed his head as she spoke.

When she had finished saying whatever it was to the man, he turned and called out. He was looking at the two intimidating entomancers in the heavy armor. They nodded their heads and moved to open the door.

Eris walked in, wearing a lovely flowing dress. Black with golden accents that matched her hair perfectly. Her hair was done up around her head, and she looked adorable. Judging by her appearance, I put her age around fourteen or so. Not quite out of adolescence just yet.

She walked calmly down the carpeted room toward her mother, holding a neutral expression, but I knew that face was a mask. If she was hiding behind a mask, she knew what was about to happen and steeled herself for it.

As she approached her mother, she bowed and moved to stand by her mother's side. With her so close to her mother, you could see even more the resemblances the two shared. You could also see, so sharply contrasted, how utterly different they were to each other. When Eris had settled in a small chair by the side of the throne, the festivities continued.

The queen bellowed out more commands, and one of the two knights moved away from the door, while the other stayed in place. The knight who moved lumbered over to Eris's father and grasped him by the neck, dragging him in front of the queen.

The rest of the patrons were shocked, with bewildered looks across their faces as her husband was unceremoniously dumped in on the white rug. He stayed huddled on the ground until the queen barked once more. The decision weighed heavily in the man's cerulean eyes. He was torn between obeying the queen and accepting his fate with grace or to defy her one last time and disobey her orders and continue staying on the floor.

Finally, the man seemed unwilling to lie down and die like a dog. He rose to his feet, and a bit of honor breathed some life back into him. My respect for the man grew, if only by a sliver.

I'd have gladly killed the man myself and done it with a smile, but it has to be said that anyone who would stare down the face of their executioner with dignity is worthy of respect, regardless of the heinous crimes committed while alive.

Death is the great equalizer. To face it boldly and without fear is to be commended.

Eris's father looked at the queen with no hesitation or remorse for his actions, whatever they had been, that had led him to this moment. He stared down the woman he had once been bonded to. She rose from the throne in a single fluid motion and sauntered over to stand before the man with nothing short of victory in her eyes.

The queen raised her hand, and for a moment, nothing happened. Then, strands of black chitin exploded out of every pore of her arm and hand, coating every inch in under a second, reshaping itself to form a wicked black sword. The queen raised the sword aloft, before swiftly bringing the blade down into her once-mate's neck.

Thick blood rained from the severed artery, coating the room and the queen in the hot and sticky mess; bright red painted her gown and face. As soon as it splashed across her mouth, she lost herself in the frenzy of the kill. She pounced on the dying man and proceeded to stab him over and over again.

She kept going until he was nothing more than scraps of shredded meat and blood. Only once she was satiated with her kill did she cease her maddened assault on the dead man.

She stood back up, back to the regal posture as before, though still spattered in crimson gore. Without a word, the chitin that was her weapon melted back through the pores in her skin, as if it had never been there at all. She motioned her hand as she turned to walk back to her throne, immediately there was bustling about by several of her aides to clean up the mess that was now cooling on the once-white rug.

Before she sat down on her throne, the queen knelt to look her daughter in the eyes. Eris tilted her head to stare at her mother, whose eyes had lost the gleam of power. The queen seemed an entirely different person while she held the gaze of her daughter, both staring at each other before the queen reached up to fondly brush Eris's cheek, meant to be a loving gesture—but Eris's cheek came away stained red.

The queen stood up and went to sit on her throne to continue with the coronation, but my eyes never left Eris. When her mother walked away, I saw the mask slip on her face, and horror and sorrow filled her eyes.

Once more, my vision faded to darkness and to one final scene.

I stood in what once looked like a town center or shopping plaza. I saw the ruined and splintered remnants of what were once makeshift shops or stalls, now nothing more than splintered planks of wood. They'd been cleared out of the center of the square and brushed against the crumbling stone buildings that lined the plaza.

What looked like an execution was taking place.

Several hundred men and women had gathered around an impromptu jail, hastily constructed in the center of the marketplace by magic. The crowd that had gathered was a mixture of elven and dwarven people. As I reached the center of the plaza, I recognized the inhabitants of the cells.

Eris and her mother were side by side, each bound and chained.

Eris looked exactly like she had when we first met. Wearing the same tattered and torn clothing as she had on in when she appeared out of the crystal. Her hair was dirty, slick with moisture, and matted to her forehead with sweat and ash. She seemed to be staring at the ground, her eyes unfocused; she looked as if she'd checked out of reality altogether.

Her mother, on the other hand, didn't seem to be taking her captivity lying down. She constantly railed against her cell. While she still held the same stunning beauty as before, it was marred by her utter and complete insanity. As I got closer, I could see Eris was only bound by one thin chain in her cell. Her mother, however, was bound in every possible way—dozens of thick heavy chains wrapped around her and were bolted into the ground.

She had both physical and magical shackles on her. The swirling ethereal blues and green of binding magic writhed over her irons...which looked to be comprised of pure shadowsteel.

The dwarves were taking no chances, it seemed, in letting their captive escape. The queen was even bound across her mouth to keep her from speaking. The only portion left uncovered was the top half of her face. Her hair was lank and strewn with bits of soot and flecked with blood. Her eyes were wild and unhinged. She seemed to be raving on the inside; her eyes were screaming at her captors.

She had lost all sense of herself to the madness of defeat.

She'd waged war, and she had lost.

The scene I had stumbled in on made more sense now. Eris had told me the story. Because of the mad queen, the entomancers had brought war and ruin to the world of the elves and the dwarves. This was the aftermath. The price Eris and her mother had to pay.

Several of the dwarven soldiers marched over to the cage that held Eris's mother and unlocked the door. They unlatched the shackles on the bars of her cell. She surged forward once the final lock clicked free. With nothing to support her and her feet bound tight, she didn't make it far. She careened out of her prison and crashed to the ground.

She tried to squirm her way free, but the chains held fast, and she found no purchase to freedom. Two of the men went and calmly bent down, hefting her onto their shoulders. From there, they carried her a short distance to a small post that looked like it had been created from the very street itself using earth magic.

Once she was as secured as a person could be to the post, the soldiers left with looks of scorn and disgust plastered across their faces. As the guards departed, the rest of the crowd followed suit, and soon no one was within fifty feet of the queen or the jail cells.

Shuffling from the far end of the courtyard caught my attention. A group of robed and hooded figures walked through the throng of bystanders to stand before the imprisoned queen. I counted thirteen of them and tried to get a better look at their faces, but even though they wore no masks, and I could see their faces, I couldn't remember a single detail about their appearance. Man or woman, short or tall. Nothing.

The fact that they were mages was all I could discern, and only because of the robes they wore. As they reached the post, they gathered around the broken queen, spreading out in a perfect circle around her.

Without a word, they began their ritual, arms held aloft almost in praise, fingers mere centimeters from brushing up against the mage next to them as they began to chant. I saw their mouths move, but even if I could hear the words, I wouldn't be able to understand them.

They kept up the chant for several minutes, an impressive feat on its own, but to combine it with the magic they were building up was a truly frightening prospect. As the spell reached its finale, a Script circle formed above their heads. The bodies of the mages perfectly formed the outline of the spell.

A small pentagram formed in the center. Framed within a circle, on the outside lay a constant stream of swirling letters. The words shifted and changed in a haze as they danced in lazy fashion. As the spell grew, it shifted, going through each color of the elements. Most stuck with only one element. This one, though, had already gone through five of them and didn't seem to be stopping.

At this rate, it would be the most intricate spell I'd ever seen. It shifted from icy blues to fiery reds, every color of the rainbow. As the spell went through the different colors, it slowed and settled on one I'd never seen before.

The spell shone with the light of the moon. Soft, soft white light illuminated the hazy square. As the spell chose its final color, the circle glowed even brighter, and it grew so bright that it hurt to keep looking. I averted my gaze and tried to follow what was happening through squinted eyes.

It condensed on itself, flowing in until it turned into a single blinding point. A small glowing white dot—a miniature moon suspended in the courtyard. It started to grow from a small dot the size of a marble to the size of an apple. It grew until it was well past the size of a full-grown man.

The queen stared at the minuscule moon above her head, her eyes still gripped within her madness. I even saw Eris lift her head to gaze weakly at the sight of it.

It pulsated, tendrils of pale light pierced through the smoke that drifted through the courtyard. They struck the ground with abandon. Indiscriminate beams of light that melted through the very street wherever they touched. One beam lanced out and shone upon the queen. She was bathed in the pale radiance that stopped just before her face, sparing her bare flesh.

As the light hit the chains, they bubbled and hissed, succumbing to the intensity of spell and melting under the gaze of the moon. It quickly worked its way through the shadowsteel and even burned away the powerful binding magic that held her. The light shifted, moving from her pale skin before it could burn her.

Her chains dissolved in an instant as the light faded.

She was free.

Even in her insanity, she took advantage of the opportunity to lunge out of the discarded remains of her bondage. Through her mania, she held a look of victory, hope having sloughed away some of her madness. As soon as she was free, she changed.

Black chitin formed from beneath her skin, pouring out like oil to form and shape itself to its master's whim. In an instant, she was wearing a full suit of armor. Glossy black and oozing malice. She formed plate armor that seemed to be painted on, as her curves were still plain to see. It was a little bulky and firm over her chest to protect vital areas, but light and flexible enough that she could move without hindrance. With a breath of viridian magic, the armor shifted. Black spikes rose across her frame—jagged edges across her arms and legs. Her armor formed itself in under a second, and both of her hands formed massive swords before she rushed the helpless mages.

She never made it.

A burst of moonlight rained over her as she lunged, guided by fate or perhaps a less fickle hand. When the light faded from her, she was in pieces.

Bisected neatly at the waist, the searing heat from the moonlight cauterized the wound, boiling away what little blood escaped. The queen fell to the ground and tried in vain to rise to her feet. She didn't seem to comprehend why her feet weren't responding. Her body didn't seem to understand it was no longer whole.

Having been cut off from half of her mana stream, the black chitin armor dissolved back under her skin; she no longer had the mana to maintain her devilish form. Her remaining mana would now be trying to repair the sudden damage that had been done.

The queen finally realized the severity of the situation and looked down to find her neatly hewn legs, several feet from where they should be. Even though no more light rained down from the moon, the spell was far from finished. It seemed once the spell touched a living being, it started to work its magic from the inside.

The luminosity from the spell was bright and hot enough to melt through one of the most durable materials I'd ever found, but it seemed to have a second even more insidious method of destruction. Bright white light started to drip from the severed halves of her body. It seeped into her blood and began to work its way up through her veins.

It burned as bright and hot as a star as it crept steadily toward her heart. Burning her away from the inside.

The pain, it seemed, was more than even her madness could contend with because she screamed. A twisted, tortured scream that pierced through the vacuum of silence. The first sound I experienced in this vision grated against my ears and throughout my mind. A sound no living being was meant to make. She ripped her vocal cords from yelling, and I was thankful to be returned to the silence.

This was a pain that went beyond mortality. It was a purifying light of the heavens, which brought the torment of Hell.

The white luminescence reached her heart and started to glow radiantly. All the while, the queen kept screaming wordlessly in utter agony. At the sound of her mother's cries, Eris seemed to regain a sense of herself. She railed against her chains, trying desperately to free herself. Complete misery was plain on her face.

No child should ever have to witness a parent go through that. Being made to watch as her mother was burned alive in this manner was akin to cruelty beyond measure.

Her mother may have deserved her fate, but Eris had done nothing to deserve the pain she was being forced to endure.

We both stood transfixed at the horror in front of us.

The radiance within her chest grew in its brilliancy. It burned a hole right through her, taking her heart and most of her chest with its heat. Her screams died as the light entirely consumed her. Once more, I had to avert my eyes as the heat washed over me, taking away the chilled air that had surrounded me since I had come here. When it finally died away, nothing remained of the queen.

Nothing but ash.

Eris slumped against her chains in defeat. The remaining life seemed to drain out of her. She returned to stare at the ground, though tears dripped down her face. They landed on her dirt and bloodstained bare feet, washing away some of the grime that had accrued and dried on her legs.

A swirl of bright green smoke rose from the ash pile of what remained of the queen and drifted toward Eris. It flowed into her mouth, and she jerked, her eyes going wide. She panicked for a split second, before she paused, staring at the ashes of her mother.

The mages held a posture of superiority about them as they watched Eris sob. They weren't satisfied with just the annihilation of her mother as guards marched over to the cage that held Eris. Her time had come.

The casters nodded at the soldiers next to her cage. They unlocked the chains and the door simultaneously. No longer held up by the chains, Eris fell to the ground and curled in on herself. She didn't even put up a fight as she was dragged out of the cage by the men.

The mages started speaking to one another, but from the way their mouths moved, I could tell they were speaking normally, and not the convoluted language of Script. Though I could not hear what they were saying, the veil that prevented sound from reaching me had returned in full, and I was grateful for the reprieve.

As the soldiers dumped Eris on the ground right next to the spot where her mother was destroyed, she kept looking at the ashes as they drifted about in the breeze. She wouldn't look up from the ground; one of the men yanked her by the hair to force her to show her face to the mages.

Her eyes were empty. The head mage spoke directly to Eris. She stared weakly at them, though she didn't seem to be present enough to understand what the man was saying. The mage produced a crystal from within his robes and sat it on the ground in front of Eris. It was the same crystal that I had found in the loot room. This was the prison that Eris was sentenced to.

They quickly formed their circle around Eris, who wasn't even chained, huddled on the ground. Uncaring.

The coven of mages all raised their arms in unison and began to chant once more. As they worked their way through the many different verses of

Script, their hands started to pulsate with an obsidian mist. Heavy black clouds of smoke rose from their palms and drifted toward the ground.

As the first tendrils of mist reached the ground, they crept along drawn toward the crystal, and toward Eris. When the first cloud of smoke reached the crystal, it seemed to glow with ethereal light, but the light was continually drawn back into the void.

Once the first part of the ritual had been completed, the head mage spoke to one of the soldiers. A younger-looking dwarven male. He seemed to have some semblance of sympathy for Eris because he was gentle when he walked over to her and picked up one of her limp arms.

The young soldier drew a small knife from his belt; it was double-bladed and elegant in its construction. It was more ceremonial than functional, more of an athame than a dagger. He swiftly and as gentle as he could be, sliced a thin groove through her wrist. He moved her dripping arm over the crystal. A ruby red drop welled from her wrist and dripped onto the obsidian gem.

It hissed as it landed; smoke rose from within the crystal and devoured the blood. Once the drop was gone, the smoke changed color, now a verdant green. More dripped from her arm. Before it could land on the ground or the crystal, it changed. It shifted into the same green mist that rose from the dark glass.

Faster and faster, her blood turned to smoke. Then it reached her hand, and it too dissolved. It ate her away, slowly turning her entire body into a whirling green cloud, suspended in the air by magic. Then, as if the wisps were magnetized, it was drawn toward the crystal. The green and black smoke merged into one inside the shard of crystallized void.

All that remained of Eris or her mother was ash and a pretty bauble.

The head mage calmly walked over to the prison that housed Eris, picking up the gem and slipping it inside the folds of his robes while the rest of the coven drifted back out of the square. I was left alone, and the edge of my vision blurred one last time. Bringing an end to the memories.

My sight was slowly taken from me, plunging me into darkness, a place where light never shone.

I expected to be shown another memory, or be taken out of the hallucination, but neither happened. I stayed in the perpetual darkness for a very long time. What could have been hours or days passed in utter darkness. I felt, for a time, what Eris must have experienced for all those centuries, trapped in the void.

It made me see her in an entirely new light. Eris had endured more than any one person should ever have to bear, had gone through such tremendous pain. And yet she could still find the strength to smile. To hold out hope for love when I myself didn't know if I could love her back. My pain paled in comparison, but that's the thing with pain. It doesn't care what someone else can endure. It only cares about how much damage it can inflict on you at that moment.

*If Eris can find the strength to live with her torment, maybe it's time I do the same? If only it was so easy.*

I sat alone with my thoughts, but just as I was truly about to feel despair, a strange presence flicked through my consciousness. Whoever or whatever it was brushed lightly against my mind. It was gentle, and I felt kindness in the touch. The figure lingered beside me, close enough that its hot breath brushed the nape of my neck. Warm lips pressed themselves to my cheek. Incredibly soft, which left me feeling a sense of peace that had eluded me for many, many years.

The voice was familiar to me, one I hadn't heard in a lifetime. It reminded me of my mother as the figure whispered in my ear.

"Save her, Sam. If you can."

As the presence pulled away, tears welled up in my eyes. I didn't want her to leave me.

*Not again.*

It couldn't have been my mother, but even a facsimile was enough. I tried to speak, but no words would come. I couldn't say any of the things I had wanted to all those years ago, the things I never got the chance to. With one final brush of fingers over my cheek, she was gone.

# Chapter 21 - The Compass Kingdom

When I came back to my mind, I was caught between the two states of being, and I jerked up out of reflex. I stifled my racing heart and wiped a thick sheen of sweat from my forehead. As I laid back, I sank into comfort; I was too comfortable to be lying on the floor.

I shifted, finding myself in Eris's lap. She was staring at me with a mixture of confusion and concern in her eyes.

She was confused at my reaction, taking it to be shaking off the remnants of a nightmare. "Shh, it's okay, love. You just had a bad dream." She spoke softly, running her fingers gently through my hair, and trying to reassure me.

No doubt, she could feel my conflicting emotions through our bond.

Eris smiled down at me, but it was sheepish and filled with chagrin. "Looks like we got out of hand last night."

"I'll say," I said as I sat up again.

I'd been lying in Eris lap, and as I looked at her, the events of the previous night flooded back to me. I froze and looked at her neck. The blood was gone, and she was wearing the same clothes she had on last night.

"Are you all right?" I asked.

She nodded. "I'm fine now. I drank the health potion you left out last night, and the pain went away quickly."

*Good.* I stood from the floor and helped Eris to her feet. The room was still in disarray, and there was absolutely no saving the bed from the bloodstains. Eris went over to the mirror and inspected herself, trying and failing to fix her bedhead. I smiled as I watched her, but my smile quickly fell as she tilted her neck.

The morning sun fell across her face and throat. It was plain as day and unmistakable; outlined roughly just above her collarbone was a silver-white scar in the shape of my teeth.

"Godsdamn it!"

*We left it untreated for too long. Her body's natural healing had already started by the time she drank the potion.*

Eris turned, confused at my outburst. "What's wrong?"

"Just look at your neck. That scar will never fade away completely, not for the rest of your life...which could be for a long time."

Disgust writhed in my chest and sickened me. We'd lost control, and Eris had paid heavily for it. I didn't know how long entomancers' lifespans were, but even if it was the same as a human lifespan, it was too long.

Eris picked up on my words. "We live for about five hundred years or so. Longer than the dwarves, but not nearly so long as the elves."

Five hundred years was a long time to bear such a noticeable scar. It wouldn't be so bad in the shadows, or inside a building, but in direct sunlight, it would be hard to hide. I walked over to her and ran my fingers over her neck, tracing the scar. Eris shuddered at my touch and leaned into me, laying her head against mine.

"I'm sorry, love."

It was all my fault. I'd hurt her. As soon as the thought entered my head, the ice-filled smoke inside gripped its talons into my heart. Ice water filled my veins, and pain radiated through my body.

*"Poor knight. You brought harm to your queen. An offense punishable by death, but lucky for you, there's no one left to dole out your sentence. No family left for the last cast-off wretch of the Hive."*

*That's your queen you're talking about, Aspect. Watch yourself!*

*"Once, perhaps, but I find myself blissfully unburdened as of late, so I should thank you for that, knight. You have some use after all,"* the Aspect replied, laughing darkly.

*What are you talking about?*

But whatever it meant, it refused to share, only to chuckle in the back of my mind before fading away. It stayed silent and left me in confusion.

Eris could sense the emotions inside me, and she was worried about me. I knew as soon as she looked at me that she thought that I blamed myself for what happened. She reached over and held my hand, intertwining our fingers.

"I don't blame you for this, love. And you know, I actually like it a bit," she said, grinning slightly.

I chuckled softly and shook my head. I couldn't think of one good reason to bear such a noticeable scar, especially since I had yet to see her wear any clothing that could reasonably be considered modest.

"Mind explaining why?" I asked.

Eris stopped and looked down, blushing at the question. She fidgeted with her hands, as I went in the bathroom in the hall and cleaned myself off. She'd wiped away most of the blood, but there were still some trouble spots. I cleaned myself off as best I could with the bucket of water next to me and went back into the room to change clothes.

I was out of fresh clothes, so I chose the cleanest shirt I had, a dark burgundy that clung tight to my chest and my black canvas pants. *They'll just get dirty from the East Kingdom roads, but I'll buy some new clothes when we get to Central.*

By the time I'd dressed, Eris had picked up all of our stuff and handed it out to me. I stowed it in my inventory, and we left the safe house. We were only a few miles from the Compass Kingdom, and breakfast could wait.

350

I saddled Lacuna, and we set off, Eris in front as usual. She didn't say anything for a little while, and she hadn't answered the question I'd asked her. I was beyond curious, so I nudged her a bit.

"Got an answer?"

"Well, yes, I do…it's because you're my husband and bond-mate. You're the person I've pledged myself to, and bearing this scar is proof of that. I am yours, as you are mine. Until eternity," she said, smiling.

I leaned down and kissed her cheek. "You're weird, y'know that?"

She laughed, her whole body shaking as we rode. "You're not the first person to tell me that, and you can blame my parents."

*Oh, right. I really need to talk to her about that.* "Hey, so, we need to talk," I said with hesitation.

Eris tilted her head to stare at me with one eye. "What about?"

"After what happened last night, when I woke up, I had your blood in my mouth. I passed out, and I think I experienced your memories."

Her breath hitched in her throat. "What?"

I didn't really know what to say, and I really didn't want to bring up what I'd seen. I wanted nothing more than for Eris to wipe those feelings, every one of those awful memories away. I had too many of them myself to carry any more.

*But I can't do that, not to her.*

I could never let myself forget the torment and misery that she'd gone through. If she could go through that and still have the strength to smile, then the very least I could do was help to shoulder some of her pain.

Fear and apprehension drifted from Eris, along with curiosity. She wanted to know what I'd seen but was a little afraid of the answers.

"I saw your childhood. How your father treated you…and I saw your mother's coronation."

Eris winced at that, knowing exactly what I'd seen. She sighed and nodded. "Was that all you saw?"

"No," I said, refusing to elaborate.

"What else?" she prompted.

I didn't want to answer her; the sights in the Mnemosyne were too vivid. It lingered still in my eyes. Eris suffering as she watched her mother die was one of the worse sights I'd seen. *At least Micah hadn't suffered. It'd been quick.*

"Sam?" she asked, her voice stretched tight with worry. I let go of the reins for a moment, and Lacuna slowed to a stop. I held Eris and rested my chin on her shoulder and whispered, "I…saw the price you had to pay."

I left the rest alone, and she didn't need the details. I just held her closer, trying to push away both of our pain. She relaxed at my touch, melting into me. There was an unvoiced fear spiking through her that needed an answer.

"You don't have to be afraid. Nothing I saw could ever scare me away."

"So, you can feel my emotions too," she said, not asking, just confirming.

"If I concentrate hard enough, yeah. Why? Is that a problem?"

Eris threw back her head and laughed at that, leaning on me as she shook. It was a laugh filled with warmth. The sound was addicting, and I'd have paid every gold I owned to hear it again.

"Problem? No, of course not. It's just surprising. You shouldn't be able to. I'd have said it was impossible. And you definitely shouldn't be able to access the Mnemosyne since you're not an entomancer. I don't see how, but I like it," she said, giving me a radiant smile.

Eris started humming softly as I pushed Lacuna to a walk. Having a deeper connection through our bond made her incredibly happy.

As we rode, Lacuna's hooves plodding through the dirt joined Eris's humming and formed an offbeat song as we passed endless trees and green fields. We both enjoyed the presence of each other and didn't ruin the moment with our words.

When we entered the outskirts of Grange, we passed an Alliance patrol. The first of many.

They patrolled on a frequent, infrequent schedule, never making the same loop twice. It, more than anything else, deterred banditry and thuggery in the area. You could never predict when the next patrol would pass by, and one shout would have the whole territory alert in seconds.

A rash of cattle mutilations and arson several years ago cost the Merchants Guild some serious coin, enough that they strong-armed the Alliance to devise new routes and schedules.

As it was, this area was as safe as we were likely to find. It wasn't quite midday, and thousands of farmers were toiling away in their fields under the harsh light of the sun. In under an hour, they would flock by the hundreds to the dozen or so taverns that cropped up every quarter mile.

If farming was king in the East Kingdom, then alehouses were their mistress. Not outright acknowledged, but ever-present and somewhat necessary. You couldn't have one without the other, after all.

By my estimate, it would be full dark before we would reach the Central Kingdom, so I made plans to stop at an inn when night fell. As we approached the first gate, I quickly put Eris's hood up. The guards should let us pass without trouble, but it was better to be safe than stupid.

Four men guarded the first gate, a giant black wrought iron monster, thick, heavy bars latticed over one another. It stood out sharply in comparison to the whitewashed limestone walls that encompassed the whole of the Compass Kingdom.

One of the guards commanded us to halt. From his lapel, he was the sergeant in charge of the others. He wore a striking blue and gold tunic and matching pants over his sparse armaments, along with a short-brimmed hat with a long plume atop his head.

A statement that suggested a superiority complex, if I'd ever seen one. The Alliance didn't enforce a strict uniform with their soldiers, as they didn't like spending the coin to outfit the many dozens of thousands of men under their command. The only piece of the uniform they did issue was a chest plate with the Alliance crest embossed across the majority of the metal.

A sword inside a clenched fist, surrounded by five stars, representing each of the kingdoms.

"Afternoon, sir. May I inquire about your business inside the East Kingdom?"

I nodded my head at him, discreetly reached inside my purse and withdrew a single gold coin, slipping the guard the money. "Just a little business and pleasure is all, sir."

He returned my nod and offered a sly grin. "Of course, sir. Head on in."

He turned and barked a sharp command that wasn't so much a word as a whistle. After a second or two, the gate started to rise slowly. Within half a minute, we were inside a stretch of white tunnel lined with torches that burned steadily even during the day, as light could never make its way deep enough to keep the place lit.

The two-gate process was an admittedly smart system of defense. Two different gates with separate opening mechanisms and two different sets of guards to open them. Who were assigned at complete random, making it much harder to bribe and coerce the men who were stationed there.

We made our way through the dark tunnel. Lacuna's hooves clacked loudly against the stone, only to echo throughout the tunnel. Before we'd even made it halfway through, the opposite gate had already started to rise.

By the time we reached it, we had just enough room to squeeze through without ducking our heads.

As soon as we had passed through, the gate began to shut. *Paranoia much?*

The streets were awash with hundreds of people going about their day. Grain merchants were everywhere, buying and selling wheat and barley by the bushel. A few produce vendors here and there, but as most of what was harvested here went to the other kingdoms, there wasn't as much of a need for it here where it was grown in excess.

Wheat and grain had a nearly universal appeal even here in the East Kingdom. And even if you didn't need it wholesale, wheat and wheat by-products were still in high demand. Bread, flour, and even ale were staples everywhere and required a steady amount of grain.

*You'd think with how well this kingdom's exports sold; they could afford better roads.* The stone streets were rough, uneven, and even missing tiles. All topped with caked over with dirt and mud that the workers tracked with every step.

Eris was having a blast. I don't think she'd ever seen so many humans at once; she kept darting her head back and forth, as we wove through traffic and proceeded to the main road. It was adorable to watch, and I left her to her own devices while I steered Lacuna toward the Central Kingdom gate. About twenty minutes later, she seemed lost in thought, before turning around to ask me a question.

"There are thousands of men and women, but I've seen very few children?"

"Oh, that's because it's not that easy for NPCs to have kids. Well, human NPCs at any rate."

"Why?"

*Truth be told, I'm not entirely sure of the answer myself—all us players have are theories.* But I didn't want to spout off some of the more "out there"

355

conspiracy theories, and so I settled for the one I put the most stock in, and by far the most common theory.

"Well, I personally think it has to do with how rapidly humans reproduced back on Earth. We spread like a disease, and it quickly became a huge problem that led to shortages in almost every major resource. So here, on Nexus, the theory is that Ouroboros restricts how many humans can have children."

"That's a little sad to hear, but it makes sense. Compared to the elves or dwarves, humans far outnumber either race, and the demi-humans are bordering on extinction. I wonder if an entomancer and a human can have children? What do you think our children will be like?"

"That's something I don't have to consider, because players can't have kids at all."

Eris whirled around with a shocked expression. "You can't have children?"

I shook my head. "None of us can. The AI can simulate life, but actually creating it is an entirely different story."

Eris didn't say another word, just turned around. Her shoulders slumped over while we rode, so to cheer her up, I put my arm around her and pulled her into my chest, kissing the top of her head.

"Don't think about it so much, nothing you or I can do to change it, so there's no point in dwelling on it."

"Right," she said but was quiet for a long time after that.

My nonchalance toward her stung, but not being able to have children was something I was grateful for. *This world is too dark for children. And us players aren't fit to be parents anyway.*

We stopped for lunch at a quaint restaurant about fifteen minutes later when the sun was highest overhead. Eris was still in her head and didn't touch her food, but I savored the spicy sausages I ordered and half a loaf of fresh bread with butter. I drank my fill of their local ale and paid a gold for our food to the ecstatic owner.

We lingered for an hour or so until the lunchtime rush abated, and the roads cleared as the populace went back to work. We climbed back on Lacuna, and I pushed her a little faster to make up for the lost time. As the hours went by, Eris still hadn't come back to her usual self. I knew what troubled her, but there was nothing I could do, nothing she could either, that would fix it.

"I know it sucks, and I'm sorry. I wish I could do something to cheer you up."

"Thank you, but it's not like even if we could conceive that it would change anything. My race was doomed the moment we raised our hands in war. I'm the last one left, maybe the last of the entire Hive. Nothing I can do will ever restore us to what we were. I'm the queen of a dead kingdom."

After that, we didn't speak for a long time, but she perked up a little as it got twilight. The streetlights were lit, and Eris marveled at the many flickering flames as we rode past.

The traffic thinned to almost nothing as darkness crept in. Except for the occasional guard or drunkard, the streets were barren. Most career thieves and criminals wouldn't dare let themselves be caught on the main roads. I started to look for a place to stop and rest, and before we'd gone a hundred feet, we passed by an inn.

It was a large white building, built in the half-timbered style so common in the Compass Kingdom, the wooden support beams flush to fresh white plaster and freshly stained bay windows. A gray shingled roof that looked easy to climb, and the makeshift ladder bolted to the side only confirmed it. If you needed a quick escape route, there were several options here. From the quick glance, it looked like a Trapped Lodge, an establishment built and operated with the sole purpose of relieving their patrons of their coin…by any means necessary.

These places thrived on the tourist traffic that came and went like wildfires. The people who lived in the city or frequented enough times knew to avoid these places like the plague. They paid hefty dues to the Merchants Guild to keep their operations running, which is the only reason the Alliance let them continue.

*No way in the nine Hells am I risking Eris or myself by tempting fate that hard.* I guided Lacuna through the dead streets, keeping a low profile as much as I could, though more than one pair of eyes peered at us from the rooftops or out from darkened alleyways. *Thieves Guild oculars. That didn't take long.*

I withdrew and dropped three gold coins in purposeful succession—one after the other. The coins pinged off the stone like the cracks of a whip and destroyed the thin silence. A message and a toll rolled into one payment.

"Phineas Carn, Crescent Rose, noon."

The absence was like a vacuum when they departed, and when I turned back, the coins had vanished—three taps on a nearby windowpane. Message received.

No further trouble followed us as we made our way deeper into the East Kingdom, past the sleeping houses and places of business. After maybe another ten minutes of riding through the sleepy streets, we came across another inn.

It was a rather boisterous place, as through the large bay window, I could see many a patron drinking and dancing, and the muffled sounds of music crept through the glass.

A glance at the vaulted, dark, wooden roof told me this place was as free of danger as I was likely to find inside the kingdom. I made my way around the small barn by the side of the stone building and stabled Lacuna. It wasn't my ideal location to house her for the evening, but she was smarter than the average criminal, so I wasn't worried about horse thieves.

I gingerly climbed off her and helped Eris down. She held my hand tightly as I opened the door. The first thing that hit me was the loud music. It was audible from outside, but I wasn't prepared for how noisy it would be once we stepped inside. A mixture of drums and a lute with the soft vocals of a woman.

She was thin, with long golden blonde hair and sharp eyes. Her face held delicate features, high cheeks, and a round chin. She wasn't beautiful, but I'd call her cute.

What stood out was her voice. It was soft, yet clear enough to resonate through the tavern, and it lent itself well to singing. The lute player and the drummer were both handsome men with similar features as the woman. All blond with slight looks and wearing matching blue and white clothes. *A family of musicians?*

I ignored them and focused on maneuvering my way through the bustling tavern, not so easy when I was dragging Eris through the crowd and kept having to stop or collide with drunken or dancing fools. I finally reached the check in station.

A stocky, handsome woman operated the counter. She was built large, not with fat but with a decent amount of muscle on her. She wasn't a former adventurer, no. Her build came from everyday hard work. The muscles were too unrefined to be from combat training.

She had thick features, both in her face and elsewhere. She was quite busty; her tight tunic and apron showcased that all too well. Her long, brunette hair was tied back out of her face, and her light brown eyes lit up at the sight of me weaving and bobbing my way through the crowd of sloshed customers. I couldn't help but laugh right back. *I must have looked quite the character.*

She kept up her laugh as I reached the counter, it devolved into several snorts before she could regain her composure enough to ask. "How are you tonight, sir? What can I do for you?"

"A room for the evening would be lovely, with a bath if you have it," I said.

She nodded and a sly grin graced her lips. "One room for just the two of you, eh? With a bath. That'll be ten copper."

I pulled out a gold and handed it to her. Her eyes lit up at the sight of it. *Gold must be uncommon here if that reaction is any indication.* She bit into the metal, satisfied by the authenticity of the coin. "Let me run to the back and get your change, good sir."

I shook my head. "No need for that. Consider it a tip. Though if you could have a meal brought for the two of us up to my room, I would be forever grateful."

The innkeeper was a little flustered as she nodded enthusiastically. I'd probably just made her month. Her smile was as wide as it could be while she brushed her long hair to the side. "Of course, my lord, right away!" She handed me a silver key with the number one stamped on the bow.

"Please, none of that lord business, I'm the furthest thing from a noble."

"Master, then?"

"Oh, gods, that might be worse. How about you call me Duran?" I asked. "And this is Eris."

Eris smiled out from under her hood. "It's nice to meet you."

"Nice to meet ya both. My name is Sylvia, but you can call me Syl," she replied with a smile.

"Lovely to meet you, Syl," I said.

360

She merely nodded and added, "I'll be by with your dinner as soon as it finishes."

I let go of Eris as we headed up the stairs to the left of us. They were well made and didn't so much as creak as we made my way up to the second floor. As I unlocked the door to our room, it opened into a rather spacious area. The wooden floor and walls were well maintained, and the bed was large and fluffy, with freshly laundered sheeting and what looked like feather pillows.

The nightstand held a small oil lantern. Eris crawled on the bed while I lit the lamp. The darkened room filled with soft lambent light. In the far corner of the room was our washtub. It was in the same room as the bed in this inn. I didn't mind that fact. We both needed a bath, and the tub was just large enough to accommodate the two of us. I quickly heated the large jug of water on the small fire stone and poured the steaming water into the tub.

Climbing into the bath, we washed clean. The few bloodstains that lingered on my skin came free with some scrubbing. Once we were clean, I drained the dirty water into the jug, ready to be emptied and refilled in the morning.

Eris climbed out first and got dressed, and just as I had thrown on a clean pair of pants, there was a knock at the door. My stomach rumbled greedily at the prospect of food, and I knew Eris must be hungry since she didn't have lunch.

I opened the door to find Syl standing there holding a huge platter with two mugs of cold ale and plates filled with cubed steak and cheese, along with a steaming pile of carrots and potatoes. The smell that wafted past my nose was heavenly, and my stomach voiced its agreement. Syl chuckled at my rumbling belly.

"Oh, where are my manners? Please come in," I said.

Syl walked in and set the tray down on the small table in front of the bed. I grinned at the thought of the food. "It looks delicious."

"Sure does," Syl replied.

I looked up from the meal to find her decidedly not looking at the food. She was looking at me with a hunger in her eyes and a smirk on her face. I looked down to find I had neglected to put on a shirt, and my heavily muscled chest was bared to her. *Oh.*

She arched her back to stretch her rather large chest even tighter over the fabric of her thin shirt. Her nipples were hard and poked out prominently.

Syl reached out to place a hand tentatively on my chest. *She wants me as a meal—nope, not going to happen.* Syl noticed my hesitation and misconstrued its meaning, seeming to take it for excitement on my part as her smile grew even more sexual. Her fingers were rough and calloused from work, but it wasn't unpleasant.

But I still wasn't comfortable with her touching me. I backed up as Eris crawled over the bed and sat down beside me. She was staring at me with a smirk peeking out from her hood.

"Ah...this isn't—" I started to say.

"What? I don't mind. She's rather attractive in a rugged way."

Syl seemed to take Eris's words as confirmation. She hastily unbuttoned her shirt to let her rather impressive breasts spill out. They were large and round, but perky enough to hold their shape as they burst forth and jiggled with temptation. Her chest was tanned as if she spent time naked outdoors every day, and she had rather small nipples compared to the size of her breasts; they were pink and fully erect as my eyes traveled over them.

I wasn't the only one looking. Eris had her eyes glued to them as well with a curious and somewhat covetous look on her face. *She seems wistful of*

*Sylvia's generous assets.* Though I rather liked Eris's chest, even I couldn't disagree that the pair of breasts in my face were anything short of spectacular.

Eris stood off the bed and walked over to get a better look, nearly pressing her face to Syl's breasts. She reached out a hand and with a nod from Syl, touched her. Syl let out a soft squeak, likely at the heat from Eris's hand, but she soon acclimated.

Syl ran her hand through Eris's hair and dislodged her hood, baring her ears and eyes. Her eyes widened a bit, but she quickly smiled. "I've never seen such a cute demi before!"

My sudden panic at Syl seeing Eris was replaced by a pang of jealousy. Eris was enraptured by Syl's chest, and her fingers played lightly around her bust and nipples. Admittedly it was a provocative scene, but watching Eris with someone else was difficult.

I tried to suppress it, but when Eris suddenly stopped and pulled her hands back from Syl, I knew she'd felt my disapproval.

"Sorry, Syl. I can't," Eris said.

Syl looked up with a regretful expression and even seemed a little hurt. "Is it my looks?" she asked.

"Of course, it isn't," she said with a shake of her head. "But my bonded doesn't like to share, it seems."

A nod of understanding replaced the sad look on Syl's face. Even if she wasn't happy about being turned away, she could at least take solace that it wasn't her looks that factored into it. She slowly buttoned up her shirt, giving Eris one final long glance at her breasts, and a mischievous grin. Once she was presentable again, she bowed to us and bid us a good evening, shutting the door behind her as she left.

Soon as the door latched, I sank back onto the bed. It was as fluffy as I imagined and was heavenly after the day's ride and eased some of my aches and pains. I sat up as Eris crawled towards me, her eyes asking me why. I sighed heavily and leaned back into her shoulder. Her arms came up to wrap around my neck. She leaned over to rest her chin against my collarbone and kissed the base of my throat.

"I'm touched that our bond matters to you, love. At first, I feared you only accepted it out of necessity, and I'm glad that isn't true. But I really didn't mind. She was rather striking, and I would have liked it if we both could have spent the evening with her."

I kissed Eris back. "I did promise you I would give us a chance, and I can't deny any longer how I feel about you. I care about you, and because of that, I don't know if I can share you."

Eris smiled wide at me. Her lips pulled back over her bright white teeth as she attempted to split her face in two with her smile. She kissed me quickly and ran her hand over my cheek. "Took you long enough to figure that out, love," she laughed.

"What can I say, I'm a slow learner," I said, but a thought struck me. "Do entomancers normally involve others in their bonds?"

Eris nodded, her chin digging into my shoulder, "All the time, it wasn't uncommon for a prominent member of the nobility to have several bondmates. It was considered normal."

"I thought you didn't want our bonding to be like the others?"

"I don't, and it's not. You just admitted yourself that you care for me. I'm not a tool or a plaything for you, so what does it matter if we bring in someone else to spend time with? I see no reason why we shouldn't."

I leaned back into her, trying to come up with a reason other than the fact that I simply didn't like the idea of it, I didn't think I could bring myself to sleep with someone else, even if Eris wanted it and wanted to be a part of it. A pit formed in my stomach as I considered it. "We just got together, let's not rush things okay?"

She hugged into my back. "It's fine, love. I promise," she said, but she couldn't hide the slight disappointment in her voice. Eris pulled my head back to kiss my forehead, my nose, and then my lips. "But if I can't have her and you together, then you'll have to work extra hard tonight."

I laughed, and the laughter took away the uneasy awkwardness that had been lingering in the air. "As long as it doesn't involve any more poisoned rabbits."

"I think we can do without," she said.

I leaned over and traced my hand over her scar. "Still, I'm sorry about this. I—"

"I like the scar, Sam. So, shut up and kiss me already!"

Eris straddled me and pushed me to the bed, her lips already pressed against mine. And I relented, giving in to her and returning her affections.

In the morning, I begrudgingly climbed out of bed, covered in dried sweat, and exhausted. We'd spent hours tangled up together and didn't manage to fall asleep until light was breaking over the horizon. My gaze caught the tray of food left forgotten on the table by the bed. I brought the food over to the nightstand and gently shook Eris awake. She opened her eyes and smiled when they focused on me. She languidly sat up and stretched while letting out a gigantic yawn.

"Breakfast, love," I said.

She giggled and blushed. "Don't you mean dinner?"

"Whatever it is, hurry up and eat. We have a meeting in Central at midday."

She performed an exaggerated bow. "Right away, master."

I laughed at her and kissed her, 'None of that, my bonded." I leaned over to feed her a cube of steak and cheese. She opened her mouth and wrapped her tongue around my fingers, dragging the food into her mouth with just her tongue.

"Impressive," I said while grabbing one of the ales and draining it. It was room temperature and tasted a little stagnant, but ale was ale, and I happily drank it while shoveling a considerable mouthful of meat and cheese down my gullet, washing it down with the second ale. After scarfing down the food and drink, we got dressed. I had to resort to wearing the same set of clothes from yesterday as I didn't have anything else. Eris or other circumstances had absconded with all of my clean clothes. *Oh, well. I planned to buy more today anyway.* I wanted to take Eris shopping for some clothes she would enjoy wearing, but I secretly wanted my wardrobe back.

I pulled out a decently clean set of clothes for Eris. This one was solid black with a deep collar. The black was striking against her porcelain skin; it paired almost too well with her shaggy blonde hair. For a second, I was taken back to the memory of Eris's mother walking to her throne. Eris looked like a younger version of her mother. *Albeit much cuter, less prone to acts of genocide.*

I had to convince her to wear the skirt while we were in public. She wasn't happy about it, but had to admit, running around with nothing but a shirt in these crowded streets wasn't a smart plan. Not when a stiff breeze would show off the fact that she refused to wear underwear of any sort. Her traveling skirt was still short, but it did reach past mid-thigh, at least.

We made our way downstairs to find a much quieter setting than last night. The bar was empty and spotless except for the smoldering coals of a fire that had recently been put out. Syl was operating the check-in station, but she looked too refreshed to have been there all night. Must have caught some sleep at some point during the night, though I wondered who watched the counter if she wasn't there. She smiled a little sleepily as we made our way down the steps. "Good morning Duran, Eris," she called to us as we approached.

"Morning," we both said simultaneously, then immediately laughed in unison.

"How was your evening?"

Eris spoke up for both of us. "A little lonely, if I'm being honest, though D more than made up for it."

Syl grinned wickedly. "I'll bet he did."

The two girls shared a laugh at my expense and exchanged a few pleasantries. Before long, people started bustling around getting things ready for the day, and it was our time to leave. I bid Syl a fond farewell, while she made a not-so-subtle innuendo about coming back soon.

As we exited into the streets, I was grateful that the walls and buildings were high enough to block the harsh light of the sun from blinding us as we walked out. We made our way to the stable, and I fed Lacuna breakfast and brushed her coat while she ate. Soon as I was finished, we climbed into the saddle and rode into the waking city.

We had woken up and set off at the perfect time, as people were going to work and bustling about with chores, but most of the farmers were already in the fields outside the city working. So, we made our way through the cobbled streets without much trouble.

The city had long since lost its charm for me, but Eris was still fascinated by all the new and unfamiliar sights and smells. We rode past many stone buildings and shops while Eris looked with wonder at it all. I could see how amazing it must seem to someone who had never experienced such a thing. She was in heaven, enjoying every little aspect of the trip. It warmed my heart to see the joy and wonder on her face as she twisted her head back and forth to people watch.

Within a few hours, we made our way to the gates to the Central Kingdom. Our progress slowed significantly as we got closer; more and more people were cropping up, trying to accomplish the same thing as we were: gaining access to the trading hub of Nexus.

"What are all these people doing here?" Eris asked.

"The same thing we are. Central is one of the busiest places in the world; it never sleeps, as some markets and stalls stay open twenty-four seven. It is also home to the seat of the Alliance, and where the five kings live."

"So, the kings don't live inside their kingdoms?"

I shook my head. "Too much hassle going back and forth since they have to meet nearly every day. Much easier to have a gigantic castle built for the five of them. Besides, the kings are mostly figureheads, squabbling back and forth over every little thing, with nothing much ever getting done. The Merchants Guild is where the true power lies in the Compass Kingdom."

"Human politics are very confusing."

I started to reply, but I found that I couldn't disagree. "Humans are generally confusing creatures," I said.

"You're not confusing."

"Oh, I wish that was true."

When we finally made it through the mass of people enough to see the gates, some semblance of a line had formed and was moving along at a snail's pace. Since this was the capital of the Alliance, security wasn't messing around in the slightest. Three teams of four guards each were at a makeshift checkpoint. There was an additional team of archers with longbows stationed atop the ramparts. They gazed down at us with cold contempt.

After twenty minutes of walking along, it was almost our time to make it through the gate. I noticed one team of guards checking through saddlebags and forcing people to take down their hoods, comparing faces to a sketch of someone—a criminal, perhaps.

"Shit."

*This isn't good; if they force Eris to take off her hood, it will cause no end of trouble. Even if they let us through, too many people would see her face and know that she's a demi.*

"What's wrong?" Eris asked.

"They are stopping all travelers and making them take off their hoods. They seem to be looking for a criminal, and if they see your eyes and ears, it will cause an issue."

"Do you think they will attack us?"

"No, nothing to that extreme, but they will ask all kinds of questions and probably detain us for a while. Demi-humans are a rarity, enough that the guards will probably call someone from the auction house to try and buy you, and I really don't want the hassle or exposure."

"What are we going to do?"

I reached into my inventory and pulled out a small bag of gold — fifty coins clinking in the canvas bag. "What I usually do. Bribe them."

As more and more people were being searched and let through, it was finally our turn. I wrapped my hand around her waist and held her tight. She wouldn't be going anywhere. The guards stepped forward as Iacuna reached the checkpoint.

"Hold up there, sir. Mind if we search your bags?" The guard peered at Eris—the bottom half of her face, at least. "Can you remove your hood, please, miss?"

I put the most conceited voice I could. "Is there a problem here?" I asked in a raised tone.

The guard, a younger gentleman in his mid-twenties or so, seemed startled by the tone of my voice. "Um...no, it's procedure. There is a dangerous criminal about who escaped custody last night, and we are still looking for them."

I barked out a harsh laugh. "And you think she's hiding them underneath her skirt perhaps? Quit wasting our time and yours. I have places to be," I tossed the bag of gold at him, he fumbled with the bag and peered inside. His eyes lit up like it was Christmas, and he waved us through without further questions.

"Of course, sire. I won't keep you further."

He shouted at the gate guards, and it opened slowly. As we went through the tunnel, I heaved a general sigh of relief. "That was close."

She nodded. "It seems money buys a lot for humans, what a strange culture."

"Money buys power, and power earns money. It's a cycle." I leaned down and kissed her head. "But gold and power can't buy everything."

As we made our way through the tunnel, it went much the way of the East Kingdom's gate, though this tunnel was wider to accommodate large wagons and the like escorting cargo to the markets.

Within a few moments, we had reached the end of the tunnel, and the large metal gate rose slowly to open up the way into the Central Kingdom.

# Chapter 22 - Central Kingdom

The gate opened to a crossroads. The front road led to one of the smaller markets, which in turn led to even more market squares. The right and left cobblestone roads led to the back alleys that housed hundreds of warehouses.

The Crescent Rose was several miles further ahead, past most of the markets. Though our meeting wasn't set until noon, so we had some time to kill shopping before heading that way.

As we rode through the busy streets, we passed an overabundant guard presence throughout the streets. Several of them popped into back alleys, and all of them kept a close eye on the comings and goings of the customers perusing the stalls.

*Must be a dangerous criminal for the guard to be so twitchy; usually, they can't be bothered to get off their asses. Whatever. Long as they stay out of our way, it's none of my business.*

I ran through the list of things we had to do. *Clothes shopping for myself and Eris, and I need my armor repaired before I meet with Phineas, though the craft markets will be further down.*

We passed through the first of the weapons and armor vendors. There were hundreds more scattered throughout Central, along with numerous food courts, which piqued my interest. Usually, they had quite a variety of meats and ales, and I'd worked up a thirst.

Eris, for the most part, kept quiet, and people watched as we rode through the bustling crowds. The scents of cooking food wafted towards us long before we'd ever set our sights on the food court.

Our breakfast of meat and cheese could only stave off hunger for so long, and a rumbling from Eris told me she was feeling hungry as well, so we stopped at the first courtyard we rode by. It was large, with wooden stalls crammed tight next to each other, and the gray cobblestone worn smooth by thousands of boots. I stabled Lacuna with an elderly gentleman on the next street over. He ran a temporary stable for merchants and had a reputation for quality. I paid a couple gold extra to make sure he'd take care of her for the day. As soon as she was situated, Eris and I found an unoccupied table.

I paid the woman manning the stall and walked away with two plates piled high with roasted meats and vegetables. We dug in and devoured the food in minutes.

After eating, I stopped by one of the liquor vendors and purchased ten casks of yellowhammer ale to be delivered to Gloom-Harbor. I owed Gil for all that he'd done for me, and a few casks of his favorite ale would be a good start. I paid five gold, and the merchant promised to have them delivered in under five days. That taken care of, we still had to find clothes for Eris and me.

The next square was for the women, a bevy of female merchants and vendors selling anything and everything a woman could dream of—dresses, jewelry, and perfumes by the thousands. I ignored most of it, though a few things caught my eye, and an idea popped into my head. *Eris won't get the meaning of it, but she'll love it when I explain it to her.* We passed by several jewelry stalls until I found the items I wanted.

A pair of solid gold rings, each a perfect circle, gleaming under the light of the sun. They caught my attention amidst the several others dotted around. For some reason, I had to have them. Paying an outrageous two gold for both, I took Eris aside down an empty side alley.

I didn't think the ceremony of getting down on one knee was needed here, but just handing it to her felt wrong. So, I compromised a little.

"I have a gift for you."

She'd seen me purchase the rings, and I'd seen the quizzical look as I paid for them. Entomancers didn't seem to have the equivalent practice, and humans on Nexus didn't spend money on frivolous things like wedding rings. This was a bit of an old-fashioned tradition, but since we were married, I wanted to do things right.

"Hold out your hand."

She did so without hesitation. I gingerly took her hand in mine and placed the ring on her finger. It shrank to fit her slim finger perfectly. She admired the glint of the ring on her finger but didn't understand the significance of it.

I explained to her, back on Earth, married partners would receive golden wedding bands to symbolize their bond of matrimony. As I walked her through the custom, her eyes welled with tears. She hugged me and drew my face down to hers in a passionate kiss.

"I love you, Sam. For now, until eternity."

"Until eternity."

She took my ring in her hand, mimicking the motion I'd made. As before, it fit perfectly around my rough hands.

I would eventually have them both enchanted. *When we get back to Gloom-Harbor, I'll get with Markos, see what works best.*

Thinking of the quirky mage made me wonder how our Gloom shroom business was going and how the Gloam was progressing. *I'll ask when we get back.*

With my little marriage ceremony over with and Eris whistling happily to herself, we meandered among the frilly lace gowns and sparkling tiaras. Nothing that would do for either of us.

Eventually, we found a stall selling more modest traveling clothes and the like. There was even an armor section, but I skipped over that, Eris hadn't worn her chestplate after the first day, and with her chitin armor, anything we bought would likely be inferior, but I did help pick out over a dozen different tunics and skirts for her.

Some were like the ones she'd been wearing, but others were cut much more to her size and would hug her curves better. A few had plunging necklines, and I had to veto those; her nipples kept popping out whenever she moved.

With her clothes sorted out, she changed into one of her new outfits. A long black skirt that came down to her knees and a purple sleeveless tunic with a modest neckline, which hinted at her breasts without revealing them.

With her situated, I needed to sort out my own wardrobe conundrum. We swept past the cooking and general outdoor gear market section along with the pet and animal market. I steered clear of the slave auction house as I wanted nothing to do with them, and I didn't want Eris to see the men and women in cages.

Finally, we arrived at the men's apparel section. It was much smaller than the women's, but men generally hated shopping. It was a sacred rule among us.

Much like the shop I'd purchased Eris's clothes at, I found one selling all manner of tunics and matching breeches and pants. I avoided any of the tights and hose, along with the finer doublets that were meant for fashion rather than functionality, but I picked several sets of cotton and linen shirts and some sturdy canvas pants.

With my purchases made and safely stowed in my inventory, we made our way to the crafts district. Having my armor repaired was the last item I needed to take care of, and no way was I going to meet my informant with shoddy, torn armor. Regardless of my appearance, I didn't want to look like an easy mark. *I don't need a knife in my back today.*

As we reached the market square, where all the craftsmen, blacksmiths, leatherworkers, and weaponsmiths plied their trade. A myriad of smells assaulted me. I'd been here a few times in the past, but I always forgot how pungent the air was.

The sulfuric odor of molten metal combined with the sharp scent of steel. All with the undertone of dyeing leather, which gave off the most repugnant odor imaginable. The smell didn't seem to faze Eris. I, however, was forced to breathe through my mouth, though the mental illusion of every breath I took coating my tongue with the foul air made me want to gag.

I suffered through enough to wander over to one of the armor workers. He was stout, with arms so heavy with muscle that they looked larger than my head. He had a rough lined face and a perfectly waxed bald head and sported a neatly trimmed beard. The man had the general appearance of someone who took time out of his day for basic hygiene. His white shirt and black leather apron were singed and torn from the day's labors.

He grumbled a rough greeting, using grunts rather than actual words. Without a reply, I retrieved my armor from my inventory and slid it across the table with a single word. "Repair."

"Five silver." He spoke, his voice was hoarse as if speaking caused him great pain.

I slid him a gold. "How long?"

He pondered for a moment, looking the armor over with a keen, expert eye. He scratched at his head before answering. "Two hours."

I frowned. *That would be cutting it too close. I need to get there at least half an hour before to set up in case of trouble.* I pulled out another gold and slid it across to him. "How long now?"

The man smiled knowingly and held up a single finger. *An hour. Perfect.*

I nodded and let him get on with his job. Taking hold of Eris's hand, we moseyed around the square, looking at the various tradesmen working their craft. It was a fascinating experience to see, watching them mold metal and leather into beautiful works of art.

The hour flew by, as walking arm in arm with Eris was a delightful experience. She dragged me every time something caught her eye, pulling me along, but I didn't mind, because she was having fun.

We soon found ourselves back in front of the nameless armorsmith, who, without a word, unceremoniously handed me my gear and went back to work.

It was nearly flawless.

He'd had to replace almost all of the metal. The chestplate was entirely new, but the shoulder guards had been left untouched. My vambraces were also new, and he'd used a much stronger metal to form the bulk of it. The tears in the leather and studs had been replaced, but he didn't have the skin of an elder dragon to patch the holes and cracks, so he'd stretched what leather he could and sewed new pieces of what looked like silver drake's skin over to reinforce the thin areas. The bright silver skin of the drake paired well with the black and gray bane wolf fur and complemented the azure leather nicely.

*All in all, I'd say he improved it quite a bit.* I donned the armor; the weight settled around me comfortably. It was heavier than I remembered, but with my increased *Strength*, I could handle it just fine.

With my gear in the best condition I could reasonably hope for, it was time to make our way to the meeting place. Which was obviously a tavern.

The Crescent Rose. A bar that wasn't your normal bar. I held Eris's hand tightly as we passed by the merchants' square entirely and made our way to the slums.

*Even in the height of civilization and commerce where gold flows like rivers, there's still enough room for the poor and the desperate who can barely eke out enough copper to feed themselves.* More than anyone else, beggars and the poor made excellent spies. Going largely unnoticed by most, they overheard everything and would happily spill those secrets for a pittance.

I made my way through the winding labyrinth of side streets and alleyways, filled to the brim with the hungry and the despondent. After dropping a bribe to a child who had to have been no more than five or six, he showed us the way to the Rose.

It had moved since the last time I'd been here, but I knew I was in the right place when I saw a single red door and a large gentleman next to it.

The door was always red. No matter in what part of the city the Rose resided, the door was the giveaway. The man standing next to the door was the following factor of authentication.

The doorman was always standing guard outside the Rose, day or night, rain or snow. He was there. I'd never seen him take a single step in all the years I'd known about the place.

In my younger days, Mika, Lonny, and I had bets on who'd witness the doorman moving first. I'd always had a competitive streak, and so I set up on the roof a nearby building. For an entire day, I watched nonstop to see doorman move. Sleep, hunger, and thirst had won long before doorman budged an inch. At this point, I was convinced he wasn't human. *A golem wrapped in illusion magic maybe, or something.*

The doorman was waiting for us when we arrived. Pale from lack of sunlight and not a shred of hair anywhere on his face, his coal-black eyes stared straight ahead. Dressed in tight black cotton underclothes and leather armor, he didn't so much as turn his head, but I knew he'd been aware of us long before we came into view.

"Password?" Doorman asked. His voice, the deepest baritone I'd ever heard, sounding like two stones colliding against one another.

"To the king, who walks in shadow."

"Accepted."

He opened the door for us and stood still, waiting for us to enter. Eris was still riding the high of sightseeing and decided to run over and greet the large man.

"Hello, I'm Eris."

The doorman paused before nodding his head. It was by a fraction of an inch, but unmistakable.

"A pleasure, miss."

Then he went back to his statue impression. As we went inside, Eris asked me who he was.

"That was Mr. Doorman…the, ah…doorman."

"I like him."

I chuckled. "In fairness, you like most people."

Eris laughed. "True."

The tavern was dark when we exited the hallway. A quick look around told me there wasn't anyone we needed to avoid. The Rose hosted all manner of criminals and deviants, so I was always cautious.

The Rose wasn't like any other tavern I'd ever been in before. There were not any obnoxious bands playing music at the loudest volume they could manage, nor were there noisy, annoying patrons. It was a dark place with sharp corners and dim lighting.

The center of the room was lined with wooden support beams, and the entire far wall housed the bar, in the opposite corners, were tables and booths, all far away from prying eyes or ears. This wasn't a place to hang your hat after a long hard day's work. This was a tavern built for shady backroom characters, dealing shady backroom deals.

There was barely enough light to move around without tripping over anything; shadows danced on the walls as the torch flames flickered. I chose a booth by the back with a clear view of the door. My contact had yet to arrive, as he was one for punctuality but was rarely early.

I kept my head low, and my hand tight around Eris's waist as I made my way over to the bar. The bartender was a well-dressed man by the name of Jackson, mid to late thirties, wearing fine dark clothing and a tailored vest with a red silk pocket square. Jackson had a clean-shaven face and styled dark brown hair that was beginning to gray. He bore a puckered scar from his neck to the base of his jaw, and his bored eyes stared silently at me.

"Ale," I told him and slid him a coin. He nodded and poured me one, keeping out of reach and sliding it to me, waiting for me to leave before taking my money. We went back to the booth, and Eris slid in first while we waited for my contact. It took him nearly twenty minutes to arrive, while I'd drained my ale in half that time. I limited myself as I needed my wits about me to deal with the man.

As my contact walked in the door, I snapped my eyes to him, taking his features in instantly. Not expecting trouble, but certainly ready for it. Phineas noticed my presence almost immediately; his eyes lit up darkly.

Phineas Carn was a weasel of a man, in every sense of the word. His thin, pinched face constantly looked like he had just tasted something foul. His small, beady blue eyes darted back and forth, looking for his paranoia induced enemies everywhere, while he ran his sweaty palms through his lank and greasy dark hair.

He withdrew a sweat-stained handkerchief from the pocket of his hip-length coat and dabbed at his forehead.

*Gods, I hate dealing with him.* Though he had eyes and ears everywhere and usually had reliable information, it didn't matter that I didn't trust him as far as I could throw him. If he came through for us, it would be worth the headache.

"Good afternoon, Duran," he whispered, sliding into the booth.

"Phineas."

He glanced his eyes over Eris, who kept quiet under her hood, his eyes trailing over her form with curiosity before coming back to mine. "Who's she?"

It was a fair question since I'd never once brought a guest with me when I met with him, but I didn't feel like explaining anything to this man. I especially didn't want him seeing Eris's face. *He'd happily sell us both out for that payday.*

Eris went to open her mouth, but I spoke before she could. "No one you need to concern yourself with. Now can we get down to business?"

Eris frowned at me for speaking for her. *I'll apologize later, but I can't risk Phineas knowing too much.* I placed a hand on her warm thigh and squeezed. She immediately lost her frown and grinned at me, taking my hand in hers and absentmindedly brushing her hair out of her face. In the process, she knocked her hood off.

The tips of her ears caught the fabric before it could fall off completely, but the damage was done. Her compounded eyes were visible, and one of her ears was sticking out.

Phineas went wide eyed at the sight of her, his face paled as he looked into the depths of the abyss. His panic was soon replaced by excitement. My knife went to his throat, and I stared him down.

"You never saw her. One word to anyone, anyone at all, and I will make your last moments so painful that you beg me for death, and it will not come. Do I make myself clear?"

He gulped in fear as perspiration bled on his face. "C-c-c-crystal."

Phineas was many things. Intelligent, ambitious, a backstabbing deviant, and above all else, a coward. *He won't risk his life by defying me.*

He nodded at me frantically, but he still had questions about her. I sighed as he asked, "She's a demi…yes?"

"Yep, now can we get down to business?"

"Where did you find her?"

"She found me. Now. Can we get down to business?"

Phineas grinned a sly smile, showing off his blackened teeth. "Of course, of course, of course."

I stifled the need to strangle him and asked my questions.

"My guild was attacked over a week ago by an unknown enemy. Hundreds of troops and a full guild to raid us. I need to know who it was."

"I'm assuming you've ruled out the Alliance?"

I nodded at him. "First thing we eliminated."

Phineas pondered over the question for a moment, drumming his fingers on the wooden table in a staccato rhythm, which was all for show. Despite the utter contempt I had for the man, he had a superb intellect and never forgot anything. Either he knew the answer right away, or he knew nothing, but his thinking was an act.

"Rumors have been making their way to me for months now. Nothing concrete, mind you, just hearsay and secondhand accounts. But according to my sources, there is a person or persons who have been making waves recently. I don't know who, but they have incredibly deep coffers, buying up anything and everything of value. Unique trinkets, artifacts, weapons, and armor. You name it." He paused, glancing between Eris and me. "Hell, they're even buying slaves of all races at prices like I've never seen before."

"Damn," I sighed, letting my breath out long and slow. "That's not anything we haven't figured out already." *I knew they had deep pockets already. If they're buying slaves, then I was right about my hunch. It must be who Darren and his ilk were working for, and we let him slip through our fingers.*

Though slavers were a dime a dozen around here. *Might ask around the auction house, see if I can bribe my way into some information, or beat it out of them— one of the two.*

"That's all you have for me?" I asked, skeptical.

He nodded his head. "Unfortunately. You could try asking around the merchants and slavers, see if anyone would be willing to talk, but I wouldn't bet on it. The kind of money that's being thrown around keeps lips tight."

"Godsdamn it."

I sighed deeply, rising from the comfortable seating. This was a waste of time, and questioning every Tom, Dick, and Harry, I could get my hands on was likely to end up the same way. *What other choice do I have? No other leads and far too many questions.*

"Well, thanks anyway. If you hear anything, I want to know about it first." I slid across a small bag of gold. Not a fortune, but too much for the little information he'd delivered. If it saved me time and energy in the future, I'd consider it worth it. "C'mon. Let's go."

Eris hooked her arm around mine, and I helped pull her out of the seat. Once she was standing on her own two feet, I dropped her arm, only to have her wind her fingers through mine.

"Have a good day, Duran," Phineas called to me as we left.

I ignored him, putting him entirely out of my mind as we walked back through the dark hallway towards the door. *If he can't help us, I'll have to find another informant who can.*

Which meant I would have to call Wilson and perhaps even Evelyn. See if their contacts could come through for me. "Hassle upon hassle," I muttered, turning to Eris as we left. "Looks like we'll be spending a few more days in Central."

"Oh, that'll be fun. We can explore some more. See a few more sights."

"That we can, love," I said as I stepped outside, into the darkened alleyway and right into the fist of an unknown assailant.

It crashed into me like the fury of a god, knocking me to the ground and sending my head spinning. I spat out a mouthful of blood and teeth onto the street, which was already covered in blood.

Too much blood to have come from me.

I looked up to see Doorman, dead on the street. His throat was slashed and spilling all-too-human blood onto the stone. *I guess I found my answer after all these years.*

Standing only brought more pain as a foot slammed into the side of my face, sending me right back to the ground.

More pain as my opponent kicked me—sharp pain to my chest, ribs, and stomach. I was grabbed roughly by the hair and dragged out of the doorway. I fell on my back as warm blood poured out of me, pooling and mixing with Doorman's.

My attacker stood over me, through my swollen eyelids, I could make out the smug, smiling face of Darren.

"Surprise," he taunted.

Footsteps scuffled from my left, and I turned my head to see Eris fighting five of Darren's goons, and it wasn't going well.

Eris summoned a swarm of insects. Spiders and cockroaches poured out of the filthy alley, but the second they appeared, Darren paled, letting go of me to deal with her.

He pulled a syringe from his long brown coat and jabbed the needle into her neck. A second later, she slumped over, unconscious. With the stream of magic cut off, the bugs fled back to their homes.

"Tsk, tsk, tsk. Can't have you ruining my plans with your little insects, girl. I won't have you fuck things up twice," Darren said. "Take her while I deal with him."

I stood to my feet, fighting back the pain to face Darren.

"You're not going to fucking touch her!"

Three of the goons rushed me while the largest goon, a thick built man with dead eyes, carried her over his shoulder. The men were big and clumsy in their black leather armor. All clearly used to their size and intimidation getting them whatever they wanted. From their movements, I could tell they only had the barest hint of how to actually fight. *Even wounded, I can take them.*

The first guy, tall with a shaved head and a wispy beard, put all of his weight on his right leg as he swung a wide right haymaker.

I stepped toward him, threw my left hand just over his bicep, and brought it around back to me, clenching tight. With his arm trapped, I rotated my shoulder and brought his entire torso toward the ground. He struggled against me, but I had the leverage. I brought my knee up sharply, slamming it to his face.

Blood rained from his broken flesh, but I wasn't done. The other goons were on me, but I kept a lock on the one in my grasp and kept his body between the others. With a twist, I pulled bleeding goon's arm from his socket and shoved him towards his comrades.

He careened into one of them, taking him to the ground, but I didn't manage to get both. The other one, a lanky man with a pockmarked face and thick, curly hair, threw a few jabs at me.

I slipped his punches and hit him with a left hook. Teeth flew as his head snapped to the side, and he staggered from the blow. I brought a low roundhouse to his chest and fractured his ribs. He went down and stayed there, clutching his side.

The final goon was getting off the ground, and I didn't bother fighting him. I took my hunting knife and threw it, burying it to the hilt in his heart. He crashed to the ground as he bled out.

It'd taken me only a minute to dispatch the three goons, but it had given the brutish one holding Eris time to escape.

*Godsdamn it!*

A dark chuckle bubbled from my heart. *"Lose something, knight?"* the Aspect asked, laughing.

*Fuck you!*

I tuned out the insidious laughter of the Aspect to focus on Darren.

"You're going to tell me where she is, right now!"

He'd been leaning against the alley wall, hands in his pockets, while I fought his men, but he pushed off with a laugh.

"No, now I'm going to savor this moment," he said, taking a shiny object from his pocket and slipping it on his fingers.

*Brass knuckles. Shit.*

*"Hope your Exoskeleton can hold up,"* the Aspect snickered.

I was tired of the mind games, and it wasn't helping me. I settled into my stance and watched Darren's feet. He had good technique, and his leather armor was well suited for quick movements. Darren brushed an errant lock of his auburn hair that fell to his forehead with his left hand and swung with his right.

He feint almost worked, as my eyes gravitated to his hair, but his hips gave him away, and I stepped back as his knuckles grazed my nose.

Darren followed his sucker punch with a kick to the groin. I twisted my leg to deflect it, but his boot collided with the side of my knee hard, and I stumbled. He flicked his knuckled hand out in a jab, and I blocked, but it was just a fake to set up his cross. His left hand hit me square in the jaw, almost in the same spot as his first hit. Pain flared to life from the left side of my face, and I fell to the flagstones, spitting out a thick gob of blood.

The pain was intense, but I'd had worse. I stood up, and a warning flashed across my vision.

***Warning! Proximity to Hive Queen Greater Than 100 Meters Penalty Activated: -20 to all Stats***

My strength fled, and I sagged as exhaustion set in. Darren took the opportunity to smash my face with his brass knuckles.

Absolute pain obliterated my world, and I lost consciousness. When I came to, blood poured freely from the side of my ruined face, and Darren was smiling.

"Doesn't feel too good, does it, asshole? How's it feel to be on the receiving end of the worst beating of your life? Not fun, is it?" he shouted as he hit my face again.

I blacked out again.

When I came to, Darren was kneeling over me, his too-white teeth grinning a malicious smile. "Really need to thank the weasel for coming through for me. It'd have taken me ages to find you on my own."

*Phineas! That rat bastard! I'll skin him alive when I find him!* But I had more pressing concerns at the moment—namely, the man beating me to a pulp.

My face was a mess of pain, but I could still fight.

Darren stood and drew his scimitar. I aimed a kick to the side of his leg, hitting the peroneal nerve that runs up the shin, locking his leg in agony.

He dropped to the ground and seized up, screaming in pain. I had a few seconds to breathe.

*"Once more, allow me to offer you power, knight. They've absconded with your queen, and you need me to get her back."*

*Hell, no. I'm not making a deal with you. I can handle this on my own.*

I opened my inventory and pulled out a health potion. I uncapped it and brought it to my lips to take a sip when my hand locked up. The glass bottle slipped from my fingers and shattered on the stones.

*"Whoops."*

*Go to hell!*

It just laughed. In the time it took for whatever the Aspect did to wear off, Darren shook off his pain and stood with his scimitar once more.

I drew my blade and prepared to engage him. Darren swung, keeping his movements light. He was quick with his sword, but I parried each of his strikes.

He switched from slashes to thrusts, and I countered. I swung, but as I reached the end of my attack, my hand locked up again, and my blade slipped through my fingers.

I could do nothing as Darren kicked my sword away and thrust forward, stabbing me in the chest. It went through my armor and even my *Exoskeleton* but stopped before it pierced anything vital.

*"Care to keep this going, knight? You've wasted enough time already. Just imagine what vile things they're doing to her as we speak. I bet they're pawing over her lovely porcelain skin right now."*

I screamed wordlessly, tearing my vocal cords as I seethed in pitch black hatred at the voice in my head. I'd have killed myself just to kill it if I could've, but I was frozen and seconds from death.

*Fine, you godsdamned bastard. Deal. Give me your power.*

*"At your command, sir knight."*

**Warning! Forceful Activation of Abilities!**

**Hive Guard**

**Chitin Blade**

**Warning! System Corruption!**

**Forceful Activation of Passive Ability: Hive Mind**

My pain vanished as *Hive Guard* took effect, pooling black over my skin and healing my injuries, allowing me to fight back. I knew I'd just made a mistake, but I didn't have time to waste.

*Worry about the rest of that shit later. Right now, Darren needs to die!*

He was enraged when my body healed itself, screaming in rage, he swung at me. "Why won't you fucking stay down!"

On reflex, I brought my hand up to defend myself, but what came up wasn't my hand. A long black sword of chitin enveloped my arm, jagged with uneven lines and wickedly sharp. It met his scimitar and nicked the edge.

Darren backed up when he realized the danger and came at me carefully.

The learning curve for using a sword attached to my arm was steeper than I'd have guessed, and Darren sliced me a few times while I got used to the difference.

Darren was gifted with the sword. He kept his form light and mobile, and his footwork was spot on. He put his body behind his attacks and was giving me a run for my money, but he wasn't in the same league as me.

I parried his sword and brought my blade along his forearm, slicing a deep groove into it. He fumbled as his hand became slick with blood and nearly dropped his scimitar. He passed it to his off-hand and thrust at me.

In his non-dominant hand, his weapon was little more than a club as he clumsily tried to fight me. I caught his sword on my vambrace and brought my blade to slice through his wrist, severing the flexor tendons and median nerve, stopping him from holding his sword anymore.

It fell from his limp hand, clanging off the stone, while Darren stared at his bleeding hands and arms, wondering where everything went wrong. *Fucked with the wrong person, asshole.*

Soon as I took a single step, Darren snapped out of it and looked at me with fear. He paled and took off at a sprint, trying to save his skin. His goons followed his lead, and the two left alive limped away as Darren fled.

*Like hell he's getting away again!* I sped forward, tackling Darren to the ground and bashing him with the flat side of my sword. While he was dazed, I got off of him and dragged him to his feet, placing my sword against his throat—a hair's breadth from ending his miserable life.

"Tell me where she is, now!"

Darren tried to back away, but a quick slice on his neck dissuaded him of that. The cut wasn't deep, just enough to let him know that I could have taken his head if I'd wanted.

"Look...if I tell you where she is, you'll kill me anyway."

I shoved him back against the alley wall. My blade still against his throat. "I can guarantee that if you don't tell me, I'll torture you until you do. So how about you save me the time and spill your guts before I spill them for you."

Darren tried to put on a stoic face, attempted to brave the pressure he found himself under, but I could see the cracks in his psyche. At heart, Darren was a coward, even worse than the weasel. Darren preyed on the weak and those who couldn't fight back. A scavenger. Nothing more.

"P—promise me, you'll let me live, and I'll tell you. I swear!"

*You'll suffer for your actions, but not until after you tell me what I want to know. I'll let you think you're walking away from this.* I softened my glare on him. "Fine, but if I ever see you after this..."

"You'll kill me. I got it. Never see me, I swear," Darren interrupted, "She's at the slave auction house, in the warehouse, where they keep the merchandise. She'll be bound, but no one will touch her, I promise."

I dug the blade a little deeper into his neck. Blood dripped down beneath my sword. "You could be lying."

"I'm not! I swear!"

"Tell me about your master," I demanded.

Darren backed up as far as he could go on the wall. Blood ran down his neck and arms to drip onto the street. He shook his head, violently.

"No way, worse you can do is kill me. Nothing compared to what he'll do to me. Like nothing you've ever seen before, man. No way. Kill me or let me go, but I won't talk."

I thought about pushing him because I knew I could eventually get him to talk, but I had a better plan. I didn't need him to talk.

With only a second to steel myself, I bent low and bit deep into his neck.

His blood spilled into my open mouth, and I braced for the transition. As the Mnemosyne took hold, Darren's memories spilled as fast as his blood.

Flashes rolled through me. The first was of Darren and a man meeting in a tavern. The location looked like a seedy bar in the North Kingdom. The man across the worn table was handsome. A thin, yet rugged face, with short brunet hair, a thick goatee, and bright blue eyes. He lifted a hand to take a drink, showing a heavy black gauntlet with a mana crystal embedded in the center. The two of them conversed for a moment before the image faded.

The second memory started in the middle of a battle. Darren, Wolf, Mikhail, and Slip were assaulting a caravan, killing merchants, and robbing them.

The guards were killed, and the survivors were brought out. Several rabbitmen were among the caravan. Two of them resisted and grabbed the guards' fallen weapons, only to be cut down where they stood. The others gave up after the deaths of their comrades. When the quick battle was over, the newly captured slaves were thrown in the back of a prison wagon.

In the back were two small children. They were very nondescript, except for their ears. Longer than the elves but not nearly as long as Eris's. They curled backward slightly, which marked them as different, but their eyes were normal. Which discounted them as entomancers, but they were, without a doubt, non-human children. *Demi-human perhaps? Not rabbitmen or wolf-men, they lack the ears.*

The final vision was of a dark warehouse. The wood was in clear need of repair, and the room housed half a dozen cages that lined the back wall. Darren and his men stood in the room with a new man.

He was wearing a pristine white suit, with a wide brimmed hat that shadowed his features. The man wielded an ivory cane in his off-hand.

Darren handed over the bound demi-human children as the man passed Darren a heavy sack of gold.

The man fiddled with his cane, tossing it from hand to hand with a flourish. He balanced it and rubbed the tip of the ivory, drawing my eyes. Embossed into the pale bone was a familiar symbol.

The hand clutching the barbed hourglass.

*I found you, bastard!* The man in white was my target.

The visions faded, and Darren winced in pain as blood dripped from his wound. Only a second had passed, and I leaned back, letting go of him, spitting out the rancid tang.

"Thank you for your help."

"I'm free to go, right? You promised."

I shoved my chitin sword through the bottom of Darren's mouth, into his brain and out the top of his head.

His eyes glazed over, and his jaw went slack, opening just enough, so part of my sword was visible poking through the roof of his mouth. Blood poured out of his lips to soak into his shirt.

I withdrew the blade as Darren slide down the wall to lay in a heap on the pavestones in an ever-growing pool of his own blood.

"I lied."

# CHAPTER 23 - CHAINS OF THE PAST

"Good riddance," I spat, stepping over his rotten corpse.

As soon as the fight ended, my nascent power flooded out of my system, leaving me weak. *I feel different, strange.* The magic inside my heart burned furiously, but inside that heat, a blizzard raged. The icy black magic was stronger; it pulsed through my heart, melding with the fire of the Hive magic.

*I just made a deal with the devil, wonder what it's going to cost me?*

I picked up my fallen weapons and stepped inside the doorway to the Rose, stopping to look at the doorman. "Sorry you died because of me," I whispered to the corpse.

My apology fell on dead ears. It was for my benefit alone. *The dead have the luxury of being unburdened by such concerns as want.*

Once more, I walked through the darkened hallway of the Rose. Phineas sat in the same booth, looking smug and content, counting a huge pile of gold. *That just further damns him. He sold us out!*

He looked up as I approached. His small eyes bulged at the sight of me, as he choked back a yelp of fright and tried to leap out of the booth.

My foot caught his knee, dislocating it with a sick pop, followed by a high-pitched shriek of pain. A few of the other patrons looked around at the noise, saw us, and went back to minding their own business. *Wise of them.*

"Hello, again, friend."

Phineas ignored me and attempted to hobble away on his one good leg. I kicked his other leg out from under him, sending him crashing into a nearby table. They toppled over in his wake.

"Where you off to in such a hurry?"

He climbed to his feet, and I kicked him right back down. He sprawled out over the tables and chairs. I knelt and shattered his arm at the elbow. He screamed even louder this time, his cries echoing through the hushed bar.

Our little show had garnered the interest of most of the shady patrons, who had stopped their dealings to watch me break every bone in the weasel's body.

"Get the fuck up!"

Phineas obliged and weakly rose to his feet, supporting himself as best he could with one leg. He leaned against one of the support beams to balance himself.

"Duran, I'm sorry, I couldn't turn down the money," he confessed. Not even bothering trying to lie to me.

I grabbed him by the collar of his shirt. "You're sorry? Fuck your sorry!"

I threw him across the room to slam against the bar top. Jackson gave me an exasperated look as Phineas bled onto his counter. I grabbed Phineas by the throat and spoke to the bartender.

"Ale," I said, tossing him a gold.

Jackson sighed, but poured me the drink, sliding it to me with a warning. "You know I called the guard, right?"

I took the ale, downing it, washing the last remnants of blood from my mouth, and shrugged. "Won't make a difference, but sorry for trashing the place. I'll pay for the damages."

Jackson gave me a half nod and a grunt before going back to minding his own business. I eased my grip on Phineas, he gasped, trying to breathe normally again. *Enjoy those breaths. You won't have many more.* As he stopped wheezing, I clamped tight over his windpipe again.

"Tell me what I want to know, and this stops," I said.

He struggled against me, but he was far too weak. After a minute, I let him breathe.

"I can't. He'll kill me." He coughed.

In a rage, I took hold of his hand and slammed my empty beer mug down on it. Fingers snapped, twisting in odd directions and glass shattered, piercing the soft flesh. Crimson ran out and down the dark wood. Dark enough that you couldn't even tell it was blood.

"Tell me!"

Gripping his hand tight, I pushed up the sleeve of his coat, took the jagged edge of my glass handle, and ripped chunks of flesh from his arm. Ichor welled from the split gashes in his skin, spilling even more onto the counter. Phineas gurgled as I mutilated what remained of his hand, turning it into nothing but so much shredded meat and gore. Flecks of bone peeked through the hues of pink and red.

"Kill me. Just Kill me."

*Like hell, you're getting off that easy.* I raised the glass shard to his temple and dug in, ruby droplets slithered down his temple. I was ready to flay his very face from his skull if need be.

"Stop…just stop. I'll talk, I'll talk."

I nodded to him and lowered the handle from his face. "Give me a name."

Phineas sighed deeply, defeated. He hung his head and whispered the name.

"Magnus. The name of the man you're looking for is Magnus."

I sliced a shallow line across his throat, carving his flesh. "What else do you know?"

"The auction house. It's where Darren spends his time. I think his boss is there."

I cut another light gash, right next to the first. Phineas shook his head, his eyes never leaving the bloody piece of glass in my hand. "That's all I know, I swear. I wouldn't even know that if I hadn't overheard him talking about him to his friends."

It was all I would get from him, and he'd outlived his usefulness.

I crushed Phineas's windpipe.

*Slitting his throat would be too quick of a death.* His face turned purple as he was deprived of all oxygen, his eyes bulging out of his skull as he slowly suffocated to death. He attempted to run away, but a stretched-out leg caught him and sent him to the floor, from where he did not rise.

Phineas choked his last and died, all while pleading with me to spare him. *Pathetic.*

I walked over to the table where Phineas sat, scooped the large pile of gold in two bags, and tossed the smaller one to Jackson as I left. "Have a good one, Jack."

"Watch your back, Duran."

Back in the alley, I found the corpses of Doorman and Darren right where they'd been. The nameless goon was right where he fell. That much hadn't changed. What had changed was that I now found myself surrounded by nearly a dozen guards — all with their weapons drawn and pointed at my throat.

"Howdy, fellas, fancy seeing you here." I smiled.

All of them shouted at me in unison. Each one was shouting a slightly different version of the same thing. Get my hands in the air. Do not resist. Drop my weapon—the usual drivel.

My knee-jerk reaction was to pull out my sword and slaughter them all. I didn't have time to deal with these clowns.

I twitched, my hand milliseconds from reaching for my sword when a voice stopped me cold. A voice I hadn't heard in a very long time.

"Don't do it, D."

I looked around until I spotted the source. The one man I'd hoped to never see again.

Pushing himself through the circle of soldiers in the alleyway, he stood in radiant crimson plate mail that shone bright even in the dim lighting. A long golden cape trailed down to his knees and fluttered here and there in the slight breeze that rolled through the alley, and a heavy longsword was belted at his hip. Almost as unadorned as mine except for the large ruby fastened in the pommel and the golden inlay of his cross-guard.

His face hadn't changed since the last time I'd seen him, over fifteen years ago when we'd stood blade to blade and tried to kill one another. He was still handsome, and his chestnut hair hadn't changed much. But his brown eyes were so much colder than when I'd known him.

"Lonny. It's been a while."

I took note of his armor, especially of the golden crest on his chest plate—hands clasped in prayer surrounded by a halo.

I scoffed at the man I once called a friend. "You joined the fucking Cardinals?"

He nodded. "They've treated me fairly over the years, D. They gave me a family, after yo—after everything that happened."

"Surprised I never ran into you when I was training."

His face darkened. "The other paladins are quite displeased with you, not to mention the High Priest. By Whisper's lips, I've never seen him so enraged before. You earned plenty of enemies that day when you fled."

I shrugged. *They can get in line. It matters little to me.* "So, you're the leader of the strongest guild on Nexus. Quite an accomplishment, old friend. And while this little chat's been fun—" I eased off my sword and moved to leave, "I've got places to be—"

"Hold it!"

*Shit.* "What do you want?"

He motioned at the bodies, an incredulous look on his face. "You killed three people, and you ask what I want."

"In my defense, I only killed two of them." I pointed at Darren. "Him and his crony over there killed the doorman and attacked me. I killed them. There's no crime against self-defense."

Jostling armor moved behind me. I turned to see one of the guards coming out of the Rose. He ignored me and spoke to Lonny. "Sir, there's another body inside the tavern. The description the owner gave of the killer matches this man."

*Thanks for the sellout, Jackson!* "Would you believe he came at me with a knife?"

The look Lonny gave me was withering. He wasn't in the mood for jokes. *Well, I'm not in the mood for your self-righteous bullshit, so that makes us even.*

Lonny went for the handle of his sword, a warning in his eyes. "D, you know I have to take you in. Not counting the bounty still on your head, you killed three, maybe four people here. I can't just ignore that."

*This isn't what I need right now! Godsdamn it, Eris is in danger!* I didn't have the time to waste, but I didn't have the time to get killed either.

Lonny joined the Cardinals. Even as a level one hundred blade master, Lonny would've been a dangerous foe. *He's twice as deadly now as the last time we fought.* He wouldn't just beat me; he'd reduce me to a bloody smear on the wall. *Maybe I could win with Dance, but no way could I get them all in time.*

Darren said she wouldn't be harmed, and even if I hated to admit it, I believed him. Slaves were only valuable in perfect condition. So, I could trust that she would be safe at least until she was bought. Of course, if Magnus was at the auction house, then all bets were off. I didn't have much time to waste, if any at all.

"Fine, I'll go with you."

As the guards moved to arrest me, I hastily unequipped my armor and weapons, stowing them in my inventory. *Can't afford to have them confiscated. I'll never get them back.* I didn't relish standing there in my simple pants and tunic, but it beat losing my gear.

"Why do you always have to be so complicated, Durandal?" Lonny asked.

"Why'd you have to go and destroy our guild, Ascalon?" I countered.

Lonny sighed deeply and shook his head. I knew he held some regret over what he'd done, but it didn't change the fact that he'd ruined everything. Over petty jealousy and grief, though it wasn't solely his fault. *Most of the blame falls on me. I'm to blame for what happened, but Lonny was the one who drew his sword first.*

The bitterness of that day still lingered in his eyes, still haunted him all these years later. *I'm sorry for my part in your pain, Lonny, but I lost someone that day too. You just never saw past your own grief to notice.*

"You know why I did what I did, but our past doesn't change anything. It doesn't change what has to happen right now."

"Yeah, I know."

Things could have gone so differently for us, but we both responded to our grief with anger, at ourselves and each other. It didn't matter that we destroyed everything we'd built in the process.

We lost Sophia, so we took everything from each other.

I held up my hands and let the guards bind them with chains. Lonny was too rough with me as he escorted me out of the alley and to a nearby jail. Jails were like the markets in Central; there was one on nearly every corner.

Lonny walked through the prison like he owned the place and threw me in the furthest cell, removing the manacles around my wrists and shutting the door.

"Court is in two days, and King Elias will set your bounty then."

The cell was a damp gray affair. A lone metal cot bolted to the wall and wet straw for a bed. There were myriad tiny cracks in the stone walls that made up the room. Gray stone walls, gray stone floors, and a gray stone ceiling.

Water dripped through one of the larger cracks in the wall to pool onto the stone floor, bringing a moldy chill to the room. The only window was three feet above my head and had bars through it, letting only a small amount of light into the cramped room.

Either I'd be forced to pay the bounty or serve a year in jail. *Though Elias likes using prisoners to pad the ranks of the Alliance. Ten to one odds, that's what he tries with me.*

Quite a few of the poor who found themselves shanghaied into service never left. It beat begging at any rate. *Pay, serve, or die.* Since it was nearly impossible to jail players for long periods of time, it was always one of the three. The most drastic option was execution; sent back to level one was a harsh punishment, though.

*I've got plenty of gold, and I need to get out of here now. I don't have the time to waste.*

Before Ascalon could leave, I ran to the bars as he turned to walk away. "Lonny, wait! I can't afford to spend two days in here. Whatever price Elias sets won't exceed a thousand gold. Not for something like this."

I pulled out a heavy bag of gold from my inventory, fifteen hundred gold, most of the money I had on me. "This is well over a thousand gold! Take it and release me. It'll more than cover my bounty."

Lonny looked surprised at my outburst. "What's gotten into you, D? I've never seen you balk at a few days in jail."

I held up my hand to show him my ring. The one sign of proof I could leverage to convince Lonny I was speaking the truth.

"The man I killed was a slaver. His thugs kidnapped my wife and nearly killed me. Please, I need to save her!"

Lonny peered at my hand through the bars. The glint of gold was unmistakable, but his face darkened, his jaw clenched tight. I knew what he was thinking. Pure hatred crossed his face, and I'd just damned myself.

His voice cracked, harsh and bitter. "So, someone managed to get you to say yes after all this time. Good for you. Too bad Sophia isn't around to share in the good news."

I slammed my fist against the bars. "Godsdamn it, man. I loved her too!"

He got right up in my face and roared at me, spittle flying out of his mouth. "Loved her! You fucking killed her!"

He turned and stormed out of the room, fury and pain clouding him, just like they had all those years ago. "Rot in here for all I care."

Then he was gone, and I was left alone. Alone with my thoughts. *He's not wrong; she died because of me, because I didn't see what was right in front of me.*

The Screaming Cliffs were Sophia's favorite place on Nexus, though I never understood why. We stepped out of the teleportation gate, and the wind immediately swept up around us, constant gusts that sounded like the wailing of the dead.

The muted brown and gray cliffs were high above the sea, and it always felt like the wind was trying to push us off and into the dark, turbulent waters below.

Sophia took my hand in hers and pulled me toward the cliffs. She'd dressed up, forgoing her usual leather armor and shortsword in favor of a cerulean dress with a revealing neckline, the hem stopping just above her knees and blowing about in the wind. Her walnut hair was pinned into a ponytail, her bright hazel eyes sparkling with excitement and nervousness.

We stopped just shy of the edge, and Soph pulled out a large blanket and an assortment of cooking supplies. She busied about setting things up and getting a fire built. A hard thing, considering the location. When I tried to help, she only fussed at me.

"Uh-uh, I don't think so," she said, handing me a tankard of mead. "You sit and relax. I'll be done in a few minutes."

I laid back on the blanket and sipped at the mead. It was homemade, blackberry and cherry mead, Sophia's specialty, and it was delicious. The most delicious drink in the world.

I cast a sidelong glance at her. She was smiling as she worked. *It's good to see her like this again—she's been so withdrawn and aloof lately.* For a time, I stared out over the cliffs, enjoying my drink and the comfortable silence between us. The clinking of pots and pans and the howling wind melded into a song.

Sophia got the makeshift kitchen set up and started cooking for the two of us, boar steaks and scalloped potatoes with even more mead. My favorite meal. I savored the food while Sophia and I talked. To this day, I can't remember what we talked about. Everything and nothing, perhaps. It all blended and faded into the abyss.

But I remember all too well what happened next.

The midday sun faded into warm twilight as we brought our outing to a close. I helped Soph pack everything up, and we were just about to head to the gate when Sophia stopped me, tugging on my arm.

I turned back to her. "What is it?"

"Um, there's something I have to tell you," she said, her face flushed with embarrassment as she picked at her fingernail, trying to work up the courage to speak.

"Go on," I pushed, unsure what she was getting at.

She huffed but smiled at me. "Duran," she began before shaking her head. "No, Sampson. I love you."

*Oh…this is what she wanted to tell me.* It wasn't like I didn't know. I'd known how she felt about me for years, even before we joined the Ouroboros Project. I knew.

"Soph—" I started, but she cut me off.

"No, let me finish. I'm in love with you, Sam. I have been for a very long time now, and I couldn't spend another day without telling you." She stepped forward to take my hand. "I love you, Sam, and I want to be with you, forever." She pulled a ring from her pocket and knelt. "Will you marry me?"

I pulled away, letting her hand fall from mine.

*I'm sorry, Soph.* I couldn't marry her. Not because I didn't love her—I loved her as much as I ever loved anyone, but even years later, the ghosts of my failures were too strong.

I was still suffering because of Micah, because I'd failed to protect my family. My excuse seemed reasonable at the time. I didn't want to fall in love with someone else, only to lose them too.

Even though that's exactly what happened anyway. I didn't know what my answer meant to her.

"I can't, Soph. I'm sorry, but no. I can't marry you."

She wasn't shocked, as I'd thought she'd be. She'd known what my answer was going to be. She stood from the ground and gave me a sorrowful smile.

"I knew you'd say that, but it doesn't hurt any less."

"Soph, I'm so sorry."

"I know you are, Sam."

I held out my hand. "C'mon, Soph. Let's go home. We can talk more there."

She shook her head. "I'm not going home."

"Why not?" I asked, shocked. I tried to go to her, but she pulled away from me, going to look out to the sea.

"I'm tired, Sam. Tired of this world. It's as brutal as anything we survived back on Earth, and I'm so tired. Tired of the killing and the bloodshed. I never wanted to be a warrior, yet I've killed thousands."

"You don't have to fight if you don't want to. We can leave the guild, go settle in the Compass Kingdom. We don't have to fight anymore."

"No, Sam. There's too much blood on our hands to ever come clean. This world feels as real as the one we left. That means what we've done, we've done to real people. For years and years, we've gone on slaughtering whoever stood in our way, and I can't carry that weight anymore. I'd rather die than keep on living with this guilt."

"The one thing that's kept me going was you. I thought that if you could come to love me that would be enough, but that was a pipe dream."

"I love you, Soph!"

She smiled at me, but it was hollow. "I know you do, but not as I love you. And it doesn't matter, anyway. It was just an excuse for me, something to cling to when my world fell apart. I loved you with everything I had, but it still wasn't enough to hold back the nightmares."

"There's too much pain, Sam. I just can't take it anymore."

She stepped to the edge of the cliff, and I wasn't fast enough to stop her. I pushed as fast as my legs would carry me, but it wasn't enough.

"Sophia!"

"Goodbye, Sam."

She let herself fall over the edge. Down to a place she couldn't come back from; a place I couldn't follow.

Sophia took her own life. There would be no coming back for her.

Lonny blamed me for her suicide, and I couldn't even defend myself. Not then.

I paced the confines of my cell. Trying to think up a way out of here. *Without Lonny's help, no way I'm getting out of here. And now, he'll probably try and obstruct my release, just to spite me.*

Eris would pay for my past sins. Would pay the too-high price Lonny forced on her, sold to Magnus or someone even worse to be abused and discarded. *No, I won't let that happen.*

With each circle I made in the cramped cell, I grew more and more desperate. Through our connection, I knew she was still unconscious, but she could wake up at any moment, and I didn't want her to be alone when that happened.

She'd never voiced it, but she was terrified of being alone. Scarred by her time in the abyss. That thought alone sent waves of hatred and self-loathing through me. *I failed her. Put my revenge and bloodlust ahead of her safety. I tortured Phineas because I wanted to, as much as I wanted information.*

*Eris is going to pay for my failures.*

"Fuck that!" *Never again will someone I love pay for my actions!*

I promised Eris I'd protect her, and by the nine kings of Hell, I was going to keep that promise. I dug out my lockpick set from my Inventory. My rake and tension wrench would make short work of the flimsy lock on the cage.

Jailbreaking from the inside was a new experience, and working the tumblers from the opposite side meant I seized up the pins more than once.

After a few minutes of raking and failing, to try again and again, I managed to set the final pin.

Only to receive a couple of hundred volts of electricity shooting through me.

I locked up and dropped like a stone to the floor, unable to control myself as the electricity surged into me and spasmed through my muscles. I cursed when I could finally move again.

My wrench and pick had fallen out of the lock and slid against the wall out of reach. *Should have figured it was trapped. My own damn fault for not thinking ahead. Eris has my head out of whack.* Even though I figured it would go the same way as the lock, I pulled out a teleportation scroll and attempted to use it.

A bright purple Script circle appeared above me on the roof of the cell, shredding the scroll as it activated. *Nullification magic, of course.* That meant this was a cell built to house players. *Expensive and annoying.* Which meant my options were limited.

I resorted to brute force as my last resort, kicking the iron gate with all my strength. After a few well-placed kicks, I found myself making a lot of noise and getting nowhere. A few more halfhearted kicks before the vibrations started to hurt. *This is wasting time.*

A nudge brushed my subconscious—an itch in the back of my head. Eris was awake and was wondering where I was. She tugged on our connection, making sure I was alive. I couldn't communicate with her, but I knew she was worried about me, and herself. Her emotions rose when she found herself alone, but she was fighting to stay strong. Trying not to let herself cry.

"Damn it!" I screamed and slammed my fist into the side of the wall. Right where the small crack was leaking water. It crumbled, just slightly where my fist struck it. *I'll tear this whole fucking jail apart if I have to. Nothing is going to stand in my way!*

Utterly consumed with rage, I ignored everything, even the damage I was doing to my hand, and smashed my fist into the again and again. Leaving smears of blood and scraps of skin along the cracks and not getting anywhere.

*"Allow me to help,"* the Aspect whispered.

I ignored the sibilant voice, but when I went to hit the wall again, my fist was encased in hard chitin. Cracks and chips started sloughing off the stone. With each hit, more crumbled under my fury. The wall weakened until daylight poured through the large cracks I'd made, bathing me in soft sunlight. Soon a fist-sized hole was through the two-foot-thick stone wall.

*I'm not done yet!*

With even more renewed determination, I reduced the entire wall to rubble in a few short minutes. When the hole was large enough, I bolted through it in a flash and raced as fast as I could to the auction house.

# CHAPTER 24 - THE AUCTION HOUSE

The first few streets were the worst. I was sure that Lonny and his goons were about to round the corner and chase after me, that it had my nerves shot to hell.

I kept my head low as I pushed through the throng of people, customers and merchants were everywhere as they bought and sold by the thousands. My pace was as fast as it could be and slow enough that I wouldn't attract attention or run headlong into someone.

Soon as I could, I got off the main streets and took back alleys. I turned down a particularly decrepit side street and nearly ran over a couple who had let their passions overwhelm them and were locked in an embrace, kissing.

I skirted around them, hopping over a sleeping bum in the process, and was nearly out of the alley when two guards walked past.

I'd spotted them in time, but one turned their head as I ducked behind a trash bin. The thud of their boots stopped, and I heard a mumbled. "What was that?"

The other guard stopped as well, slurring his words as he spoke to his comrade. "Why'd you stop?"

"Thought I saw something."

A shove, followed by more slurring. "Well, go check it out then."

Heavy footsteps approached, and I held my breath, hoping they would stop and leave, but no such luck. They crept closer. A few feet from me now.

*Damn it, I don't have time for this hide and seek bullshit.*

When the guard was within reach, I jumped out from behind the bin and brought the side of my palm to the unfortunate guard's neck. I held back, trying not to crush his windpipe, but put enough force behind it to bring him to his knees, breathless, to clutch his neck. I kneed him in the face, breaking his nose and sending him to the stone, unconscious.

The drunk guard stumbled over his words in an attempt to shout while also drawing his weapon. He rushed me and stumbled, tripping over a rock and tumbling to the ground. I took two steps and kicked his teeth in before he had the chance to stand back up.

*What a waste of time.* I stepped over the bleeding drunk and left the alley.

The route to the auction house was clear after the scuffle with the guards. Pulling up the map to check my location, I waved away the blinking notification tab. *I'll deal with it later.*

I ducked through another back street and hopped the gate to the auction house. It was located in the Market District, but it looked as if it belonged in the Noble District. Where everything in the market squares felt cramped, with as many stalls squished together as possible. The road to the slave market was vacant and clean. Freshly paved stone and large red brick walls topped with wrought-iron spikes lined the entirety of the square.

In the center stood the primary residence for the Slavers Association. It was called a house, but it was as extravagant as any high noble's mansion.

The palatial home was built of spotless white stone with matching marble columns. The dark oak shingles were trimmed in gold and accented the stone perfectly. Large windows on the second and third stories offered a brief glimpse of the ostentatious wealth that was present here—bedrooms and offices that held more gold and marble than a bank vault.

I'd forgotten how profitable the business was. "Bah," I muttered.

The worst kind of blood money. *To sell a being that has all the intelligence of a flesh and blood human, just because you don't consider them real. Disgusting.*

Flanked on either side of the grand manor were two large warehouses. Built of sturdy wood, they'd stood the test of time, but were much worse for wear. Broken and rotten planks were scattered across the two buildings and detracted from the opulent house.

As I walked into the courtyard, I was surrounded by even more wealth. People were busying about in the large square: rich men and women crowding each other to get a look at the wares.

They all crowded around a makeshift stage. The wood was of excellent quality, but the construction was clearly sub-par. It still dripped wood stain that was too thickly applied. A thud caught my attention as one of the wooden gates to the warehouses was forced open.

Several large cages rolled out to rest near the stage as the massive crowd shuffled against each other to get a better look. Elves and dwarves were locked in the cages. Men, women, and even children. People whose only crime were being born differently and being unlucky enough to be caught outside of their respective kingdoms.

I slipped through the crowd as quickly as I could and moved to get a better look at the faces of the slaves, studying each of the cages carefully.

Eris wasn't among the group currently for sale. I turned my gaze from them, feeling sadness and shame well up inside me. *It's wrong to treat NPCs as slaves, but there's nothing I can do. Bad things happen to people who don't deserve it. It's a harsh world we live in.*

As much as I despised slavery, I wouldn't step in and stop it. I was a part of the problem. *But I'm just one man. One man can't change the world, and to believe otherwise is a fool's dream.*

No. I couldn't help the slaves. My one and only priority was Eris. She came before all others, and I couldn't right every wrong I came across. *Yeah, maybe telling myself that will help me sleep at night.*

I ignored the slaves and focused on my surroundings. Watching the comings and goings of the number of guards that were scattered around, keeping an eye on the merchandise. There were four by the stage. Their hardened gaze fixed firmly on the cages, periodically glancing at the crowd to keep an eye on them, but it was clear what they were being paid to protect. But beyond those four, there were two more on each of the warehouses, standing by with compound bows at the ready.

*I can't go waltzing through like I own the place. I'll get tagged the moment I act out of the ordinary.* With no clear plan of action coming to me, I settled in and waited for an opening.

I stood out sharply compared to the rest of the crowd, all wearing expensive outfits and jewelry, while I was wearing my usual cotton shirt and pants, still filthy from being in jail and climbing through back alleys. I was getting a few sidelong looks from the people close to me, but the mercenaries hadn't yet noticed me, so I quick-equipped my armor and sword. With my shabby clothes, I looked like exactly what I was—an outlier. *Least with my gear, I'll look like a warlord, or one of the bandit kings, instead of a homeless beggar.*

Nothing happened for a few minutes; the buyers all craned their necks to get an eye for the slaves. Dozens of whispered conversations broke out, each one talking about prices. The door to the auction house opened, and a man in a dapper white suit strolled out, his head shrouded by the large brimmed hat he wore on his head, but the shadows ended at his thin mustache and goatee.

It was the same man I'd seen in the Mnemosyne without a doubt. *Magnus.*

I gnashed my teeth, biting my tongue hard enough to bleed, just to keep from drawing my blade and rushing him. *Wait! Eris comes first. She comes before all others.*

Magnus swept his hand to the first cage, where a stocky dwarven male resided. Built like the world's beefiest child, he stood maybe four feet if he was an inch, shirtless and stacked with more rippling muscle than any human could have managed. Dwarves were built for heavy labor, and it showed.

The bidding started at a hundred gold coins and soon grew to nearly a thousand before being sold to a stoic faced woman with long mahogany hair in a stunning yellow dress.

"Next up, is one for the gentlemen in the crowd," Magnus spoke, his voice crooked and sharp, like broken piano wire.

The slave that was rolled up was a beautiful elven woman. Even in the thin rags she was dressed in, her beauty could not be denied. Long golden hair covered her ears entirely, but she had the tall, elegant grace of the elves. That was as unmistakable as her thin pointed face and shallow cheekbones, which all too visibly gave away her race. Her blue eyes, while striking, were jaded and bitter. She knew the exact fate in store for her.

The hungry, lustful looks from the men in the crowd made all too obvious the role they had in mind for the elven slave. Her gaze haunted me; it took away her ethereal beauty and made her far too human in my eyes. She looked up for a moment, and her eyes bored into my very soul.

I averted my gaze; I didn't want to see any more of that bottomless misery. I didn't want to see the judgment in them, rightfully condemning me.

I had kept my eye on the guards throughout the auction, but it didn't seem like there was a good opening anywhere. I was about to risk it when a hand slipped through my arm. I looked over in confusion.

A girl had sidled up to me and was leaning heavily on me. She was gorgeous, though something about her nagged at me. Everything about her screamed nobility. From the flowing black dress she wore to her expertly applied makeup and hair—all tailored to perfection. Her scarlet hair was done up atop her head and shimmered in the sunlight, giving the appearance of flames alight, but her emerald eyes sparkled with more compassion and intelligence than I expected to see of a noble.

"Pardon," she said with a smile, leaning over to whisper in my ear. "Follow me."

I was a second from jerking my hand back, but something about her stopped me. Everything about her told me she was nothing more than an arrogant noblewoman, but some ineffable quality about her made me hesitant to put her in that category. She was a lovely woman, but she didn't seem conscious of it. *Women who know they're beautiful usually use their beauty as a weapon, and I'm not getting that from her.*

"Who are you?" I asked as she tugged on my arm.

She gave me a knowing look and a smirk, hinting at the mischievous. It wasn't sexual or evil, more like playfully devious. A smile meant for a partner in crime about to pull a big score, rather than a girl wearing a thousand gold outfit. I didn't exactly know what to make of it, or her for that matter.

When we were free from the crowd, I swiveled my head to see if anyone was looking, but everyone was staring at the stage. All eyes were on the elven girl, even the guards, such was her beauty.

The stranger pulled me along and toward the back of the warehouse. There was a thin street between the building and the large brick wall. When we were out of sight from the stage. I stopped and pulled my hand back.

"All right, spill. Who the hell are you?"

She absently swiped at her spotless dress, brushing away imaginary dust. Her long, thin fingers sparkled with elegant jewelry and were capped with long black nails, resembling talons. "Angry, are we? Well, I suppose you have reason for it. I'm a friend, Duran."

"You know my name?"

"I know many things. You may call me Morgan."

I jabbed a finger towards her, nearly touching the small golden amulet wrapped around her slender throat, a large ruby nestled in the center. The size of the gem alone was impressive, but it sparkled in the sun, casting blood-red light across her chest. "What do you want?"

"I'm here to help you, of course. I've a vested interest in you and your bond mate."

"Eris! Where is she?"

Morgan pointed a finger to the warehouse. "She's in there, and you better hurry. You don't have long before he returns."

With that, she left, walking back to the stage. Before she left my sight, she stopped and turned back to me. "Keep your wits in there, Duran, and keep her safe for me," Morgan said, walking away with a chuckle.

*What the hell?* Morgan walked around the corner with a final glance back as she disappeared from view.

"Hey, wait!" I called, running after her, but when I rounded the corner to the square, she was gone. *Where the hell did she go?*

I shook my head. *What the hell am I doing?* I could've slapped myself for getting so distracted at a time like this. I needed to focus on the task at hand.

There wasn't a door on this side of the warehouse, just a rugged ladder leading up to the roof. It might get me in faster, but with the added risk of running into someone. The only people on the roof were the guards. *I could try and blend in, act as if I belong.* But I quickly discounted that idea—way too many unknowns.

In truth, there were too many unknowns for this whole thing. I had no idea what I was walking into. A hundred different things could go wrong here, and if something could go wrong, it inevitably would. *Keep my wits about me, eh?*

I skirted around the ladder and went looking for a door. I hated the narrow space between the warehouse and the tall brick fence that lined the property, didn't like being so boxed in. It was just high enough that I couldn't scale it easily or quickly, and the wrought-iron spikes that lined the top of it made that idea very dangerous to try.

Rounding the second corner, I found a large sliding door meant to load and unload heavy cargo. I ducked right back around as several workers lifted large wooden boxes off a wagon and brought them into the storehouse. Peeking out again, I watched them for a minute or so. All of them were intent on their work, so they didn't notice me, but it also didn't allow me a way in without being seen.

*Short of marching in and slaughtering them all, I don't have many options.* That was the most drastic option, and I didn't want to resort to it if I didn't have to. *Much as I hate slavery, it's legal, and the heat that will come down on not just me, but Eris and even the guild, will be too much.* The Merchants Guild would never let me live if I went against them.

The direct route was out, so I backtracked to the ladder and climbed up to the roof. Despite looking like a rotten and crumbling mess, the ladder held and didn't so much as creak as I ascended. I was on the roof in five seconds and stopped just before the lip, spying on the guards before I pulled myself up.

Only one man was up on the roof, and I didn't see the second one. There was nothing on the roof except for the guard and a raised doorway that led into the warehouse. Caution told me to wait, but the darkness in my heart demanded action, so I hopped up and silently as I could snuck the forty or so feet to the man. Who was too busy watching the slaves down below to notice the danger that was right behind him.

I unsheathed my hunting knife, passing it to my off-hand and positioned myself behind him. I took the man's forehead in my right hand and yanked him back while kicking the back of his knee and bringing him to the ground.

He didn't even have time to shout as I clamped my hand over his mouth and shoved my knife into his carotid artery. It stuck out the other side of his neck, and blood drenched his chest. He gurgled, trying to speak, but too much of his life had been lost for him to form any cohesive sentence. He slipped into unconsciousness a moment later, and death would follow in minutes.

As long as the large crimson pool the guard was lying in didn't spill over the side of the building, no one would know he'd died up here. With one guard taken care of, I crept to the doorway that housed the staircase to the second level of the warehouse.

I jiggled the knob, making sure it was unlocked before I carefully opened it a hair and peered inside, looking in at the exact wrong time as soon as I cracked open the door. The second guard walked through without a care in the world.

The door smashed into my face, knocking me back on my ass.

"What the fuck?" he asked as he walked through the doorway, gazing down at me with as much shock on his face as there was on mine. Neither of us ready for the other. He cast his eyes towards his partner only to find him dead in a pool of blood. His eyes widened in alarm, and he went to shout a warning, but the door to the building had shut on its own behind him, and he wasted precious seconds fumbling with the knob.

I took advantage of the situation to sweep his legs out from under him. He fell to the ground with a grunt of pain, and I scrambled to pin him before he could go for his weapon. I managed to get on top of him just as his hand grasped the handle of his sword. With a twist, I broke his hand and quickly

416

covered his mouth to stifle the scream of pain that escaped. At some point, he had the wherewithal to chomp down on the side of my hand with his teeth, tearing through the soft flesh until he hit bone.

I pushed the pain down enough to reach for my knife a second time, bringing it out and plunging it into his eye. He died with his teeth still entrenched in my flesh.

I had to break the man's jaw to unclench his teeth. As soon as I was free, I tore a long strip of cloth from the dead man and tightly bandaged my hand. It was the same hand that I'd torn the flesh of my knuckles from in the jail, so at least I had one undamaged hand. I could heal it later with a potion, no problem. The pain was uncomfortable, but the last thing I needed was the health potion side effects right before I rescued Eris.

With my hand bandaged, the two men dead, and no alarm sounded, I opened the door to the entrance of the warehouse and slipped inside.

It was stifling hot as I shut the door to the roof behind me, and it reeked. Mold and rot along with the stench of unwashed bodies packed too tightly together. *Only one thing that smell could be. Least I'm in the right warehouse.*

I made my way down the steps, finding myself on a brace of catwalks that lined the entirety of the warehouse. A quick peek told me there weren't any more guards patrolling this level.

I hadn't taken so much as a single step onto the metal catwalk when I received a notification.

**Warning! Proximity to Hive Queen less than 100 meters!**
**Penalty Removed.**

With a rush, my strength returned to me. *I haven't checked my notifications since before I killed Darren. I've probably leveled up.* I weighed the pros and cons of leveling up at that moment. *I want to get to Eris, but the extra strength can only help me. Well, my wits are telling me to level up. I have a feeling I'm going to need it.*

I opened my notifications tab to read the bombardment of notifications.

*Combat results*

*5 Killed: (Human) 7,500 Exp*

*4 Downed: 6000 Exp*

*Mercy Penalty: -2000 Exp*

*Total Exp Gain: 11,500 Exp*

*4900/4900*

*Level Up! (x2)*

*Level 51!*

*2600/5100*

*20 Stat Points Available!*

*New Ability Available!*

*New Class Abilities Unlocked!*

The previous abilities caught my eye again. *Hive Guard,* in particular, tempted me as it had saved my life more than once. But it was nothing more than a health potion and recovery potion combined. *Incredibly powerful, but I have access to both potions, so I'll save that one for later.* What also surprised me was the appearance of locked abilities. The new ones I unlocked appeared from a drop-down menu.

*Second Tier List*

*Chitin Armor*

*Chitin Sword*

*Arachne's Blessing (Locked)*

418

*Scorpius's Blessing (Locked)*

*Mantearia's Blessing (Locked)*

*Apocrita's Blessing (Locked)*

*Hive Mind (Corrupted—Error!)*

*What the hell does that mean? Why is that ability corrupted? Does it have to do with the deal I made?* I pushed those thoughts aside and focused on picking. I'd leave the newer ones alone for now. While *Chitin Armor* and *Chitin Sword* were tempting, I already had armor and a weapon and could hold off.

**Chitin Shield**

**Aura of the Arachnid**

They were the two that would benefit me the most right now. The aura seemed powerful, but I didn't know precisely what it did or how it worked, so it made my choice clear. I selected *Chitin Shield,* and the ability unlocked in my interface.

I read over the description quickly. I could deploy and retract it at will, but the longer I had it out, and the more I used it, the higher my battle fatigue would rise.

*With my Durability so low right now, I'll have to use this sparingly and not rely on it too much.* Both my main stats were maxed now, so I could focus on my sub-stats. It seemed *Durability* would be critical going forward, so I added ten to it, and ten to my *Attack Damage.* It ensured I could continue to take a beating and hit hard.

My stats were settled. I moved along, careful of my steps against the metal so that I wouldn't alert anyone below. There were more men inside, working with boxes moving them around, but also large cages in which even more chained slaves resided. More dwarves and elves, even several rabbitmen as well.

*So, these are the ones I saw in the memory. I wonder what clan they belong to?* Their ears were the only way to differentiate them. *I've never met enough of them to be able to tell the difference between the clans.* Their ears twitched as I slunk along, and I knew they were aware of my presence, but they kept quiet and didn't give me away.

It hurt to see so much misery in one place, but I couldn't let it drag me down. I had a job to do, and I couldn't afford to be distracted. *Eris is here, and she comes before anyone else.* So, I left the rabbits in their cages and moved on, passing by even more pens until I found a secluded section.

It was locked away tight as a vault from the ground, but I had easy access from the catwalk.

I peered down and scanned the cages for her. My heart swelled when I spotted her dark blonde hair. My relief boiled to rage as I took in the rest of the cage.

She was bound by heavy shackles, and even then, she still struggled to free herself. She railed against the chains, her face twisted in fury.

She wasn't alone in the room. Darren's goons from the alley were here, and so was Magnus.

I still couldn't see his face; his wide-brimmed hat obscured it, but I did get a better look at his attire. His suit was of the latest fashion, and there wasn't a spot on it—a slew of large jewel-encrusted rings brandished across his slender hands. And he had his gaudy ivory cane with him as well. He leaned on it while talking with the goons.

Their voices rose, enough that I could make out snippets of conversation. Money seemed to be the topic, and the thugs appeared to be upset about the lack of it.

I dropped to all fours and crawled forward as lightly as I could, trying to pick up more of what was said. As I crept closer, I got the gist of it. Magnus had a deal with Darren and wasn't paying up. Darren and his men had been promised a hefty sum for bringing him Eris, but with the death of Darren, Magnus didn't want pay.

"My deal was with your superior, not with his underlings. Your boss was sloppy enough to let himself be killed. As such, a new deal must be negotiated."

The flunkies were understandably upset at the turn of events. They wanted what he'd promised, and with the looks on their faces, they were going to get the gold by any means necessary.

One of the men, the large, brutish one with the dead eyes, pulled out his sword and waved it around. "We had a deal, little man, now pay up or get hurt!"

The brute kept thrusting his sword randomly in the air like a raving lunatic, but he made the mistake of waving his sword too close to Magnus.

So fast, I could barely see it. Magnus withdrew a short blade from his cane. With a single fluid motion, he severed Brute's hand clean from his arm. His dripping hand dropped to the ground, still holding onto his weapon.

You could have heard the drop of a pin; it was so quiet. Brute didn't even register the loss of his hand for a solid second. Magnus wiped the steel and sheathed his blade with a distinct click. With that singular sound, Brute dropped to his knees and screamed, trying to stop the stump of his arm from spurting blood everywhere. He fumbled for a health potion on the nearby wooden table and clumsily uncapped it, pouring the entirety of its contents down his gullet.

After a moment, his hand regrew, and he stopped his bellyaching. Magnus was standing in the same position as before. If I hadn't seen him move with my own eyes, I couldn't have told the difference. The set of his shoulders seemed to convey a sense of superiority to them. With good reason. He moved faster than nearly anyone I had ever seen before—less than a second to sever Brute's hand and return.

A truly marvelous display of skill. *Could I have done it? Maybe…with a lot of practice, so could Wilson and Evelyn. But beyond the three of us, I doubt many could replicate such a feat.* Magnus had just become my priority target. The others were children compared to him. That level of speed and precision was genuinely terrifying.

The other men were looking at Magnus with a new light, not as stupid as they appeared. They mumbled a few words of apology and gratefully accepted the still decent-sized bag of gold on the table and bowed to him respectfully, departing.

I didn't want them to leave; they'd all participated in the abduction of Eris, and I wanted them to suffer, but I'd let my anger and bloodlust cloud me before, and it was the reason I was here. *I can't be so careless again, not when it comes to Eris.* If I disregarded my position to try and take them out, it would be a foolish mistake. Those chumps were merely hired thugs, small fish compared to Magnus.

*He's who I came here to find. Once Eris is free, and he's dead, I can find the rest, but not before.*

Magnus was the threat, and he would die first.

The men unbolted the heavy door and shut it as they left. Magnus looked at the door, and with a flick of his wrist, the bolt slammed home, locking the door.

Which was impossible.

*What the fuck? What was that? Did he use magic? That's not possible.* My thoughts ran rapid-fire through me, my mind not understanding what just happened. *You can't use magic like that; he didn't even use Script!*

It wasn't possible to use magic without Script. I believed that to be fact, up until I met Eris, whose own spells didn't use the language. *But she still has the strange smoke that pours out when she uses magic; there's still an aspect of tangibility to her magic.* Casting required a tangible element to cast. You couldn't just wave your hand and affect change like that.

What Magnus had done was simply impossible.

*It looked like telekinesis magic, but every telekinesis spell used Script.* I knew several mages who used telekinesis magic, but they had to use Script circles to cast. It didn't make sense that he could do that. It went against the rules of magic. *What is he?*

*Guess it doesn't matter, he'll be dead before he knows it.*

Magnus strutted over to the cage that housed Eris, tilting his head to peer down at her, speaking in his unnerving voice. "Look at you, such a beautiful specimen you are. A shame, the fate that awaits you, dear. A waste, in my opinion."

He chuckled darkly and walked over to the table with an assortment of goods and items arrayed on the wood. He set down a large black key on the table and picked up a large syringe filled with a noxious green liquid. The needle was the length of the blade of a dagger and dripped with whatever poison resided within it.

Magnus started walking back to the cage, preparing to inject Eris with whatever was in the syringe. I wasn't about to let that happen. I drew my sword, activated *Dance of the Immortal,* and leapt over the railing.

I landed just shy of him and was finally able to see all of his face.

It was long and thin with sharp edges and a wicked, malicious set to it. Even in the gray-washed landscape, his teeth glinted within his cruel grin. He sported a dark goatee, and his purple eyes flashed with devilish light.

I moved to cut his head off when a thought struck me, *Purple eyes? What the—?*

Before I could finish the thought, Magnus moved. His blade came up and blocked mine, stopping me cold.

*Impossible!*

He smiled nauseatingly at me. "Well, well, well. What do we have here? An intruder? How rude of you to interrupt my fun."

# CHAPTER 25 – AN OFFER MADE

The color was still drained from the world; every hue of gray surrounded me. "How are you able to move?" I asked.

*Dance is still active, and this shouldn't be possible.*

Magnus just laughed, raising his hand and with a snap, shattered *Dance of the Immortal*. His purple eyes faded to blue as color bled back to the world. Time returned to normal, and I sagged to my knees as my battle fatigue raised. *Not good, not good. How is he doing this?*

"How did you disrupt my ability?"

"Easily." He grinned.

Eris struggled against her chains and cried out. "Sam!"

She kept on, railing against her chains to no avail. *She's as helpless as I am here.* I fought down my rising exhaustion and rose to my feet. All the while, Magnus stood there, calm and collected, waiting for me to stand. With a nod of his hat, he spoke. "A pleasure. Sam, was it?"

"Go to hell, Magnus," I shouted.

He laughed, a sick, twisted sound that grated in my ears. "Now, where did you learn that name?"

"From your cronies, they couldn't hide you from me!"

Magnus laughed and sauntered forward, twirling his cane while the warped floorboards creaked under him. "Darren, I imagine. He could never keep his mouth shut, but he had his uses."

"Had being the operative word. I killed him," I said, glancing around the warehouse room.

The vault door was locked tight, and I wasn't reaching it without dealing with Magnus. But I had to get Eris out of her bondage first.

There was a table pushed along the wall with a few items scattered across it. Potions and poisons in equal measure, a scattering of small knives and weapons along with a large black key.

Magnus just smiled at my words. "No matter. He can be easily replaced. And from what I hear, you took out his entire crew. My, my. You've been a busy little bee, haven't you?"

I didn't bother responding, I lunged forward with a quick thrust. I'd aimed at his heart, but my sword bit through empty air by Magnus's left arm. He hadn't moved, I'd watched his hips and feet, but I still missed.

He flicked a finger on the flat of my blade, sending a metallic twang reverberating up the sword. "Missed me," he taunted.

Before he even finished his sentence, he struck. A twitch of his fingers a split second before was my only warning. I just managed to bring my blade up in time to deflect his attack.

His smile only twisted further. "Color me impressed. Not many can block me. You have talent, young man."

I growled in frustration and swung at him; he sidestepped my sword with a flourish of his hat, still smiling at me. "Quite agile as well, my, my. You're a rare find."

"Fucking stand still!" I yelled, attacking him with everything I had, but he was too fast. With the barest second to spare, he dodged every single one of my attacks. I could do nothing to hit him.

With my barrage of attacks having done nothing, I backed up, giving me some space to try and come up with a new plan of attack. *He's too fast, so the direct route is out. I'll have to catch him by surprise. But how? I've got Chitin Shield now, but that's my last ability unless I want to rely on the Aspect again, but I still don't know what the first time cost me.*

*Poison Blade* was active and dripped its vile substance down my blade but was useless if I couldn't even land a hit. Magnus was circling me, keeping his distance but watching me like a hawk. I moved, my footwork light, but I was so focused on Magnus that I stepped to the side and bumped into the wooden table, knocking over the many vials of potions and poisons.

*Poison!* I turned, keeping my blade in front of me and hiding my left hand from Magnus's view while I grabbed one of the vials of poison along with the large black key.

He didn't notice my theft but chuckled at my clumsiness. "Watch your step, Sam, wouldn't want to hurt yourself."

*He's fucking toying with me!* The fact he wasn't taking this fight seriously sent fury rolling through me. I wanted to rush him, but that would only hasten my death. I played it cautiously, getting in close and probing his defense with a few quick thrusts. As before, he nimbly dodged every one of them, but I surprised him with a low kick to his leg. It connected just below the side of his knee and put Magnus off-balance, which I followed up with a vial of poison to his face.

He shook off the kick quickly, and out of reflex, brought his cane-sword up to deflect the glass bottle. He sliced it in half, the glass shattering and raining harmlessly on his suit, but a splash of whatever poison resided in the bottle sprayed across his face. He cursed as it stung his eyes and entered his mouth.

Magnus's humor disappeared. His gaze screamed malice, and he stopped playing around. His hand twitched, but before I could move, a sharp pain streaked across the side of my face. A deep gash opened under my cheek. Hot blood poured down my cheek, but I couldn't stop and worry about a minor inconvenience.

He frowned as he watched my blood soak through my armor. "Ah, a pity. I was slightly too high. You must forgive me; I'll make sure to hit your neck properly next time."

His hand moved once more. I didn't even try to deflect a blow I couldn't see and instead threw myself to the side as he struck. A slight pain lanced through my left side, but I could tell at once it was a flesh wound and didn't hit anything vital.

I just managed to rise to my feet when my instincts screamed at me. I stepped to the side just as death passed my ear, and a thin line scratched my neck—another too close call.

His frown turned positively sour as he struck again. Decades of trusting my gut on the battlefield were the only thing keeping me alive right now. I was surviving by the skin of my teeth. I was solely focused on keeping my head attached to my shoulders and couldn't do much else. *He's too fast for me to go on the offensive. I'm going to have to pin him down somehow.*

Another slice at my neck, but I parried it with the flat of my sword. To which Magnus's smile returned. "You're proving slipperier than I first gave you credit for. Well done."

"Glad I'm amusing y—" Another strike pierced my side as he moved. Too fast for me to see, his blade struck my right side this time.

The wound was deep, and blood trailed down to soak into my pant leg. It trickled down my thigh, growing heavier with every step I took on the uneven floor. *All right, I'll have to use my shield now.* I stepped closer to Magnus and gave him the opening he needed, he thrust with his blade, and I brought my left hand up and activated *Chitin Shield*. Black chitin pooled out of my skin and tore through my leather armor to form a small shield, about two feet in width and length, and perfectly round. It solidified in less than a second and stopped his thrust cold.

Magnus's cane-sword sank into the chitin but did not break through, leaving his sword lodged in the shield and giving me the best chance I'd have to end this. I brought my sword up and slid it into his chest. Dead center, I speared through his heart—a fatal wound.

He was dead.

Magnus sagged against me. I pulled my blade out and waited for him to drop to the ground. Which didn't happen. He stood stock-still; blood fountained from his chest, but not nearly the amount that it should be given I'd hit his heart.

He lifted his head in a grim smile, a shadow of pain across his face. *I hurt him, should have killed him, but guess he has more tricks up his sleeve than I first thought.*

Magnus inclined his head to me. "I must commend you on your performance thus far; you've put on one hell of a good show here, young man," he said. "Nobody's forced me to use so much power like this in…well, ever, truth be told."

Magnus gave me a theatrical bow, flicking his hat in the process. A tip of the hat to a well-deserved actor.

"Time for the second act."

Without warning, Magnus stood before me. His sword pierced through my *Chitin Shield*, chestplate, and studded leather with ease, hitting dead on my heart. The only thing that saved me was my *Exoskeleton*. It stopped him from killing me on the spot. I fell back, hitting my head on Eris's cage.

I still had the key in my hand. With the *Chitin Shield* covering my left arm, Magnus hadn't noticed. *I need her help. I can't do this alone.* With a look, I slipped the key into her hand. The chains that bound her bore the same lock as the cage, an oversight on Magnus's part, but a blessing for us. I left Eris to free herself and stood up, trying to hold him off as long as I could.

*I only have a few more minutes left in me; battle fatigue is nearly maxed. I'm going to have to play this smart.* I had to deactivate *Chitin Shield* as it caused my battle fatigue to rise much faster while active. It retracted back under my skin, leaving me feeling naked and my left arm very much exposed. The tattered remains of my vambrace hung limply on a few strands of leather. *Gil's going to murder me when he sees it.*

Magnus practically glowed when my shield disappeared. "Can't keep it up, eh? What a shame."

I slashed at him in anger, but he didn't dodge this time. Instead, he parried with his cane-sword. *He's slower. Not by much, but it's there. Did the poison actually harm him? Or is it the chest wound that should have killed him?* Whatever the reason, I was grateful. I wouldn't have survived much longer if he'd been at full strength.

I couldn't just rush him with a flurry of attacks; my fatigue was too high for me to be reckless. I needed to be precise with my attacks. A creaking groan startled the both of us, even though I'd been expecting it. Eris walked out of the cage with anger on her face. Pure hatred for the man who'd imprisoned her.

Raucous laughter roared from his mouth, and he clapped his hands. "Ho! Snuck the key from right under my nose. Clever, clever." He held up his hand, stopping the fight for a moment. "All right, Sam. Let's stop this before someone gets hurt."

"What?"

"You've impressed me. You fight well, and you've proven to have quite a sharp mind behind that thick skull of yours. Something lacking in most of my subordinates. I'd like to offer you a job."

I scoffed at him. "Why the hell would I ever agree to that?"

"It saves your life," he said, walking over to the table and reaching for a health potion.

"You touch that potion, and all bets are off," I said just before his fingers brushed the glass.

"Fair enough," he said, his grin deepening. "How about a gesture of good faith?"

"What do you mean?"

"I haven't been entirely forthcoming with you, dear boy," he said. "My name isn't Magnus."

*What?*

"Bullshit!"

"Unfortunately, not. Believe you me, I wish I were. If you think I'm hard to kill, oh, you haven't seen anything yet. No, I'm merely a humble servant to my master."

I backed up, placing myself between Eris and Not-Magnus, "Then who the hell are you?"

He took off his hat and swept it across his chest as he bowed. "You may call me Liam."

Liam stood from his bow, and with a flick of his wrist, rolled his hat up his arm and to the top of his head.

"So, what do you say, Sam? I'll pay you better than anything you could dream of, and I'll even let you keep the girl. She's what brought you to me, after all."

*We could keep fighting, but there's no guarantee that we'll win. Not that I want Liam to live, he deserves to die, but I don't want his death at the cost of mine, or Eris's.* I turned to Eris, who'd been quiet so far. "What do you think?"

She shook her head, her eyes never leaving Liam. "No, you didn't hear the things he said to me, the delight he took in my imprisonment. He needs to die. The world will be better off without him."

"But—" I began, but my voice was taken from me. The Aspect rose up without warning and took over. I could do nothing to stop it. *"I want to kill him. He annoys me. Let's pull him apart and see what makes him tick!"*

Eris stopped dead and looked at me, her eyes wide. "Sam, what did you do?"

*"He desired more power, and I gave it to him,"* the Aspect said, laughing.

I couldn't control my voice, but I could still see and hear, could still move my body, but it felt as if I was sharing part of myself with another entity.

Eris sighed deeply, and her voice sounded a thousand years old. "We will speak of this later, Aspect. You've overstepped yourself, now. Give him back."

The Aspect retreated into my heart, and I had control again. "Thank you, Eris. I'm beginning to regret dealing with that monster," I said, raising my sword.

"Hand me your knife."

I unsheathed my hunting knife and passed it to her while Liam scowled at us. "So that's your answer?"

I nodded. "You heard the lady. Fuck your offer."

"Very well, a shame. You had such potential."

The brief reprieve from combat allowed my battle fatigue to drop just a tad, not by a significant amount, but enough to let me stay in the fight for longer than I otherwise would've been able. Liam came at us fast, putting all of his speed to work, but I parried him again. *He's definitely slower than before. With me keeping his sword busy, Eris can summon her insects to attack.*

"Eris, use your magic!"

The half-second my head was turned to Eris, Liam sliced a gash down my arm, adding to the ever-growing puddle at my feet. The wound in my side still bled freely; this new wound only added to my trouble.

"Shit!" I hissed in pain.

I kept my sword up and backed up to Eris. She was focused on her hand, bringing her verdant smoke to summon horde of creatures. As soon as her magic began, Liam snapped his fingers.

As if a phantom gust of wind blew in, the green smoke dissolved into nothingness.

Liam wagged his finger at Eris. "Now, now. No outside guests allowed for this performance."

Enraged, Eris ran into the fight, swinging wildly, getting nowhere. She was untrained in combat, and it was painfully obvious, her anger only making it worse. Liam was able to keep her at bay with ease, but I attacked at his side, forcing him to switch priorities.

He blocked my sword, but I swept at his foot. He didn't fall for the trick a second time, shifting his balance and catching the kick on his shin.

Eris took the opportunity to try and stab him, but he caught her wrist and took the knife from her. While holding me off with his cane-sword, he brought the hilt of my knife to her temple with as much force as he could muster. With a sickening crack, Eris dropped, blood trailing down her head.

"You son of a bitch!" I screamed, putting my entire being into killing him. He kept me from landing a fatal blow, but each block with his sword was weaker than the last. *His battle fatigue has to be at least as high as mine, and even if I don't understand how he's ignoring the laws of magic, his mana must be close—*

It hit me like a sledgehammer.

*Even if I don't know how the hell he's doing it, he's still using magic, and that means I can shut him down.*

433

Magic was magic, no matter if it was using Script, smoke, or even nothing at all. It was still magic, and magic couldn't defend against antimagic.

I activated *Aura of the Antimage*, and it pulsed out along my skin, dispersing around me. Coating everything around me in an antimagic field.

It hurt less than the last time I used *Aura*. The Aspect burrowed through my heart and spread through my veins; it was a part of me now, and it wasn't going anywhere. As soon as the aura spread beyond my skin, the Aspect returned to its home in my heart.

It still wasn't the most pleasant feeling, but from the look on Liam's face, he was in far more pain. He no longer held his sick smile; now, it was twisted in agony. He dropped his cane-sword from his hand, and it clattered against the floorboards.

Liam looked down at his chest. At the rapidly growing stain of blood pouring out of it.

He stumbled to his knees, his heart pumping out his lifeblood with every beat. Liam's air of theatrics died and was replaced by utter panic. He stumbled over to the table and tried to grab the health potion that promised his salvation.

Only to find Eris's iron-clad grip around his ankle.

Blood ran down her face. She looked at him with fire in her eyes. "You're not going anywhere."

Liam fell to the ground, tripping while trying to dislodge Eris's hand. He was weakened from the blood loss and couldn't beat her strength. He kicked at her face, but I plunged my sword through his thigh, aiming for his femoral artery.

Blood soaked through his white pants, pouring freely into the dirt. With my final attack, *Aura of the Antimage* ended, and my battle fatigue maxed.

As if my bones were made of jello, I folded, bumping my head on the table and falling to stare, unmoving as Liam laughed. He didn't miss the subtle pop as my aura timed out, and he immediately snapped his fingers, stopping the massive flow of blood from his chest and leg.

"Looks like you overdid yourself, Sam. How unfortunate," Liam said.

"And it looks like you forgot about my magic!"

Liam turned sharply to see Eris and a stream of smoke slipping from her hands as she summoned her insects. They came, crawling from the darkened corners of the warehouse en masse at the command of their queen. Spiders, ants, beetles, and cockroaches. They all came, and from the look on Liam's face, he could do nothing to stop them.

Even if he didn't show the same symptoms of mana depletion, he was running out, and keeping himself alive was taking the remaining mana he had left.

"Devour him," Eris commanded.

Liam panicked when he couldn't stop the rising horde. He looked to me with pleading eyes. "Don't do this, Sam. Stop her!"

But it wasn't my decision to make.

I couldn't move, couldn't even speak. I couldn't tell Eris to stop even if I wanted to, so I just stared as the swarm crawled over his legs and up to his chest.

The spiders reached him first, scurrying up to his face and neck and sinking their venomous fangs into every inch of exposed flesh. The fire ants were slower, but they worked their way under his clothing to bite and sting his legs and feet. Both were sickening to watch; my phobia of insects was out in full swing, but I physically couldn't look away.

The cockroaches were the worst. Spurred by the command of the Hive Queen, they crawled to Liam's chest and burrowed into his open wound, a dozen of them at a time, eating away at the bloody skin to crawl deeper inside him. His shouts were deafening, raking at my ears and pounding through my skull. Liam screamed and screamed until his mouth filled with spiders, choking off the horrid sound.

It took four minutes for Liam to die. The timer for my fatigue kept track for me, and in the end, I don't know what killed him. The blood loss from the deep gashes, the lack of air from the spiders, or the cockroaches that ate their way to his heart.

Honestly, I didn't want to know. All I cared about was that he was dead.

Liam had been, without a doubt, the most dangerous foe I'd ever faced.

Eris sat up off the ground and crawled her way over to me, pulling my head into her lap. For the first time in my life, I was thankful for my battle fatigue. It kept me from shivering at her touch. I felt horrible at myself for even thinking about it.

I loved Eris, knew I loved her from the bottom of my heart. But for a single split second, I was deathly afraid of her.

I managed to shake off the feeling by the time my battle fatigue wore off and chalked it up to my phobia of insects. I sat up and immediately pulled out a couple of potions: two health and a mana. I handed a health and mana potion to Eris and downed mine while she did the same to hers. My health steadily rose back into the green.

I knelt and cupped her cheek in my hand. "I love you, Eris."

My words cracked the dam, and Eris couldn't hold back her tears anymore. She broke down and cried. I kissed the top of her head and held her till she stopped a minute or so later.

I wiped the remnants of tears from her streaked face and kissed her lips. A chaste kiss, but I put my love of her behind it, and pressed my forehead to hers, enjoying her warmth again.

As with all things, though, our embrace came to a close, and I stood to my feet, with some resistance from Eris, who clutched at my sleeves. "Why can't we stay like this for a few more minutes?" she asked.

"Can't love, we've lingered here for too long as is. We don't need anyone coming in and finding us here. C'mon, let's loot the place and go," I said, pulling Eris up with me.

She knocked the dust off her clothes while I perused the room. The glint of light off of Liam's sword caught my attention again, and I stared as my fury rose at the symbol etched to the bone.

*Magnus.*

*Damn it! I thought I'd had him!*

Realizing that Liam wasn't the man I'd been looking for was a sucker punch. I'd come this far and fought through a mountain of enemies, only to end up with a name and too many loose ends.

*Magnus has been the root of all of this. His thugs have made my life hell, not to mention the attempt on our castle. This will not go unpunished.*

*"Let me skin him alive when we find him. I'll be careful not to end his life too quickly,"* the Aspect promised.

Eris felt the anger and looked at me with concern. "Sam, we need to talk."

"Yeah," I said.

I needed to know what I'd gotten myself into but was hesitant to actually find the answers.

"You made a deal with it?"

"I didn't really have a choice in the matter," I said and preceded to tell her about what happened, how it had taken over my body and nearly gotten me killed.

She sighed, running her hands through mine. "I don't know what this means, but it won't be good. For whatever reason, the Aspect is different and isn't bound by the old laws."

"So, what do we do?"

"I don't know."

I let out a deep sigh, echoing hers. *Oh well, it's my own fault for agreeing to it. Not that I had a choice, but I guess I just have to live with it now. And figure out how to get rid of it as soon as we can.*

*"Good luck, knight. I'm a part of you now. Until eternity,"* it mocked.

*Fucking perfect.*

"Let's ransack what we can and get the hell out of here," I said.

The bodies of the guards had long since vanished, and Liam's corpse was gone as well, leaving behind a paltry few items from his inventory. I took his gear and the cane-sword since it seemed to be hero-tier.

I had no idea on the patrol schedule of the guards, and people could still come looking for their dead comrades, only to find us instead. A prospect I didn't relish coming to pass.

Eris nodded, finding the logic in what I was saying. She took the few potions and coins on the table while I looked past the cages and tried to find anything.

*Liam worked for Magnus; there has to be something. Some lead to follow or clue as to his whereabouts.*

I quickly searched the contents of the room, took the vials of health and mana potions Eris handed me, as well as a bottle labeled "sleeping draught." It bore the same bright green liquid as the syringe. There was nothing more evident in the room, though my gut told me I was missing something.

This place was built more like a vault than a mere holding room for valuable slaves.

438

A second, more thorough run through the room led me to a secreted safe hidden in a false wall panel. The slight discoloration in the wood was my only tip-off, and if I hadn't been listening to my gut, I'd have missed it.

Using a metal crowbar I found next to an empty crate, I forced the handle open. I put all my weight into it, shearing the metal and making a lot of noise. I shattered through the lock and tore the door off the safe. It swung open, only to fall off its hinges, nearly crushing my foot as it tumbled to the ground.

Sitting inside the rather large safe were several boxes of papers and a wooden chest with an intricate lock built into it. A glance through the documents told me they were bills of sale. It seemed Liam kept detailed records of all his dealings. I noticed the names of a few high nobles and aristocrats, and I even saw William Curran's name a few times. *It seems the Northern King likes his slave girls. I wonder how his queen feels about that?*

I tucked those sheaves into my inventory, never knowing when I'd need to blackmail a monarch.

I kept looking through the papers, hoping for a lead on Magnus, but there was nothing. Not a single scrap to indicate the man even existed. For how many slaves Phineas said he was buying, and how detailed Liam was, the documents were missing for a reason.

I couldn't help but let out a disappointed sigh. *Of course, it wouldn't be that easy. What was I expecting to find, a bill of sale with Magnus's name and his exact location and weaknesses? Life doesn't work that way.*

I'd have to find him the hard way. The way that would demand a much higher price.

I had his name, and that was a valuable piece of information. There were powerful beings I could call upon to ask for help, though it would cost me dearly. *If I have to resort to calling upon them, it'll make the deal I made with the Aspect look favorable in comparison. But I'll do whatever I have to if it means seeing that bastard brought to heel for what he's done to me.*

With the documents out of the way, I picked up the chest. It was heavy, incredibly so. I struggled to heft it out of the safe and down to the ground. Once it was on the ground, I was able to get a better look at the lock.

It was a complex number with two keyholes and looked to have a few built-in fail-safes. You needed two keys turned in tandem to open this chest. One glance at the lock told me I had no chance in hell of picking it. *I imagine this lock would even give Wilson trouble.*

So, I broke the wooden lid of the chest, bypassing the lock entirely. Sitting inside the chest was gold. It was filled to the brim with gold coins, thousands of them. A small fortune, at least.

One look at the money, and I was already thinking of ways I could spend it. I would sort out exactly how much gold it was later when we were away from the slave house, but I tried and failed to store the entirety of the chest in my inventory…*of course.*

With the destruction of the lid, the chest no longer functioned as a storage container. Which meant I couldn't carry it with me. I could take as much as I could carry. Around five thousand gold was the most I could hold at once since I had no stat points in *Carrying Capacity*, and that wouldn't even dent the pile.

I hated to leave that much wealth on the table and walk, but I didn't have any other options. Eris didn't have anything to store it in, and it would only slow us down if we tried.

I scooped as many coins into my purse as I could. It ended up being three thousand two hundred and fifty-three coins added to my wallet. Not even a fourth of the coins still in the chest. *Oh, well. I still made a profit on this trip.*

With one last covetous glance at the chest of gold, I wound my arm through Eris's and unlocked the heavy door to leave this wretched place.

# Chapter 26 - Escape

The heavy iron door groaned as I forced it open, scraping against the metal frame in protest and echoing throughout the massive warehouse, announcing our presence to any who still lingered. I didn't bother shutting the door behind me. *Let them loot the place for all I care.*

Walking through the ground level of the warehouse was more intense than sneaking over the catwalks. The heat was lessened slightly, but the pungent odor of tightly massed bodies and waste was revolting. I resisted the urge to vomit and started breathing through my mouth.

Huge wooden crates lined the walls and were stacked in haphazard piles at random throughout the warehouse, creating a very maze-like environment, and there were plenty of cages mixed with the crates. A few were empty, more than likely the once homes of the slaves that were auctioned off outside, but most of the pens held the less valuable ones: the young elves and dwarves or the too valuable ones like the rabbit men. *The nobles just go crazy for bunny-girls, much too valuable to just auction them off.* More than likely, Liam would have held a private event for them and raked in a mountain of gold.

I tried to ignore them, tried to ignore their pleading or judging eyes, but I could feel them like daggers in my back, begging me to save them. *I can't help you. We've been here too long already, and I have to get Eris out of here. She comes before all others.* I didn't have the time to waste helping them.

I could ignore the looks from the slaves, could leave them to their misery, and whatever awful fate awaited them. It would only further damn my soul to whatever pit of hell I'd resigned myself to, but I could do it. However, there was one gaze I couldn't ignore.

Eris was wide-eyed, staring at the horrors of this place. Her face held such sadness at what she was seeing. I tried to put it out of mind, but she felt such conflicting emotions that she'd inadvertently opened our connection and spilled her overflow of feelings into my mind. Considering the many lifetimes she'd spent locked away herself, she couldn't bear to see others going through what she did.

She tugged sharply on my arm, forcing me to stop walking, which had been me dragging her more than anything.

"Sam, we have to help them."

"We don't have time to waste. Look, I'm sorry, I know how this must pain you to see, and I don't exactly like it either, but this world is a harsh one, and we can't right every wrong we come across. Bad things happen to good people. It's just the way it is."

I yanked on her hand, trying to force her to keep walking. The bay doors were just a few yards away, and freedom from this place was so close, but Eris wasn't having it. She dug in her heels and wouldn't budge, using all of her considerable strength to stop me in my tracks and pulled away from me.

"No, Sam, I'm going to help them, whether you like it or not. I love you, but you're better than this, I know you are."

I stared at the bleeding marks on my arms where her fingers had scraped the skin free from my arm.

*Godsdamn it!*

She was right, though; I knew she was from the beginning. I just didn't want to listen. Much as Eris thought I was good, I wasn't. *I'm a monster, but she's right, I can't just walk away. Not when she's begging me to right a wrong against innocents.*

"Fine," I sighed.

The smile that lit her face put the sun in the sky to shame. She squeezed my hand tight and mouthed, "Thank you."

I managed a half-smile, which I quickly dropped as I got down to business. *Staying here means staying on guard. Let's get this done and get out.*

"Right, let's make this quick."

Whispers around us told me that our conversation had been overheard, and a few death glares withered into ones of relief. They crowded against the bars of their cages, each of them begging to be freed—their voices combining into so much incomprehensible noise.

"Quiet!"

As if a switch had been flipped, they obeyed—instant silence.

I walked over to one of the cages. A slight elven male resided in it. His thin features even more so, as malnourishment emaciated him. He flinched back as I got close, but I ignored him and looked at the lock on the cage. It was different than the one that housed Eris. The key I took would be useless.

"Does anyone know where the key is kept?" I asked. It wasn't in the vault, and there wasn't a key in Liam's remains. I don't want to waste any more time on a scavenger hunt.

"Here," one of the slaves spoke up from a cage along the far wall.

As I got closer, I noticed the slave was one of the rabbitmen demi-humans. A small girl, maybe six years old. Her black hair was a tangled mess, and her gray bunny ears had dirt and filth on them. Her blue dress was ragged and soiled with grime. It looked as if she'd been wearing it for weeks.

Her face was equally dirty. Except for where her tears had washed away the dirt, leaving thin streaks down her face. She looked up at me with wide, unblinking eyes. *Such bright blue eyes.*

"The key is kept over there," she said in a whisper, pointing at a small office hidden behind even more crates. The door was ajar, and I spied a desk and a rack of keys hanging on the wall

Not wasting any more time, I took off at a sprint and hopped over the crates in my way, barging into the office. I knocked aside the door with my shoulder. It slammed against the wall with a thud to rattle the single window in the cramped space.

Four different keys lined a small wooden shelf on the wall. The only thing inside the office besides the large plain desk and chair was a small potted plant that resided on the desk—likely an attempt to bring a little life into this den of iniquity and vileness. A nudge sent the plant crashing to the ground.

*"Whoops."*

*Stop doing that!*

The Aspect laughed as I pocketed all the keys and hurried out of the office.

"Eris, catch!" I tossed her two of the four keys, and we set about freeing the slaves. As I opened the little rabbit girls' pen, I handed her my extra key and sent her to help with unlocking the rest of the cages.

Within five minutes, we had all twenty or so unlocked, and the group of former captives was huddled together in an awkward attempt at solidarity. They still bore looks of confusion and sadness, but there was a splattering of hopeful faces in the crowd as well.

Eris finished unlocking the final cage and rushed over to join me. Her hand around mine was a comforting warmth in this dank, decrepit place.

Though the current slaves had been freed, this place held the weight of too many lives sentenced to bondage. That kind of darkness leaves a stain that will never fade. Save for under the purifying light of fire.

*Let the former slaves escape under cover of smoke. Burn the place down, and while the slavers are busy figuring out what the hell is going on, we'll be long gone.* A solid plan with a decent chance of succeeding.

I had a thought and cleared my throat, speaking loudly to the crowd.

"All right, you're all free. You can walk out that door right now if you so choose. In the back room, behind the heavy iron door, is a chest filled with gold. Take what you can carry with you. I recommend traveling in groups to avoid getting recaptured. Use the gold to buy what you need any way you can."

"You have five minutes to grab what's here. After that, I'm taking a torch to this fucker. Okay, speech over. Good luck to all of you."

After my words, I walked over to one of the crates and splintered it with a kick, grabbing a few planks of wood and a discarded rag in one of the nearby cages. It was filthy with all manner of nastiness, but it would serve as decent kindling.

The slaves had started bustling about after I finished speaking. A few had found metal pipes and were in the process of ransacking the crates looking for anything of value. Grunting from behind me caused me to turn. A couple of the dwarves were carrying the chest of gold. They dropped in the middle of the room and went through counting it and dividing it equally among the twenty or so slaves. They counted the money like machines. A blur of hands counting and stacking coins by the thousands.

I left them to deal with the loot and set about getting ready to burn this place to cinders.

I was walking hand in hand with Eris, making my preparations, when she stopped dead. It was sudden enough that my hand was nearly yanked from hers.

"What?" I started to say when I noticed the look she had.

446

Her face was wide in disbelief, not in fear, just like she couldn't believe what she saw. I followed her gaze to see her staring at two children huddled together by themselves, away from the main group of freed slaves. For some reason, they seemed familiar to me.

I was trying to figure out why, when it hit me like a ton of bricks. I had seen them before. In the flashes of memories from Darren. They were the strange children with long, curved ears—the not quite demi-humans.

Eris let go of my hand and walked unblinking towards the children. I called out to her, but she paid me no mind. I called again much louder this time—still nothing. The children had heard me yell and looked up to see Eris walking towards them. They looked at her with confusion on their faces before it crumbled into dawning realization.

*They know what she is.*

This turn of events more than piqued my interest, and I rushed over to stand by Eris. I brushed my hand against hers, and she jumped like a bolt of lightning had struck her. She whirled around at me, before calming herself once she realized it was me.

"Eris, what the hell?"

"I'm sorry, Sam, you startled me."

"Obviously," I replied, "You mind telling me what's going through that beautiful head of yours?"

She stared at me, incredulously, motioning towards the children. "Do you not see them?"

"Yeah, the kids with the long ears. What about them has you in such a frenzy?"

Something clicked on Eris's face, and she turned away from to kneel in front of the children. They seemed a little wary of her but not nearly as much as they feared me. They shivered in fright just from looking at me.

*Great. Durandahl, Hive Knight, and monster to children everywhere.*

Between Eris and me, they chose Eris gratefully, rushing to her and huddling into her knees. They disregarded the dirt they accrued from the floor onto their clothes, and both of them clung onto her legs, burying their faces to hide from me.

Eris looked from them to me, and with an apologetic look, asked me to back up a tad.

"Sure...no problem."

I crept back on the floor, well out of arm's reach, and sat down next to one of the few remaining crates that we hadn't splintered to pieces, waiting to find out what was going on with Eris and the strange children.

Eris gently cooed at the frightened kids, brushing their disheveled and dirty hair through her fingers, trying to get the kids to settle enough to stop hiding away. She started humming to them. The same song she kept singing to herself since we'd met. The kids' ears twitched at hearing it. *Seems they're familiar with it, even if I'm not.*

I put the many others bustling about in the warehouse around me out of my mind and watched Eris as she soothed the children's fears. She was acting like a big sister or mother to them. *It's a good look on her.* That errant thought sent a trill of panic through me. *Where the hell did that thought come from?*

While I worked through my miniature existential crisis, Eris managed to assure the children that I wasn't going to hurt them and that they were safe. They finally removed their heads from her chest and blinked at me. I managed a weak smile and a half-wave, which, from the looks I received, I doubted did me any favors.

"So, care to enlighten me on what's going on?"

Eris looked from me back to the kids. "It's okay, you can show him," she told the little children.

448

I didn't know what they meant to show me, but I gave them my full attention. Slowly, a haze appeared around the children's eyes, like heat from a hot summer day. Distorting and twisting around and around. When the shimmering air in front of them stopped, their eyes had changed.

Where once they had both been brown and very nondescript, now a slew of colors filled them. They were not the eyes of humans. The boy's eyes were a deep black with a purple shine around his iris.

The girl's eyes were yellow around the entirety with two pinpricks of black for the iris. They were both larger than a normal humans, but not quite as big around as Eris's.

*Are they entomancers like her?*

When I asked this question, Eris told me no, they weren't. She had a sad look on her face as she confirmed that she was still alone. However, it went away when she next spoke, answering my question.

"They may not be entomancers, but they are still Hive. They are arachne."

"Arachne...like spiders?" I asked, trying and failing to keep the fear from rising in my voice.

"Yes! They are arachne spiderlings, the youngest of the brood."

She started speaking to them, but not in any language I was familiar with. It used mostly clicks of the tongue and the lower muscles in the throat. It was bizarre, and to top it off, my interface couldn't even translate it, leaving me feeling like I was being left out of the conversation, though I didn't necessarily mind.

*Keep the freaky spider kids away from me.* I'd gotten used to Eris, and while my once-phobia of insects and spiders had been significantly mitigated, I was still terrified of the creepy things. Even if they looked mostly human, hearing the word spider sent angst and fear through me. *I'll happily face Liam again or a horde of crater snakes, but keep the tiny crawling, flying, biting, and stinging bastards far away.*

Eris could feel the fear that was still present in me, and she frowned at me, but her eyes were sparkling. She had some idea cooking in her head and wiggled her fingers, letting a few drops of magic slip out.

I sighed, knowing exactly where this was going.

Spiders came crawling through the wooden walls and seeming out of nowhere from the dirt floor, skittering over one another to reach their mistress. The children's eyes lit up at the sight of all the things crawling towards them, like a long-lost pet finally returning home. They picked them up with small squeals of delight and let them crawl up and down. Under the command of Hive magic, I knew the spiders were no threat, but I still froze when they climbed over me.

Eris would get her feelings hurt if I freaked out about them, so for her, I stayed still and let the bugs skirt over my hands. I'd seen her use her magic enough times before, but I still hated the feeling of their many legs skittering over my skin. Eventually, my fear subsided, and I came not to mind the bugs so much, though I heaved a sigh of relief when they finally departed from me, back to their hidden nests.

The sight of the spiders had done its job, and the children were in excellent spirits as they played with Eris. She kept talking to them in their strange language, and I left them to it.

I stood up from the ground and went to check on the progress of the rest of the freed slaves. In the few minutes I'd left them to their own devices, they hadn't wasted a single second. Most of them were garbed in much nicer clothes than the soiled rags they'd been wearing. Nothing too fancy, but sturdy clothing meant for traveling.

Most of the elves and rabbitmen wore makeshift shawls to hide their unique traits. As long as anyone didn't get too close, people wouldn't be able to tell them apart from humans.

The dwarves were a little more difficult to disguise, but they'd belted short swords and daggers to themselves in an attempt to dissuade anyone from attempting to recapture them. Each and every one of the once slaves had small packs filled with all manner of pilfered goods, and the chest of gold on the floor was now empty.

They were as ready as they could be. It wouldn't be easy to get them out of Central and the East Kingdoms, but with the gold we had, I didn't think there wasn't anyone we couldn't bribe to secure safe passage.

"Everyone ready?"

A slew of affirmations rang through the storehouse. *Right, time to burn down this bitch!*

I picked up two of the jury-rigged torches and lit them with one of the sconces that hung along the walls. Both pieces of timber wood went up quickly, even without an accelerant. The flames crackled and devoured the rag covered wood hungrily. Before they could eat through the cloth and singe my fingers, I tossed them in opposite sides of the warehouse.

One landed in a pile of splintered crates and quickly scattered to the fresh tinder. The second torch hit the far wall and tumbled to the ground, at first, I thought it wouldn't catch, but the flames licked the jagged planks at the base of the wall with determination. Soon enough, it caught, and fire crawled up the walls. Dense clouds of smoke started filling the building, so we beat a hasty retreat through the bay doors and out into the loading area.

Thankfully it seemed the workers had finished their jobs, and the place was deserted. I motioned for everyone to follow and took off at a quick pace and kept us along the brick fence. My head was on a swivel to make sure no one spotted us.

A few hundred feet later, we arrived at a heavy gate, manned by a single guard stationed in a rough wooden shack next to a lever to swing the gate open and closed. He was facing the opposite direction as us. The entrance looked to open into one of the many backroads that would lead us back to the main gate to the East Kingdom.

I put my finger to my lips and made it a point to make sure they knew to be quiet. Fearing recapture, none of the freed slaves made so much as a peep. One of the braver rabbit-men, a wiry, middle-aged man with light brown hair and what once was a neatly trimmed beard, now matted and dirty. His blue eyes were sharp as he crept up to me.

"Can I take him out?"

I passed him my hunting knife. "Knock yourself out."

The rabbit-man crept along the wall far faster and with more stealth than I'd have managed. He reached the guard in under three seconds and, without hesitation, slit the guard's throat and dropped his body out of sight. A few seconds later, the gate swung open, and the rabbit-man poked his head out to wave us through. *Damn, he's got some skill.*

"All right, through the gate, quickly," I whispered urgently.

In a flash, all twenty of the freed slaves were through the gate. Eris took charge and made sure to lead them through quickly, though she'd taken the hands of the spiderlings, prioritizing their safety. I rejoined the group, and as I shut the gate behind me, the rabbit-man warrior approached me, handing me back the knife. Not even a speck of blood on it.

I held up my hand. "Hold onto it for me," I told the man.

"Thank you, Lord!" he said, his bunny ears shook in excitement.

"None of that now. Name's Duran, what's yours?"

"Lyahgos, sir."

I put my hand on the rabbit-man's shoulder. "Okay, Lyahgos, I have an important job for you. The trip out of here is going to be long, and I can't keep an eye on everyone at once. I want you to come to me if you hear anything out of the ordinary."

He nodded vigorously. "What about if we get attacked?"

"Kill any enemy that tries to harm us, don't wait for my approval."

"Right, sir!"

We both rejoined the main group. Who, in our absence, had nominated Eris as the temporary leader, as they deferred to her and followed close behind her. The backroads were quiet, with only a few wagons making their way through the dead streets. We received a few funny looks but nothing that would cause alarm. It was merely strange to see a group this large.

As we got closer to the front gate, I had all the former slaves put their hoods up and stick close. There was a reduced guard presence today, but there were still hundreds of people trying to use the gates at once. I was thankful for only one team of guards.

*Guess they caught that criminal from the other day, or they gave up. I doubt we could get all the freed slaves through without incident if they were still checking everyone.* We meandered over to the rapidly growing line of people and tried to act as inconspicuous as possible. With her holding the kids, I couldn't keep Eris close to me, but my eyes never left her for a second.

With a nod to Lyahgos, he took my spot by Eris as I approached the guard. A lazily dressed man with a thick, bored face, and unkempt dark hair. Food stains littered his tunic, and he waved people through with barely a glance, though, of course, he perked up as we got close.

"Reason for entering the East Kingdom?" the guard asked, stifling a yawn.

"Heading home after business," I replied.

He glanced at the crowd of men and women with me. He could see that a few of them were dwarves and elves. He gave me a once-over, and I was relegated to playing the part of a scum-sucking slave trader, I put a sneer across my face and tried to look like Darren as much as possible. *Least the scumbag's good for something, even in death.*

He gave me a knowing nod and a poorly disguised look of disgust at the freed slaves. He waved us through, and I slipped him a few gold as I passed. *Nothing much, but maybe enough to keep his mouth from flying off the handle about the rich slaver who had over a dozen slaves in tow.* It wouldn't matter once we were gone, but the fewer people who knew about us, the better.

We still had half a day before we reached the gate to leave the Compass Kingdom. A lot could happen between here and there if we weren't careful.

We made our way slowly through the darkened tunnel. It was much more claustrophobic with this many people shoving against one another. There was plenty of room to spread out, but it seemed the freed slaves preferred to keep close to another. Half a minute of stifled walking, and the gate opened, bringing in much needed fresh air.

Once we were through, the slaves thankfully stopped crowding around each other so much and walked in smaller groups of three or four. *All right, no way we can stay in this large group and make it out of the Compass Kingdom unnoticed. It's best if we split into smaller groups and head our separate ways.*

With a whistle, I got everyone's attention and brought them to a small alley between a small shop and the guard barracks. It was off the main road with just enough room for all of us.

"All right, we're clear from the worst danger, and with the money in everyone's possessions, you shouldn't have any trouble getting out of the

East Kingdom. Just toss gold at anyone who bothers you, and keep your guard up."

Some of the freed slaves looked a little disheartened that I wasn't going to escort them the entirety of the way through the kingdom. *I'm not their babysitter, and they're all adults who can take care of themselves.* The dwarves all had multiple weapons strapped to themselves and looked as if they knew how to use them. Even a few elves had knives and the like at their waists.

One of the oldest dwarves made his way through the crowd and walked up to me. "By Lachrymal's Heart, I can't thank you enough for your kindness, sir. On behalf of all of us here. Thank you."

He held out his hand for me to shake.

I coughed and dropped my gaze, feeling disgusted with myself. "If you want to thank anyone, thank Eris. I was originally going to leave you all there."

The old dwarf didn't seem concerned with that in the slightest. "Still, Lachrymal smiled upon us, and I won't shirk the man whose hand played a role in my freedom," he said, still holding out his hand.

I took it after a moment of hesitation. His hand was all callous and muscle, and he could've crushed mine like a twig if he'd wanted. I looked down to see an old, well-worn brand etched into his forearm.

An emerald inside a teardrop. *Lachrymal's Chosen.*

The dwarf was a member of Aldrust's elite guard. Tasked with protecting the king and keeping Lachrymal's Heart safe.

After he let my hand drop, he went over to Eris and gave her a handshake as well, to which she blushed scarlet.

The dwarves and the elves formed a small band, and with one last farewell, they departed, giving us a lot more room in the alleyway. *It makes sense for them to travel together. Aldrust and Yllsaria are neighbors, after all. Just a few*

455

*days' ride between the two nations. Hope they make it there safely, would hate for them to run afoul of one of the bandit kings.*

With the elves and dwarves gone, it just left the rabbit-men, who were standing around looking forlorn and skittish. *Guess I'd be nervous too, despite how close the Northern Mountains are. They only have four members, and the trek up to the Pale Everlands is perilous, so I've been told.*

To add to their list of problems, Lyahgos was the only one combat trained in the party. The other two were girls just out of their teens, and the little girl. The way they carried themselves told me there were unfamiliar to battle. With just one warrior, even one as skilled as Lyahgos, that trip would be dangerous. *Hell, even if he decked himself out in high-tier gear, just one warrior isn't going to cut it. Whatever, it's not my problem to solve the problems of others.*

I waved to Lyahgos. "Farewell, hope you have a safe trip."

Lyahgos went to say something but stopped himself. Unsure if he should speak.

"C'mon, spit it out."

"Would it be all right if we traveled with you?" he asked.

*Huh, didn't expect that. Guess saving them bought some goodwill.* I thought about their request. *Do I care if they join us? No, not really. I'm sure we can find a place for them at Gloom-Harbor, but that does raise an interesting question.*

"I don't have a problem with it, but why don't you want to return to the Everlands? I'm sure you can hire a couple of guards at the Adventurer's Guild'. Probably wouldn't even cost you that much since its only about a week's ride."

Lyahgos shifted his stance, kicking at the loose trash in the alley. "We could do that, but it would defeat the entire reason why we left the Everlands in the first place."

"Why's that? I admit I'm curious as to why you're here. It's rare for your kind to leave your homeland."

He sighed, and it was filled with weariness. "It's just not safe for us there anymore. The whole territory is teetering on the brink of war."

*What?* "Since when do the clans fight among themselves?"

"It's not the rabbitmen that are fighting each other."

*That leaves only one option.* I leaned against the wall of the wooden guard barracks. "Why are the wolfmen so aggressive? They've never been so ruthless before."

*Wolfmen are clever hunters, but they've never desired all-out war before. It'll kill their main food supply.* Lyahgos shook his head. "I don't know, word is something precious was taken from the Aminah clan, and they're blaming the wolfmen for the theft."

"Huh, who'd steal from them? That's asking for a death sentence."

"No one knows, or what exactly what was taken, but we escaped before more blood was spilled, only to end up as captive slaves. The Morrigan sure loves her games."

*Can't argue that one.* "Well, I don't mind you tagging along, but we'll need supplies and a few horses if you guys are coming with us."

At the mention of horses, Eris's eyes went wide. "We left Lacuna!" she shouted in a rush.

I chuckled and walked out of the alley, the others in tow. Eris wasn't privy to most of the features players had available to them. I pulled out a small scroll from my inventory—a summoning scroll, specifically, for mounts, pets, and familiars.

I poured a little mana into the scroll to activate it. One of the only times I ever used my limited mana. The scroll unfurled itself, and a bright circle formed on the parchment. It was a smaller Script circle; only a few lines of script flowed over the shining blue pentagram. With a flash, the scroll shredded, and the magic circle transferred to the dirt road next to me. Lacuna appeared in the center of the circle amidst a shower of brightly lit sparks.

As soon as she appeared, the circle faded and disappeared from the world. I walked over to the gigantic horse and stroked her face. "Sorry for leaving you all alone."

I helped Eris on Lacuna, and she, in turn, helped the kids on. One of the children, whose names I still didn't know, sat in Eris's lap. *Need supplies and horses for the trip. Last I remember, there's a general store near the entrance. I'll need to ask after the horses, though.*

*Lots to do.* And I didn't want to linger here any longer than we had too. Lonny had almost certainly realized I'd escaped by now and probably reported back to the Alliance and the Cardinals. It would take nearly a full day for the information to spread through the kingdoms, but I wanted to be long gone by the time it did.

With a goal in mind, we made our way through the busy streets. Eris and the two spiderlings sat atop Lacuna as I held her reins and walked beside them. They'd concealed their eyes once again, and Eris was wearing her cloak. From a distance, no one could tell her apart from a human.

We were forced to stay in the center of the street as we walked along, too many people on either side of us weaving in and out as they hurried along. Over the next few hours, we made our way to the East Kingdom entrance without any serious trouble. Nearly running into half a dozen people as they obliviously walked out in front of us didn't qualify as trouble to me.

I spotted the store right where I had remembered it. We hurried across the street. Weaving as best we could through the masses, we reached the front of the store. I hitched Lacuna and Lyahgos and the others came with us inside the store, as it was their supplies we would be purchasing. Let them pick out what they wanted and pay for it.

The store was a simple two-story wooden affair, and even though it was unadorned, you could tell it was crafted with time and care. As we made our way inside, the same level of care could be seen on the interior as well—not a speck of dust or item on the shelves out of place. Manning the counter was a spry youth in his late teens or so. He must be running the store for his parents.

"Afternoon, all. What can I help you find today?" he asked. His voice was light but held traces of masculinity. It teased what it would mature into. His hair was a dark brown, so dark it looked black in the muted light of the store, and he was sporting the beginnings of stubble on his face.

"We need a weeks' worth of provisions for six people," I told the lad.

"Of course, good sir, any preference?"

I jerked my head towards Lyahgos. "Ask him."

The rabbitman approached the counter and began discussing the types of provisions they would all need. I let him do his thing. Eris and the children walked through the aisles, browsing their wares. It was her first time being in an enclosed shop like this, so she browsed while the others purchased what they needed.

I browsed myself and picked out some more supplies for Eris and myself. I topped up my health and mana potions, bringing both back to ten and two weeks of rations. Nothing fancy, but I bought plenty of dried meat of all kinds. *Rather not live off game for the next week.* I paid the youth two gold, even though it was more than what my supplies cost. I slid the extra gold to him with a warning. "You never saw us, and we didn't buy anything, got it?"

He took the gold with a nod of understanding. "Good lad," I said, turning and leaving. With my purchases secured, it looked like the Lyahgos was finished buying what they needed as well. They all had new cloaks that covered them nearly to their shins and sturdy traveling packs that seemed to be stuffed full to bursting with supplies.

We regrouped at the entrance to the shop. With all of our supplies taken care of, it was time to get horses and get out of the East Kingdom. Asking the lad at the counter, he pointed us in the direction of the entrance, telling us that there was a horse merchant near the front gate. I tossed him another gold for his trouble. *Hopefully, that shuts him up.*

We left the shop and had a late lunch, scarfing down our food quickly and setting off again. After helping Eris and the kids back on Lacuna, I set a steady pace, and we made it to the gate in twenty minutes.

After a few minutes of rest, we started looking around for the horse merchant. I found him a few minutes later. The lad had given us the wrong directions, or the merchant had moved, but he was not, in fact, next to the main gate. He was about five minutes further up the street. We had passed him without realizing it and were forced to backtrack to find the man.

We ended up paying nearly fifty gold for two sturdy horses and saddles. The rabbit-men tied their packs to their new mounts and climbed up. They were large horses but couldn't match Lacuna's size.

Once everyone was situated on their horses, I led them all out of the front gate. After making it through the gate, we were finally out of the Compass Kingdom. *It'll be a cold day in hell before I set foot back here anytime soon.* Though that was my usual attitude whenever I came here. I was too much of a homebody, and I smiled at the prospect of getting back to the castle soon.

"All right, let's get going!"

# Chapter 27 - The Obsidian Throne

Once out of the Compass Kingdom, we sped away as fast as our horses would let us. With Lyahgos and the others, we could ride for longer, switching riders when one grew tired. I stayed on the reins for the most part, as Eris was busy with the two spiderlings.

After nearly a full day of riding, they were finally comfortable enough that they stopped being afraid of me. According to Eris, they spoke Rachnaran, the language of the arachne. A language that my translator couldn't understand.

And I was kind of okay with it. I didn't know how to act around children, especially half-spider children who didn't speak English.

Their names were Tegen and Cheira, and they were kind of cute, but I left Eris to take care of them, which she took to with abandon.

She spent most of her time with them on the trip back. Making sure they were okay and had someone to talk to besides each other. It was incredibly endearing to see her like that, but it also meant most of her time was spent with them, and we didn't get to spend much time together.

I busied myself with keeping a fast pace, but even still, there was only so much distance we could travel without breaking the horses wind, and I didn't want that to happen to Lacuna.

When it got dark the first night, we stopped and set up camp in a large clearing just off the main road. There weren't any trees around, but I wasn't worried since we had so many people in one group. Lyahgos helped get his people's tents set up while I worked on ours. Eris dug out the fire pit while Tegen and Cheira hunted.

Despite their young age, the children were fierce hunters. They crept over the grasslands like ghosts and managed to bag a large buck single-handedly and carried the several hundred-pound carcass by themselves—much to the entire camp's amazement.

Eris praised them for nearly an hour while I cleaned and cooked the meat. The rabbit-men's diet mostly consisted of vegetables, but they weren't opposed to eating meat, so when the deer was prepared, we all sat around the fire and ate, told stories, and just enjoyed each other's company. Eris laid her head on my lap after the meal, and I stroked her hair while Lyahgos and I talked.

It was a perfect day, one of the best I'd had since coming to this world.

I leaned back and sighed with contentment, reaching to wind my fingers through Eris's. I wanted nothing more than the moment to stretch on forever. That thought caused me to chuckle. *I've really become a sap, haven't I?*

*Eh, guess I don't mind so much.* Though I couldn't deny the change I felt in me, even from the relatively short time we'd spent together. I was a better person for Eris being in my life.

After too many years of holding on to all my bitterness and self-loathing, my past mistakes and failures, Eris was the person capable of breaking through all of it.

I may have been a hybrid now, something more and less than what I was, but it was because of Eris that I'd regained some of my humanity. I couldn't make up for my past, the awful things I'd done. But having someone who sees the monster you've become and still loves you for it?

That kind of person is worth changing for.

I leaned down and kissed her cheek. "I love you."

Eris smiled, basking in my affections. "As I love you, my bonded."

We stayed like that for some time, letting the fire die, but too soon, Eris took the children and went to get some rest along with the rest of the camp.

I volunteered for first watch, mostly because I had too much on my mind to be able to sleep, and because our tent was now occupied with the spiderlings.

While I kept watch, I pulled up my interface to check my stats and character page

*Combat Results*
*1 Killed: (Human) 1500 Exp!*
*Total Exp: 1500 Exp!*
*Exp: 4100/5100*

*Character Name: Durandahl*
*Level: 51*
*Exp: 4100/5100*
*Race: Hybrid (Hive)*
*Class: Hive Knight*
*Reputation: Wanted Criminal*
*Bounty: 1300 Gold*
*Stats (-)*
*Strength: 100 (Max)*
*Sub-Stats (-)*
*Attack Damage: 30*
*Constitution: 100 (Max)*
*Sub-Stats (-)*
*Health: 25*
*Health Regen: 25*

*Durability: 15*

*Endurance: 75 (85)*

*Sub-Stats (-)*

*Battle Fatigue: 10*

*Battle Fatigue Regen: 10*

*Agility: 50 (60)*

*Sub-Stats (-)*

*Attack Speed: 15*

*Movement Speed: 10*

*Wisdom: 25 (35)*

*Sub-Stats (-)*

*Mana: 20*

*Luck: 0 (30)*

*Charisma: 0 (10)*

One of the rabbitmen girls came and relived me a few hours later. Charlotte was in her mid-twenties with long, chestnut hair and a cute, round face. Her eyes were the same blue as the others, and her long bunny ears were gray and spotted with a little black. She yawned and sat by the embers while I went and got some sleep. When we set off in the morning with the spiderlings happily chatting to one another, I had a thought. *I haven't asked, but I guess those two are coming with us.* I brought up the subject, and Eris surprised me.

"They'll be coming with us for a short time, but I have to get them back to their home."

"They have a home? Where?"

"The Silvanus Darkwoods."

*Shit, really? Well, I guess that explains why no one's seen the arachne in a thousand years. I'm not looking forward to that adventure.*

The Silvanus Darkwoods resided far to the south, past the South Kingdom and the Salted Mire. The Darkwoods were shrouded in mystery and terror, and in all my years here, not a single person who entered ever returned, which earned the Darkwoods a much more infamous name.

Slaughter Woods.

*An apt name if it's actually the home of the arachne. Given how swift the spiderlings are, I'd hate to fight an adult.* The spiderlings were confident that we could pass through unharmed. They assured me—well, they assured Eris, who then assured me—that we would be fine as long as we brought the children with us.

"Do we have to go?" I asked.

"Of course, we do. We have to bring Tegen and Cheira back. Plus, I would very much like to meet the queen."

"The queen of the spiders, color me terrified."

Eris playfully smacked my arm, smiling at me. "Oh, you worry too much, it'll be fine."

*Yeah, the spider queen, who kills any who intrude on her territory. Yeah, I'm sure she's a beacon of patience and morality.* But I kept my mouth shut.

*Can't blame her for wanting to go. She just learned more of the Hive survived. I couldn't imagine how happy I'd be if I found out some of my family survived.* The age-old hurt returned to my heart when I thought of them, but it wasn't as painful as it used to be. *Maybe I can finally put Micah and Sophia's ghosts to rest. It's been too many years since they died. It's time to move on from my grief. I need to start living in the present.*

The days blurred together in a mix of riding and camping. At night, when it wasn't my turn to watch, I crawled into our tent, but we had two new additions, and I was relegated to sleeping by myself while the spiderlings snuggled up to Eris. After an hour of tossing and not being able to sleep, I climbed out of the tent and went to keep watch again.

Charlotte was the one keeping watch tonight while Lyahgos got some sleep.

She looked up with a nod and went back to keeping watch, though her eyes were wasted as she'd hear anything long before we saw it. *She's kind of cute, if not very sociable. Eh, I guess we're mostly strangers, I was the same way before I met Eris.*

I pulled out my flask and took a few long pulls before I tapped Charlotte on the shoulder and offered her some. She took it and sipped politely, but from the look of disgust on her face, it was too strong for her. She passed it back, and I took another drink while waiting for dawn to break.

When the sun finally rose, I woke the others, and we packed up camp. It went that way for the entire trip home. Ride as much as we possibly could, then set up camp and eat, followed by me trying and failing to get a wink of shut-eye. I'd quickly gotten used to having Eris by my side, and with her absence, I couldn't sleep more than a few fitful hours each night. By the time Castle Gloom-Harbor peeked over the Rolling Hills, I was utterly exhausted.

We rode up to the front gate, and with the passphrase, the man at arms lowered it. I climbed off Lacuna and stabled her before I got the rabbitmen settled. I grabbed the first maid I found and told her to get Amber. She departed with a bow.

I went over to Lyahgos. "Head inside. Amber, our head maid, will get you all settled in and find the best job for you."

"Right, sir!" he shook my hand and left with Charlotte and the others. I was about to head inside myself when a voice called to me. "Greetings, Duran. How kind of the fates to ordain this meeting."

I found Markos walking up from the direction of the gate. His shaggy hair was slick with sweat, and his ordinarily pristine white robes were soiled with dirt and bits of filth. I walked over to the man and clapped him on the shoulder.

"Good to see you, Mark. How goes the Gloom shrooms?"

"Good news and bad news on that front. Our supply of Gloom mushrooms is gone."

"What?"

He held up his hands, backing up automatically—the vein at the base of his throat pulsed with fear. *I shouldn't have yelled at him.* "Sorry for yelling, you just surprised me is all. Tell me what happened."

"Well," he said, fumbling over his words and his robes. His hands twiddled absentmindedly while he worked up the courage to speak. "When I introduced the Gloam to the Gloom mushrooms, they spread quickly, and assimilated the weaker strain, converting the entirety of our stock to the gloam."

"How is that even possible?"

"I'm not sure, honestly. The winds of chance blew in the wrong direction, leaving us in a mess."

I turned from Markos. *I'm no botanist, let him sort it out if he can.* "Fix it if you can. Miguel will be sending a ship to collect our next shipment in a few days. If we don't have any Gloom shrooms to give him, let him have the new stuff."

"Of course, I'll do what I can."

"Good man."

I left the mage to his work and went inside the castle. My little chat had gone on long enough that the entire guild was aware that we'd returned.

When I opened the door, I was met with the hulking face of Gil, eyes nearly bulging out of his skull.

"D.! What the hell did you do to my armor?!"

I grinned sheepishly. "Man, you wouldn't believe me if I told you."

Gil grumbled under his breath, his hands pantomiming wringing my neck, but before long, he composed himself, though I could tell he was still mad. "You better explain everything."

"Of course. By the way, did you get my gift?" I asked, hoping to appease his anger.

My diversion had the exact effect I wanted as his eyes lit up. "It arrived a few days ago, and I can't believe you bought that much ale. That many casks will last me a good while."

*Good, hope it gets you off my back about the armor at least.* I smiled at him. "Glad you liked it, now where's Wilson? We need to call a meeting."

A whisper behind me alerted me to the rogue's presence. "I am here."

I turned my head to speak, and Wilson was just over my shoulder, leaning against the railing to the second floor. "I'm glad you made it home safely, old friend," he said.

"As am I. Could you do me a favor and call a meeting? I want to go over everything, and I'd rather not do it more than once."

"Right away," he said, inclining his head and vanishing back into the shadows. Soon as Wilson left, Gil swept me up into a giant bear hug. Which I returned as best I could.

"I missed you too, buddy," I said.

By the time my ribs stopped creaking, Eris had joined us, flanked by Tegen and Cheira. Her face split into a wide grin when she saw Gil. She padded over to him and hugged him.

"Gil! It's good to see you again."

468

He returned her hug gently, patting her on the back. "It's good to see you too, little miss."

The Aspect made its displeasure known, writhing up from within my heart to rage wordlessly that another man put his hands on what was ours, but I shut it down. *I'm in control, not the other way around.*

*"Now, why don't you believe that?"* it asked.

The deal I'd made with the Aspect was still a mystery, and what it made me give up frightened me. *But I'll deal with it as it comes at me—nothing much else I can do.*

This whole trip had aged me fifteen years, and I wanted nothing more than a hot bath and twenty uninterrupted hours of sleep, but business came first. *Gotta let the others know what I learned. Well, what little I learned, at any rate.*

Wilson took care of getting everyone to the guildhall. I sent Eris and the children up to Eris's room while we conducted business. After a week on the road, we all needed a bath. She leaned over and kissed me.

"I'll see you upstairs in a little while."

"Soon as I can," I promised.

I walked the guildhall while Eris went upstairs. It was midday, but the stone hallway was chilly. The soft light of the torches along the wall did little to warm me as I went. *Has it always been so cold in here?* I put my discomfort out of mind and opened the wooden door, each of the faces of the guild carved into the oak. *Alistair won't be back to join us for some time. Should I remove his face for the time being?*

*No, he'll be back soon enough, and it'll be good to have a reminder that I need to be more careful in the future.*

I sat down at the head of the table and waited for everyone to join me, a laboriously long process that took over thirty minutes. *Glad to see some things never change.* One of the maids came in with several pitchers of ale and glasses.

When everyone finally decided to grace me with their arrival, we got down to business.

First things first, I told them about our trip, of the difficulties we faced on the road. More than a few laughed at me when I told them of the fight with Wolf.

"You fought a werewolf by yourself and lived?" Evelyn asked.

I nodded. "I would've died without Eris, but we scraped through by the skin of our teeth."

"Haha, good on you!" Yumiko said, laughing.

*Figured the vampire would get a kick out of me slaying a werewolf.* And I was right. Her blooded eyes were positively sparkling. I also told them of Darren and the slavers. Of Phineas's betrayal and his revelation. The name of the man who started all of this.

"Magnus?" Wilson asked.

"Yep, why? Does it ring a bell?"

"No, I've never heard it before, what about any of you?" he asked the room. A slew of head shakes, and noes resounded through the room. *Course not, looks like I'll have to go the hard way.*

"Well, see if you can find anything else out. That's our last shot before I have to resort to the more drastic methods."

Gil looked at me incredulously. "You're not thinking of calling upon *her*, are you?"

I picked up my glass of ale and drained it. "What other choice do I have? The Alice is the best bet for information."

"Yes, but you know what kind of price she'll ask. Do you really want to be indebted to the fae?" Wilson asked.

"Course not, but I want that bastard, and I'm willing to play her games if that's what it takes."

470

"Fine, call up the queen of the fairies, but on your head falls the consequences," Evelyn said.

"Thanks for your concern. You're all heart."

She scoffed at me and returned to conversing with Adam. Though I managed to get her attention again when I brought up the fight with Liam and what he could do with magic. Everyone looked rightly shocked at the news. *I witnessed it with my own eyes, and I can hardly believe it.*

And lastly, I told them of the arachne spiderlings and what was really lurking in Silvanus Darkwoods.

"I guess what I'm getting at is that Nexus is home to a lot more dangerous foes than we previously thought. We're going to have to bolster our defenses and work on getting stronger. It feels like the calm before the storm is coming, and I want to be ready for anything," I told the room.

I sat back down and poured another drink while everything settled. It was a lot to absorb at once, and I saw a few cups being drained and refilled. I didn't blame them. I drank mine much slower and waited for everyone to be on the same page. Then I spoke about our upcoming trip.

"We'll be heading that way in a few days after we've rested. If you guys want to accept a few contracts while I'm away, that's fine. Just be sure to vet them to the highest degree you can and make sure to have Wilson approve anything."

"Speaking of, I left Evelyn in charge for a few days and went to investigate the theft quest."

"Ah, right." *I forgot all about that.* "What'd you learn?"

Wilson sighed, taking a sip of his ale. "Nothing much. I learned the thief was a woman, pretty from the description, with brilliant red hair. Other than that, she's a ghost."

"What was taken again? A ruby amulet, right?"

He nodded. *Pretty redhead. Sounds like Morgan. And wasn't she wearing a ruby necklace when we met?*

I chuckled. "Best to let this one go. You're not going to find her."

"Yeah, my thoughts too, it's too big of a haystack for one woman," Wilson said, sighing.

### Quest: Thief Taker Abandoned.
### Reward: 0 Exp

With that taken care of, we got down to the more mundane items on the roster. Even with me only being gone for two weeks, small things still piled up and had to be addressed. It droned on for another hour, and I was grateful when it ended.

With our debrief complete, I dismissed everyone and went to take a bath.

Eris was getting the spiderlings settled in. I let them bunk in Eris's room, but they didn't want to sleep alone, so Eris went and slept with them, sparing me a kiss and an apologetic look as she left. *I don't want to sleep apart, but maybe it's a good thing. Perhaps some time apart will do some good.* We'd spent nearly every waking moment together, and I hadn't had a moment to myself where I could just relax.

I stripped out of my arms and armor and sat them outside my room with a message to Gil to repair them at his convenience, before returning to the bathroom. I stepped into the steaming bath. The hot water soothed my anxiety and relaxed me.

It made the prospect of sleeping apart from Eris much more bearable to think about, and I let the weight of my exhaustion settle in. I quickly washed my hair and didn't even bother to comb it or dry it before stepping out of the bath and managing to stumble into a pair of pants and a shirt before leaving the bathroom.

I was dead tired from nearly five days straight of no sleep, but as I settled into the bed, the emptiness of the room got to me. *It's too quiet and cold without Eris.* I sighed and tossed and turned for half an hour before realizing sleep would be eluding me for some time yet. I grabbed the fresh bottle of whiskey from the nightstand and walked out to the balcony.

*Hopefully, the booze with take the edge off and let me sleep.* I grimaced as the bite of liquor seeped down my throat. *It's new and strong. I like it.* I savored the taste, and before I knew it, half the bottle was gone, and the night sky spun like it was dancing.

I set the bottle on the railing and watched the stars, while the night air chilled my burning face. A raven flew through the air, dipping and gliding in a circle. It was mesmerizing, and in my drunken stupor, I couldn't stop looking at it.

The raven swooped down to land on the railing, cocking its head at me to stare, unblinking with its large red eyes. As we gazed at each other, a shiver ran through me that had nothing to do with the night air—*time to call it a night.*

"Goodnight, bird," I slurred as I turned my back on it and went inside. A fluttering of feathers behind me startled me, and a soft voice spoke quickly, a woman's voice.

"I'm sorry."

*What?* I turned, only getting a glimpse of long dark hair and pale skin, before everything went black.

***

I awoke an indeterminate amount of time later. My head fuzzy, and in a fog, it pounded in time with my heartbeat, and I had the urge to vomit. Once my nausea settled, and the blood wasn't so loud in my ears, I sat up and took note of my surroundings.

The location was unfamiliar to me, though, it was incredibly reminiscent of Gloom-Harbor. Nearly the same dark stone made up the room. A dark rug lay across the floor, almost the entirety of the floor. It looked plush and incredibly expensive.

When I shifted, I sank into luxury. I was on a bed, but to call it a bed was wrong. It was enormous, easily twice the size of mine back home, which had been bordering on the excessive already. Fifteen people could sleep without touching each other. The bedspread matched the rug, and it was very low to the ground. I rolled off, and my bare feet hit the carpet.

*Well, I'm not tied up, that's a good sign. Maybe I'm not a prisoner…or whoever kidnapped me is confident that I'm not going anywhere—not a pleasant thought.*

Next to the bed was a nightstand, though it, like the bed, was twice the size of what it should be. *Gods, it's like a giant lives here.*

On top of the dark wood sat an unlit lantern, along with a match.

I lit the lantern and let the soft light fill the room. The room was mostly spartan, beyond the bed, nightstand, and a large wardrobe in the corner made of the same wood as the rest of the furniture. There were two doors in the room, one in front of me that likely led to a hallway, and the second was about six feet from the bed, leading somewhere. *Maybe the bathroom?*

I used the nightstand to steady myself as I rose out of bed, and something crinkled under my fingers as I did so. It was a piece of parchment. I picked it up and smoothed out the creases. There was just enough light in the room for me to read.

It read.

*Dear Duran,*

*If you are reading this, please dress in the attire provided in the nightstand and exit the room. A servant is waiting to escort you to the throne room. You are a guest here, and no harm will befall you, though, I advise you to not stray off the grounds. My guardians are overzealous and are trained to kill on sight.*

I read the paper and crumpled it in anger. *Damn it, the note all but said I'm a prisoner here.* I'd given Gil my armor to repair and stored most of my inventory in my room. I had nothing here.

They'd even taken my clothes. I was completely nude, except for my hairband. *And I'm clean as well. I don't smell like my soap either, so someone bathed me while I was unconscious. That's creepy as fuck.*

I quickly tied my hair back and opened the drawer of the nightstand. Nearly a dozen outfits were arrayed for me, each a different color, but keeping with a similar theme. Nothing flashy, but all of them elegant. Each of these would cost at least a hundred gold apiece.

I picked one at random and tried it on. It was made of black silk, with silver accents. It sported a sharp v neckline and fit me perfectly. The pants matched and were cut to my figure perfectly. *So not only was I bathed, but fitted for clothes as well. Whoever is behind this spent a fortune on making an impression. They've got the money to burn and want to show off.*

I had a good idea about who kidnapped me, and I was so screwed.

Though I hoped I was wrong, I took hold of the lantern and opened the door. The dark wood was smooth, and the brass handle opened without a sound. As I stepped out, I found myself staring at a maid.

A literal maid. In a maid outfit.

*Now that's just too much.*

She was young, but not indecently so. I'd place her in her late teens or so. Short, russet hair cut just below her small, square chin. When she shifted in the candlelight, her hair seemed to change from red to brown and back again.

Her eyes were golden-brown, like pools of honey. She was gorgeous, but the lifeless, almost robotic expression on her face made her seem inhuman.

She looked to me, inclined her head, and spoke in a curt tone. "Follow me."

She turned on her heels and walked without looking back, expecting me to obey. *My knee-jerk reaction is to start trashing the place, but that's the wrong play here. I need to stay on Magnus's good side. For who else would have abducted me?*

The maid led me down hallway after hallway, each of them so identical that I wasn't sure we weren't going in circles. The same rugs along the floors and the same number of doors, windows, and torch scones on the walls as we walked. *The castle itself is a trap. If I don't know my way around, I'll get turned around and picked off with ease.*

I tried to memorize the route but lost it after a confusing series of turns, but after almost five minutes of walking, we made it to our destination.

The maid pushed open the heavy door and walked me inside the throne room.

It was huge and resembled a cathedral rather than a throne room. Huge stained-glass windows lined the sides, showcasing wild scenes—things I'd never seen before and couldn't accurately describe. Lands and architecture not native to Nexus and a slew of strange creatures and monsters. All like nothing I could've imagined in my wildest dreams.

I was so focused on the windows that I didn't realize that I'd arrived at the throne. It was a tall black throne that looked to be made of obsidian, and it shimmered in the moonlight that poured through the windows.

Sitting on the throne was a rather unremarkable man.

I was expecting a towering giant; instead, he seemed somewhat ordinary-looking. Shaggy golden hair fell in his face, nearly covering his bright green eyes that sparkled even in the darkness. He sported a neatly trimmed beard and seemed to be in his late twenties or so—no more than thirty years of age.

Laugh lines at the corners of his eyes and mouth gave him a much kinder appearance than I was expecting. He was dressed simply, but his outfit was at least as expensive as the one I wore. A simple emerald green tunic with a black cloak that draped around his slight but muscular frame. He wore no crown, nor did he have an air of the monarchy, but I was, without a doubt, looking at a king.

He smiled as I took him in, showing off his polished teeth, and spoke to the maid. "Thank you, Jasmine, you may leave us."

She curtsied and left, sparing me a curious glance before she shut the door behind her. I turned back to the man on the throne and kept my guard up.

"Welcome, Durandahl," he said. His voice was smooth, not soft, or light. It held the right amount of gruffness in his tone, but it was a warm voice.

I inclined my head to him respectfully. *Let's act nice, shall we?*

"Magnus, I presume."

His eyes lit up with a fraction of surprise. Which only made him smile even wider. "I'm impressed. I'm partial to my privacy, so I'm keen to know how you came across my name?"

I thought about lying to him but disregarded it. *I have a feeling he's far more dangerous than he lets on. He dismissed the maid and left me alone with him. It's better if I'm upfront with him.* "A man named Phineas told me after I tortured it out of him."

Magnus frowned. "I see…I'm unfamiliar with that name, which disturbs me. It means someone's been talking that shouldn't."

"Let me solve the mystery for you. He learned it from one of your henchmen. A man named Darren."

Magnus sat back in his throne, propping his chin under his hand in thought. "Thank you for your honesty. That's a rare trait these days. *Hmm*. I'll need to have a talk with him about the need for secrecy."

I stifled a chuckle, which Magnus didn't notice. "Might be a bit of a one-sided conversation."

"Oh?"

"I killed him."

Magnus stared at me for half a second before letting out a hearty laugh. It was a good laugh. Full of mirth. He nearly doubled over from it. It took a lot of the tension out of the room, and I relaxed a bit.

"Any particular reason why you killed him?"

"He made himself my enemy."

That earned me another laugh. "It seems you are as stubborn as I am when you want something. I think I like you."

*Well, there it goes.* I'd had enough of the jovial tune Magnus was playing and dropped the humor from my face. "Yeah, you like me, liked me so much you kidnapped me, not to mention the fucking army you sent after my family."

Magnus stopped laughing and looked at me strangely, almost admonishing. He smiled a dopey grin and spoke. "Ah, yes, I do hope I can convince you to forgive me on that front. I'll admit I didn't handle that the best, but I can't exactly take all the blame for that."

"The fuck you can't!"

He wagged his finger at me. "As a matter of fact, my men had orders not to engage unless they were attacked. You were the one who jumped the gun and attacked first. By the time my messengers got there, your guild had killed all of my men."

478

"Your messengers were a guild of vindictive assholes with a grudge against us."

Magnus held up his hands and shook his head. "Which was a blunder on my part. I should have vetted them more thoroughly before sending them out. One of my lieutenants vouched for them, and I took their word for it. A mistake, I admit."

"What were you even doing there? Why send an entire army after us?"

"I sent those men to reclaim something I lost many years ago. It was supposed to be a simple meeting, not a bloodbath."

I threw up my hands and resisted the urge to strangle him. "What were you even after in the first place?"

"Something personal that I'm not inclined to share with you."

"Then what am I doing here? Why did you bring me here?"

At my words, his eyes lit up with humor again. He leaned back in his throne and smiled at me. It was a knowing smile that said he knew something I didn't. "Oh, I'm not the one who had you brought here, I'm afraid."

I did a double-take at his words. *What?* "Then who did?"

"I did."

I turned at the new sound. It was a woman's voice. Dark and rich with just a hint of bitterness. I'd never heard the voice before, which confused me, until she walked out.

She was beautiful, that much was clear, but it was the sharp edge of a blade. Beauty meant to cause harm to any who stepped too close. She had long, golden hair that flowed down her back like a river, and a dagger point chin. High cheekbones complimented her long ears that poked out from under her hair.

I knew her, even though we'd never met.

She looked the spitting image of Eris, though older and so much crueler, as her bumblebee eyes regarded me with curiosity.

"So, this is the human who's stolen my daughter's heart?"

*Oh, Hell.*

### 

# End of Book One

# AUTHOR'S NOTE

## Thank you for reading my novel!

It means the world to me that you've made it this far and are reading this. I hope you enjoyed the novel and are excited about the sequel. On that note, if I could beg a favor? If you're reading this and you enjoyed the book, then please leave a review. Reviews decide whether an author lives or dies, and taking a minute or two to write a single sentence review makes our day. If you loved the book, please tell me your favorite parts, or if you hated it, go right ahead and troll me into oblivion, I probably deserve it. But whichever you do, please leave a review. And this isn't a purely selfish request. The more reviews this book gets, the faster I can get the sequel in your hands. The sequel will be published regardless, but if my publisher picks up the sequel, it will happen much faster than not. So please, by the nine kings of Hell, please review my book. I'm on my virtual hands and knees here, guys. It's a little embarrassing. Can you quit looking at me like that? :D

Thank you. -Grayson Sinclair

# ABOUT THE AUTHOR

Grayson Sinclair loves books, has loved them since he was a child. Reading has always been a passion of his, even when he really should have been focused on other things, like school. The worlds in books were always more magical and exciting than anything real life could offer, and he hopes a few of you will get lost in his worlds for a short time.

His website is Graysinclair.com, or you can find him on:

- Facebook (https://www.facebook.com/GraySinAuthor)
- Twitter (https://twitter.com/EpsilonUndying)
- Reddit (https://www.reddit.com/user/EpsilonUndying/).

While you wait for the next book in the Trinity of the Hive series, why don't you check out the short story by Grayson set in the same universe? **Swords of Legend: In Remembrance.**

https://bookhip.com/NAWGLX

# About the Publisher

**Starlit Publishing** is wholly owned and operated by Tao Wong. It is a science fiction and fantasy publisher focused on the LitRPG & cultivation genres. Their focus is on promoting new, upcoming authors in the genre whose writing challenges the existing stereotypes while giving a rip-roaring good read.

For more information on Starlit Publishing, visit their website: https://www.starlitpublishing.com/

You can also join Starlit Publishing's mailing list to learn of new, exciting authors and book releases, including **Grayson Sinclair's next book!** https://starlitpublishing.com/newsletter-signup/

For more great information about LitRPG series, check out the Facebook groups:
- GameLit Society
https://www.facebook.com/groups/LitRPGsociety/
- LitRPG Books
https://www.facebook.com/groups/LitRPG.books/

# My Recommended Reading

**TJ Reynolds** - My best friend and fellow author. He's been a truly wonderful friend, and an excellent rival (I'll match your writing speed one of these days). And to top it off, he's a phenomenal writer. You're missing out if you don't give his books a chance.

https://www.amazon.com/TJ-Reynolds/e/B07XXJF5QL

**Emilie Knight** - A very close friend as well and an excellent dark fantasy writer. It's hard to make it in pure fantasy, but she has the chops for it. She was the second person to read the very first draft of Hive Knight (I'm really sorry for making you suffer through that), and I returned the favor by reading her first draft. Her writing blew me away, and when she makes it big in the next few years. I'll be saying I told you so.

https://www.amazon.com/Emilie-Knight/e/B07BMCHMFB

**Jaeger Mitchells** - Literally one of the nicest people I've ever met and a great friend to me. He helped me when he didn't have to and when it didn't earn him anything in return. I will always be grateful for his support and I hope this is can be my way of supporting him in turn.

https://www.amazon.com/Jaeger-Mitchells/e/B07JNB9Z1Y

# THE LitRPG Guildmasters

**Who we are:** The LitRPG Guildmasters is a group of dedicated LitRPG and Gamelit authors trying to spread the word of our favorite genres. By working together and introducing new people to amazing books we hope to expand the genres that we love. Sign up to our Newsletter to get a **free book** and follow us on Facebook to keep up to date on our latest work. If you love LitRPG check out the LitRPG Guild Website, our Discord server, and the LitRPG Adventurers Guild Facebook Group.

### LitRPG Guildmasters Titles:

Altered Realms: Ascension by B.F. Rockriver

Brightblade by Jez Cajiao

Ethria: The Pioneer by Aaron Holloway

Grim Beginnings: The Ashen Plane by Maxwell Farmer

Primeverse by R.K. Billiau

Shattered Sword by TJ Reynolds

Tower of Gates: Hack by Paul Bellow

Cipher's Quest by Tim Kaiver

Watcher's Test by Sean Oswald

Star Divers by Stephen Landry

Fragment of Divinity by Jamey Sultan

Hive Knight by Grayson Sinclair

To learn more about LitRPG, talk to authors including myself, and just have an awesome time, please join the LitRPG Group!
https://www.facebook.com/groups/LitRPGGroup/

Made in United States
Orlando, FL
22 November 2024

54263751R00296